a fall of
stone

*All the Very best,
hope you enjoy.*

First published in 2003
by Barny Books
First published in this edition in 2004
by Richard Neath
www.richardneath.co.uk

Typeset and printed in England by Alphagraphics 68 Darlington Street Wolverhampton

The right of Richard Neath to be identified as the author of this work has been asserted
in accordance with section 77 of the Copyright, Designs and Patents Act 1988

A CIP record for this book is available from the British Library

ISBN 0-9547021-0-7

For Max, my wife and best friend.
For Al (the real Al) my best mate.

Glen Sligachan & The Cuillin Ridge

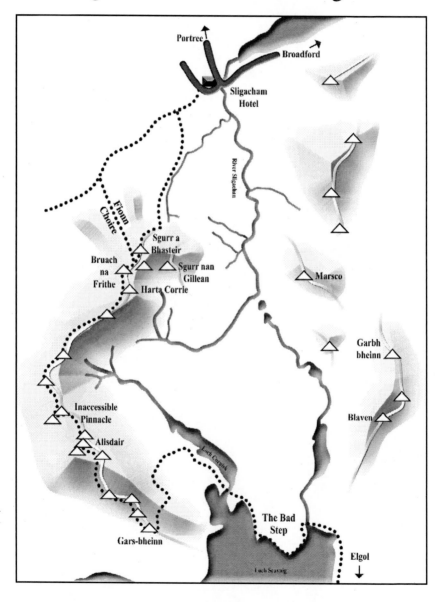

Introduction

I never read introductions.

I'm always too keen to get into the meat of the book. I've browsed the shelves, looked through my favourite authors, glanced at the interesting titles. I've picked up the ones with the eye catching covers, read the sleeve notes and had a peek at the picture of the author on the back page. I may have flicked through a few of the initial pages, read a paragraph or two. Then and only then, if it's grabbed me, if it makes me want to sit down and read it right there in the shop, will I make my way to stand under the 'Please Pay Here' sign and dig in my pocket for some hard earned cash.

By the time I've got home, or am sitting in a favourite pub with a coffee and a cigar, I'm simply too keen to get right into the story to be bothered reading long introductions that drone on about the author's life and who they would like to thank with regards to the finished article.

No more.

I am now a confirmed 'Introduction Reader'. Never again will I delve straight into a book after giving a cursory glance to the first page or two headed 'Introduction'.

Why the sudden change?

Quite simply, it's because I wrote this book. I moved from reading them to actually sitting down and writing one.

The introduction is the chance for the writer to share a bit of themselves with the reader. To say "this is me, this is what I did, what I do, who I am." It's a chance to perhaps explain a little about the story that follows, to give a few background details or explain any liberties taken that could be construed by the reader as 'errors'.

And yes, it's a chance to thank people who've helped, badgered, bullied, beaten or encouraged the writer through the tedious re-writes, computer failures, nervous breakdowns and other every day hazards that seem to happen ... well ... every day, when writing a book.

This book is fiction. The events are fiction, although they certainly could happen. The characters are all fictitious and no one would ever persuade me to admit anything to the contrary. The place names are all factual and the mountains all exist. Anyone who knows the Skye Cuillin intimately will realise that I've taken a few liberties with the geography; used a little writer's licence to help the flow of the story. For instance, you can't see The Bloody Stone or the Inaccessible Pinnacle from Harta Corrie;

they're both hidden behind other mountains.

I hope you'll allow me these discrepancies.

The book was written largely in pubs around the Wolverhampton area. Mainly during the day, during breaks in my real work (I was a financial advisor) and mainly in quiet corners where the staff would often regard me as some sort of deviant, sitting and scribbling for an hour or so, asking for coffee re-fills and chuffing cigars. I calculated that, in the three years that I took to write it, I drank around fifty gallons of coffee and smoked enough cigars to double the gross national profit of some small African countries.

I need to offer thanks to a few people, even though they already know how much I appreciate their help, love and understanding.

To Richard Eaton of 'Eaton Estates' for his assistance in printing each of the rewrites and for his genius in turning my initial thoughts for the front cover into reality. To his sister, Caroline, for putting up with my annoyingly regular use of her printer. To Ali, Elizabeth and the Isle of Skye for providing the inspiration for the second part of the book. To my parents, for reading my initial copy and for their honest opinion and quiet, subdued excitement at the prospect of having a son who could just conceivably be an author. To any of my friends or family who toiled through initial, pencil-scrawled manuscripts and helped sculpt the final version. To Peter Morris and Kevin Walley - friendly solicitors with helpful information during my troubles with the first edition. To the 'two Dans' - AlphaGraphics' own comedy double act, for all their help and expertise. To Paul and Lisa Harris for their kind words of praise and monumental efforts in selling my book from their shop 'Harris Home Furnishings' in Lower Gornal. And to the two people to whom this book is dedicated; Al (the real Al) for his continued friendship, no-nonsense cajoling and encouragement and Max, my wife and best friend, for sticking by me when it all seemed to be going pear shaped and for her understanding, love and support.

As I make alterations in preparation for the printing of the second edition, I also thank you, the reader a) for deciding to read my story when there were probably equally interesting covers alongside it on the shelf and b) for actually taking the time to read this introduction.

I hope you enjoy reading it as much as I enjoyed writing it (though I hope it doesn't take you quite as long).

One last thing - for those of you who's Gaelic is as basic or non existent as mine, *pòg mo thòn*, pronounced pok muh hoan, or as close as I can get it (sorry Ali), roughly translates as 'kiss my arse'. That's not aimed at you, dear reader, but *is* relevant to the story.

Richard Neath

An irrational fear?

I've always hated rock-fall.

The mere thought of it is enough to give me nightmares.

Its unpredictability terrifies me. It injects a liquid panic that courses through my veins, seeps into my every cell and oozes through pores that gape and swell to the push of fear's tide.

There *is* nothing that can be done. There *is* no action available to a climber, other than to run, or curl into a tiny ball, waiting for a bulls-eye but praying silently for mercy. Even crouched, deep in a dark cave, safe and secure amongst damp, lichen encrusted rocks, clattering, spinning missiles exploding out of harms way in the bright mountain sunshine, fear *still* finds a hold. Irrational, but there none-the-less. With a swarm of projectiles buzzing to earth like angry bees, the air is suddenly a horrid, semi-solid place, a battlefield where the mountain always wins.

The mountain can do what she likes. We are quite simply of no relevance to her, but a minor irritation crawling upon her weathered hide to be swatted away with a few well aimed rocks.

She is shedding her skin.

Shaking off her loose bits.

Getting her own back.

Richard Neath

PART ONE

Sleeping in the sunshine

I'm sure the sound I can hear is that of a helicopter way off in the distance, probably somewhere over the southern tip of the island, blades whirring in the morning stillness. I blink my eyes to clear the drying sweat, tilt my head over to one side to gauge the direction of the sound and, at once, I'm in the middle of a clattering battlefield of flying shrapnel. What seems like a thousand falling rocks spiral their way down from the ridge and I raise my arm in a pitiful show of protection, praying that I'll live through the storm. The smell of exploding fragments fills the air and spinning missiles transform the peaceful June morning into a nightmare place where death is an eye-blink away. A chunk the size of a grapefruit clips the corner of a boulder six feet to my left. I watch as it disintegrates in a puff of dust and smoke. A splinter, thimble sized but sharp as a razor, catches my cheek, drawing a fine line of blood.

Then, all is quiet. The smell of shattered rock hangs for a while like the lingering odour of a dead firework. Danger past, I slip into a kind of sleep.

Now, a light breeze is beginning to stir the stunted grasses of the corrie and the sound of water trickling between scree and boulders is calming, relaxing. Glen Sligachan lies a mile to the east and its river will be slow and sluggish after days without rain. There will be salmon now, but more likely sea trout, lying beneath overhung banks in the deep, clear pools. On any other day, the base of the glen and its jewel of a river would only be half an hour's walk away and I imagine how good it would feel to creep along the banks in the gathering darkness of a June evening.

Dawn on Skye is often cool, even in June and *especially* deep in the heart of the Cuillin, but on a fine day the temperature, driven by the warm air of the Gulf Stream will often soar into the 70s.

Today will be a warm one. Already a sheen of sweat has built on my back and the dawn sky is tinged with yellow and scarlet over the twin peaks of Blaven. A light dusting of cloud stirs on Alisdair's summit ridge, curling and swaying in the breeze. Banachdich is clear and all of the ridge between; places where, only yesterday, my boots left scrapes and scratches on the weathered surfaces and my hair was blown by a mountain breeze which cooled my skin and took the edge off the heat at noon. The rocks and boulders over which I scrambled stand out sharp against the lightening sky and as I watch, two figures make their way across the summit ridge of Dearg, heading towards the Inaccessible Pinnacle.

I pluck at a piece of heather by my side, marvelling at the intricacies of its tiny flowers, a deep mauve, almost purple, which catches the early morning sunlight. The moss-covered ground is soft at my back and, although I'm apparently stuck at an awkward angle, I feel an extreme calm steal into my mind.

Staring absently into the blue expanse above, I think of Rachel; of her smile and her hair, that shock of unruly red, cute yet alluring and incredibly sexy. All of life's pressures have simply fallen away. I am relaxed, totally and utterly at peace.

Perhaps a thousand feet above me, a pair of buzzards soar effortlessly on expanding thermals, their high pitched, mewing calls echoing off aged, storm weathered rock. An updraft of warm air from Harta Corrie carries them higher and higher on outstretched wings, broad and powerful.

Warm sun now bursts over Blaven's summit ridge and I squint against its sudden glare, raising my arm to shield its brightness from sleep weary eyes. Marsco erupts into brilliance, its southern ridge shines a vivid gold. The Bloody Stone is, as yet, still in shadow, sitting squat and unmoving way down the glen to my left. Boulders are strewn around its base like mountain cast-offs, their covering of moss and lichen glittering with a sprinkle of early morning dew.

Behind me, Gillean towers, sentinel of the glen; the last summit, and final craggy obstacle on the Cuillin ridge. A short while ago I sat in the pre-dawn chill on a rocky ledge, somewhere between its spiky crest and the domed, fairly unremarkable top of its close relative, Bruach na Frithe. Between fascinated minutes watching the warmth and glow of the sunrise spread in the east, my eyes had flicked from one summit to the other - 'where I've been, where I'm going; where I've been, where I'm going'. I'd sat, legs pointing out towards the terrifying void of empty space below, wondering what the day would bring.

My kit is still up there somewhere, abandoned and scattered amongst the rocks like Autumn leaves. My sleeping bag will still be warm and the burner on my stove would probably raise a blister on a careless fingertip. A half empty mug of hot fruit juice is also there for the taking, cooling in the breeze, maybe the odd wisp of steam curling from its surface. For as long as I can remember, dawn has been my favourite time of the day. The *birth* of a new day always inspires me and today, despite everything, I'm still inspired, still glad to be alive.

Up on the ridge, the climbers I saw earlier are beginning their ascent of the Inaccessible Pinnacle, their matching red jackets stand out, stark against the dark rock. Moving with exaggerated care and unaware of my presence, two thousand feet below, they climb without ropes, every move taking them closer to their summit.

A clatter of small rocks wakes me from my daydream. I watch as they bounce and cascade down the final slope of the buttress to my right. Terrified of another rock-fall, I'm powerless to stop my pitiful whimper and once again raise my arm above my head and shut my eyes, waiting for the onslaught. This time, through the protective darkness, the distant, almost surreal sound of voices trickles its way into my confused mind. Then, way above me a shout rings out, clear and obtrusive in the early morning stillness.

"He's down there." A pause, "Hey, hey, he's down there, at the base of the buttress. See, there look?"

For a second, even through my confusion, I'm sure I recognise the voice, a strangely familiar and altogether comforting sound. My memory tries a few options, then becomes hazy once more. Calm.

"Aye junior, Ah see him. On ma way; stay where yeh are."

There's a stern edge to the second voice and again the sound tugs at my memory - Liam? William? Don't know, something like that.

The voices fade and I feel the pull of sleep's approaching tide. It tries to carry me away again and this time I give in, letting it wash over my senses. Then I'm sliding, slipping ever faster into an inky blackness.

Nice.

I like to sleep. In my dreams, the rocks can't touch me.

Safe.

Chris Stevens

The offices of Chris Stevens Financial Services, Independent Financial Advisers stood between Lester Briggs Funeral Directors and Penn Fields General Stores at the northern end of the Penn Road.

Its blue-rinse tinted glass and sharp, high-tech, shiny plastic, purple sign, contrasted garishly with the drab, down-in-the-mouth appearance of its neighbour's frontage. Set into the brick surround of the mahogany door, a plaque of the shiniest brass proclaimed that 'Chris Stevens, FLIA, MLIA (dip) Independent Financial Adviser' had an associate by the name of David Charles.

I had, for the last few years, drifted aimlessly within the ocean that *is* the insurance industry. Dissatisfied and disillusioned with the whole God-awful thing, knowing that, although I could do the job well, deep down it really wasn't me. At thirty six years of age, with fifteen years of selling Financial Services behind me, I was a comparatively rare breed, an adviser who'd managed to survive the relentless changes in regulations that had been thrust upon the Industry over time.

Chris Stevens, now there's a *real* survivor.

To me, he had fallen from grace, done the unthinkable; lost sight of any scrap of decency that lay within him, sold his morals in the name of greed and stolen from the very people who sought his advice.

I hated the man.

He was a disgusting low life. A be-suited sleazy piece of scum that oozed an almost poisonous, noxious slime that masqueraded as a well-dressed, well-off charm.

His handshake suggested courtesy and good breeding. His short, smart haircut, greying at the temples confirmed the characteristics of his handshake.

His suits shone pure Savile Row, clean and crisp in their tailoring. His choice of tie was Conservative with a capital C, not quite 'old school', but just the right mix of tradition and high-power to blend in with his business contacts. Shoes were classic, if a little light and soft, almost balletic, the same design by Gucci that he'd worn for years.

Everything about his appearance was smart and practical. People meeting him for the first time would get the impression of success, but without the pretences of unashamed wealth. He was though, unashamedly wealthy.

Car choice was classic, young businessman. BMW M5, leather seats, air-con, all the trimmings - no flash 6 or 7 series, no ostentatious Porsche, or swanky, open top Merc; just steady, business-like Germanic dependence.

He could play the 'lad' with true rugby club drunken abandon. Yet in the eight years that I'd known him, I'd only witnessed insobriety on a couple of occasions.

He'd developed a fondness for the new breed of respectable clubs; the sort springing up in major towns across the U.K. advertised on billboards in florescent pink type, along with the alluringly naked head and shoulders of a pouting blonde apparently trying to reach something stuck in the corner of her mouth with her tongue. Clubs where it's perfectly acceptable to watch naked, beautiful, young girls dance erotically with expressions of vacant boredom, while the clientele, laughing with bawdy, testosterone boosted bravado, slap their thighs and swig back champagne, Red Bull and Vodka and try to stuff £10 notes into impossibly small G-strings. £20 buys a 'private' dance, where a gyrating sex god straight out of any top shelf mag' would stop just short of doing, what even Clinton would have trouble denying was 'sexual relations'.

He lived the life of the successful businessman in all he did. From the designer cuff-links, all the way to exclusive holidays at the drop of a hat in far away exotic places. Holidays spent by the pool immersed in self-help books, evenings in the bar chatting politely with the other guests. I'd never seen any holiday snaps but I knew, that if I did, they would consist of soul-less hotel complexes of marble and shimmering, ornately decorated pools. There would be no colourful, native markets or dark, atmospheric washing line draped alleyways. No essence of the country visited or local people met. Just ornate concrete and tiles, blue tinted disinfected water, tasteful pastel parasols, stagnant, unsatisfied looking waiters and the merest hint of ocean somewhere in the far distance.

He played a part; that was all; and played it, as with all of his sham of a life, to the best of his ability.

So that's him. To those who feel they know him anyway.

But to those who *know* they know him; a lying, immoral, greed ridden, untrustworthy, unethical, thieving criminal low-life bastard.

The former outnumber the latter by about a thousand to one. I'm one of the latter. Like I said, I hated him. With a great big overpowering passion.

There was a change coming, like a storm at sea, seen approaching from unmistakable distance, building and growing. The blackness of my thoughts had darkened during the previous weeks as a series of events unfolded during the normal process of my work. Events that had initially simply itched at my subconscious, had suddenly bloomed, flourished, then spawned fruit that rotted where they hung.

I had, over the previous few weeks, perhaps even months, found myself questioning my boss's motives. I'd also found myself staring into the sun-tanned, distinguished face during meetings, searching for what, I had no idea. I *knew*, there was something … well … not quite right about the office, the business, my job, my employer. Trying to rationalise my concerns and worries simply pointed me in the direction of my own dissatisfaction, my own disillusion; I really didn't like my job much. During the last monthly sales meeting, Chris had spotted my stare and raised his eyebrows in question. He'd been able to hold the returned stare for long enough to allow a nod of inquisition before I even realised what was happening. I'd nodded back in recognition, raised a stupid grin in return and averted my eyes.

I'd simply had a feeling, a nagging, gnawing, grating sensation. Something was not right - I just hadn't known what. Something like a cancer was eating away at the very fabric of the business and I'd lived in dread of him calling me to one side and, with a fatherly arm around my shoulder, saying clearly, but in hushed tones - "I know that you know."

The insistent "beep, beep" from the pedestrian crossing roused me from my brooding with a visible start - *this* morning, of all mornings, I'd good reason to be a bit jumpy.

A month ago, no, let's be honest, more like a week, all I'd had was a vague feeling of unease, a hunch about misdeeds at the office. Then came the Trevor Talbot bombshell and Friday night's escapade.

I'd hoped it was all coincidence, a few snippets of jumbled, garbled information that may have had a perfectly logical explanation. I knew the industry well. Insurance Companies can give the world's worst customer service, their record keeping, despite legislation, can be crap. Policies often get lost, mislaid. Information is often wrong, values are incorrect, names spelt with an extra 'L', Miss instead of Mrs, retirement ages misquoted. The list goes on. They talk a good game but, for all their sincere, gushing promises, the tacky adverts with ageing T.V stars peddling policies for the over fifties', their regulations, best advice rules and larger than life smiling corporate faces, the basic premise still rules supreme - sales, sales, sales and more sales make the financial services world go round; always has and always will. Whether bicycle clips, raincoat, flat cap and a nice cuppa, or designer suit, lap top and a gin and tonic, it's all the same; just a different number of noughts on the end of the cheque.

Pedestrians crossed and I glanced around but felt no strange stares or quickly averted glances. I *looked* as though I'd just got out of bed, *felt* like I'd never even been, but wished I could go straight back there. At least, as far as I knew, my thoughts had been in my head and not spoken out loud.

I lit another cigarette.

The nicotine cleared my thoughts.

The business -

Eight staff in total, comprising three Advisers, the two Principles (Chris and David), one wife (of David) and two secretary/telephonists. David was ... well that was difficult to say. He was undoubtedly, a major financial backer of the firm. He'd appeared on the scene and was introduced to all concerned as a 'new partner'. Along with the smell of expensive cigars and even more expensive cologne, came a noticeable increase in liquid assets. Chris had new office furniture delivered and decorators blitzed the whole place one weekend; tired and drab, to vibrant in the space of forty eight hours. New carpets followed, then a new phone system, fax and drinks machine.

Things were good. Business was buzzing. New clients flowed through the business sausage machine, sweeping through with a swish of expensive overcoat tails and a satisfying rustle of designer suit material. I even dealt with a few personally.

On at least three occasions my client was ushered away by Chris once the paperwork was signed. That same swish and rustle followed them straight into Chris's office for a 'private meeting'. Usually there was plenty of old school stuff; firm handshakes and arms around the shoulders.

I hadn't a clue what was going on behind the scenes and, at the time, couldn't have cared less. The commission rolled in, right after the clients rolled out.

I was happy to be ignorant.

Shortly after the arrival of the enigmatic Mr Charles, Chris announced to a stunned gathering that he would be taking a back seat in the selling side of the business. He went on to explain in clipped tones that he would be spending more time in administration and marketing. He would, he assured us all, be looking after his existing clients and a few select corporate introductions from Mr Charles, "So," his voice had dropped to no more than a hushed whisper, "no raiding my client bank!" He delivered it as a joke, the 'nod, nod, wink, wink' of the sales manager wanting to be your best mate. We all understood its real, intended meaning.

Chris then moved to the leafy suburbs of Wolverhampton. In a sleepy village, the house was such a divergence from the norm that we all wondered whether he'd finally taken up with one of his lap dancers on a more permanent basis. Surrounded by fields on all sides, a long conifer edged driveway lead to a large cottage of white painted brickwork and black timber. Mature trees dotted a garden which extended to over five acres. Roses grew around the doorway and twined their way up walls and trellises. The whole picture was straight from a chocolate box.

A bus pulled up at the pedestrian crossing, startling me again from my daydreams.

I'd been gone five minutes. Five minutes where I'd been totally and utterly lost in my thoughts. Going absent while standing in the street was not good and I shuddered at how many people must have walked past me while I stood and stared like a vacant wino.

More to the point, had anyone from the office seen me? I was late for a meeting, a meeting that I'd never expected to go ahead. I looked a mess. I'd stood in the street, an almost certainly soon to be 'ex' financial adviser, in a totally vacuous state.

Not good. Not good at all.

I slumped against the wall at my back, ran my fingers through my hair and scanned the office frontage for signs of life. Through the shifting, reflected images of passers by and speeding cars, I could make out the shadowy shapes of my colleagues. They'd held back the meeting just for me and now shuffled around the office between desks and coffee machine, their routines disrupted, their diaries rearranged. Steve sat in his corner, unobtrusive and calm while Andy (the 'other' Andy), prowled the carpet, anxiously kicking his feet together.

Tina sat by the front door, behind a desk that she polished daily and kept clear of clutter. Tina was a dream Secretary. Efficient, understanding and dependable.

There had been a time, eight years ago, when I first joined the firm, when I'd interpreted her friendly nature as something other than what it was. I admit to being automatically drawn to her; her attractiveness was as unnerving as it was all-consuming.

I soon realised, as feelings of stupidity washed over me like breaking waves, that I was way off the mark. Tina was just Tina, the same with everybody she met; friendly and nothing more which was for the best really as I'd been married for ten years.

My wife, Rachel, was my *best* friend.

Our courtship had been a low key, laid back sort of affair lasting for three years during which time, we built on our friendship, explored each other's feelings, each other's world. They were worlds that crossed at many points, at many junctions; our joint love of the outdoors, of mountains and high places, of picnics in the summer by gurgling rivers dotted with dancing insects. And of painting. Her talent and eye for colour, light and shade, my boundless but often ham-fisted enthusiasm. She painted what she saw, in perfect reproduction, while I bumbled along, an enthusiastic amateur in the presence of a talent I could never match. While she produced beautiful images in watercolours, oil or pastels, I was apt to wander about, capturing scenes in the black depths of a camera.

We had split once, following a period of niggling arguments that, with hindsight, we put down to 'growing pains'. We were, undoubtedly heading towards a serious commitment.

On Valentines Day eleven years previously, I met her from work following a six week period when we had not spoken at all. Armed with a bunch of flowers and with a red velvet box containing a diamond solitaire ring hidden in my suit pocket, I marched into battle.

She'd been shocked upon arriving at her car. I'd hidden, leaving the bouquet on the roof of her Nova and crouched low, watching from behind her boss's Range Rover. She'd read the note accompanying the blooms, shaking her head and searching the car park through a curtain of salty tears.

"I've missed you, I love you. Get in your car if it's over, don't if it isn't."

That's all it said. She read it, tears rolling down her flushed cheeks. She re-read it, desperately glancing round the car park, making no moves to get in her car.

That's when I knew - knew the ring was right, that the proposal was right and that our lives would be right, together.

She had said yes, blubbering and getting tears and smudged mascara on my suit shoulder. We married a year later, bought a house in the meantime and had moved twice since.

Our house was detached, old, full of character, partially draped in a ridiculously aggressive ivy that really needed attending to and had an annoying damp problem. The garden was our pride and joy. The result of hundreds of shared hours spent digging, humping soil and rocks, planting seeds and cuttings, laying gravel and wood chips. Times all shared, all special. It was now one of my greatest and simplest pleasures to water the garden in the evening, my thoughts free as air.

My nightly garden watering had, for the last twelve months, been wracked by thoughts of how to get out of the industry that I had stumbled blindly into all those years before. Little else took up space in my daytime thinking either.

For the past few weeks though, darker subjects had swayed in my mind's breeze. Thoughts of mysterious, missing legacies. Policies that Insurance Companies knew nothing about. Lump-sum investments taken out, with policy documents all present and correct. Policies that showed nowhere on companies records. Policies in trust to charities that, to all intents and purposes, didn't exist other than in the records of Chris Stevens and Associates and in the hearts of the generous clients.

Glancing both ways along the street, I stepped into the road, straightening my tie as I went. I felt my cheek, reminding myself that, yes, I had shaved and yes, it was a shoddy effort.

At the far side of the road I stopped on the kerb. Ranj from the general stores waved a cheery good morning. I barely noticed. My mind was already struggling to find a composure that would allow some degree of normal behaviour. I checked my tie again, then, with my hand once more stroking skin for signs of stubble, walked the three steps across the footpath and into the offices of Chris Stevens and Associates.

The doorway swallowed me like a hungry whale.

Trevor Talbot

Twelve months previously, the firm had held a seminar at a local hotel aimed specifically at a market that Chris had coined 'The Wealthy Greys'.

Affluent ladies and gentlemen with a minimum age of sixty, they represented a niche market with high disposable assets. Typically widows or widowers with estates measured in several hundred thousands or even millions of pounds. Keen to maximise their income, mitigate Inheritance Tax, or use Legacies to gift money to charities by way of Investments written into Trust, they were a lucrative vein of revenue waiting to be tapped.

It was this final need that Chris saw as the biggest earner. Life Insurance Bonds that would, once suitably wrapped up in a Trust, reduce the Taxable Estate of the donor and pay out on their death to the charity of their choice. A very plausible and highly laudable marketing plan. Good for business as all fees to the firm were up front and usually subject to no claw-back. Relatively easy to set up as far as any compliance issues were concerned, most of the cases being set up as a limited advice basis (where no other area was discussed) and, doing a bit for charity in the meantime.

All very nice and public spirited.

I'd set up dozens of such investments in the past twelve months, usually measured in tens of thousands of pounds, but also a couple which broke the magical £100,000 barrier. It was good business, lucrative, relatively easy. Times were, or should have been, good.

Trevor was a client of Chris', looked after personally for many years and with an investment portfolio of over £7,000,000. It comprised everything from stocks and shares, gilts, PEPs, ISAs, Guaranteed Bonds and Unit Trusts. The single biggest client of the firm, he was Chris's baby, personally and exclusively handled by him and him alone. I'd met him once officially. He'd visited the offices with his chauffeur and been whisked away to see Chris, a veritable blur of expensive British tweed and Italian leather. He seemed unimaginably old. Grey skin lay in folds over almost skeletal features. His high, prominent cheekbones were tinged with pink, giving the impression that he was wearing blusher. Despite this aura of almost decrepit antiquity, he'd been incredibly sprightly, moving with a surprising grace and fluidity across the office. His tweed jacket, leather patched at the elbows, had been crisp and fresh. Matching trousers hung comfortably, but with a razor-sharp crease that defied belief. His bald head was liver spotted and a large, hooked nose was criss-crossed with blood vessels like that of a heavy (or recently 'ex' heavy) drinker. I couldn't help thinking that he looked, in spite of his sprightly demeanour, as though a large glass of scotch would probably kill him.

Half way across the floor, he stopped, turned to me, smiled and spoke in a clear, subdued voice with no trace of accent whatsoever.

"I don't think we've met," a liver spotted hand moved purposefully towards me. His handshake was firm and positive.

"Andy, pleased to meet you Mr Talbot." I'm sure my voice had quavered a little.

"Delighted. Keep up the good work."

That had been one damp and dreary day in the middle of an equally damp and dreary March. Then, as May was preparing to blend seamlessly into June, I'd had the call.

I'd been watering my beloved garden, the still night air surrounding me like a well fitting cloak, while water cascading from the hose had painted the garden in a deeper darkness. Rachel appeared at the back door.

"Andy, telephone for you."

I glared at my watch, the dimly illuminated dial lit by light from the kitchen window, told me what I already knew. It was 11.30.
"It's a bit late isn't it? Who is it?"

I spoke as I crunched across the gravel to where Rachel, resplendent in 'piggy pattern' pyjamas, stood in the doorway. She leant towards me and whispered in my ear "It's Mr Talbot."

I stared open mouthed.

"What?"

"It's Mr Talbot, he apologises for calling at home and so late, but he'd like to meet with you."

I took the phone as though it was going to bite me.

"Hello, Andy Perkins."

For the briefest of moments the phone appeared dead, then, that same clear, but low voice broke the silence.

"Andy, a thousand apologies for phoning so late and curses on me, at your home as well. I'll be brief. I need to see you sometime early next week. I understand this is somewhat irregular and would appreciate our conversation being strictly between us."

"But Mr Talb ..."

"Please, it's Trevor and I know what you're thinking. Mr Stevens would not approve. Nevertheless, I need your opinion."

"But ..."

"Andy, please humour me. Shall we say next Monday, around 10.30 a.m.?"

Without waiting for an answer, he continued.

"Good, good. My address is The Stables, Colwood, do you know the village?" He continued, again without waiting for an answer, "Two hundred yards past the village shop. Buzz the dinger on the gate, I'll let you in." He paused for a second before continuing, "I will look forward to our meeting and, Andy, please apologise to your delightful wife for my disturbance. Goodnight."

"Yes, thank you ... I'll see you then ... "

The line was dead, only the dialling tone evidence that I was holding anything other than a lifeless lump of plastic.

"Buzz the dinger?" I spoke out loud and Rachel's face appeared in the kitchen doorway.

"Mr Trevor Talbot, multi-millionaire, successful business man, semi-recluse, enigmatic character has just asked for a private meeting with me and asked me to *'buzz the dinger'* to be let in!"

"Isn't he one of Chris's clients - not to be handled by mere mortals?"

"Christ yes, I met him a while ago, just a brief hello really. What the ... "

The week passed without further incidence and, by the weekend, I'd largely forgotten about the call. Sunday evening, in the middle of Antiques Roadshow, Rachel reminded me.

"I bet you'll be wearing you're best suit tomorrow won't you?"

"Mmhh?" I really hadn't got a clue what she was getting at. Then it dawned. "Shit, yes. God I'd forgotten about Mr T. Christ. Wonder what he wants?"

"You haven't told Chris have you?"

"No Rach, I haven't. I know I hate the job, but I'm not quite ready to start signing on just yet. Anyway, between Stevens, Charles and Talbot, I reckon there's a chance of ending up in the River Severn wearing concrete boots."

I regretted my choice of words instantly. Rachel flinched, turning to look at me, open-mouthed.

"Joke ... Rach, Rach, I was joking. God I bet that painting's going to be worth a bloody fortune. Look, probably been in an attic for a hundred years."

Rachel turned back towards the TV and I breathed a low sigh of relief. I knew though, from the expression on her face, that I'd sown a seed of doubt.

'The Stables'. In my mind the name conjured up a quaint, ivy covered cottage with small, tidily kept lawn, rose bushes and the odd willow thrown in for good measure. What greeted me was as far from this image as was humanly possible.

Massive Oaks towered over a ten-foot high brick wall. Set into the wall were equally high wrought iron gates crowned with brass points that glinted in the spring sunshine. An impressive, square, brick built, Georgian, three-storey house sat in the middle of manicured lawns, a gravel driveway, straight as a die, leading up to its front door. Pillars were set on either side, supporting a canopy under which sat a black Mercedes, paintwork gleaming and reflecting the sunshine.

I couldn't shake a strange feeling of being watched and, scanning the windows of the house, I imagined pairs of eyes studying me. The strongest sensation though, was one of clinical efficiency. What should have simply been an impressive country home of immense monetary value, gave the impression of being a fortress. The place had an unfriendly atmosphere. It felt dead.

Reaching for the buzzer, I had to fight an overpowering impulse to get back in my car and simply drive away. Instead, with a feeling akin to jumping off a high bridge, I reached out and pressed the button in the middle of the intercom system.

For the whole of his working life, Talbot had stuck to a principle, a work ethic from which he'd never sway. His principle was a fairly simple one and encompassed the belief that there was always a deal to be done, that his work was his life and that his customers were always, on the face of it, right. When out of their company, he always worked on the theory that they were largely stupid, ignorant and constantly looking to rip him of.

However he felt, he never let these feelings interfere with his dealings with them. He was always the perfect gentleman, smart, courteous, ready and willing to please. He'd always spent a great deal of money entertaining his larger customers. Days at the races, big football matches viewed from executive boxes and opulent luxury. Fine wine, excellent dining, gifts for the ladies. He strongly believed that a £10,000 night out in the presence of his best clientele would return ten fold or more into his personal bank account. It was a theory that had served him well from the day when, as a self-employed builder working on the bank's money, he had built his first house. Now, with a vast fortune easing him through his old age, he was probably the biggest property developer in the Midlands.

His first meeting with Chris Stevens had been six years previously, a typically lavish affair at Worcester racecourse to promote his new housing development in a pleasant green belt area, south of Stourbridge. Chris had bought one of his houses and, in doing so, bought into a very profitable friendship.

Over £4,000,000 had been diverted, largely legitimately, into corporate bonds, gilts, unit trusts, life assurance bonds and various pension schemes over the years. All through C.S.A. - it was a relationship that created wealth on both sides. Talbot benefited from the financial knowledge and expertise of Chris, swelling his personal wealth through sound investment decisions and often swathing large chunks from his Tax bill, both corporate and personal.

For Chris, the commission cheques and occasional fees charged, kept rolling in.

As Talbot sold off portions of his empire, scaling down for full retirement, and turning assets into cash, the outlook for C.S.A. was indeed rosy.

Inheritance Tax planning was sure to be of concern, although with an estate the size of Talbot's, all the planning in the world would make little difference. Unless he willed it all to charities or political parties, the tax man was going to be rubbing his hands.

With the advent of Stakeholder Pensions, CSA were sure to do well. Talbot had to offer pension planning to all of his employees and, being such a highly thought of boss, so caring towards his staff, he was sure to make contributions to the scheme.

All good news to CSA. A business relationship that worked in perfect harmony.

I, of course, knew nothing of Talbot's details. Living in Wolverhampton, Talbot's reputation preceded him and it was difficult to drive around the area without seeing notice boards and advertising hoardings proclaiming 'Another quality development by Talbot's' or 'Property for let - enquire through Talbot's'.

Of the relationship with CSA though, I was quite in the dark. I'd seen him in the office a few times and met him just the once.

There was a secrecy surrounding him that was absolute. Chris's personal assistant would never allow a file to be left on her desk that contained details of him. This, though, was not exclusive to Talbot - Chris's work was never on show.

I therefore, had no knowledge of the £750,000 life assurance bond written earlier in the year for Talbot with Midland Mutual Assurance. Neither did I know that Talbot, near demi-God figure around Wolverhampton was, at the age of eighty two, not expected to see another Christmas.

Locking the car, I straightened my tie in the driver's mirror, grinned, showing my teeth, for signs of toast my toothbrush may have missed and turned towards the house. I was taken aback at the sight of a smiling Talbot, dressed immaculately in black trousers and a deep purple silk shirt, open at the collar.

"Never go into a meeting without checking for spinach in your teeth or snot dangling from your nostril."

Talbot's words and impish grin forced me to smile back.

"Absolutely right Mr Talbot, wise words indeed."

"Please, it's Trevor, don't stand on ceremony, this is an informal meeting." He pointed a bony finger at me and continued, "Should have said to come in casual gear. I've seen enough suits to last a thousand life times."

I stepped forward, hand extended in greeting, aware that I was still smiling, like meeting an old friend after years apart.

"You have an honest face," Talbot whispered, his keen eyes scanning mine as our hands clasped together.

He didn't shake, just gripped, firmly, searching with his eyes as if to confirm the validity of his opening statement.

"Please, come inside, I've made coffee."

Outside, the day was cool and bright but the hallway into which I stepped was sombre; windows to the front were tinted with a subtle hint of green so the resulting light was tinged emerald. Swirling motes like a million inquisitive insects gave the whole vision an almost mystical quality. A staircase rose from the middle of the hallway through ten steps before splitting left and right at a small landing then rising to first floor level. The steps were startling. Adding to the sombre nature of the hallway, they were highly polished granite, mottled with tiny flecks of crystal mica.

A huge chandelier hung above the staircase and I struggled to stifle a smile as an image flashed into my mind of Del-boy, Rodney and Grandad trying in their own inimitable fashion to clean it.

"I laughed too when I saw that episode, fit to burst my stomach." Trevor was standing to one side by an open door, a smile shinning across the gloom and, for a moment, I imagined the words had been in my head.

"Only Fools and Horses. That's what you're thinking isn't it? Everyone remembers that episode when they see my chandelier. Please Andy," Trevor gestured through the open door, "the coffee will be brewed to perfection by now."

The room into which I now stepped emitted a warmth that had little to do with conventional heating. The furniture was straight from the most exclusive gentlemen's club. Studded leather furniture comprising high, wing-backs and thick cushions in deep mahogany.

Two chairs and a three-seater settee guarded a huge, beautifully simple oak fireplace. On each side of the fireplace sat a large vase. I knew enough from watching Antiques Roadshow that they were expensive and Chinese in origin. Highly coloured with dragons and ornate birds in unfeasibly shaped trees, they looked somewhat out of place in the otherwise traditional English surroundings.

"Been in the family for hundreds of years. I'm fairly sure they're four or five hundred years old. Last time I had them valued, they reckoned they were worth £250,000 each. Three quarters of a million for the pair."

I felt a prickle of unease crawl up the back of my neck. Trevor was either the most perceptive of men or he was a mind reader.

Between the cluster of chairs was a large smoked glass coffee table, on which, a gleaming and ornately carved silver tray was laid with two china mugs, plain white and pristine, rimmed with gold, a large cafetiér, white matching pot of Demerara sugar and a selection of biscuits. Trevor gestured to one of the chairs then, reaching forward and pouring coffee, added one sugar and offered the mug to me.

"Black, one sugar I believe?"

"Errr, yes, thank you." Trevor obviously took more care in preparation than I did when it came to business meetings. I never took my coffee any other way and he knew that.

"He's quite a character, Chris, your boss."

It wasn't a question or really a statement, simply a prompt for further conversation.

I replied, trying to remain as diplomatic as possible, not really knowing where the conversation was going. "Well, I suppose he is. Like all bosses, he has his moments."

"Is he a good boss? Do you enjoy working for him?"

"Yes, like I say, he has his quirks, but ... yes ... I suppose I do ... in a way ... look ... Mr Talbot, Trevor, ... I'm a little confused as to the reason for this meeting ... Chris is very, well ... protective about his clients. He wouldn't approve, I'm sure."

A blue fire flashed in Trevor's eyes and, for a second I imagined a rage of biblical proportions was to be released that would turn the quiet contemplation of the room into a swirling vortex of crashing furniture. Then, as if simply a product of my imagination, it was gone and a calm peace returned to his face. He was standing, his movements so quick, I hadn't noticed him rise from the settee.

He strolled to the large window, arms behind his back and, after a moment of awkward silence, his voice cut across the void.

"I've known Chris for many years ... six or so ... yes, must be. Bought one of my houses you know. Done a lot of business with him. Always thought he was ... smart in business. Trustworthy. Trust him?"

I wasn't sure what I'd heard.

"Sorry, Trevor, I didn't catch ..."

"Do you trust him Andy? Would you give him your lottery winnings to invest?"

"Well ... that's an odd question. You know it's not something I've really given much thought to. But yes, I trust him. I don't see any reason not to. I've certainly never been given any reason to think otherwise."

"How much do you know of me and my relationship with Chris?"

"Trevor, I'm not sure I like where this is going." I felt a warm rush of heat up my back. "CSA always operate a strict confidentiality - Yvonne, Chris's secretary never even lets your file sit on a desk without her being there. If you think Chris has been divulging information about your dealings with him, I think you're sorely mistaken. I for one ..."

"No, Andy, you miss the point, I'm not concerned about office tittle-tattle. I feel sure you have all developed theories about the 'mysterious Trevor Talbot'. What I'm concerned about is my relationship with Chris and, while I expected nothing different in your answer to my question, your reaction tells me a lot about your own personal ethics. You like to see the best in people, even if the worst is easier to spot. I may be wrong, God knows I have been in the past, not often mind you, but your reaction shows me that my 'problem' with Chris is not one that I will have with you."

For the briefest moment, the previous rage glinted in Trevor's eyes before a calm settled itself over his tired features.

"You see Andy, I believe I have a big problem with Mr Stevens."

The same stiffly prickling sensation began its crawl up my neck and I struggled not to shiver. Trevor's gaze changed swiftly from the mellow friendliness of a favourite Uncle to that of the steely determined stare of a spurned and angered businessman. Under the unrelenting glare of Trevor's piercing eyes, I felt like a rabbit, stunned into frozen terror at the onslaught of brilliant white headlights - desperate to flee to the safety of nearby undergrowth, but unable to galvanise into any form of movement.

"Mr Talbot, Trevor … I really have no idea what you're talking about. Chris never lets on …"

"I know," Trevor interrupted, "you've been very clear on your office and its embracing of the ethics of confidentiality. I wonder, though, how does your firm, or more accurately, Mr Stevens stand on fraud?"

I rose from my seat and cleared my throat; acting as mediator to my employer's dubious business activities was certainly not in my contract. It was time for a rapid exit.

"Midland Mutual," the words came from Trevor, still staring out to the lawns beyond, "you've dealt with them I suppose?"

… Midland Mutual, yes, a traditional society, recently gone through a re-organisation. Big in with profits, bonds and traditional whole of life assurance policies. Mutual in its organisation, a head office, no regional offices, advisers working from home. My best friend worked for them, Manager was utterly disliked, bit of a twat, a real company man through and through, Spanish or something like that …

"Yes, Trevor, of course, they're a trad …"

"I know they're a traditional mutual; good with profit performance. I have policies set up with them by your Mr Stevens, have done for years. They've done alright for me." He paused. "Earlier this year, I did an investment through CSA, a large amount of money all told, in one of these bond things your boss is constantly pushing, 'reduce your I.H.T. bill Trevor and give a bit back to charity', that's how Chris sold it to me. I'm not short of a few quid Andy, as you well know. Great idea I thought, what with this bastard cancer that's killing me, 'yes Chris, good idea, I'll give a bit to cancer research, do my bit.'"

This time the pause stretched on interminably, I was about to speak when Trevor turned, red faced, features like thunder.

"You see Andy, I thought I'd check on my investment, what with the economic climate and all the shit that's going on at present. Chris had said the best thing to do was to forget about it, wouldn't be paying out until I'm dead anyway. 'Leave it to bumble along' his exact fucking words 'let it ride and do some good when you're gone.' £750,000 all told. I don't let that sort of cash bumble along, even if it is for some other fucker when I'm dead."

Trevor was on the verge of apocalyptic rage, his whole face coloured bright red, no signs of the grey pallor that had struck me at the start of the meeting.

"Trevor, please, calm ..."

"It doesn't fucking exist," spittle flew from his mouth as he spoke and arced across open space, back-lit by the sunlight streaming in through the window.

"I've spoken with their people and all they tell me is that I must have the wrong policy number. I've checked a dozen fucking times and phoned them twice. The policy number I'm giving them is straight off my document. They have no record of it. *It never fucking happened.* It's a fucking ghost policy, an apparition. Read my God damn lips Andy, it doesn't exist, it's a pseudo-policy ..."

"I'm sorry Trevor, I didn't know."

"I know, you've already told me about your wonderful confidentiality ethics." He was calming down, the rage seeming to drain away, leaving a tired old man who seemed ashamed of his temper.

"No Trevor, I mean about your illness. You mentioned you have cancer. I'm sorry, I didn't know."

"Had it for years, thought I'd beat the bastard twice. It's in my liver now. Not good when it turns up there. Death knell and all that. Perfect you see, for a bit of Estate reduction. Gifts to charities being exempt or whatever. I argued that I could just leave it in my account and will it to them. 'Yes Trevor you could, but they give you an enhancement for large sums in this policy, plus potential to get some better growth. Turn your cash into £770,000 in a year, plus an extra 1% on death', that's what he said."

He continued to cool down, losing his flush, his colour reverting back to a more normal shade. He reached out to steady himself and sat heavily into the leather chair he had previously vacated. At that point I thought he looked utterly drained. For the first time I was looking at an ill man.

"I'm sorry, I shouldn't have ranted at you. I need some help. If my worries are correct, Mr Stevens has shafted me over good and proper. It's not the money, it's the principal of it. In a few months I'll be dead ... that doesn't worry me, Christ I've had a great life - wrung every drop out of it. Done things that most people only dream of. But if my dying swells that bastard's bank account by three quarters of a million quid, I swear I'll haunt him for the rest of his life."

The next two hours passed in a blur of information that left me reeling and punch drunk. Revelations that, at first, stunned me to silence, then brought on a flood of questions, anger and disgust.

David Charles, the enigma that turned up at CSA the previous year, was an old friend of Trevor's that had, in his words, 'gone rotten as a carrot'.

He was involved in various interests, lately becoming more and more intricately entwined in the drug trade. Cannabis mainly, in all its forms, from normal strength grass to chemically enhanced resin that 'hit you like a sledgehammer and left you reeling in a hallucinatory daze for hours'. He also dabbled with designer drugs, specifically ecstasy and good old Charlie, but, a traditionalist at heart, preferred his grass roots of cannabis.

Trevor had unwittingly become embroiled in the business when he loaned David £100,000 for a supposed property development that turned out to be a shipment of Colombian finest. He'd threatened to go to the Police there and then and continued to threaten until he received nearly £200,000 in cash a month later in used notes as a return on his investment.

"I was stupid Andy," Trevor confessed. "I didn't need any more money, was already well on my way to my grave with this cancer and certainly didn't want to end my days as a drug dealer. I've been no saint in my life Andy, I'm not saying that, but drugs, Jesus, I've never even smoked a joint. Money though, that's my drug. The more I have, the more I want. I couldn't help myself. It was all so easy and, as I didn't touch the stuff myself, didn't see the shit it caused in people's lives, I felt I was exempt. Cocooned from it. It's bollocks. I'm as guilty as the pimp that strings a twelve year old up on heroin, so she'll fuck his clients. Guilty. Stupid. Greedy."

Regular deals over the intervening months swelled Trevor's cash reserves and, he admitted, caused him not insignificant problems as what to do with it. "But Christ Trevor, investing in insurance bonds? I mean … all the paperwork, it leaves a trail you know? Client identification, money-laundering legislation. The system's tight. How …?"

"Stevens has a 'friend' in a dozen insurance companies. It doesn't present a problem. I told him I was done with the drugs thing. Wanted out. Decided to put my ill-gotten gains into trust for charity and scribe a line under my past."

Trevor paused, sighed and seemed to slump deeper into his chair, a wasted carcass that appeared to shrink into itself.

"God that sounded so pitiful, so pious. *Scribe a line under my past?* Crap, I was terrified of getting caught and ending up dying in prison."

I collected my thoughts and spoke again.

"What about money laundering regulations though Trevor? I mean, every case I write has to have proof of ID and such like."

"Yeah, I gave my passport every time and Chris duly noted the number on his little bull-shit form. But Christ Andy, what does that prove? I put £30,000 from my first deal, a third of my drug profit straight into a unit trust with Chris. The cash had gone straight into my business account with invoices to prove it was payment from work I'd done to help out a builder friend of mine. All bogus, but Andy, my business turns over £60-70 million a year. £30k just gets lost. I paid myself a dividend, so I even paid Tax on it. That's a laugh, I thought, paying the Inland Revenue tax on drug money. Then I wrote out a personal cheque, showed my passport and away I went.

"The paperwork matches for that, I've checked. All present and correct Sir."

"What about the Midland Mutual case?"

"Ah, that was a bit different. I gave him cash. Said he'd 'make it disappear', if that's what I wanted. One of his contacts at Midland Mutual would need a cut, £10,000 all told. He even gave me a brochure 'Key Features' he called it. Very nice, very glossy, all plain English and easy to understand. Thing is Andy, when he said he could make it disappear, I didn't quite have this in mind.

"We sat for an hour, filling in paperwork, chatting and setting out the trust forms. He had me fooled."

My mind was racing. A feeling of utter confusion clouded my thoughts. I hadn't a clue what Trevor wanted me to do, but knew that whatever it was, it wasn't going to improve my day much.

"I know what you're thinking Andy … 'what's this got to do with me? What can I do?'"

Again, that flash of intuition, second guessing, mind-reading or whatever it was. Quite frankly it un-nerved me with its unerring accuracy.

"I want you to check. That's all really. Do a bit of digging for me. Perhaps miracles actually do happen and they find an administrative error, that some dizzy school kid's typed in the wrong policy number and shoved the paperwork in the wrong filing cabinet … I just don't know. Thing is Andy, if he's done it to me, if my fears are correct, how many others has he done it to? People who can ill afford to lose their life savings? People trying to do a good thing on their deaths, leave a bit to a deserving charity and meet their maker with a sense of well being. Shit Andy, if my thoughts *are* right, I dread to think what he's done already. I'm a good man you know. I've done some things in my life that I'm none too proud about, but basically I'm alright. I pay my Tax, look after my staff, try to put something back into society.

"Yes, Andy, the whole drugs thing was wrong, 'bad shit' I think would be the modern phrase. I'm not proud of it, not one bit. But, God, I tried to put it right, give it away to charity. It's caused me some sleepless nights, I can tell you. Imagining the local papers banging on about the local businessman dying and leaving nearly a million quid to a cancer charity. Praising my generosity and public-spiritedness, while all the time the cash came from drugs. I'd got it right in my head though, you know? Made my peace if you like. Come to terms with what was done, was done. Now it looks like the only thing to be done is me. You know the true irony Andy? You want to know what *really* sticks in my craw? I thought of Chris as a friend. Priceless, don't you think …?"

A heavy silence hung over the room, broken by Trevor's laboured sigh that seemed so desolate and utterly without hope. It was one of the saddest sounds I'd ever heard.

"Why me?" The sound of my own voice was startling and unexpected. For a moment, I wondered whether I'd actually spoken or simply thought the question. Trevor looked across, his eyes red with what looked like tears and, for a moment, one fleeting second, I saw a small boy lost and hurt.

"You have a trusting face. When I met you in the office that time, I was struck by your honesty. I'm good with people you see. It's a gift I reckon. I saw high moral values and integrity in you, it came through in your handshake, refreshing, unusual. It reminded me of what I believed in when I was your age."

I dropped my gaze, studying the shine on my shoes, the patterns of the carpet, anything, in fact, to avoid having to observe the pain and tormented anguish in the face opposite that appeared to be broken and pleading for help.

"Look Trevor, I'll see what I can do. I'm not promising anything though, working at CSA is, well, difficult sometimes. Chris has a habit of knowing what's going on." Gazing at the ceiling, I felt like I was stepping from a comfortable place of warmth and peace into a cold void, a world where demons lurked and pain was never too far away. "Give me the policy number then. I'll phone from home this afternoon."

Trevor moved to a chest of drawers on the far side of the room

I watched as if in a dream; watched the key being inserted, the twist of Trevor's wrist and heard, as if from below water, the click of the lock as it turned, half expecting the drawer to burst open, flung by the demons that had infected my life during the last few hours, to hear the accusations and warnings to '*leave well alone*' scream across the void of carpet space between them. Instead, Trevor removed an envelope containing policy documents.

There was no blinding light, no fearsome portents of doom. Just an old, sick man needing help.

It didn't help me though. A sheen of sweat seemed to have sprung from every pore to accompany a tightness in my chest and heavy weight of despair that had settled on my shoulders as I walked slowly to my car. Trevor stood, old and frail, in the doorway, watched me all the way to the gates then, as they swung open to allow me through, he simply melted back into the building with a seamless grace.

Allowing the engine to bumble along at low revs, I turned back towards home, a feeling of dread threatening to crush me as I increased speed and instinctively reached for a cigarette.

The Nissan's engine purred, rising in note as I tramped down on the accelerator at the apex of a bend, propelling myself back up to seventy in the first few yards of the next straight. Trees and hedgerows flashed past in their early summer vibrancy and despite the morning's revelations I felt quite at ease.

Later, sitting in the overly warm lounge of The Dick Whittington Public House, a coffee and cigar to keep me company, every word of the meeting with Trevor replayed itself in my mind.

I couldn't help thinking that, if Chris had shafted Trevor out of his money then it was his own tough luck. Let's face it, Trevor was blatantly trying to launder drug money. What honour can possibly come from such dealings? OK, he was only trying to do the right thing; give his ill-gotten-gains back to charity. But they *were*, after all, extremely ill-gotten, not just a couple of thousand quid from a building job that he'd paid no Tax on.

Drug money.

As my coffee cooled and my cigar uncoiled smoke into the sunlight streaming through the window behind me, my thoughts turned to CSA and, more accurately, to Chris.

Trevor was very hesitant to describe Chris's involvement in the actual drug dealings. It had been, however, quite clear that he was more than just a sleeping partner and that his new property was being used as what appeared to be a storage depot. For want of a better description - *headquarters* for the deals.

Ideas and images streamed through my mind. If £750,000 could be shifted relatively easily through the finance industry, as regulated as it was almost to the point of strangulation, how easy would it be to make £10,000 or £20,000 disappear? If Chris had the audacity to carry out such a scam with Trevor's cash, what hope for any of his other, less well healed, 'wealthy greys'?

The policy documents, spread out on the table in front of me, were allegedly, the real thing. If the policy didn't actually exist, the cash having been diverted into Chris's own accounts, then they had to be fake.

I decided my first task would be to check against my own policy documents. I'd put a rather modest £10,000 into a bond with Midland Mutual a few months previously, drawn by the promise of a good return. Their pedigree was strong, past returns had been amongst the best in the industry, no secret there. I'd even called in my best friend, Al to arrange it, forsaking my own commission to help my best pal towards his target. As I left the pub, I hoped that this was all one big mistake. In my heart though, a cancerous seed of doubt had already taken hold and, if I was true to my gut-feelings, I knew this was no administrational error.

My spare room served as my office. It was a place solely for work. I never entered unless it was to phone clients or prepare reports. It wasn't part of the home, but a necessary evil; shut up when not in use.

Working largely from home had its advantages, but the ability to shut it out at will had always been important to me. I never entered it at the weekend. Weekends were for me and Rach. Chris knew it and respected it. He never called at the weekend or outside normal office hours.

On the desk, pride of place went to a green leather blotter and, behind that, an antique lamp with brass fittings. Trevor's policy lay on the blotter, neatly piled with the acknowledgement letter sitting on top. Next to it, arranged in the exact same way, my own policy. It took only a few minutes of examination to realise that they were exact facsimiles of each other. Through a magnifying glass, the type was exactly the same. The format of letter and documents were exact. I felt sure that if any differences were to occur, it would be in the schedule. Computer printed on flimsy paper and in poor quality type that, in fact, made it distinct in itself; it would be difficult to reproduce.

Nothing. Right down to the Society details, address and associated organisations printed in tiny blue type at the foot of the page, the pair were identical. If there was indeed a difference, I for one couldn't spot it.

As a last resort, I'd held the two documents up against the light of the window, looking for the watermark that accompanies most brands of paper. A single rose-like pattern embossed into the bottom left corner of each individual sheet, save for the actual schedule, stared back at me. Same print, colours, spacing, format and even make of paper.

No difference.

Trevor's was a Midland Mutual policy in every way, save for the fact that it didn't exist.

"Hello, Midland Mutual, how may we help?"

"Ah, good afternoon, it's Andy Perkins from Chris Stevens Associates. Can I speak to someone about a client's policy please?"

"One moment."

A rendition of 'Green Sleeves' played, apparently by a twelve year old on an old electronic organ, briefly filled my room. The phone was on speaker, a Dictaphone placed next to it to record the conversation.

I absentmindedly clicked my lap-top. I was quickly becoming frustrated by my lack of success at completing 'Free-Cell' game number 15662. It was my third attempt and again, my free cells were full and a statement asking me if I wished to try again, flashed onto the screen.

"Good afternoon, customer services."

"Hi, it's Andy Perkins, Chris Stevens Associates. Could I have a value on policy number Y22469/01 please?"

"One moment please sir."

Silence filled the space. The barely audible click-click-click of expert fingers on a computer keyboard drifted back from the phone.

"I'm sorry sir, could you give me that again please?"

I repeated the number, knowing it would do no good. A warm flush spread rapidly through me and a persistent buzzing in my head made me think the phone was playing up.

"I'm not getting anything for that number at all. What's the clients name and address?"

I dictated the details and was provided with a list of other policies held by Mr Talbot. As the old man had said, 'all present and correct sir'.

I was fighting a rising panic, now desperately wanting to finish the call.

"Not to worry, I'll check with the client and get back to you. Sorry for the trouble."

"No problem," a pause, "anything else I can help you with today?"

"No, thank you. Thanks for your help."

Pushing the 'end' button on the phone and then 'stop' on the Dictaphone, I re-wound the tape and re-played it. I felt myself slump into the chair, a deep confusion and a feeling of utter despair in my chest.

No Admin error then.

Trevor was right, the policy didn't exist. £750,000 just simply disappeared. It was indeed a 'ghost policy'.

The rest of the day dragged. Even the weather, grey and damp after the morning's sunshine, strove to depress me. No matter how I tried, the work simply wouldn't go away. I'd got a report to finish, half a dozen calls to make and I needed to nip into the office to grab a file for my one 'official' appointment of the day.

I shuffled papers, dialled numbers, spoke to a few clients and left a few messages, by which time it was 4.30 and I needed to be away for the office.

Rach would be back at 5.30 and, yet again, she'd be returning to an empty home. Given that I reckoned I'd be with the clients for an hour, perhaps an hour and a quarter, I banked on being back at around 8-8.30. Time for something to eat, a brief chat about the day and then to bed. It was an aspect of the Industry that I detested above all others.

I left a note, signed it with 'Love you xx' and left.

The traffic was relatively light, being the hour between the school run and rush-hour and within fifteen minutes I was heading towards Leominster and my meeting with the Shuttleworths. They had a bond maturing and were looking for ways to invest the proceeds by way of something more open-ended. All-in-all, a simple piece of work. Good for commission, quick, easy and simple to explain. The life blood of my business.

My mind was elsewhere though. The CD player mumbled away in the background. Capercaillie usually sped my mind away to my beloved Scottish Highlands. Today though, I hardly noticed. Trevor's situation unrolled like an endless newsreel across the projection screen in my head. Snippets of our conversation played over and over and the policy documents imprinted themselves into my memory, perfect in their duplicity.

Brake lights suddenly filled my vision. The Volvo I'd been

following, had slowed to allow a lorry to pull out from the left.

I stamped on the brakes and felt the judder of the anti-lock brakes under my right foot and the slide of my rear tyres, stepping out towards the verge.

With no hint of the slow motion that people talk of just prior to an impact, I lifted off the brakes and swerved out onto the far side of the road. The Volvo flashed past on my left, its driver unaware that I'd even been following him.

Headlights flashed me and I just had time to see the smoke flare from the tyres of the oncoming Escort as I mounted the low grass embankment on the far side of the road. I came to rest at a shallow angle, completely on the grass. The Escort sped past. I'd overtaken the Volvo and the rumbling lorry, now having reached about fifteen miles per hour and had time to jump out of the driver's door and hurl some well timed and frantically chosen abuse at the grey haired driver, as he accelerated away.

An inspection of the car revealed mud splattered paintwork and a cracked right wing mirror that I'd caught on a low branch.

Lucky that time, *very* lucky indeed.

The rest of the journey passed without incident. The music managed to do its job of calming me, taking me away to a place of rolling glens, mountain streams and jagged peaks.

The three cigarettes, chain-smoked, for the rest of the trip also helped.

The Shuttleworths were a likeable couple; both retired school teachers, both very tweedy, incredibly courteous, friendly, rather scatty in a wonderful, easy going sort of way and very comfortable, financially.

I enjoyed seeing them, mostly because of Edward's passion for photography and fishing.

He'd recently returned from a trip to The Karluk River on the West coast of Kodiak Island, Alaska. He reckoned his passion for salmon fishing had been sated to such a point that he'd swapped his rods for his camera and wandered the banks snapping off a dozen or more reels of film.

I was in the middle of helping Edward re-live the experience and had started on my second coffee, when, out of the corner of my eye, I saw a photograph on the Shuttleworth's portable TV that caused my jaw to drop.

Trevor Talbot, resplendent in dinner jacket and velvet bow tie, stared back at me from the top left hand corner of the screen. The news reader was speaking about the huge impact he'd had on local business over the previous fifty years and how he would be sadly missed.

"Sorry, Edward, can I just listen to this a minute?"

"… local charities and the community in general have also benefited greatly from his generosity. Trevor Talbot, who died peacefully at home, earlier today at the age of eighty two. And now to the weather for our region, Stephanie, what's in store for us tomorrow?"

"I was with him this morning. Jesus. Edward, I was with him just this morning."

An awkwardness settled over our meeting, so I made my apologies and was gone within half an hour. A cheque for £28,000 and an application for a 'Celebration Bond' tucked into my briefcase.

I phoned Rachel to say I was on my way and waited for the barrage of questions about Trevor. As none came I presumed she'd obviously missed the news.

Parking on the drive, I stopped before reaching back into the car for my briefcase. The sky was beautifully mottled with high patchy cloud. Stars were sprinkled haphazardly amongst them. The moon poured a brilliant liquid light through a wispy gauze of vapour and its massive silver orb was surrounded by a vivid halo. A natural wonder, its glow shone with all the colours of the spectrum and, from the other side of our high garden wall, the tinkling of water from the garden pond permeated the night-time stillness.

Peace, tranquillity, a welcome respite from the days events. I was home, a minute away from a welcome hug, a smiling face, a glass of fine Merlot and a steaming bowl of sea-food pasta (I made a point of having red wine with almost everything).

Conversely, I was also possibly two minutes away from having to talk about everything that had gone on today - two minutes from having to re-live the events - two minutes from having to fill Rach in with the details when all I wanted to do was sit, eat and cuddle (in that order). A simple need at the end of a complicated day - to be able to look at a beautiful, familiar, friendly face and try to forget the fact that I could well be a load of miles up shit creek, with no paddle *and* a boat that's sprung some serious leaks.

The kitchen was warm, welcoming and homely as usual - made even more so by a large saucepan of pasta simmering on the hob. Its rich, tomato aroma made my mouth water.

Rachel sat at the kitchen table reading a novel and looked up as I stepped through the door. As always, her face lightened my day. No matter how bad the daily grind had been, a glimpse of her warm smile and round hazel eyes framed by an untidy mop of red hair never failed to lift me.

"How ya doin' gorgeous?"

"Not bad thanks. More to the point, how are you?"

"Oh ... I ... Jees ... don't ask."

"I heard about Trevor on the news. What on earth happened? I mean, were you there?"

"No. I caught it on the news as well, the Midland News, just the last few sentences. The clients had their telly on ..."

"That never ceases to amaze me. How can they be so inconsiderate as to leave the telly on when they've got a visitor? I think it's rude. If I'd got a ..."

"Rachel, for Christ's sake, it doesn't matter. What happened? The report, what did they say?"

"Not much really ... he was found in his study at home by a gardener or something. Heart attack apparently. Been suffering from cancer and hadn't got long left by all accounts. I was worried, didn't know whether you were there or what. Your meeting, could have been a bit awkward ... with Chris ... you know?"

Leaning across the table, I kissed her lightly on the lips, pleased when she stroked the back of my hair and held me for a moment.

"Yeh, first thing I thought was that I was glad I wasn't there at the time. I tell you Rach, he was a nice bloke, would have liked to have got to know him. What else did they say on the news?"

"You know, the normal stuff, 'fine upstanding member of the community, respected in business, blah, blah, blah'. And that he was dead, leaving no known relatives and a personal estate of some hugely obscene amount. I didn't catch the exact figure, but reckon it had a mass of zeros on the end."

I stirred the pasta and filled a glass of wine from an open bottle on the work surface.

"Want a top-up?"

"I've already had two glasses. You trying to get me drunk?"

"Might be, I've had a hell of a day and could do with a pick-me-up."

"Fill me up, grab a bowl of 'slop' and tell me all about it."

I was surprised by how easy it came. Every detail of the conversation, my uneasy feelings on arrival at Trevor's house, the missing policy (which raised questions of whether it would come out when his estate was calculated - something that honestly hadn't entered my head before Rach raised it).

It was 11.30 when, with the final dregs of wine swilled and the pasta leaving me with a warm, full feeling, the conversation dried up.

"What are you going to do now, you know, about his missing money?"

"I'm tempted to forget about it. Trevor's dead. It was drug money so never existed 'officially'. This scam though ... I honestly don't give a damn about Trevor's cash, but ..."

I gazed out of the curtain-less window onto a garden draped in blackness, my face, dog-tired and full of worry, gazed back at me.

"If he's done it to Trevor, what's to stop him having done the same to others? Those policy documents, Christ you should see them Rach, they're works of art. If they've come from Midland Mutual, then someone there is as bent as Chris. If they haven't, well, Chris is some sort of master forger."

As I uttered the words, they stuck solid in my throat, as though they possessed a mass.

Unwittingly I'd become embroiled in major fraud and, in a bizarre twist of fate, I'd ladled a huge slice of 'lady luck' right into Chris's lap.

Trevor's executors would find no trace of the policy. No awkward questions would be asked, no enquiring phone calls would be made to Midland Mutual.

"The policy documents, Rach, they're on my desk upstairs."

The following day I called the office, putting on my best 'God I feel shit voice' and had Tina cancel all of my appointments.

"Tell Chris I'll probably be in tomorrow, I think it must have been something I ate."

My first cigarette of the day, usually the best, made me feel ill, it was drizzling and dull outside and my head throbbed from the half bottle of wine I'd drunk the night before.

And I *did* feel ill, quite genuinely, but it was nothing to do with anything I'd eaten. It was more to do with a leaden feeling of utter hopelessness brought on by 'Trevor-Gate' as Rachel had coined the whole situation. She'd left for work an hour before and now, toast and coffee finished, I sat at my desk staring blankly at the documents piled on its surface.

Dialling a number, I checked my watch.

Six rings, a beep, then "Hi, this is Alan Jones of Midland Mutual, sorry I can't get to the phone at present, please leave a message and I'll get back to you as soon as I can."

Another beep.

"Al, it's me." A pause. "Al, you lazy bastard, pick up the goddamned phone," another pause, "Al," shouting now, "come on, come on, I know you're there."

"Fuck me chappy, it's the middle of the night."

Al.

Tall-ish, dark-ish, some would say handsome in a 'mid-thirties, losing his hair, a bit on the rough side, sort of way'. Often caustic, always up for a laugh, told you everything straight and loved a debate on any subject.

I'd known him for twelve years. We'd met while we were both working for National Life and had hit it off almost immediately. We shared a mutual love for fishing and, when Al left to join Midland Mutual, the fun of the job at National had largely left with him.

It was around this time that I started suffering from alarming headaches. I put up with them for a while, ignored them really, until, being unable to cope with the kaleidoscope of flashing lights and blurred vision that visited me on a daily basis, I went to my doctor.

What really forced my decision to seek medical help was suffering what, at the time, I was convinced was the beginning of a stroke.

It was around half past ten one night. The road from Bromyard was deserted, damp and windswept and I'd made apologies to my client (a young nurse with an interest in alleviating the financial effects a long term illness could bring), as I could only clearly see her if I turned my head to the left and looked out of the right corner of my eye.

She'd been concerned, wanted me to have a lie down until it passed, but I was adamant I'd be OK. I simply needed to get home.

It did pass. Ten minutes of cautious squinting into my journey, I could see clearly, fifteen minutes in, it felt like a bowling ball had fallen on my head from a great height and after twenty minutes and almost as many miles, a strange coldness settled into my shoulder. Icy tendrils crept along the base of my skull, into my neck and then marched into my chest, freezing my heart.

I tensed my left hand, staring unbelievingly at the clenched fingers, realising that they were dead and lifeless. There was no feeling whatsoever.

I thought I was going to die.

A farm entrance appeared in the pool of light thrown by my headlights. I screeched to a halt, sliding off tarmac and crunching onto gravel, finally coming to rest at a drunken, abandoned angle half in, half out of the gateway. I sat there gawping at my claw-like hand through eyes that seemed to vibrate in time to my pounding head. My left leg had the same creeping coldness and I realised that I was dribbling from the corner of my mouth.

Instinctively, I reached for my mobile phone, intending to dial 999 but only succeeded in sending it flying into the passenger foot-well where it clattered off the chrome door sill, the battery parting company with the handset. I let out a moan of fear and frustration. Then, as quickly as it had started, it passed. A warm glow spread from the base of my neck downwards like the warmth of a fine malt whisky. My useless left hand moulded itself around the steering wheel and the pressure in my chest eased until my heart resumed its steady, rhythmic beating.

The twenty five miles home dragged on in a never-ending, dream-like trance.

Specialist consultations, tests, scans and more consultations proclaimed that nothing was wrong. I was suffering from stress with occasional bouts of acute anxiety.

I quit National Life ten minutes after the final diagnosis, telling my boss to 'shove the job right up his pipe until he could taste it in the back of his throat', a childish comment really, not at all professional, but, nonetheless, one of the most satisfying. I spent the next six months relaxing.

I'd been scared. I expected a phone call from my specialist at any time. Always, it was a tumour, buried deep in my brain, inoperable, terminal, life-ending.

The tumour though, it turned out, was my job.

Through the whole episode, Rachel and Al had kept me from despair. Rachel with her love and Al with his straight talking, no bull-shit unsentimental common sense.

Friends which any man would be eternally grateful for.

"It's after nine for God's sake."

"Andy, as I never cease in telling you, you dumb tosser, some of us have to work for a living. Not all of us sit around in our nice IFA office, waiting for the money to roll in."

I smiled, Al was successful, up there in the top ten salesmen at

Midland Mutual. He never had any problems writing business. He just liked to have the banter, knowing it would wind me up.

I didn't bite, instead I reeled off a brief, very brief, outline of my situation, highlighting the fact that all of it hinged on a Midland Mutual policy, then waited. I could sense Al *coming round* from his sleep, like a diver decompressing or the gradual clearing of cloudy thoughts following a night on the beer.

After what seemed like an age, I heard a sigh. "Bloody hell Andy, what are you going to do?"

"I thought you might have an idea or two."

"Erm, I ain't even up yet mate, so don't expect any sign of conscious thought from me for a while. Tell you what, give me half an hour. Come round then, I haven't got any appointments 'til this evening."

I stifled a smile and replied, "I thought us IFA's had it easy?"

"Do you want any help or what? ... oh bollocks. See you in half an hour."

The phone was dead in my hand and the brevity of the moment gone, I looked at the pile of paperwork scattered on my desk and silently wished, not for the first time, that I'd never heard of Trevor Talbot.

Al

Al lived in an end-terraced property, described in the literature, when he bought it as a '... delightfully presented cottage-style property of traditional character, set in the rural Midlands'.

It *was* delightful. It was set in the rural Midlands (less than half a mile from, amongst other things, Chris Stevens' grand country retreat). It was well-presented, with modern kitchen, double glazing and a spacious conservatory.

It wasn't however, a cottage.

"It's a terraced ex-council house, Al."

"Bollocks, it's a cottage, it said so in the bumph."

Al was adamant. He did, however, just the once, at that point somewhere between a half and two thirds of a bottle of whisky when the tongue really begins to loosen, spend half an hour singing the praises of ex-council houses. Specifically about how they could almost certainly survive a nuclear blast; definitely survive being hit by a runaway truck and how he'd reduced two drill bits to useless swarf just trying to put up a picture. I asked him if he was sure the offending drill bits had been masonry drills and not wood drills. He replied that he didn't know there was a difference. I made a mental note to never ask him for advice about D.I.Y.

Despite what anyone said, it was a cottage and he loved it. He would sit in the garden with a glass of whisky and a cigar on summer evenings, watching the night develop. He was proud that he had badgers visit from their set in the nearby woods and a sparrow hawk that would zoom in and take blue tits from his bird table.

If there was a slight drawback, it was the neighbours.

Loud parties, late night D.I.Y., ear-splitting music, overhanging, light-blocking trees, screaming kids or unsociable cats making deposits in the borders were the complaints of normal mortals. Like Al's unusual garden visitors, where Al had badgers, his neighbours were a rarity also.

They were naturists.

Visions of lithe Swedish blondes cavorting with a beach ball could not be further from the truth. Al had Geoffrey and Enid.

Geoffrey, in his late fifties, was a retired director of a local office stationery company. He was bald, fat, saggy and very pink. I can honestly say that I'd never seen anyone quite so pink. He didn't have the burst blood vessels of a drinker. He was just uniformly pink. A very pale body left in the hot, mid-day sun for a couple of hours would go a similar shade.

Spring, Summer, Autumn and Winter, the pinkness prevailed.

Enid was a similar age. Grey haired, slim, if a little on the skinny side. She stood five foot nothing and possessed the most disproportionately large breasts I'd ever seen. In her prime, I could imagine her being an impressive creature, turning heads whether dressed or otherwise. Her prime though, sadly, was well passed and gravity had imposed its will on her prize bosom creating a sagginess to almost rival her husband's pinkness. Al reckoned that, when she knelt to weed the borders, they brushed the soil and ended up muddied and encrusted with grime.

They were not fair weather naturists either.

If they were at home, rain or shine, snow, sleet or hail, they were, well … open to the elements. Enid, resplendent in wellies and a woolly bobble hat, scarf blowing around her nakedness while she swept leaves in a November gale was a sight to see.

Al had been at his 'cottage' for just over two years and during that time had spent the total sum of £17.40 on its refurbishment.

Doormats, front and back, both saying 'welcome' had set him back £12. The £5.40 was for a poster in a Perspex clip-frame from a car boot sale. Taking pride of place above his lounge fireplace, it depicted a man in a rowing boat, casting a fly in the centre of a mist-shrouded lake. The positive mental attitude caption under the scene extolling the virtue of taking time to savour life, had been replaced by a typed message on a square of yellow card.

'Don't let things get you down, say bollocks to the world and go fishing'.

It was pure, undiluted Al.

Other, largely less contentious, pictures hung on his walls, but they were only new to the property. Not new to Al. He was quite proud of the fact that he had been able to lift the contents of his large flat in Wolverhampton and place it straight into his new 'cottage'.

"Why decorate if it doesn't need doing?" It was a philosophy with which I found it difficult to argue. Having spent £1,000's on our home, I still struggled to find the hole, down which I'd poured all the money.

There was a brick built storage shed at the bottom of his long, weedy garden. It housed a mass of fishing tackle, his rarely used gardening equipment and, on the wall facing the house, a circular, straw disc used for archery targets. Al wasn't an archer, nor did he stick things to the straw and blast them with his shot-gun. I've never seen a better shot with a catapult though. Nine times out of ten he could put a ball bearing into a space the size of a matchbox from twenty five yards. Better than I could achieve with an air rifle and telescopic sight. It was his party piece, much practised and as near perfect as he was ever going to get. He boasted one drunken night, his beloved 'Black Widow' cradled in his arms like a much doted upon child, that he could kill a man from thirty yards, probably more. I slurred that I hoped he never decided to take a shot at me, drained my glass and fell asleep.

The driveway consisted of tired looking, lumpy, broken tarmac gently crumbling beneath the tyres of his old, temperamental, but excruciatingly fast, Audi Quattro. A truly bizarre car for someone who allegedly didn't like driving; like paying for the upkeep of a yacht when afraid of the sea.

The doorbell buzzed abrasively and was loud enough to raise pigeons from the surrounding fields. I'd actually bought him a cable free, top notch replacement as a house warming gift. It had unfortunately been crushed, still in the box, under a beer-keg at the house warming party. Sacrificed to alcohol; not a bad way to go.

"It's open." The shout was accompanied by a brief glimpse of a blurred, frosted-glass-distorted head and shoulders from the kitchen at the rear of the house.

A strong smell of bacon assailed my senses and, as I stepped into the hallway, a machine gun rattle of spitting fat and the gurgle of percolating coffee told me I was in for a second breakfast.

He was hunched over his cooker, flicking oil over a couple of fried eggs that were sliding about in a large stainless steel frying pan. His face was a picture of concentration and I couldn't help thinking how alarmingly domesticated he looked, albeit in a very slightly manic sort of way. With a red and white striped apron over his tee-shirt and green combat trousers, he handled the spatula as though it was a martial art weapon. He barely looked up as I entered the room.

"He-he mateeeey," (he often reminded me of a mad pirate) "in the shit then, as per usual?"

"Nothing I can't handle me old mucka."

Later, having demolished bacon and egg sandwiches, two cups of coffee and a couple of rounds of toast each, we sat, pouring over the late Trevor's policy documents.

"I'm utterly stunned by this mate."

Al leant forward, re-reading the type on the covering letter.

"First things first. If you'd have come to me yesterday with these, I could have saved you a lot of time with the magnifying glass."

He looked at me, his face a picture of smug certainty.

"Our Mutual Reward Bond, you see Andy, has a maximum investment amount. £500,000. It ain't possible to put £750,000 into it. Any extra would form a completely new policy. He'd have had to have done two policies." He tapped the paperwork with the end of a teaspoon and held up his hands to still my disbelief.

"I'm not saying Stevens didn't know, he probably just banked on Talbot never bothering to check. But Christ almighty mate, not only has he sold a plan that doesn't exist, he's sold one that *couldn't* exist."

He shook his head and looked out of the window towards the fields bordering the end of his garden.

"I know one thing me old mate and that ain't two."

I looked up, incredulous, Al's ability to make light of a situation never ceased to amaze me. My face must have looked a picture.

"What? Oh come on, I don't know why you're looking so worried. Listen, I'm going to light a fire in the lounge in a minute, let's use the paperwork to get it going." He waved the paper and I felt the draught of air from its rustling sheets. "Forget you've ever seen it. It doesn't exist. The policy, it's not real is it? He's been shafted, yes, but ..."

He counted the points off on his fingers.

"One, he's dead now anyway, so it can't hurt him. Two, the policy doesn't exist, nor could it have. Three, the money itself didn't officially exist, therefore, couldn't have been invested anyway. Four, no one knows you went there apart from me and Rach and we ain't gonna say anything. And five, he's dead anyway."

"You said that twice."

"I know, just making sure you were listening. Bloody hell, get involved in this and you're likely to end up at the bottom of Edgbaston reservoir." He threw his hands up in the air in frustration, "Andy, Andy, listen to this - *drugs, drug money, £750,000 of it.* For Christ's sake, forget it."

A glint came into his eye and a smile spread across his face that was pure mischief.

"Let's burn it."

"What about the Police?"

"He hasn't sold them any dodgy policies has he?"

I laughed.

"You know what I mean. This isn't right."

"Life ain't right, life ain't fair, if it was, Chris would be scraping shit off the walls of Birmingham main sewer and we'd be fishing in the Bahamas from our Cruiser." He shook his head "Forget it, I'm serious."

Reaching across and pouring another coffee, he smiled his infectious smile.

"Fishing, Friday?"

Password

Ripples spread across the flat-calm surface as a large carp rolled, tight against the semi-submerged boughs of a fallen tree. They looked like a wind-flung, black silk scarf in the dark water beneath the dense foliage. Overhead, idyllic, fluffy white clouds, baby cumuli-nimbus, drifted in a barely perceptible breeze. Being completely surrounded by woodland, the pond rarely rippled even in a strong gale. On some days, the sound of wind-blown branches would roar like ethereal express trains, while the surface of the water would rock merely to the push of inquisitive fish.

I was crouched amongst brambles and nettles, expectant, tense and yet relaxed all at once, I watched as a good fish, perhaps fifteen pounds, maybe a touch more, drifted slowly from the left, straight towards the bait. It stopped and looked straight at me, its mouth clear of the surface, gulping air as if trying to speak. A branch was knocking against my left shoulder. It was becoming annoying, threatening to unbalance me.

The carp, surely aware of my presence, suddenly spoke, quite clearly.

"Andy, Andy."

This wasn't right. Carp can't speak. A shake, gentle at first but getting more insistent; then everything was blurry and indistinct, the trees on the far side of the pool gradually faded to exactly the same shade of cream as my lounge wallpaper and the carp grinned, developed a shock of red hair and a wonderfully sweet smile.

"Been busy?"

There was no reproach in Rachel's voice, even though a pile of washing up sat undone, greasy and festering in the sink.

I just smiled.

"Sleeping like a baby. I've been home half an hour, it's 6.30."

Now clearly in focus, her smile was that of the deepest contentment.

"I've got the promotion, Graham called me into his office this afternoon. Head of Marketing, car allowance, executive pension, health scheme, £34,000 a year."

"You little beauty." I jumped up and gave her a great big hug, kissed her solidly on the lips and then held her at arms length.

"Why didn't you wake me? Why's your hair wet?"

She was in her dressing gown, obviously showered and, on other nights, would be looking forward to a meal, an hour or two in front of the telly, then bed.

Tonight she obviously intended to miss out on the meal and telly, at least for the time being. She let the dressing gown fall open and, underneath, the flimsiest black gauze covered the contours of her body. Hugging in some places, loose in others, she looked edible. She stood, hands on hips, her smile replaced by a mock pout, and tilted her head to one side.

"Come upstairs and help me celebrate."

Rachel was muzzled against my chest, breathing deeply, but awake, released, like me. The room was dark, save for a lamp giving off its warm orange glow in the far corner of the room and a stillness, a calmness, had enveloped the atmosphere.

"I burned the documents."

Rachel stirred, as if weighing the words I'd spoken, in her mind.

"Trevor's policy?"

"Yep. Saw Al today, spent all morning and a good part of the afternoon with him. He was lighting a fire in his lounge. We needed some paper. It all went up quite well really."

Lifting her head to look into my eyes, her expression was one of confused disbelief, then she shrugged, a look of understanding creeping slowly over her face.

"S'pose it's for the best. No one needs to know do they? I mean, it didn't exist did it? What's your plan then?"

I considered my options and decided that I hadn't really got a clue.

"I've no idea. Get on with the job I reckon. Forget all about it. Shit, I don't know. A part of me wants to dig a bit yet, you know, just sort of have a little probe? Speak to a few people, ask a few questions. I just want to make sure he hasn't ripped anyone else off. I won't rest until I know. Let's face it Rach, I couldn't work for him if he's shafting people left right and centre."

The following few days went by as usual.

Work was much the same, a constant procession of appointments, reports, presentations, highs, lows, telephone calls and an endless stream of strong, black coffee with clients at desks in the office, sitting at kitchen tables or perched on the edge of soft settees.

Immediately following Trevor's death, Chris was conspicuous by his absence and, when he finally appeared, he was accompanied by a 5 o'clock shadow and a gaunt look that hinted at a deep sense of concern.

He looked like a man who'd lost something.

Something important.

Yvonne, Chris's secretary, was in the middle of typing a letter, when he bowled into the office, uncharacteristically dressed in jeans and a polo shirt. His brisk "Morning" cut through the atmosphere like any icy blast, raising heads and eyebrows alike.

"Yvonne, can I see you in my office? Now please?"

"Morning Chris, I'm just finishing this letter to Foster Hydraulics, I won't …"

"I don't care what you're doing, it can wait."

The last word of his reply was cut short by the slam of his office door, leaving behind a silence so complete and intense, that it hurt my ears.

She hastily clicked her mouse to save her work but mainly to hide her computer's information from any unauthorised eyes. Grabbing her shorthand pad, she followed her boss into his office. Shrugs and raised eyebrows passed between me and Steve like Chinese whispers.

"That can't be good eh?"

"No, I think our leader is in a bit of a mood."

Steve smiled, nodding at the closed office door.

"Perhaps one of his Armani suits shrunk in the wash? That's the first time he's been in since that big client of his died isn't it? What was his name? Terry Talbot?"

"*Trevor.* Trevor Talbot," I replied.

"Thought we'd got rid of him for a while there. Knew it was too good to be true." Steve stared vacuously at Chris's office door. "Like a bad penny though, that bastard. Keeps coming back."

I was genuinely shocked.

Steve was a true gentleman. Married, two lovely kids, a Labrador and a nice sensible Volvo that was owned, not financed. He lived in nearby Walsall, owned a detached, four bedroom house with ivy growing up the walls. It was just one amongst countless others in the area, each with a similarly sedate, sensible car, manicured lawn and a neighbourhood watch sticker in the porch. He was a devout Christian, got involved in charity work and cleaned his car on a Sunday morning between church and a roast lunch with the family.

I'd never heard him swear. In the two years I'd known him, not a single curse had passed his lips.

"Christ almighty Steve." I held up my hands in apology at my blasphemous language. "Sorry, no offence, but, I mean, mate, I've never heard you swear before. What's he done to you? I thought you two got on?"

Steve spent a moment looking at his desk, probably reciting a quick prayer of forgiveness for my outburst.

"My neighbour, about four houses down, nice old lady. We give her a lift to church, when the weather's bad and she doesn't want to walk. She's got a lab like us ..."

"Steve, I don't need her life story, what's she got to do with Chris?"

"She spoke to me a week ago, wanted advice about where to invest some spare money she's got. She's a client of Chris's ..."

A cold burst of creeping fear spread across my neck, reminding me of the headaches I used to suffer. This was nothing neurological though, just a dawning fear. This was it, the floodgates of fraud and scam that I dreaded. The knowledge and doubts that I harboured weighed heavily on me for the first time in days. Their combined weight pressed me into the seat like a physical presence.

I wasn't listening to Steve's drone. I knew exactly what was being said. Chris would have warned him off with a little jovial pat on the back, a chat about his hard work in the past building up his clients and, about there being plenty of people out there for everyone. No need to tread on each others toes.

"... kept banging on about client etiquette 'loads out there for all of us'. Finished by slapping me on the back and giving me a piece of advice about the office code of principals."

Steve shook his head, the light flashing briefly on his baldpate.

"I tell you, Andy, he was deadly serious. Stopped short of threatening me with my job. Only just though. I couldn't believe it. I would have done the business in his name, if he'd wanted, I just wanted to help out. Business is business after all. Got to be good for the practice wherever it comes from."

He looked from me to Chris's door again.

"Bastard."

"What was her name Steve, just hear me out here."

"Alice. Alice Brownhill." Steve sighed. "She's 89. In fairness, she's been a bit off lately. Real Trojan though. Still walks her dog twice a day. Turns out she attended one of our seminars at the Friendly Hotel, late last year. Never thought to speak to me though ... she didn't want to impose."

Steve slapped his desk with both palms, rose from his seat and reached for his case.

"Anyway, mate, gotta go. Late as usual. Got to be in Kidderminster in half an hour. More of the great un-washed to try and sort out. I'll never make it in time."

He patted me on the shoulder, as he swept past.

"See you."

"Yeh, take care mate."

I was alone in the outer office. The atmosphere seemed to be electrically charged while the pressure of my thoughts threatened to explode from my head. I was sure I could hear raised voices from Chris's office and wanted to leave but, at the same time, press a glass against the door and listen.

Instead, I did neither, but walked over to the back door and stood outside, studying the brickwork of the surrounding buildings and smoking a cigarette like a condemned man. Mind in a turmoil and unable, or unwilling, to think of any logical solution.

Weekends were always quiet at the office. I'd not been in since my first few months at the practice. I'd basically decided that if I couldn't do the job in the time between 9am and 9pm, four days a week, I shouldn't be in the industry.

I did, however, have a key and access to the alarm code. All of the associates were given full office access after serving three months probation. Chris would present the 'key to the office' in a typically grand ebullient ceremony, usually in the pub with the other advisers present.

His staff turnover was very low and even if it hadn't been, security was assured. No associate ever left without returning the key and the chances of getting one cut was slim, very slim. I'd never seen such an intricate cut on any key before, or since.

The alarm code was changed on a regular basis and Yvonne was quite taken aback when I asked for it.

"Don't see you in on a Saturday much?"

"No, I've got a bit of work to do and I need a bit of peace and quiet. I need the mainframe as well."

Saturday morning and the other Andy arrived ten minutes after me. He looked totally different out of his suit.

"Bloody hell mate, you've put a bit on haven't you?"

"It's the jumper, don't be fooled, I haven't had to buy a new suit for three years. Still a thirty four inch waist."

Andy two, as he was known (because he'd joined a month or so after me), was a likeable thirty eight year old. Ruddy faced and thinning on top, he reminded me of a slimmed down Father Christmas. His face always beamed, giving the impression of joviality even if his mouth was turned down at the corner. Trustworthy, honest and sincere, he was generally good company.

I didn't want it today. I'd things to do that were strictly outside of my working remit. Activities that would, if discovered, result in me being stripped of key, alarm code and job in one flamboyant swish of Chris's Armani suit jacket.

I'd been taking notice of Yvonne and trying to watch her as she accessed her computer, trying to get a fix on her password. I was fairly confident I'd succeeded and felt that Saturday was the best time to try a bit of unauthorised access.

The system was fully integrated, but each staff member had only limited access. Each client bank was protected by a password unique to the individual Adviser. Only Chris and Yvonne had unlimited access. Their passwords alone unlocked Chris's client information.

Two days earlier my terminal had blinked a message for me to change my password before access was allowed. I'd been in early, first in fact, apart from the cleaner, which was just as well or I'd have had to wait in the rain for a staff member with the alarm code.

Yvonne had arrived ten minutes later, passing the cleaner in the doorway, on her way to her other job and had mouthed "Good Morning" to me whilst continuing her mobile phone conversation with her sister, who had just given birth to a baby girl. 7lb 4oz, Vicky Louise; her third.

She'd made a coffee, phone still clamped limpet-like to her ear, sat down at her desk at 8.30 a.m., glanced at the clock and finished the call with a promise to visit that evening.

I'd watched as she click, click, clicked at the key board waiting to see if her access was interrupted by a password change request.

"Bugger, I hate having to think of a new password. It seems like it's every week." She spoke to herself and looked across the office searching for inspiration. Her eyes hadn't roamed far when a gentle smile transformed her face and she typed in her choice.

Click, click, click, click, click, a pause, then a final click.

Her day had begun.

I did the counting in my head. Five clicks, V-I-C-K-Y, then a final one, the system requiring at least one number within the password. "Could be wrong" I thought, but didn't think so. It was all too convenient. What would have been the thing most prominent in her mind as she sat down?

By my reckoning, I needed nine chances to get in, ten if I included zero; I honestly didn't think I'd need them though. How many times had I simply added a '1' to the end of my password? Then, usually when I needed to change it, I just added a '2' then '3' until I got bored or received a flash of inspiration and started all over again with a fresh one.

Yvonne's previous password had, I'd noted, comprised of eight characters. She hadn't just changed the digit.

'V-I-C-K-Y-1'. Got to be.

"What brings you in on a Saturday morning anyway fat-bloke? You struggle to get your arse out of bed during the week."

Andy two was at the coffee machine. Peering at the selections myopically, as if he'd never seen them before, he traced a finger down the choices. He looked as though poised on the brink of a choice that could have repercussions for the rest of the world.

"Less of the fat bloke. It's the jumper, it sort of hangs funny." He was facing away from the coffee machine now, holding out the woolly garment as if attempting to do a curtsy.

"Sort of hangs funny? It certainly *ought* to be. What did they do? Just slit the sheep's belly, gut it, chop off the legs and sow up the opening?"

"I'll have you know, this is top quality stuff. Helen's friend gets it direct from the manufacturer."

"Yeh, the local abattoir. No, mate, honest, it's nice. Really it is."

I paused to allow my woolly colleague time to turn back to the drinks machine then added "Park the trawler out back did you Cap'n?"

"You've just got no idea of style have you?"

He slouched across the room and sat in a swivel chair on the other side of my desk. Looking as though he lived there, he tilted the chair way back, put one leg up on my desk, stretched, yawned, sighed and with a little shake of his head reached for his coffee.

"Helen's in town looking for a birthday present for her mom. Bloody dragon. Mother-in-law, not Helen."

"Still having problems there mate?"

A big shrug, another shake of the head and then with arms raised to the ceiling he let out a mock scream of frustration.

"You could say so. She just won't let ..."

"Andy, are you here long? It's just ... well, I've got loads on ... I mean, for me to be in on a Saturday ..."

"Chill out chap. She's going to phone when she's ready, shouldn't be long."

I relaxed. "OK then, but at least get me a coffee if you're going to take my time and disrupt my work."

We sat and chatted, had two coffees and smoked a shared cigarette on the outside steps. As the conversation waned, I even considered telling him what was going on but thought better of it. His mobile went and Helen requested a lift, her shopping done.

"OK love, I'll be five minutes. Right mate, I'm off. See you Monday."

"Yeh, cheers. Have a good weekend."

He waved over his shoulder as he trotted across the car park and, for a fleeting second, I considered calling after him. The words actually formed in my throat, stuck and came out as a stifled cough. Watching my friend drive away, great bubbles of adrenaline seemed to burst, turn into huge, pterodactyl size butterflies and flap for all their might in the confines of my stomach. The pull of the front door was immense.

I could resign, become a bin-man or a window cleaner. Give it up. Forget all about it.

"Oh sod it."

My desk faced the front door, so I'd have an early warning if another of my colleagues had decided to work the weekend. My terminal sat, blank and lifeless, a pale plastic blob with single, large black eye staring at me - awaiting instructions. The button clicked into its shallow depression, the gentle pluck of noise prompting a manic whirring and fizzing as circuits flowed with electricity and the machine came to life.

Initial access was universal. The password was a gratingly ironic 'HONESTY', chosen by Chris as epitomising the ethos of the firm. 'McAfee V Shield' appeared briefly to tell me that the virus checker was working, then, against a mid-blue background impregnated with 'C.S. Associates - Financial Advice for Life', a whole host of icons spluttered into focus. I couldn't believe what I was doing, or what I *intended* to do.

Two photographs sat on my desk, next to the monitor.

The first, taking pride of place, was Rachel, sitting astride the summit cairn of Blaven, my favourite mountain. In the background, my favourite sky-line scribed a jagged arc against my favourite sky; a limitless expanse of the deepest ocean blue and the Cuillin. Ask a child to draw you a mountain range and the resulting scribble will not look dissimilar to Skye's mighty Cuillin Ridge.

In the photo, miles of shattered rock, pinnacles, precipices, scree slopes and the most unlikely paths, spread from left to right. Only Rachel's woolly hat and thick fleece jacket gave away the fact that it wasn't taken on a mid-summers day. To the right of her head, Sgurr Alisdair's spiky summit reached towards heaven, the highest point on the island - I'd have given my house to have been there right now, the events of previous weeks having been catapulted somewhere into infinity.

The second photo was me and Al. Late September on the River Severn, each with a salmon almost exactly the same size. Fifteen pounds of pure joy that created smiles almost wide enough to split both of our faces.

Happy times.

Friendship, love, big mountains and big fish. I really believed life got no better.

Back on the screen, my icons were immobile, awaiting instructions. Driven by my nervous right hand, the cursor rolled backwards and forwards across the blue background, agitating icons here and there into flashing up their contents as it passed.

The mouse felt small and smooth under my palm, an utterly insignificant piece of plastic. Silently, it sped across its black mat, in turn, propelling the silicone pointer towards its destination. Client files.

Double-click.

More whirring, fizzing and electric popping. A pause, more whirring and then the screen blinked magically to dark green, a box in the centre listing, alphabetically, all CSA's staff.

Yvonne.

Double-click.

```
please enter your password.
```

This was it. I had never felt such tension.

Even thinking back to a stupid, careless slip on Tryfan, a rocky mountain in North Wales, that had almost propelled me over a three hundred foot expanse of utter nothing to my certain, instant and brutal death, I truly thought that I'd had never felt such tension, such raw fear.

V-I-C-K-Y ... a pause.

It had to be.

I *could* still hit cancel, close down the screen and leave.

1.

I only had to hit enter.

One simple click.

One simple click, that's all it would take.

Click.

```
sorry, incorrect password.   please re enter.
```

"Shit."

Like a rapidly breaking, news-story-nightmare, the truth of the situation started to sink in. I realised, as I sat there in the empty office, staring at a blinking message on a computer terminal, that actually, I only had one more chance. It seemed downright stupid to get fired over this. No, I wasn't going to get fired. If the next one was wrong, I couldn't risk a third try. I'd have to forget it, perhaps try again another time.

But if not VICKY1, then what?

"Jesus, I could have the actual password wrong. No, got to be Vicky. *Got to be. It all fits.*"

I spoke out loud and startled myself. Without thinking, I glanced around the office as if making sure I *was* actually alone.

I needed to speak to someone.

"Andy? Hello mate, it's Andy. Yes, I know you've only just left. Listen mate, ... oh yeah, hiya Helen, you alright? (he was hands-free) ... good ... you found something then? ... yeah, OK ... yeah, see you soon. Andy, if someone had forgotten their password ... right, yeah, OK ... stupid, yes, I'm thick with a memory like a sieve ... yes, alright, whatever Andy ... fu ... sorry Helen ... Andy, Andy, listen, please. Hypothetically, I've forgotten my hypothetical password, I've tried, hypothetically, to get into the system a couple of times ... yes, I know ... yes ... yes ... ANDY ... sorry mate but I'm a touch stressed here. If I go out of the system, can I just go back in and try again another couple of times or what?"

I listened to him, well known as the office computer geek and my hopes sank.

No reprieve. No break his time.

"OK mate, yeah, thanks. See you Helen. See you Monday Andy."

Yep, my appeal had been quashed.

I'd wrongly thought that if my first two attempts drew a blank, I could simply exit, then go back in and have another couple of tries. Andy reminded me that, although this was technically correct, the system was a little cleverer. The computer kept count and only allowed three wrong attempts per day. If I failed a second time I could switch off the computer and go straight back in. But - and herein lay the real bastard - I would get just the one attempt, then 'good night nurse', all over, system locked. Yvonne would come in on Monday to find her access denied.

Oopps.

Out onto the fire escape for another cigarette and to let my nerves return to somewhere approaching normal. I wracked my brain and arrived at two, *most likely*, possible choices.

'7', surely everyone's lucky number and '4', the number of Yvonne's house.

Back at my desk I stared at the message on my terminal. It seemed to be mocking me, goading me into a rash and ill-conceived decision. I pondered the choices. Each number had its merits but, strangely, neither felt right.

I keyed V-I-C-K-Y again, then paused, two fingers hanging over two separate keys.

"Shit, shit, shit - it could be either."

My heart pounded in my ears while my fingers hovered over the two separate plastic squares. '4', had to be. The finger hanging over the '7' lowered slowly to the desk top and drummed with its neighbours to a beat in my head. The finger over the '4' dropped until it was touching cool, hard plastic. Yvonne wasn't, to my knowledge anyway, at all superstitious. Had *I* ever chosen 7 as my digit?

No. It wasn't logical.

And '4' was of course? A house number? An accident of geography? Yeh right, real logical.

"OK, OK," I agreed with myself, "not really, but at least there's some logic to it. Right, OK. Lets go then. '4' it is."

Still I hovered, unconvinced. The beat tapped out by my right hand was being filled by my left index finger. At each snare beat, the plastic square, imprinted with its three symbols shuddered at the tiny impact.

"Ahhh, bollocks" - click.

sorry, incorrect password.   please re enter.

"Noooooooooo. Ah well, it was a long-shot anyway."

Propelling the icon to cancel, I gazed at the name screen again.

"Damn, damn, shit, damn, damn, shit and shit. I was convinced that was right. VICKY - got to be."

As if in a daze, I stared out across the office, looking at Yvonne's desk in the corner. She was single. No kids. Her desk top photos were of her sister's two children. Rebecca and Simon. Two children. Now a third, Vicky. Vicky was her sister's third. Her third child. Child number three. Slowly everything seemed to click into place, like the final pieces of a difficult jig-saw. V-I-C-K-Y-3. Yvonne's previous password had comprised eight characters. REBECCA plus a number? I probably wouldn't have bet my life on it but thought it stood a fair chance.

V-I-C-K-Y-3.

The more I thought about it, the more I became convinced it was probably about right.

I stood for a second or two then set about pacing the carpet. Subconsciously, I reached for my smokes and lit one, for the time-being, forgetful of the strict non-smoking policy in the office. Over and over, I turned the idea around in my head.

"VICKY3, makes sense. Logical. Yvonne's a fairly logical lady is she not? Not worth getting in the shit over though. One in eight now. They're still not great odds."

I contemplated losing my job on what was now effectively a throw of the dice. My cigarette burned lower and the trail of ash, absentmindedly flicked on the carpet as I paced around the office, grew more widespread. I sat back at my desk and clicked on 'Yvonne' again. If I thought about it, I wouldn't do it. Simple as that. Anyway, I could doubtless explain it away as a stupid mistake or at least use the rest of the weekend to compose a real stinging, sarcastic resignation letter to present Chris with on Monday.

"Sod it."

V-I-C-K-Y, a slight pause 3, no pause whatsoever, ENTER.

I didn't see the change to the welcome screen. My eyes were shut tight while my pulse seemed to be trying to escape from my ears. I somehow expected a siren to go off or a cage to slam down around the desk, sealing me in until Monday morning.

"Yes, yes, yes. Oh you little beauty."

The search table was laid out in front of my eyes and I relaxed.

"BROWNHILL, ALICE." I spoke the words as I typed in the name, unaware that I was doing so. The client screen appeared and I hit print, hearing the mechanical printer whirr into life and the first of three sheets drop into the tray. Personal details first - address, telephone number, full name, date of birth, any employment details etc. The second sheet listed any notes made by the Adviser at previous meetings, then finally a full list of any policies held.

I was very aware of the time, and of the fact that, at any moment, any one of my colleagues, or even Chris, could walk into the office.
I hit 'search parameters' and immediately entered 'age 60+'. After a few seconds the screen changed to a list of names; an alphabetical list of anyone in Chris's client bank over age sixty.

"Bloody hell, three hundred and forty eight. Too many."

Age 70+ still brought up over one hundred. Age 80+ delivered thirty nine.

"That's just about right. Print away."

It seemed to go on for an age. I paced backwards and forwards across the office, flicking yet more ash, this time, at least, grinding it into the carpet. I willed the job done - watched the sheets pile up.

With a pile of paper hidden in my brief case, the computer shut down and alarm safely on, the drive home seemed to fly past.

Rachel knew what I was intending to do and was waiting when I got back. Sitting at the kitchen table, lost in her latest book.

"Well, how'd it go?"

"All done. Thirty nine clients over eighty years old to trawl through. V-I-C-K-Y-3, told you I was right."

"Vicky3? How did you arrive at the three?"

"Genius, pure genius. It's her sister's third child. Obvious really."

"Andy," her eyebrows raised, a look of knowing spread across her face "you're lying to me. I can tell, you know I can. What happened?"

So I told her. I have to admit to getting carried away in my story telling. A strange excitement bubbled away and threatened to boil over as I babbled on.

I suppose it was the realisation of what I'd done. Taking a gamble on my job for the sake of a fairly rash and ill-conceived idea.

"Bloody hell, I can't believe you did it. The God-damn name could have been wrong. I mean you didn't even know *that* bit for certain."

I couldn't really argue, so settled for my roguish little boy lost look and watched the wonder that is her smile break over her face.

"Fancy going out for a pint and a bite to eat?"

Monday dawned, glorious sunshine, blue skies. Burgeoning spring into summer.

My appointment level had dropped off of late and I had the morning free. I'd sat at my desk since Rach had left for work at 8.15 and by 10.30, a whole three pages of lined A4 had been covered in my meandering handwriting.

Name, address, telephone number and policy details (lump sum investments only) set out with a blank space for notes. The original computer print outs now languished in my waste paper bin, each torn into tiny pieces. By half eleven I'd spoken to six different insurance companies and had explained in each conversation that we seemed to have had some form of virus that had corrupted a number of client entry details on our computer. I was simply wishing to confirm policy numbers and detail any anomalies.

The first twenty clients, held a total number of thirty four policies. Of those, fourteen had been written in the last three months. Nine of these did not show on any computer records for the insurance company in question.

Nine policies that *did not exist*.

Agnes Whitworth had invested £45,000 into an Insurance Bond with Midland Mutual. The policy number was the right format of letters and numbers, but didn't tie up with their computer records. Written in trust, our records showed, for Cleobury Hospice.

Stanley Grainger donated £20,000 via a Capital Protector Bond with Bristol and District Assurance for the sole benefit of the NSPCC.

Gwen Hilton made an investment of £70,000 into the same type of policy with Bristol and District. Her chosen charity was Macmillan. The file notes added that she was terminal with a rare form of lymph cancer.

The list went on. Alice Brownhill, church goer and close personal friend of Steve was one of them. Her donations were split between her church, St Mary's and Christian Aid.

Her legacy extended to the grand sum of £95,000.

Their generosity and selfless actions bound them unknowingly together. United in a wish to pass some of their wealth to deserving causes upon their deaths, knowing that others would benefit from their demise.

Their deeds had also unwittingly bound them together as the victims of a loathsome man who's only concern was for his own personal wealth. His greed.

In amongst the list of unfortunate clients, Trevor Talbot sat near the top. His policies were many and varied. The whole spectrum of Financial Services, reflecting his astute business thinking and financial awareness. One policy was, however, distinctly absent.

The Midland Mutual investment had no listing. Not only had it never existed, it now had no record, wiped clean from the computer like a nasty, troublesome stain.

I couldn't understand how Chris intended to get away with the whole scam though. Trevor's money was taken as cash and had originated from distinctly ill-gotten gains; it was *never* going to be traced. Alice Brownhill though? She didn't sound like a drug-dealer to me. Her death was bound to create a problem for Chris. Even if he managed to swipe the bogus contract documents (which I felt sure, as her personal financial adviser he would), somewhere in her Financial Accounting, £95,000 would have disappeared.

It had to leave a trail, had to raise the suspicions of her trustees, bank manager, accountant; her beneficiaries for God's sake.

I stared at the list, the figures blurring into one continuous black smudge. The start of a headache prickled at the base of my skull and my eyes were sore and dry. My coffee, poured over an hour ago, was bitter and cold when I raised the cup to my lips.

I'd not touched a drop.

The pressure was beginning to tell.

From boy to man

I remember, a short life-time ago, an age when life was everything I dreamed it could be.

My parents' home, in a small village in North Wales, was for me, the epicentre of the world. I would disappear into hills that rose directly behind the two foot thick, stone walls of the cottage and lose myself in the unfolding greenery. A sheep track climbed steeply, slashing a well-trodden groove diagonally across a field where, in its far corner, a stile awaited. A brief meander through a dense wood brought me out into open pasture land once again then, after another half mile of gradual climbing, spilled me joyously onto open moorland and sweeping hillside.

The rocky ridge on the skyline was always my chosen route. It was also my playground; my slide, my swing, my see-saw. Big slabby holds and crumbling, shattered boulders of limestone and slate provided a proving ground for my later love of climbing and, by the time I was seventeen years of age, I reckoned that there wasn't a single square foot of rock that was untouched by my hands or feet.

Apart from 'Death Gully'.

The two hundred foot chimney (christened so descriptively by my father - I think to keep me off it), consisted of polished limestone walls, over which, at times of rain, a cascade of pure, cold mountain water plunged before spilling down the hillside.

The first twenty feet was an easy scramble. Holds appeared on either side of the chimney, all within easy reach, before an expanse of *just* climbable holds persuaded me up to a two foot ledge. On my first attempt to climb it, the rock was encrusted in lichen and moss, making rope-less climbing something of a lottery. I felt incredibly proud though, standing on my lofty perch, the wonderfully elevated position affording a splendid view of the surrounding valley bottom some five hundred vertical feet below me. I could see the cottage, smoke curling into the clear air from both of its chimneys. Dad was in the garden, rumbling around on his motorised lawn mower. I waived, but my greeting went unnoticed. I was, after all, over a mile away.

I searched the wall in front of me, fingers probing into cracks and over tiny ledges, the first feelings of unease forcing me to question my own ability. Slowly, another feeling wormed its way in, settling itself in the pit of my stomach. This one was quiet and persistent; it asked of my rationale at attempting the climb on my own and without protection.

Try as I might, I couldn't find a hold.

On either side of the gully, the walls were either marble smooth or crumbling and loose. The back wall was mossy and unstable, wet from the last rain and of no help to me.

I would have to climb back down.

Anyone who's been in this situation will know that to journey downwards, to *reverse* a climb can be far worse than the journey up. Holds disappear and rough, textured rock magically becomes smooth, slippery; useless.

The hillside, falling away below me, swelled the appearance of height to that of a minor Himalayan peak.

I remember, after an hour of shouting for help, feeling a strange detachment, a terrible yet somehow calming fear. I had managed to shuffle down onto the ledge so that I sat, legs dangling in space, hunched against the rock. I rationed my shouts to one minute every ten, my voice already becoming hoarse, fading with the light; becoming weaker as the wind grew stronger.

It was after 10 o'clock when I saw torch light winding its way up the slopes below and heard the shouts of my parents against the wind, now gusting, nearly a full storm.

Relief, on both parts, shrugged off any reproach at my actions. In the end a simple steadying of my foot on my father's hand provided the hold I needed to retrace my route. More so, the knowledge that someone was there for me, to support and to encourage. I never attempted Death Gully again on my own.

I remember home life being calm and serene, bucolic. Dad would retire to his study for what seemed like hours at a time, the clicketty-click of his typewriter magically transforming his thoughts into words of beauty and feeling. He wrote tales of the countryside. Innocent stories of country folk from a time long gone. Times sadly missed amongst his readers. Magazines were his life-blood, but his life's purpose had manifested itself in his novel 'Pool of Stillness'. A tale of a world long gone, of better times when a neighbour was just that, when a kindly deed was the rule rather than an exception and when the salmon ran rivers clear and pure in numbers unknown today.

I've read this work many times. Barely a year goes by that doesn't find me deep into the characters that flood with passion from well thumbed pages yellowed by time.

On the first page of my first edition, written in his favourite fountain pen is a line of wisdom that brings a tear to my eye each time I read it.

To my son, holder of my dreams. Everyone has a tale to tell.
Tell it well and let it be true and good.

I was twenty-four when the drunk driver altered my life forever. Still a child really, but one on the brink, unknowingly, of bursting into adulthood.

Twenty four is not a good age to lose a father. Just at that time when a conversation over a pint in a village pub starts to have real meaning. The time when the love of an older man, as an equal, has been earned. Golden ale and spirited games of chess in front of crackling log fires.

It's a worse age to lose both father and mother. Neither man nor boy. Too old to blubber and cry into the arms of a comforter. Too young to take out a much used funeral tie and grieve at a wake.

I found them, you see. I was following, ten minutes behind that had closed to three or four by the time it happened. I drove faster in my youth.

His car was still ticking and tocking when I rounded the corner and picked out the wreckage, half in and half out of the dry stonewall. In my nightmares, I swear I can see the wheels spinning, but I know this is purely my imagination.

To find both parents, still, yet still warm; broken and bleeding. One hundred and thirty years of life, wisdom and knowledge wiped from this earth in an instant by the selfish actions of a driver younger than I. A driver, so recently out of school who couldn't say no to another Friday night pint. To do all that, is a life-changing, near life-shattering experience.

The car, on its crumpled roof, straddled the grey stonewall, bonnet crushed against the ground, boot high in the air. Directly under it, my father's golf clubs lay like an injured animal in the damp grass (I exclaimed later, calmed by drink but still near hysterical, that they'd looked like a dead bag-pipe). It was as if the contents had been taken out and laid on the ground. They weren't scattered or strewn around. Next to the golf-bag, an old wide brimmed felt hat, pair of boots, road map and one of those reflective triangles for use in an emergency. I never thought to use it. A

life was over and its contents had seemed to just *drop out* onto the grass.
The roof had been crushed at the front, above the screen. The front seats were broken and distorted. Safety belts had turned into crushing bands, as strong as steel.

Another car, a small hatchback, was against the wall almost directly opposite and I thought, at first, the driver had stopped to help until I saw how it was embedded into the stone on the driver's side. Its driver was frantically trying to get out but I ignored him and clambered over the wall, tried to squeeze into the upturned car through the broken driver's window.

I knew, instinctively, that they were dead.

They appeared to be sleeping. No sounds came from them, no breath, no pulse.

I fell back against the wall, chest heaving, staring at the blackness above me, wanting to scream, but unable to draw sufficient breath.

I remember the noise. It dragged me bodily from my daze, a frantic banging and terrified screaming.

I remember the smell of pungent, acrid smoke.

I remember, the young lad, beating at the passenger door as flames licked under the front wheel arch.

I don't remember climbing the wall, nor picking up the piece of stone with which I smashed the back window. Nor do I remember dragging the driver out or watching him sprawl, screaming on the tarmac at the pain from his shattered leg.

I do, though, remember the alcohol fumes and realising I was staring at a murderer.

I also remember raising the stone to smash his skull.

Remember thinking, with diamond sharp clarity 'an eye for an eye'.

Sirens saved him, nothing more. I know in my heart that I would have brought that stone down and ended his life, as he had ended my parents'.

An old lady in a house set quietly in the corner of a field had raised the alarm and allowed a life to be spared.

He was banned from driving for five years and spent a paltry two of a four year sentence in prison. He spent twenty-four months behind bars and then walked free because he had been a well behaved young murderer. I often wonder where he is, what he did with his life after he had wrecked mine and ended my parents'.

I hope that he managed to get on with living. I hold no malice anymore. It was a stupid, unfortunate sequence of events that I hope he learned from; that he regrets. Sometimes, when I'm driving, especially at night, I peer at the cars around me, looking for a glimpse of recognition, knowing that it will never come. And, at my yearly pilgrimage to the place where it happened, the memories come flooding back. The smell of burning, the tick-tocking of my father's cooling engine, the screams from the other car, bathed in yellow and orange flickering light, the heat, the blackness of the summer sky and the silence from within, where my parents waited to be cut free.

I re-live the thoughts each time I visit and lay them, along with flowers and a note, at the foot of the still crumpled wall.

It took six years before I could do this without crying.

The house was sold and, only when the estate was settled, did I realise what a financial mess undercut the idyllic lifestyle of the simple cottage. All told, my father owned £12,000 more than he owed. No life assurance to ease the financial burden of death. No investments or capital to speak of to cushion hard times. I was a budding financial adviser at that time, raw and keen, moralistic and ethical, brimming over with ideas of protection, of the *right thing to do*. Scared of being pushy, shying away from the archetypal image of the life assurance salesman.

And I never knew that I could have helped them.

A few years ago, I took a couple of days over my annual visit and spent a day walking in the hills above the cottage. The rock chimney is still there along with the small wooded area and sheep dotted hillside.

A family had recently moved into the cottage, now pristine white, complete with extension, conservatory and gleaming double-glazing. They seemed a little dubious as to my request to have a look round, until I told them of my parents' accident. They knew of it, having been told by the previous owners who bought it in the aftermath of my life collapsing. We spent half an hour chatting in the kitchen, haltingly and with a distinct edge of awkwardness.

The kitchen had been my Mom's place. She could not cook to save her life, but what she lacked in ability, she made up for in boundless enthusiasm. Meals were entertaining times filled with laughter. She simply took our jokes and carried on churning out barely edible food that we became slowly accustomed to; like building a resistance to anti-biotics.
In the years that I lived there, I don't remember a single row or even a raised voice by one of us, against another.

Lifting boxes

The night rushed in, covering all in its path in an inky black, velvet cloak. Silver reflections of moonlight and stars swayed to the constant push of silky water under the bridge on which I stood. A couple of owls had hooted as the light faded, then flapped like fluffy bats from one side of the river to the other. They seemed to be checking me out.

I think I'd 'chained' four cigarettes so reckoned I'd been standing and watching the water for thirty minutes or so. In that brief time, I'd lifted thoughts around in my head like packing cases full of clutter, trying to fit them into some sort of order; a route, a map, a task, anything.

"Trevor Talbot," I muttered to my swaying reflection thirty feet below, "I wish you'd died a week earlier."

I'd uncovered £580,000 of bogus deals (give or take a quid or two), well over a million counting Trevor's missing money, but however hard I bumped the boxes around in my head, I couldn't work out what Chris's long term plans were. Stealing money from his clients had to leave a trail.

He must be building everything up to split.

Had to be.

No other answer.

His plans had a finite life span.

The next client to die would bring his whole scam crashing down.

Had to.

Dan

Daniel Soames was a normal seven year old.

From a well-to-do family, he enjoyed a privileged childhood. An only child until the age of eight, his sister was a barely perceptible bump in his mother's slight frame when his life changed forever.

Dan had a pet rat.

Mr Jingles was white, pure as snow, with piercing pink eyes and a black sock on his front right paw. He would sit for hours on Dan's lap allowing himself to be petted and pampered, would trot around the small cosy bedroom that he shared with his master and curl up on his own feather pillow at the foot of the bed.

The day that heralded the change in his young life was a hot mid-August beauty. Stifling and airless, no breeze ruffled the net curtains at his open window. Deep blue brilliance stretched from horizon to horizon in a seemingly endless exhibition of summertime. Entering the room on all fours, he squinted under the old antique chest of drawers where Mr Jingles would invariably be lying, sleeping in the shady cool. He wasn't there; just dark shadows and a few droppings, tidily in the corner.

From the other side of the bed a movement caught his eye and he scuttled across, ready to grab his friend for a much needed cuddle.

Mr Jingles lay on his side moving feebly, his white fur tinged with pink around his ears. His tail twitched in recognition at his master's approach. As Dan got closer and stooped to pick up his pet, he noticed a pool of sticky goo spreading from under the white fur and a coil of intestines that looped lazily under his barely moving abdomen.

At the same time, a hiss from under the bed drew his eye into the shadow.

A large ginger tomcat sat, hunched and bristling, its teeth gleaming from lips pulled back in anger, claws outstretched, digging into the wooden floor.

The sadness and shock Dan felt was rapidly replaced by another, more base emotion and standing calmly, he moved to the window and pulled it shut. Then, as if it was the most natural thing in the world, he walked to the soft chair in the corner of the room and sat, watching. After ten minutes the cat emerged, looked up at the window and, realising its exit was sealed, sat down next to a now still Mr Jingles and purred.

"Here kitty, come on, I won't hurt you."

Years later, Dan would realise this was his first lie. He'd told 'fibs' to his parents about broken crockery or spilled drinks, but this was a real lie, told with malice and knowing.

He spent half an hour playing with the cat, while all the time his faithful, much loved pet lay cooling in the corner, its spilled blood drying in the heat to a sticky mess. Eventually, with the cat lying stretched out on his bed, Dan took a pillow out of its case, gathered up his new playmate and forced him in. He had to hold the parcel at arm's length as the writhing, hate-filled bundle exploded in the confines of its linen prison. Screeches and hisses of pure rage filled the room as Dan carried the twisting, straining sack to his wardrobe where he removed his school tie and secured its neck.

His parents were in the garden so they didn't see Dan walk out to the shed, collect his bike and a length of nylon rope, then make his way to the track at the side of the house.

Wheeling his bike whilst carrying the pillowcase was not too difficult as his hostage was now quiet, seemingly resigned to his incarceration. When he reached the track, he turned along it and made his way to a point where the width increased in front of a gate, a turning point for farm vehicles.

Once on the ground, Tom (Dan had already named him), began to fight once more, scratching and screeching, hissing and biting, trying in vain to escape.

This simply would not do.

What Dan had in mind required Tom to be nice and still.

He pondered the problem for some time before swinging the sack around his head. Again and again the bag flew, squeals of anger and frustration cutting through the otherwise still, quiet summer afternoon. He lost count of the number of times he swung the sack, knowing only that his shoulder ached from the strain and that sweat stung his eyes.

Resting briefly, he switched arms and continued; the only sound now, the rush of air and his own laboured panting. After what seemed an age, he let the bag fly, watching it spin through the air and land with a muffled thump on the gravel twenty feet away, throwing up dust.

Nothing stirred from within the white parcel as he walked towards it, rope in hand.

The first thing that he became aware of, as he opened up his package, was the smell. Tom had voided his stomach, bowels and bladder during his flight and now resembled a pitiful creature that had crawled from a swamp and was close to death. Dan hoped it would hold out a little longer. His fingers became wet and slippery from the combination of vomit, faeces and urine, but he soon managed to tie the rope around Tom's neck.

He was breathing weakly, but seemed to be coming round.

The day was warm and Dan was in no hurry, so he sat, leaning against the fence bordering the track, waiting for the next phase of his fun.

Gradually, Tom seemed to gather his wits, at first standing shakily then making as if to move off. Dan tweaked the rope, enjoying the spectacle as Tom once again exploded in fear, cart-wheeling through the air. He scratched at the rope, tight around his neck, writhing against its pull and pawing at the air in front of his face.

Dan thought this was the most fun he'd ever had and a strange tingle ran through his body.

He played for over an hour, sometimes allowing Tom a brief respite from his taunts. He even tried to stroke him once, receiving a claw in his palm and a hiss of rage for his troubles. He answered this little misdemeanour with a kick that lifted Tom high in the air.

He walked back to his bike, paying out rope behind him without a care in the world. He was becoming bored and wanted to speed up the game, so tied the rope around the springs on his saddle, mounted it and pushed off slowly. He watched as the rope became tight and, before Tom could begin leaping and straining against its pull, peddled away. His small thighs pumped with the effort as his speed built and his breath rushed through his grimace of a smile.

As he passed his home, he was vaguely aware of a scraping, scratching sound coming from behind him. No mewing or hissing now, just a bumping, scraping of gravel and stones.

After two hundred yards he stopped and looked behind.

The cat, what was left of it, resembled a dirty orange rag. No discernible shape or form, just a bundle; blood streaked and dust caked. He walked over and prodded it with his sandal, feeling the warm damp fur against his toe and the same tingle of pleasure spread through his body.

Tom moved weakly, the last trace of life ebbing away, somewhere deep within him.

"Wow." It was the first thing that Dan had said since leaving his bedroom a lifetime ago and as he brought his heel down against Tom's head, his face lightened with a broad grin, widening as the skull crushed beneath the pressure. The tingle that had built through his body over the last hour grew as greyish pink matter oozed from Tom's broken skull. The feeling surprised, scared and pleased him all at the same time.

Life in the Soames' house continued normally for the next few months, Dan mourning Mr Jingles' passing (he was surprised at how much the loss actually affected him). Mrs Soames glowing and radiant as her figure swelled and blossomed. Mr Soames spent less time at work and more time with his wife, strutting around the house, nest making.

In early February, Dan ceased being an only child.

After an incredibly brief and fantastically unexpected labour, Emily Frances Soames arrived, bawling and howling amidst frantic boiling of water and fetching of towels. So rapid was the progression from waters breaking to full, unstoppable labour, that Mr Soames didn't have time to get the car out of the garage. It sat idling, passenger door open and expectant for its panting, blowing, grunting charge, while in the house, the full fury of a home birth broke over its occupants like a tidal wave and transformed an expectant mother into simply a mother. Dan stood while Mr Soames and his sister-in-law (there for a meal and quiet evening) swarmed frantically around their patient. He felt real joy when, amidst the blood and mucus of birth, his sister shouted her entry to the world.

For a while he saw Emily as a replacement for Mr Jingles; he could cuddle and stroke her, hold her tiny feet while she sucked at her mother's breast, dangle furry toys over her inquiring fingers and watchful eyes. He would stand at her cot for what seemed like hours (and probably was), while she slept with slowly twitching joints and constantly moving dream driven expressions.

He could honestly say that he'd never seen anything as amazing in his short life.

Well, perhaps just one thing, back in August, but that seemed somehow hidden behind gauze drapes and, try as his might, the details wouldn't become clear. They remained a hazy recollection of some life-altering experience that peeked from behind his subconscious then went back into the dim recesses of his mind.

He was eight, Emily barely four months when he reverted to his previous status as only child.

Emily was found, late for her four o'clock feed, by her mother. An instinct as old as time itself roused her from her much needed sleep and, glancing at the bedside clock, she stirred, rose from bed, stretched and made her groggy way to the nursery. She had undone the buttons on her night-dress and, in her sleep-clouded state, lifted little Emily from the cot and made to place her at her exposed breast. She sat for a moment, rocking her beautiful baby before the first tendrils of unease crept into her. She was very regular in her feeds; they joked that they could set a clock by her and yet now, as she lay in her arms, nothing stirred.

Suddenly, frighteningly awake, she realised Emily was still and cold, a blue tinge to her lips and her normally rosy pink cheeks pallid; marble white against her yellow baby suit.

Her scream woke her husband, jumping upright in bed, instantly scrambling for the door, racing barefoot across the landing into his wife's arms sobbing and bawling. Recreating the noise Emily had made coming into the world, they announced her sudden departure.

The Doctor who screeched into the family driveway fifteen minutes later, unnecessarily pronounced what the grieving, shattered parents already knew.

The death certificate, tragically premature, proclaimed her to be the victim of 'Cot Death'. No post-mortem was ever carried out.

These things just happen.

In the aftermath of such a terrible tragedy, Mrs Soames struggled to regain any sort of equilibrium. This gradually developed into her racing to the bottom of a vodka bottle and into blissful oblivion, usually during the afternoon while her 'boys' were away at school or work.

One afternoon, almost a year after Tom took his life-ending, enforced run down the farm track, and less than two months after her precious Emily became just another 'dear departed', Mrs Soames added a bottle of sleeping pills to her unusually extravagant two bottles of vodka and wrote her own death certificate.

Dan and his father sold up and moved out, ostensibly to escape the memories that haunted them around every corner of the cottage though Dan thought his father was escaping the scene of his crime. Too much work, not enough time for his distraught wife, briefly a budding, vibrant new mother. Guilt ate away at him.

Something of which Dan had no knowledge.

The new house was thirty miles away. Set, once again, in rolling countryside with neat borders and stripy lawn. Roses grew around the front door and, on cold misty mornings, wisps of grey smoke trickled from the twin chimneys.

Life, as they say, goes on.

Dan hated it.

By the time Dan was twelve, his father had gained a stone in weight, a twenty cigarette a day smoking habit, a bald patch and a friend called Betty who gradually evolved from an occasional visitor to a near constant companion. Weekend stays progressed through mid-week to permanent.

Dan was outwardly friendly and pleasant towards this new woman in his father's life. He put up with her being around because of the way he perked up and began to participate in living again.

Inwardly he seethed.

During the Christmas holiday of his thirteenth year, he was found by Firemen, sitting in his pyjamas in the middle of the patio at three o'clock, Christmas morning. Shivering and caked in soot, he stared at the remains of his home, an orange glow bathing his smeared black face. Flames roared from every window.

The whole roof collapsed as they ushered him into the waiting ambulance. Sparks flew into the early morning blackness and a roar of crumbling timber and masonry rent the air like a distant explosion, burying his father, his 'Betty', his unopened presents, the toys he had yet to play with, his clothes and a fair portion of his memories.

The firemen found nothing conclusive, finally deciding that a faulty connection on the Christmas tree lights was most probably the cause. The fire had certainly started in the lounge, but no plug had shorted. No electrical surge had created the blaze that ended two lives.

A small, bright red, glowing coal had found its way from the fire grate into the packages under the tree, melting the carpet then adding its heat to the wrapping paper.

While Mr Soames and Betty slept in their bed, tired and glowing after a particularly rampant and energetic love-making session (that had been listened to by Dan at their door) dizzy with the spent passion and bottle of brandy consumed after dinner, the eager, licking flames raced through the tree and along the wallpaper, turning it black and crinkled, before finally blazing and flaring. As the three-piece suite exploded into a fusion of light and heat, a young face peered in from the hallway. The front door stood open, creating a blast of oxygen rich air that added its fuel to the now blazing lounge. The noise was horrendous, each crackle and pop sent up blazes of sparks and fresh flares racing to consume anything that would burn.

Dan worked quickly, dropping a match into the three foot pile of old newspapers in the cupboard under the stairs, standing back as the flames reached the sloping wooden ceiling. From the front door, he watched the stair rods curl their thick, brown smoke, then burst into flame as the varnish caught. He expected to see the terrified face of his father appear at the top of the stairs at any time, sure that the noise must wake him, no matter how drunk he'd been. He waited, the smoke building, growing thicker by the second, pouring upstairs and rushing past him as he stood watching. That same tingle, almost forgotten from when he was a small child consumed him as the fire in turn consumed the stair carpet and burst upon the bathroom door. The bottom few steps were still free of flame, though the pile on the carpet smoked furiously.

Dan stepped slowly forward and stood facing the flame, feeling his hair singe and the fabric of his pyjamas begin to heat up and stick to his body. Soon his eyeballs were dry and itchy; his nostrils screamed with the intensity of the heat.

Still he stood there, knowing he was beginning to burn.

When he could stand no more, he threw himself backwards, landing heavily in the open doorway, rolling out into the front garden and smearing himself in the wet grass. Feeling the cooling dew on his skin, he watched as a face at the window stared incomprehensibly down at him. Wracked with coughing, it disappeared, momentarily appearing again, before, once more, ducking back from view. Dan could not imagine the horror, the true terror of the scene that was being played out in the master bedroom. As hard as he tried, he couldn't grasp what his father must have felt.

And he did try.

Life with his aunt, the same woman who had been present at the birth of Emily, was surprisingly good. She didn't try to replace either of his parents; she was simply there for him, striving to draw him out of his near catatonic state during the early months following the fire and then helping him to re-adjust to his new surroundings.

For the first three weeks, he did not speak.

Gradually, his story came out; of hearing the fire, of rushing from his room and half running, half falling down the stairs, through the smoke and first, delicate licking of flame. Sure that his father was still downstairs, he told of shouting for him, of screaming through smoke-raw lungs for him to get out. He was so distraught, so believable, that attention and love for this poor, traumatised child poured on him from all sources.

The only thing that he was left with (apart from an inheritance of over £750,000 after tax) was a lacy handkerchief anagrammed with an elaborate 'E'. One of Emily's christening gifts.

Prior to the fire, the handkerchief had been a constant companion, always in a pocket, never used, other than as a reminder of his sister. For the first two months after it, it never even left his hand. Any attempt to remove it brought such a stare, such a determined glare of stubborn resolve, that the recipient of the look gave up without a fight.

This dainty, lacy talisman remained in his possession always.

His life continued, but following the fire, the once confident, assertive child had somehow changed. He became quiet and withdrawn; would spend hours on his own in his room or wandering the nearby fields around his aunt's home. She became concerned for him when, on his eighteenth birthday, he disappeared in the early hours of the morning, and returned, tired, dirty and ashen faced, the following evening. In answer to her questioning, he explained simply and without embellishment, that he'd 'been out' and that he'd wanted to spend some time alone, save for the memory of his Emily.

Emily, he said, came to him, spoke with him, and was a constant companion.

He knew, he admitted, that, yes, she was dead, but he "felt her presence." She was with him all the time in some, small but important way and he needed to be with her on this, most important of birthdays.

The episode passed and his journey through college life continued, on the surface at least, normally and not without success.

He showed a talent for languages and a manual dexterity that materialised in his drawings and paintings. He would sit and paint for hours. Landscapes were his forte. Bright and airy, dappled light captured in watercolour and oil spearing through perfect boughs. His skies were beautiful facsimiles of true life. In every painting though, whether the day was bright or overcast, a corner of his canvas would depict a representation of a storm. A black, malignant, growing maelstrom of power and anger. Lightning would crackle silently from the depths of the broiling grey mass. Sometimes, the storm was merely hinted at, a dark grey smudge of malevolence at the edge of an otherwise bright day.

Along with the storms, another element was always present. Sometimes so subtle, onlookers could peer at the canvas and remark on his clever use of colour and tone for minutes before it became obvious. At others, this constant formed the major focus of his work.

A young girl - the only figure he ever included.

In what he considered his best painting, his aunt studied the scene over a period of two weeks, convinced that, for the first time, his obsession with his sister had finally been broken.

The scene was rural; glowing open fields and trees with a farm set in the distance. A track led the eye deep into the picture; winding its way into the trees, then out once more towards the farm. A bicycle leant against a fence post in the foreground and, nestling within a clump of grasses at the post's base, a subtle tinge of orange showed through the delicate blades. On inspection it became apparent that a ginger cat lay sleeping in the grass.

No young girl though.

On questioning him, he became glazed, as though his thoughts were suddenly elsewhere. He stared straight through his aunt, then, as though some spark of electricity had snapped him awake, turned, without a word and strolled to the lounge door. As the door opened and he stepped through, he paused and turned, smiling and somehow serene, calm, ultimately at peace.

"She's always there Aunt, you just need to look." His smile faltered momentarily, "Always there."

Then he was gone. With a cheery goodbye, he opened the front door and jogged into the garden, hands shoved deep into his back pockets, smiling and squinting at the clear blue brightness of the summer sky.

His Aunt watched him and, as he turned his gaze to the finches on the bird table, she swore that he was talking to someone.

She strode up the stairs and into his room which, as always, was neat and tidy. His easel stood in the light of the room's single window, on it, his latest work. It seemed to glow with vibrancy and energy, alive with the warmth of a summer in rural England. She studied every facet of the scene and, after ten minutes, her eyes were sore with staring.

On the desk lay a large magnifying glass. She swept this slowly over the trees and fields, searching, searching for any sign of a figure. Convinced that if anywhere, Dan's little girl would be in the farm, she spent five minutes studying each area of light and shade.

Nothing.

Sitting down on the bed, she put her head in her hands and sighed. He was a strange lad, no mistake, but he was a good boy, caused her no trouble. Apart from the scare he gave her when he stayed away overnight, he'd never given her cause for *real* concern. God knows he'd been through the mill. Loosing his sister and his mother, then his father, home and all his possessions in one fell swoop was enough to 'de-rail' anyone.

He *did* concern her though. The obsession with his dead sister, the stubborn conviction that she was with him always.

It scared her.

It wasn't natural.

Returning her gaze to the painting, she concentrated on the bicycle and barely visible cat lying in the grass. Her eyes swept the gravel track and then peered 'into' the trees bordering it. For some utterly inexplicable reason, the hairs on the back of her neck prickled as she searched the foliage.

There … amongst the branches … what was that?

Just a patch of light, a flick of fawn colour nestling within the darkness of the shade. Surely nothing?

Rising from the bed, she stepped closer. Unsure of herself and fearful at the same time, she held the magnifying glass up to the trees and momentarily recoiled from what she saw. It *was* brilliant. Dan must have used the glass to paint the merest representation of a face peering out from the depths of the forest. The most incredibly subtle lightening of shade formed a basic head, two flicks of light brown paint created the illusion of eyes.

As she stared, marvelling at her nephew's mastery of this most beautiful medium, the hairs on her neck continued to bristle as if statically charged. The face was looking directly at her and, from those simple blobs of pigment shone a sadness that pierced her soul. She felt a sob of misery rising from her chest.

"Beautiful, isn't she?"

Dan was standing at the open doorway, leaning nonchalantly on the frame, his face set in a non-smile.

"Yes, yes she is." It was all she could say.

"I told you didn't I? She's *always* there." His gaze became intense, great trouble seemed to flick across his face, his brow furled as if struggling with some terrible secret, an all encompassing problem fighting within him. As quickly as it appeared, the concern left his face to be replaced with the same, serene expression that had swept over him in the lounge doorway.

"Yes," he said with a terrible, longing sadness, "you're always there."

For the next few weeks, his Aunt noticed a strange melancholy in him. He was still the same deep young man, but his depth had seemed to increase. If anything, he became more introvert, never one for many words, she struggled to raise anything from him at all. So she left him alone and soon he was back in the routine of his second year of college and things seemed to return to some sort of normality.

By mid-October, his studies going well, a new, menacing element was added to his schooling.

'Big Dave' joined his course late, recently moved into the area from London with his parents. The family had followed the Father's work and settled into a nearby village. 'Big Dave' turned up at Dan's college on a nearly new Yamaha 350 and was an instant hit with both sexes. The girls liked his charming arrogance and dark, good looks. The lads enjoyed his wit and easy going nature, his choice in clothes, worldly-wise confidence and, of course, his motorbike.

Dan thought he was the most loathsome creature he had ever met and during a canteen brawl over Dan's possessive protection of his Emily's handkerchief, decided that 'Big Dave' had to go. When Dave started calling him 'hanky' or 'lacy boy', gradually breaking down his tenuous friendship with the other lads, he decided he would have to go sooner rather than later.

It took two months before the opportunity arose. Two months of critical planning and preparation that would stand him in good stead for his future, as yet unimagined profession. He learnt Dave's route home, noted the timings meticulously and every day for a week, he watched from the bushes as Dave sped past, angled hard over round the tight bend, then away, at over seventy along the lane.

Dan always left college by 2.00 p.m., having no late lessons. Dave stayed behind, catching up on the first months of missed work until 3.00.

In a strange twist of fate, Friday 13th December was Dan's chosen date for Dave to receive his comeuppance. The day was cold but dry and clear, no frost or ice. Dan stood hunched behind a large oak, a length of nylon rope, similar in many ways, to the one that ended Tom's life all those years ago, tied securely around it via a large loop. The other end was held in his lightly perspiring palm.

The lane was never busy at this time of day and only half a dozen cars had trundled around the bend in the time he waited. His hearing was buzzing as he sat in the silence then, at six minutes past three, the tinny rattle of Dave's two-stroke engine permeated the quiet. No time to waste, he sprinted across the tarmac pulling the rope behind him, frantic for a second, as it snagged in the undergrowth. Working as fast as he could, while the buzzing of Dave's approach built in his ears, he wrapped the rope around the steel post of the bad bend sign on the other side. Five, six, seven times he spun the rope, finally sliding into the ditch and holding on to his end with all his weight.

The trap had been set five seconds, no more, when he heard the blip of throttle as Dave dropped a gear and powered into the bend.

Hidden by scrubby undergrowth and below the level of the ditch, Dan saw nothing of his target's approach. In the microsecond he had to wait, he suddenly realised there was a chance, infinitesimally small, that the biker wasn't Dave. He severely doubted it, but, well, there *was* a chance.

He wasn't too surprised to realise that he wasn't *really* that bothered.

This was going to be fun, more fun than old Tom.

He felt the same, very welcome tingle of pleasure that always crept over him when exited. He closed his eyes, waiting.

He felt and saw nothing, being hidden in the ditch and cushioned from the pull on the rope by the turns around the post. He'd been worried that he may not have been able to hold the impact; that the rope would fly, burning skin as it sped through his palms, or even that his trap may not fetch Dave off the bike. (Dave wasn't called 'big' for nothing and, at six four and wardrobe-wide across his shoulders, if he simply ground to a halt, Dan was in serious trouble).

He had nothing to worry about.

He would have loved to have seen the resulting spectacle and secretly kicked himself for the rest of his life that he had been too chicken to stand up and watch. He would never miss out again.

The rope was low and tight but Dave *did* see it at the last minute. At fifty miles an hour though, he could do nothing to avoid it and instead did what most bikers would have done in the event of an inevitable impact. He stood up on the foot pegs.

The bike hit the tight rope at a point between the front mudguard and the head light, instantly slicing through the fairing and connecting solidly with the forks. It was the sort of rope used by hauliers to tie their canvas lorry covers and was good for five tonnes of pressure. Even so, it did break, but not before lifting the back wheel high off the ground. The seat came up at a frightening speed, concertinaing Dave's legs, then connecting with his backside forcibly enough to implode a number of his discs and shatter half a dozen vertebrae, shortening it by several inches. Had Dave simply fell to the floor he would have lost his six foot status and remained completely paralysed until the life support system had been turned off.

He didn't.

The force of the seat catapulted him forwards and upwards, sending him and his bike high into somersaulting flight. The handlebars ripped his kneecaps from their sockets and left them to float around in his leathers. The rope chose *this* moment to snap, whip-cracking to both sides of the road, one end flying high over Dan's head.

Dan was sure the engine had cut, such was the silence, but then it roared again, partially drowned by the wrenching of aluminium and steel, the shattering of fibreglass and the dull scrape of leather on tarmac.

The bike cart-wheeled and pirouetted along the tarmac for fifty yards, Dave somewhere amongst the flying wreckage until it hit the verge at a point on the near side of a farm entrance. It then soared gracefully over the gate, depositing pieces of Yamaha liberally around the field. Dave's flight was shorter but no less spectacular. Parting company just before the verge, he rolled along the muddy roadside, flipped up the grassy ramp and slammed feet first into the near gatepost.

Pathologists would later reveal that both ankles and knees had shattered. His right femur had disintegrated. His left shoulder had dislocated then broken and his left hand had actually become detached at the wrist. Add to this a displaced spleen, both lungs punctured and pulped and, what Dan would have considered the piece de resistance, a heart so brutally mashed that it had become detached from its musculature and moved several inches in his chest and even the least anatomically minded of people would realise that Dave was seriously dead.

Silence fell on the scene. After a second or two, a blackbird chattered shrilly and flew low over the road, pulling up as it travelled over Dave's broken form. Dan rushed from the ditch and, though careful not to leave any noticeable footprints, he was aware that time had never been more 'of the essence'.

First he gathered the rope from his side, coiling it neatly around his elbow and open palm, before turning his attention to the other side of the road. The rope here was well tangled in the hedge and caused him some concern initially. With the loop undone, he checked the oak's bark and was pleased that no noticeable scar was left. Hanging the two lengths over his left shoulder, he trotted along the verge and stared in awe and disbelief at his work.

Dave was half in, half out of the gate. Both legs had been forced through the horizontal steel bars to hang limp and disjointed, ending a foot above the ground. He marvelled at the way the leather of Dave's all in one suit was stretched and twisted and the bizarre way the left foot was facing the wrong way. The top of the gate was bent inwards towards the field, where Dave's body had crashed into it before springing backwards and slamming into the gravel entrance to the field.

Dan placed a finger to the exposed side of Dave's neck, feeling for any trace of pulse. Nothing.

Like Tom, all those years ago, in death, Dave seemed magnificent - totally broken, ultimately still and at peace.

"Wow ... Jesus ... unbelievable."

The official line was 'Accidental Death', no one suspected foul play as Dave always rode his bike at a speed that had onlookers shaking their heads in disbelief. The general opinion around the College was that it was going to happen sooner or later.

Dan even went to the funeral, grieved somewhat awkwardly and sang at the Church with his College friends, also awkwardly and out of tune.

It was his fifth kill; the first had been Tom, feline rather than human, but massively gratifying none the less.

Number two and three, his father and Betty, devastatingly effective and incredibly aesthetic. He did, however, resent the fact that he hadn't been able to watch as Betty shrivelled in the heat.

Number five, of course, had been Dave, spectacular and infinitely destructive.

Number four.

Number four had been a twenty seven year old prostitute, persuaded by the payment of £300 to wander the lanes with him until undertaking her normal duties in a woody clearing, only three miles from where his Aunt sat, nervously awaiting the return of her nephew on his eighteenth birthday.

He was proud of his performance that day. Proud indeed, having performed for over three hours; acting out every single sexual fantasy his young mind had previously perceived, plus a few that it hadn't. He'd known her enjoyment was real, couldn't believe her orgasms were fake. He looked deep into her eyes as she lay sprawled, partially clothed and panting and knew, just knew, that she had, this time, if never before, found, at least *some* level of job satisfaction.

He strangled her with his belt, carried her ten yards into the wood where a steel cover sat on three courses of brick; the capped entrance to a mine ventilation shaft. On one side, where the brickwork was broken and shattered, he forced her head and shoulders into the blackness, pushing her forward until gravity took over and she slid from his grip, leaving her left shoe on the soil. The muffled thump two seconds later sounded like a sack of potatoes landing on broken brickwork.

She was officially on a missing persons list but, as she'd been on it for ten years since fleeing her abusive father, he was probably doing her a favour.

Emily.

Well Emily didn't count.

She had wanted to die. He was sure of it.

This horrible world where grief and suffering were rife, was no place for her. He clutched the handkerchief in his pocket and remembered how it had fit so neatly into her mouth. Balled into a tiny lace parcel, it had sat snug and damp while her eyes at first showed terrible fear, then resignation. As he'd gently pinched her nostrils shut, he was sure she had, in her own small way, thanked him for his kindness.

Why else would she have stayed with him for such a long time?

At twenty one, Dan had left University prior to the start of the third year of his humanities degree, inherited the small fortune left to him by his father that had, through the prudent investment decisions of his Aunt and her solicitor, been turned into a large one, dropped straight out of the rat-race into a life of privileged excess.

Just short of £3,700,000 passed fluidly into a bank account of his choosing a few days after his twenty first birthday. A return on the original investment just marginally shy of five fold in the eight years since his father's death.

He felt he owed his Aunt something for the years of love and care she had given him. So, with a gold nibbed fountain pen bought specifically for the occasion, at a cost of over £300 (the price of a rampant sex session and a little murder on the side), he wrote a cheque for £692,411.87. Made out to 'cash', he left it, along with a note of thanks, on the kitchen table next to the pen that had written it, at 4.30 a.m., a week and a half into his twenty second year, shouldered his rucksack and strode out into the dark of a mid-August morning. He never saw, or spoke to, his Aunt again.

Cash can, despite what people, generally with very little of it say, bring happiness.

Dan travelled; India, Nepal, Thailand (he liked Thailand greatly), Australia, New Zealand, Peru, Argentina, Brazil, Mexico and into the

United States. He lived life fully, gleefully and with no remorse or questioning of his actions.

America didn't agree with him; he preferred the trusting nature of simple, less materialistic cultures. Thailand gave him the opportunity to develop his darker side, where sex and money was the order of the day. Where he could *pay* for anything, *ask* for anything and *get it* - with change.

Human life seemed to be as cheap as the sex; death and mutilation almost considered an occupational hazard.

By the time he was thirty, he was back in England, looking to settle into a life of leisure. His wealth, even with the excesses of his youth was largely untouched. After giving his aunt what he considered the loose change, he had spread the remaining £3,000,000 amongst various investments, deposits, offshore accounts, bonds and shares. He was set for life; whatever life he wished.

He found that he had mellowed and settled down in a nice house in North Shropshire with a Labrador called Mitch. He took to writing poetry and enjoyed a pint in the local pub. He got to know his neighbours and was accepted into the community, blending easily into village life. He cultured an air of aloofness, choosing not to draw attention to his considerable wealth by outlandish spending or ostentatious shows of materialism. None of his new friends knew what he was worth, he was just 'that nice bloke who lives on his own', or 'the chap with the lovely Labrador'. He liked his neighbours and the people in the village.

Only very rarely did the thought cross his mind to kill any of them.

Following a stock market 'wobble' in 1997 he decided to look for alternative investments and came across the firm of C.S.A. and Chris Stevens. It was also around that time that Mr Stevens began to branch into his own 'alternative investment' portfolio with the help of David Charles.

A three-way partnership?

Three men, all with their own skills.

Three men with their own strengths, weaknesses and passions.

Money, power and destruction.

Dan felt the old tingle of adrenaline and thought of the pleasures yet to come his way.

Six months after Dan first met Stevens, the body of a tramp was found, in a sleeping bag, near Wolverhampton town centre. The verdict was suicide, the unfortunate man having guzzled Vodka like it was soon to be rationed, then dined on a few dozen sleeping pills to finish the job.

In truth, the unfortunate vagrant had been befriended by a smartly dressed man in the wee hours of the morning, shared a couple of bottles of drink, then, having been told the pills were, of all things, vitamins, happily swallowed the capsules and drifted off to never land.

Dan was back.

The Birmingham Five

"Al … what-o-mate … how're things?"

"Ah, you know, bored, should be fishing, too much work, manager pissing me off on a daily basis." He let out a resigned sigh, then continued "Same old shit really. Anyway, how's Wolverhampton's own James Bond, uncovered any more international drug barons since we last spoke?"

I gave him a brief run down, leaving out the full details but making sure the overall figure in question came out.

"Sweet Jesus. Any ideas when you're emigrating?"

I didn't answer but paused, dragging deep on my cigarette and shuffling my feet on the gravel path of my garden.

"Listen mate, I need to ask a favour …" he cut in, "Andy, you gotta understand, best mates and all that, but, bugger me, I don't really want to get involved and, more to the point, neither should you."

"Al …"

"Go to the Police … call MI5, the Famous Five, the Birmingham Five if you like but, for God's sake, just *think* mate. Take a second. Think, before you do *anything*. I know you, you've got a plan, I can tell and believe me chappy, I ain't part of it. Sorry."

There followed a long drawn out silence, the old silent close where the first to speak loses.

"Go on then, what?"

I elaborated on the details I had skipped earlier, concentrating on the charitable donations of the unfortunate clients. Then, once the emotional blackmail had been poured on good and thick, highlighted briefly what I had in mind.

"Come round, give me the full craic and I'll let you know."

"Thanks Al, I …"

"Listen, I ain't said yes yet and, one thing's for certain …" another pause and I could somehow tell he was shaking his head, eyes closed and brow furrowed, "I am *not* involved in this. This is *your* crusade. I value my kneecaps and everything else attached to me. I'm not going to end up maimed, dead or worse. I thought my boss was a nasty piece of work, but Jesus, yours makes him look saintly."

"See you later then and Al, I think you'll find it was the Birmingham *Six*, not five. Not that it matters, Al … Al … you there …?"

Paying Chris a visit

Late May, the sky black as pitch and sky sprinkled with stars. A new moon had crept above the trees and its thin, silver sliver cast subtle shadows on fields showing the first strong signs of summer growth. Two figures were moving slowly along a mixed hedge of bramble and stunted birch, blending well, invisible pretty much, to anyone caring to look. At the end of the hedge dark shadows lurked, thrown by a high bank of conifers that ran at right angles along the edge of the field.

A pale silvery patch of light swept smoothly along the distant road accompanied by a distant, barely audible, rumble. A red flare of light bathed the trees as the car braked then moved off, blackness descending once more.

The two figures continued towards the corner, approaching it with an undisguised degree of stealth. Quiet hung over the proceedings, complete save for the odd sharp snap of dry twig or squelch of boot in the occasional damp spot along the hedge's base. There was a gate in the corner, its post set into the ground beneath the conifers.

The leading figure suddenly pitched forward, sprawling onto outstretched hands and landing heavily on his knees sunk deep into a foul, stinking wetness.

"Ahhh … Jesus … bloody hell … cow shit. Bloody hell … oohhh my God … what a stink … I'm absolutely covered in it."

I stooped down and lifted Al by his baggy, camouflaged jacket, recoiling at the pungent smell of manure.

"Watch that log mate, slippery as owl snot."

I couldn't help it; an involuntary and untimely bout of laughter wracked my chest 'til I was fit to collapse. I staggered and nearly fell myself, having to grab a handful of prickly hedge to steady my wobbling legs.

"It's not funny. Look at my bloody trousers. This is mad."

We were at the boundary of Chris's garden, 2.30 a.m. - we were not paying him a visit for a coffee and a chat.

"I should give the gate a wide berth if I were you. It's about a foot deep in cow shit."

We worked our way back to the conifers, pushed through branches that were thick and dusty, then peered into the open space on the other side.

"What exactly are we looking for?"

I stumbled over my words, not really sure myself.

"I don't really know. Just wanted to see whether ... I don't know, whether there was anything to, you know, sort of ... pin on him."

Al picked at a drying piece of manure on his cuff, "I doubt if there's going to be big boxes of snout lying about, if that's what you're thinking."

We'd had this conversation already, back at Al's house, in front of his fire, drinking whisky until after midnight. I was supposed to be fishing (or at least that's what I'd told Rachel) and had no real idea what I was expecting to find, only that Trevor had hinted that Chris's home was used as a staging post for the drug deals. Whether he stored anything here was another thing. I suppose I was just being naïve; I knew nothing about the drug trade.

Set in the middle of the old farmyard was a series of out-buildings, the closest being a wooden shed, its doors facing us, the size of a garage. Gravel in front of the doors, deeply gouged with tyre tracks suggested it was just that. Behind it was a large barn, starkly outlined against the sky.

"Right, all you've got to do is stay here and watch for any movement. I'm going to have a quick mooch about. Remember, anything untoward, give me a hoot."

(Al was a master owl impersonator).

He shrugged. "OK, but remember, if I see anything that looks like trouble, you get one hoot, then I'm out of here." He offered me his hand, which I took, grimacing at the rough texture of partially dried muck that met my palm.

I could see his smile even through the darkness "And I'll see you back at the house."

Set within the conifers was a three-strand fence of plain wire that I clambered over and, avoiding the gravel, sprinted across the yard to the barn. My Maglite torch was heavy in my pocket and the 'real tree' camouflage balaclava felt hot on my head, causing beads of sweat to trickle into my eyes.

The barn door nearest me faced the rear of the house and was comprehensively locked with the largest padlock I'd ever seen. Shiny in the dim moonlight, it glinted with a dull silver glow of utter confidence. Working my way along the side of the building furthest from the house, I picked my way carefully past a large wood pile. My left shin struck something solid and I instinctively put out my hand to steady myself, recoiling at the sticky substance that instantly covered my palm and fingers. Quickly flicking on the torch illuminated a patch of tar pooled next to a large tin. A brush, stiff and black, lay in the puddle like a small, dead, hedgehog. The whole sticky mess was sitting on top of an old packing case. A bundle of rags also sat on the case and I used one to wipe my fingers. Switching off the torch, I plunged straight back into darkness.

At the far end, more packing cases were piled against the wall reaching perhaps ten feet up the panelling. They looked as though they'd been used to allow easy access to the structure.

Two windows were set into the barn on this side, the boxes leading step-like up to one of them. I quickly moved to the end of my wall and crept around the back until I could peep around the corner. One window on this side, near the centre, facing the house, along with a single door; again, secured with a huge padlock.

Back at the rear of the barn, I carefully stepped up onto the first packing case, conscious that the scuff of my boot on the wood was like a symbol crash in the silence.

I noticed how warm it was for May. How still the air was, not a breath of breeze to stir the trees. I thought of Al, hiding back in the trees and hoped he hadn't nodded off, having drunk a fair amount of whisky earlier in the evening.

Three packing cases up, the window was level with my waist. Freshly painted, brand new framework and putty-smeared glass explained the required access. There were blobs of still soft putty on the top of the highest case, suggesting the work had been done that very day.

My precarious perch, combined with the silence and crazy situation I found myself in, pushed the first tendrils of fear into my mind.

I caught, out of the corner of my eye, a blink of red light through the window and froze. A tiny red diode, high in the corner of the roof opposite me flicked on off, on off. I ducked instinctively and waited for the sirens.

Nothing.

Risking another look, my heart froze.

Blackness stared back at me.

"I must have triggered it," I mumbled to no one but myself.

Then, with a movement of my head to the right, it was there again. I realised, just as the fear began to build once more, that it was constant; something was hiding it from me if I moved to the left.

I flicked on the torch.

A hayloft ran the full width of the building and about a third of the length. Standing upright, about six feet high, was what looked like a door;

the reflected glare of the torch beam made it difficult to see.

A dozen or so packing cases were strewn haphazardly over the hayloft. The door leant against two stacked cases, another two next to it. The outer edge of the furthest box was a mere six inches from the edge of the loft.

A plan formed in my mind and I prodded a finger into the putty, feeling it squash at the lightest of pressure.

After five minutes work with my penknife, a line of putty lay on the case on which I stood. Ten minutes later, four rough lines of creamy paste lay next to my feet and the glass would move if pushed at the corner.

Al shrunk back against the trees at my approach, blending perfectly with the foliage. "Had enough?" he whispered.

I explained what I'd found and about my putty removal.

"I think I can get in behind the cases and the door and, if I keep low, reckon I can have a look to the barn floor from the end of the hayloft."

"Yeah, right. That's presuming there's only one sensor and that whatever you're looking for is big enough to see from ten foot up." He was smiling again. "Probably got a tractor in there. Perhaps it's not taxed - you could always report him for that?"

I shook my head.

"I knew I could rely on you for a piss-take. Listen, who do you know who's put an alarm system in a barn?"

"Well ..." he scratched his balaclavered head "I don't actually think I know anyone *with* a barn, but yeh, I get your point."

We both stared out across the yard in front of us.

"Suppose he could have a vintage car or something in there?"

"Nah, not his style. Look, give me ten minutes, then we can get back and finish that whisky off, right?"

"Alright, but hurry up eh? Getting a bit chilly out here and to be honest, I could really do with a crap."

Back at my perch, I put the broad blade of my penknife under a corner of the glass and, applying a little pressure, levered it outwards, wincing as it splintered at the edge. I hadn't worked out whether I could put the putty back in, but thought I probably could. If not, I'd decided I'd drop the whole lot on the ground below, as if it had fallen out. It was the best I could think of in the circumstances.

It came out easily and I laid it on the case against the barn wall. Keeping well to the left, I squeezed through the opening and toppled over onto hard boards covered in a coating of dust and more patches of wet tar.

No alarm bells sounded and, as I peered around in the darkness, I could see no more blinking red lights.

"Just the one then, good."

My torch beam shone out over the emptiness, sweeping its pool of light around the barn floor. I picked out several tables laid out to form an 'L' shape on which sat several small cardboard boxes, a clip board with sheets of paper attached and, strangely out of character in a barn, a set of electronic scales.

"Well, well," I smiled, letting my gaze sweep along with the yellow beam of light, "surely not for weighing his home grown vegetables."

The scales were white, efficient looking, ultra modern, digital jobs. Sitting in the stainless steel pan on top was a dark package. About four inches square, it appeared to be wrapped in cellophane. From the distance I was viewing (about twenty feet) I couldn't make out exactly what it was; my imagination, however, had already decided it was about half a pound of cannabis resin, pre-wrapped, weighed and ready for despatch.

The drop to the barn floor was about eight feet onto stone, enough to break an ankle. But, more worrying, once down, I reckoned I could only get to within ten feet of the table before the sensor picked me up and all hell broke loose. Anyway, the ladder was way over on the right hand side - as soon as I poked my head up over the hayloft, the game would definitely be up. It was a quandary; from where I was, I could achieve nothing but add fuel to the fire of suspicion in my mind.

"In for a penny and all that."

I crawled to the edge of the loft, keeping low to the boarded floor.

Being a climber, I was used to the airy, helpless feeling of dropping out over a sheer face whilst abseiling, but the drop down to the stone floor was still unnerving. Falling into an almost absolute blackness scared me witless and I landed heavily, lurched forward under the loft space, stumbled into another packing case then cracked my head against a low beam.

I waited a minute before edging to the outer perimeter of the loft. I re-did the maths and reckoned I could *almost* reach the scales before being detected but, unless I chose to take up permanent residence under the hayloft, it was all going to go off as soon as I poked my head above the top of the ladder. I was terrified - the thought of a scramble up a vertical ladder, out of a small window space, down to the ground and then a mad rush across open country with the prospect of being caught by gangsters and dumped in a nearby quarry pit, did nothing for my nerves.

I edged out slowly towards the table, my torch showing the way. A glance behind me showed the sensor was still hidden from view (or me hidden from *its* view). With the gap closed to no more than four feet, I could see the package perfectly.

"I knew it. If that isn't cannabis resin, I'm tea-total."

I shrank back a couple of feet, uncertain of what to do. "Sod it, I'll hand it over anonymously, then move to Skye and become a crofter."

Al was sitting on ground soft with pine needles, leaning back against one of the trunks. His eyes were drooping when the light came on in the house. The glow was diffused as if through frosted glass, probably a bathroom or toilet. Placing his hands to his mouth, he hooted twice, standing up and seeing stars as his head connected with a low branch.

"Shit that hurt."

He started to shout, then thought better of it, and hooted again, three short sharp blasts.

"Andy, for God's sake. Come on, come on."

Time dragged by for what seemed an age, then the light went out. Darkness prevailed again.

"Phew, don't do that to me."

The next second, he was bathed in a brilliant white light as three halogen lamps set high on the house blinked into life. Accompanying the glare, his ears rang to the harsh wail of a high-pitched siren, ironically enough, like that of a police car.

"Oh fuck, fuck, fuck," he instinctively raised his hands to hoot, then realised the futility of such a signal.

"I think he's got the message, I'm out of here."

At the same time that Al was scrambling to his feet and forcing his way through clinging branches into the field, I was about half way across the loft. The ladder had been a barely remembered scramble, climbed on raw fear rather than strength. The window appeared to be closing shut as I watched. I forced my upper body over the sill and fell onto the packing cases, smashing the windowpane with my knee. I could feel the warmth of blood flowing under my camouflaged trousers, but had no time to ponder the sensation as my world tumbled away from me.

The uppermost case toppled over, pitching me into a spinning fall lit by white light, all to the disorienting wail of a piercing siren blast.

I caught a brief glimpse of a star-lit night sky before crashing onto soft grass. I was up like a shot and sprinting across the yard towards the trees as though I'd merely tripped over a kerbstone. I caught a movement to my right and sensed, rather than saw, a figure stumble onto the patio. The glint of steel flashed briefly, as, legs splayed, the figure raised what I could only presume was a shotgun and took aim.

Al was against the hedge, halfway across the field, breathing heavily and caught between the pull of his own safety and concern for his friend, when the twin blasts rang out, deafening in the night.

"Shit, Andy, Jesus Christ." Staring around dazed and blank, he whispered "Oh no."

I was five feet from the trees, sprinting at full pelt when the shots came. I never screamed or paused, but flung myself into a dive, clearing the fence and landing sprawled amongst years of pine needles then rolling forward onto my back. I heard the clatter of shot in the tree branches and realised I was peeing, freely in my trousers. Warmth flowed down my legs as I lifted myself up, grabbing a tree branch for support.

The siren still blared behind me and amongst the branches it was like a fantasy grotto, all silvery light and shifting shadows. I ran.

Al also ran, not from, but towards the trees. He was crying openly, a terrible anger exploding within him.

"You bastard, shoot my mate and you're one dead, drug-dealing fucker."

Straight through the soft ground in front of the gate, he closed the ground to the trees.

We collided, half skidding to a halt about six feet into the field and sprawling in a muddy, manure streaked tangle of arms and legs.

"Having a good time?"

"Fabulous mate, I think I've pissed myself though."

"No bother, you're in good company. I think I have too."

"Shall we get off then?"

"Probably best, eh?"

Expecting another shotgun blast at any time, we made our way at a shambling run across the field, not bothering to stick to the hedge. At the end of the first field, we scrambled over a fence, Al pulling me by the arm as I reached the top, helping me to the other side.

"I tell you what matey, I thought you'd bought it then."

"Mutual mate" I replied, resting my hands against the fence and breathing deeply.

"I was … I dunno, about six foot … from the fence and … I … I heard the shots and just leapt for it. How I cleared it … well, God only knows." I looked at his face, peeping through the opening in his balaclava, pale in the waning moonlight.

"I felt the shot go over me Al. It peppered the branches. Another foot and I'd be bleeding now."

I shook my head and looked down at the ground.

"That wasn't any warning shot you know? He was after me. He meant it. The bastard would have killed me given the chance."

"Come on, let's get going, nothing to say he isn't coming across the field right now."

We started to jog along the edge of the second field, scaring cattle from their slumber. "I doubt if he's following, I think he had a pair of boxers on, straight from bed."

"Probably right, I saw him go to the loo just before all hell broke loose. I hooted but you obviously never heard me, being in the barn."

"No, I did, scared me witless at the time, so I just scarpered."

We cleared another fence, crossed a road then passed through a gate onto another field. Five minutes later, we were dropping down a steep hill and following a path through a dense wood. From there, we dropped down an overgrown farm track, over a fence and onto another road. Opposite, in darkness save for the single bulb in the porch, Al's house waited for our return. His garden gate creaked as we opened it, piercing the stillness.

We left our boots in the porch and stripped down to our underwear in the hallway. Al went into the kitchen and turned on the heating. The small house was dark, but a warm orange glow from the lounge fire lit the room in a dappled, shifting light.

"Here mate." He threw me a towel and I wrapped it around my shoulders. My hair was stuck to my scalp, slick with sweat.

With more logs on the fire, we sprawled in opposite armchairs watching the budding flames, a large whisky each in our hands.

"What happened then? In the barn?"

"Well, I heard you hoot and, like I said, it put the wind up me. I tell you, when I came out of the window, I half expected to be greeted by a Mafia welcome party." I sipped at the amber liquid, let it warm my chest and continued by describing the layout of the barn, the tables and the scales.

"So, I'd already decided I was going to set the alarm off getting out, your hoot just forced the issue." Another sip. "Made up my mind, so to speak."

A long pause followed, both of us going through what had happened; winding down, back to earth.

Al spoke first. "I'd have shot you, you know." He spoke in a certain, matter of fact way. "He must be a crap shot. Didn't give you enough of a lead." He mimed the action of raising a gun, swept his arms from left to right and whispered "Bang."

"You'd have been dead mate, no mistake."

"Big headed wanker."

I think Al started first, laughing, fit to collapse, spitting his whisky in the process, head thrown back, his body shaking, wheezing and coughing. I joined in, unable to control myself with the relief of still being alive.

During the next half an hour, we suffered another two bouts of laughing, the last one drawing a series of thumps on the wall from next-door. We both shouted our apologies; our voices drawing more laughter, this time through closed teeth, sniggering like naughty schoolboys.

"Chappy, don't know about you, but I'm knackered." He added a huge yawn, as if to add credence to his statement. "I'm off to bed."

"Hang on." I jumped up and went to the kitchen, returning a few seconds later holding something in my right hand.

A shiny package reflected the firelight as it spun through the air and landed squarely in Al's lap. He raised it in his hand; watched it glint orange, as the cellophane picked up each flicker of flame.

"Well ... bloody hell." His head snapped up to look at me, then back to the package. "Somebody is going to be mighty pissed at you, you know. At £20 an eighth, there's got to be over a grand's worth here."

He appeared transfixed. Turning the block in his palm, he watched the fire dance on each of its eight, smooth sides.

"Jesus, you know, *I really didn't believe you*," he held up his hand to halt my reply, "even after everything you'd told me, I really didn't believe you." He looked up at me. "This doesn't happen round here."

"I know ... it's unbelievable isn't it?"

We both looked into the fire for a few seconds then, as if reading together from a script, blurted out:

"Got any Rizzlas?"

Interesting times…

I am not a good drinker.

No, that's not strictly true, I can sink a fair amount, especially whisky, but it doesn't like me.

So, it was with a thick head, aching muscles and mildly blurred vision that I woke just before mid-day to the sound of Radio One drifting up the stairs from the kitchen. I made my way down, ducked under the beam at the bottom and navigated my way along the hallway via each wall.

Al was sitting at the kitchen table, dressed in jeans and a tee shirt and looking disgustingly normal. The smell of coffee brought me round by degrees as I sat opposite him.

"There's eggs, toast, cereal or some bacon if you want," he said, adding "though I'd pass on the bacon if I were you. It's a bit past it's sell-by-date. Only a week … well ten days actually. Probably all right, but, well …"

"Toast. Coffee first. Thumping head. Feel crap."

On the table sat the resin taken from Chris's barn just a few hours earlier.

Anyone caring to weigh it would find it was a fraction under eight ounces; by three joints or so.

"What are you going to do with it then Chappy?"

"Don't know. Police? Anonymously? Don't know." I slumped, visibly.

"Jesus, WAKE-UP!"

"OK, OK." I lifted the coffee pot and slopped a half measure into a chipped mug proclaiming that James Gibbon made the best turned-parts in the Midlands.

"Tell you what, I'd like to be a fly on the wall in Chris's kitchen this morning. I'd put my life savings on the fact that he's in a bit of a pickle right now."

I looked across at Al as he took a huge bite from the corner of his bacon sandwich.

"Remember Al, I've got to work with him."

"Hey hey, interesting times ahead then me ould mucka, very interesting times indeed."

Things change

"David ... yeah, great, you? ... Listen, we've got a big problem ... really ... yeh ... right ... OK ... David, David ... please, for God's sake if you'll just listen for one minute, I'll tell you. Last night someone got into the barn and helped themselves to half a pound of red ... about 3 o'clock ... yeah ... fuck me, will you *just listen?* I think I shot him ... well, I found blood on the fence along the conifers ... no he got away ... I'd got my bloody boxers on ... no, I ain't chasing anyone across fields in my skivvies ... for a fat bloke David, you talk a right sporty game, you know that? Now, listen to me, things have changed ... what? ... that's easy for you to say, you haven't got a million quid's worth of Colombian marchin' powder in your garage. Yeah, I think we need to meet ... one hour, yeh, here. See you then." Click.

His usual rugged, good looks and immaculately kept hair and clothes are both absent as he stares out of the patio doors. The barn stands thirty yards away, sturdy and solid. It seems to mock him.

He's not slept since his forced early rising and it shows. No shave or shower. Jeans muddied from his trek across the fields, shotgun under his arm and large, powerful torch illuminating his way. The tracks had been easy to follow, all the way to the road, tram lines clear in the early morning dew, but, after that, nothing.

"Probably had a car parked on the road. Could be anywhere by now."

He raises his coffee to his lips realising it's stone cold; as cold as the trail he'd followed last night.

"Things have changed, things have changed."

He realises he's squeezing the cup, his right hand straining, tendons standing out like highly tuned piano wire.

"Oh yes, things have changed."

A deposit in the grit bin

There comes a time, I always think, when sitting back to ponder on a situation, whether expected or otherwise, is the right and proper thing to do. Rushing in with a 'gung ho', Hollywood blockbuster attitude is OK sometimes. Sometimes that's exactly right. *Quiet pondering* though, quiet and thoughtful consideration - now there's a solution.

I remember a time when at my first insurance company, Al and I had the unfortunate attention of a manager to contend with. He was a long serving employee, a company man through and through. A vicious, insecure bully who possessed the most obnoxious blend of personal attributes imaginable.

That time was a nightmare.

Again and again, we jointly reported him to Personnel; our arguments swelled by similar complaints from other staff.

He side-stepped every single one.

We were held to ransom in an industry that looks at results above all else. The team was successful; therefore, it was a direct reflection on our esteemed leader. So as a team, one day, during a subversive meeting in a local pub, we decided we'd had enough of the aggression and stress that he personally caused. Some of us decided we would suck in our pride and become 'Yes Men'. Others decided they would put in a final grievance then resign, sighting Guissepé as their reason for leaving, in the hope that at least their sacrifice would drop him, once and for all, in a mess deep enough to drown him.

It didn't work.

Al had a blazing row with him in the middle of the office. Much to the combined pleasure of all onlookers, Guissepé's parenthood was called into question along with his ability to pleasure his wife, the size of his penis and whether he enjoyed procreation with animals. The whole incident built to a stunning climax with Guissepé dripping with coffee and sitting in a metal waste-paper basket. He rose, shaking drips of sweet black liquid from his beard and wiping his eyes as Al stormed out of the building. He shouted that we'd all seen what happened and that he would be looking for witness statements from us all.

No one was surprised to find that his quest for support came to nothing - apart from perhaps, Guissepé.

He continued harassing, imposing his opinions and generally making life hell for all remaining members of his team (four out of an original nine). He was the recipient of my phone call telling him to 'shove the job' following my brain scan. Never before had a simple conversation given me such pleasure. Looking back, we did the right thing; we sat back and gave thought to a problem. We all came up with our own solutions, stuck to them and acted upon them. Democracy at work, *at work*.

My situation with Chris was slightly different.

So I drove and pondered, deep in thought. I enjoyed the scenery while half a pound of cannabis resin rolled around in my glove box and a million and one thoughts bounced around in my head - like me, they seemed to be going nowhere in particular.

After twenty miles and nearly forty minutes of pondering, my thoughts finally became crystal clear and I drove home. Rachel was out when I pulled onto the driveway, the house warm and still. I was relieved; she didn't expect me home until the evening, so my arrival at four in the afternoon would have raised some awkward questions.

Once my unused fishing tackle was back in the shed, I sat at the kitchen table staring at over a thousand pounds of illegal drug. I took it with me when I went upstairs to change into jeans and tee shirt. Somehow I didn't want it out of my sight, fearful that it would disappear if left for a second. It sat on the bathroom washbasin while I sat on the toilet. It stood on my desk while I stood, looking for a padded envelope in which to place it and seemed to watch me as I watched my words appear on the word processor. A simple letter explaining where it had come from, when it was stolen and how I had come to obtain it.

Everything, all the details were there, apart from that of an accomplice; or of course my name.

I drove into the countryside for ten minutes before turning right into Pattingham and parking next to the public phone box. I dialled, hearing the electronic beeps of each number, then the ringing tone.

Three rings.

"Hello, West Midlands Police."

I told them what I had, where I would leave it and hung up. Back in the car, I drove four hundred yards to a bend just outside the village where, sitting at the roadside was a yellow plastic grit bin. For a second, the lid wouldn't lift and a surge of panic rose like bile. I realised, after straining to open it, that I was trying to prise open the seam that fixed the whole thing together. The lid lifted easily once found and within twenty seconds I was back in the car, my package sitting in the dregs of last winter's grit. A Police car flashed past, going in the opposite direction five minutes later.

"I'm impressed lads, now do your bit."

Rachel was home when I got back and, as usual, she got the whole story out of me. Angry at my deceit at first, her anger gradually developed into concern, then laughter.

"Is that the end of it then?" Rachel asked.

Unsure, I replied that I hoped so.

"I think I'll post off the relevant client details over the next few days as well, just to bang a few more nails in his coffin," adding, after a pause, "once the drugs begin to take effect." Rachel just smiled her sad, knowing smile; the one she reserved for solemn occasions. She didn't think my comment was funny in the slightest.

"He'll get out of it, you know, people like him always do." Rachel's face was one of saddened resolve. "They *always* do."

I nodded, but secretly thought he would have difficulty getting out of this particular tight spot.

"I suppose," I said with a resigned sigh, "I'm going to be looking for another job."

"… people like him always do."

Monday morning, 10.30 a.m.

Rachel had long since left for work and I was dozing in bed, enjoying a lie in and thinking that the office wouldn't miss me today. Chris would hopefully be helping the Police with their enquiries and, later in the day I would almost certainly be at a recruitment agency, hoping they could help me with mine. In my fuzzy, barely awake state, the phone in my office seemed to be ringing from another planet, not just another room and I suppose it had been going for about a minute by the time I roused myself and answered it.

"Hello?"

"Andy, good morning, it's Chris here …"

In about a millisecond I was awake. My mind sharp and focused, though everything in the room seemed to be pulsing in time to my heart beat, the furniture throbbing and thumping, stretching then contracting; almost kaleidoscopic. I felt as though I was going to faint.

"Chris, hi … you all right?"

"I'm well thank you. Aren't you forgetting something?"

My mind raced; the last person I had expected to be talking to today was on the end of the phone asking me if I'd forgotten something. Like what exactly? Finger prints? Security camera? His birthday?

"Sales meeting … today … 10.30?"

Shit.

I composed myself.

"Chris, look … I'm so sorry, I overslept, not been feeling too good just lately …"

I realised I was sweating profusely and also that I had no real idea how I should be handling this. My brain seemed unable to cope with the input it was receiving. I may as well have been listening to a talk on quantum physics.

"Sorry, I'll be there in forty minutes."

"Make it half an hour, we'll wait for you …"

The line was dead.

This was not right.

He should have been at Wolverhampton nick as we spoke. He

should have been sweating over difficult questions and calculating the total bill he was likely to receive from his expensive barrister. He should have been crapping in a bucket under a two foot square window, barred, criss-crossed with safety wire and set high in a white painted brick wall. He should have been eating prison food from a plastic tray and having to physically hold his trousers up, his Armani belt gone along with his liberty.

Instead he was phoning me, asking where I was, telling me to be in the office in half an hour.

Rachel's words rang clear in my head ...

"He'll get away with it, people like him always do."

I was leaving the house ten minutes after getting out of bed. I'd shaved while dressing and dressed while running around the house collecting brief-case, wallet, pen and mobile phone. I looked awful. I looked like I'd been out on the town all night, had a skin-full, slept for an hour on a park bench, then gone to work. I need to wash my hair every day and it showed. I looked in the rear-view mirror and grimaced.

"I think today's going to be an interesting one," I said to myself as the engine kicked into life and I exited the driveway.

At the first junction, while waiting for the road to clear, I checked my teeth in the rear-view, dry brushed them with the tooth brush I keep in the glove box and swilled my mouth out with the last dregs of water from the bottle that happened to be rolling around in the passenger foot-well. I had one chewing gum left so ate that. Dental hygiene taken care of, I continued my journey.

I parked at the kerbside in a side road opposite the office, walked slowly to the pedestrian crossing, lit a cigarette and proceeded to blank out. Ten minutes of nothingness, punctuated by very brief instances of clarity; the beep of a horn, grind of a lorry gearbox, swish of bus doors opening.

The jangle of a little bell over the door into the office was drowned out, as I entered, by polite applause and cheers of "Nice of you to drop in, thanks for joining us, get you out of bed did we?"

They were all there, Chris, Andy two, Steve, a full compliment of administration staff and, sitting at the back, fat and pompous, a sneer masquerading as a smile - David Charles.

My mind was in turmoil as I endeavoured to keep things together. Utter disbelief on my part, but Business as normal on Chris's as though nothing had happened. I thought of Al and I creeping through darkened fields, stumbling along in the blackness, both scared of what we were doing and the possible consequences. Of what we had achieved - the block of cannabis, my drive to Pattingham, the phone call to the Police, everything.

Or rather, *nothing*.

Steve was the first to speak, the concern clear on his face.

"You alright Andy?" I felt my open mouth snap shut "You, err, don't look quite the ticket."

I instinctively looked away and mock-coughed into my fist.

"Yeah, umm … I, err, think I've got a cold coming on."

It was a lame excuse so I continued, "Like I said to Chris earlier," my composure beginning to steal back in, "haven't been sleeping too well of late, I feel a bit off that's all, nothing to worry about really. Anyway sorry I'm late, I'll try to keep awake."

"Right," Chris's voice boomed out "lets get it on eh? Conference room I think." He turned and stepped through the door on his left, not waiting for us to follow. He let it swing shut and Steve simply shook his head and held the door for David. He took a deep breath before entering and I'm sure anyone skilled in lip reading would have been taken aback at what he mouthed.

"We'll be in as soon as Andy's got a coffee," Andy 'two' said as we gathered at the machine.

We both listened to its internal gurgling.

"Sounds like my stomach after a curry" I said.

"Mate, you look like death warmed up. Sure you're OK?"

"Yeah, honest," I paused, "… listen Andy, can I have a word with you later? - In confidence?"

"Course, anything serious?"

"Well, yes really. Listen, I'll tell you about it later, OK?"

"Right, minutes from last meeting first …"

I watched as Chris droned on, my utter loathing barely hidden and seeming to increase with every second I had to listen to him. Only I wasn't really listening, his voice was just there, in the background, like static from a badly tuned radio. I drifted, re-living the events of the weekend, gone again, lost in the considerable depths of my thoughts.

"ANDY!"

"Shit, sorry Chris, I'm really sorry," adding as an afterthought, "like I said, I'm really not quite with it."

For a split second, I detected the stern set of his brow, then he smiled, a weak, false smile.

"Perhaps we would all benefit if you spent less of your weekends wandering around the countryside in the dead of night?"

My world suddenly seemed to spin out of control, downwards, spiralling away from me. And I was a mere bystander, watching as it all went on without me. Watching my world swirl down a dark vortex - the plug hole to end all plug holes. I tensed, instantly ready to run - from the office, to the Police, anywhere.

"You and your bloody sea trout. Can't you catch them in the daytime?"

His brow raised, his eyebrows lifted a fraction and his mouth, thin and chiselled, lifted into a smile that both he and I knew was tainted with a fair measure of anger.

His eyes, you see, they did not smile.

Hate glared back at me. Hate, I saw it, clear as the prickling of hairs around my collar. Burning, desperate anger wrapped loosely in a charade of joviality.

"I really do feel rough Chris," my own glare angled back at him across the flat expanse of the conference table.

I matched his anger. And he knew it.

"Night fishing for sea trout has nothing to do with it." At that precise moment, with perfect theatrical timing, a sneeze exploded from me. "As I keep saying, I'm really not well. Sorry all, but I think it's best if get off." I rose and made my way to the door, "I'll speak to Tina and get her to re-arrange my calls. Sorry."

"Andy."

"Yes, Chris?"

"I'll set up a meeting to go through your figures. Later in the week perhaps?"

"OK, whatever ... sorry Chris, yes, great. Tina has my appointment details."

His face dropped and any trace of a smile vanished.

"I know. I am quite aware of how my firm runs, thank you very much. We really do need to talk, don't you think?"

"Yes, sorry, see you all."

I slumped against the wall outside, raising eyebrows from Tina and Yvonne.

"What's up?" Tina asked, "Sacked you?"

The irony was lost on her, not though, on me.

"Not yet."

Appointments for the next three days cancelled, I sat smoking in my car, able to see the office window in my rear view mirror and imagining the meeting continuing without me. Taking my mobile phone from the glove box, I put in a short text message.

ANDY NGS HD PENN RD 2 0 CLOCK.
BRING STEVE. A.

It was 11.35; I had some preparation to do.

I drove home, taking the opportunity to shower, wash my hair and have a proper shave. I collected the paperwork I'd gathered on Chris's clients, changed into jeans and sweatshirt and strolled around my garden, delighting in the new growth all around. The fish in my pond mirrored my aimless wandering, drifting like me. *They* didn't have a care in the world though.

I seemed to carry them all.

At half past one I drove away from home, turned left at the end of our road and swung into the bus stop outside the corner shop.

Cigarettes replenished, I made my way to the pub.

I settled myself into the corner of the lounge, lit a cigarette and took a swig of bitter. Being towards the end of lunchtime, I was pretty much alone. Ron, the landlord was trying to read the paper whilst an old guy leant on the bar talking about his ten year old granddaughter and her wanting a tattoo.

"At her age, Christ, I don't know, kids today. What we going to do with 'em, eh?"

"Yeah, right." Ron never even looked up, simply turned a page and nodded his agreement. The old fella didn't seem to notice. He nursed his pint and carried on rambling about the terrible state of today's youth.

At two minutes to two, Andy's Mazda MX6 drew onto the car park and pulled up next to my Nissan. I constantly jibed him about his lack of turbo, he reminded me every time that with a 2.5 litre V6 under the bonnet, he didn't need a big hair-dryer to help him eat Nissans. I secretly liked his car and I'm sure he did mine. Both bright red, they made an impressive pair, parked facing the pub. I was pleased to see Steve get out of the passenger door and, taking the folder from the seat, placed it on the table next to my pint.

Once inside, Andy pointed to me and they strolled over. Suited up, a smart and efficient air about them, they looked like a couple of plain clothes police officers, come to interview an informant.

"I thought you might have dressed for the occasion," Steve boomed, adding "I've got to say though you look better than you did earlier."

"Pint?"

"Coke for me please. Some of us are working."

"Me too please Andy."

They sat down, both looking unsure about the reason for my meeting. Eyeing the file with interest, Steve reached over and turned it towards him, making as if to open it.

"Steve." My voice cut across the quiet pub from the bar, making him jump. "Please, I need to speak to you both before I show you what's in there. I know it seems a bit odd" I said, returning to the table, ice cubes clinking against glass, "but you really will understand soon."

I started with Trevor Talbot, my story brief but detailed, only stopping once to answer a question from Steve.

"Why *you* do you think? I mean, there were plenty of people he could have chosen."

"Don't know, I think he liked my handshake. Said I had trusting face. Simple as that."

I continued with my rule-breaking access of the computer files, drawing a nod of recognition from Andy 'two'.

"I thought it was odd, sorry, *unheard of* for you to be in on a Saturday morning." Recognition dawned on him and he added, "The phone call, five minutes after I'd left, about passwords, right, yeah, got ya."

I needed to control the conversation, desperate to get the whole story out, but needed to pose a question first.

"Lads, I haven't told you everything yet." I hadn't mentioned anything about drugs, or that Trevor's missing policy was simply one amongst many.

"OK, I need to get your understanding before I go on. Trevor Talbot's missing legacy is just the tip of the iceberg. Things have gone on at CSA that you wouldn't, no wait, *won't* believe." I paused, searching their faces for any dropping pennies.

Nothing.

"I can stop now if you want." I held up my hand to Andy 'two' as he began to speak. "The information I've got on Chris is enough, I believe, to get me killed. I'm deadly serious. You've got to realise how grave this situation is, before I continue. I can shut up now and we can just have a quiet drink. I won't be offended, believe me." I took a sip of bitter and continued. "But, if I carry on, I think you'll both be in some danger." I took another sip of beer. "It's up to you … your call."

Andy piped up. "Let me get this straight, the Trevor Talbot situation is nothing compared to whatever else you've got?" I nodded.

Steve spoke up next. "So we're working for a bloke that has ripped off a client for £750,000 and that, as you put it, is nothing compared to whatever other stuff he's up to?"

I nodded again, thinking that I'd found a couple of allies.

"I don't know about you Steve, but I'd like to know exactly what's going on."

He nodded his agreement, so I continued. Everything came out. The client information, the early morning break-in to Chris's barn, (they both thought that was a scream), the half pound of cannabis, the Police phone call, everything, finishing with Chris calling me this morning, the last person I expected to hear from. I added about his comment during the meeting; unsure whether it was innocent or otherwise.

"Have you thought about what you're going to do?" asked Steve. He was calm now but he'd literally exploded when I'd told him about Alice Brownhill and the fact that her investment didn't show up anywhere at Midland Mutual. We'd had to physically restrain him from going back to the office to pull Chris's head off.

"No idea, I really thought the drugs would have done the job, I was going to send this file in a couple of days." I sighed and drained my pint, "Then, well, dunno, get to a good job agency at least. I hear the pay on North-Sea oil rigs is quite good."

"*Is* there anything we can do? I feel at a loss really," Steve asked.

"I don't think so. Just be aware, I suppose, anything suspicious. I don't know, just watch your backs."

There was an awkward silence that seemed to spread outwards, consuming the whole of the bar.

"I think he knows it was me. Don't know how, but that comment this morning and the way he looked at me. Well, no, the way we looked at each other. He knows. I'm sure of it. He knows."

We chatted for a while, going over details and aspects of his fraud. Toying over his possible plans and how, if he knew I was onto him, he would be sure to start making moves to flee. After an hour, we drove away, in different directions, uncertain of our future and what it would hold for us.

At some point before home, a green Subaru pulled away from the kerb, slicing easily into the traffic. Three spaces behind a red sports car, it mirrored its moves for several miles. After some time, it drove slowly and unobtrusively past a modest detached house. The red sports car sat on the driveway, its engine ticking as it cooled. Its driver never noticed the Subaru roll quietly down the street, past the trees and other sleepy, detached properties

After the pub and all its revelations, I made my way home. Andy and Steve returned to some semblance of work, a work that would likely never be the same as they thought of job changes just around the corner, their heads reeling with information that had shocked them to their cores.

I, however, felt better than I had in days. The largely selfish knowledge that it wasn't just me now was a relief. The knowledge that people close to me, people who *were* involved, were now privy to the same information that had weighed me down like a skip full of bricks, calmed me.

I sprawled on the settee in front of crap daytime TV and then smashed up a few cars on the Play Station before falling asleep. While I slept, Mr McRae blasted through the forests of Finland, showing me, had I been interested, how it should be done.

Rachel came back early, kissing me awake, blooming and fulfilled with her new job, while I pondered my own, distinctly waning career.

We ate a simple meal, shared a bottle of Merlot, then, while she skipped upstairs to the draw of a hot soak in the bath, I strolled out to my workshop, my hidey-hole.

To potter, perchance, to forget.

The clutter of my brick shed seemed welcoming, like meeting up with an old friend.

I sunk into its untidiness, allowing the disorganisation to wash over me.

A flicker of lights

A cluttered shed, its sturdy bench overhung with wood-working tools. A lamp throws its light around the room, casting shadows into the corners and glinting off the steel teeth of saws, the diamond edged swirls of drill bits and garden implements hanging from hooks on the door.

On the bench, mingling with the sawdust of past DIY jobs, is a half finished model of a Porsche 911. Struggling to melt solder onto a particularly tricky joint, the modeller hears the door open behind him; a spade clangs against the frame.

"Hello love, I'm struggling a bit with the transmission, but ought to be finished soon."

Before he can turn to smile at his wife, a thumping blow under his right ear tumbles him onto the bench and, spinning sideways, he sprawls onto the sawdust coated floor.

His eyes flicker and then he is still.

Black gloves reach out and remove the soldering iron's plug from the wall, the usual tingle of adrenaline and sexual stirring causing the hand to tremble slightly. Generally, Dan manages to keep his stirrings under control nowadays, but they still surprise and please him on odd occasions with their ferocious intensity. He searches around the workroom, eyes flicking from bench to shelf, not completely sure of the way forward. There, high on the far wall, sawdust encrusted and benign looking in its stillness; his chosen weapon.

Black and Decker.

A drill, Dan thinks, holds such a plethora of possibilities for pain and drawn out discomfort. Pity, but tonight, its many talents can't be fully utilised. This has to be an accident. From a jar on another shelf, he takes a cable tie and quickly fastens the trigger into its 'on' position. He then plugs it in and, as the motor whirrs into life, flicks off the switch next to the socket.

A half finished cup of coffee sits on the bench, cold and forgotten. Careful not to allow the coffee to pool on the bench, he pours a steady flow into the workings of the drill.

Working quickly, he removes the plug and, using a small red handled screwdriver, spins the Philips screw out of its centre. All the time he keeps an ear open for the sound of any unwanted attention and flicks his eyes to the still form on the floor, ready to react to any movement. He doesn't expect any. "Just stay nice and quiet for Uncle Dan."

The plug lies on the bench in two parts, its internals open like an upturned, partially shelled crab.

Next, he takes a length of heavy gauge fuse wire (it's twenty amp and he would prefer thirty two, but beggars can't be choosers) and, doubling it over, twists it together like a rope. He removes the thirteen amp fuse and winds the new temporary one in its place, bridging the terminals before replacing the top of the plug's casing.

It presses back into its socket with a satisfying clunk.

With another 'fuse' ready in case his first one doesn't do the job, he bends down and lifts the dead weight from the floor, seating him on the small stool and laying his upper body on the bench. It's difficult to get him to stay put and Dan has to reign in the frustration that builds within him. He's tempted to just cave the lifeless head in with a lump hammer that hangs on the leg of the bench, but resists the urge. This *has* to be an accident.

Eventually, he manages to wedge the upper body; a piece of four by four under the armpit, acting as a crutch.

Next, he carefully opens out the victim's right hand, lays it palm-up on the bench and places the drill into it, now deadly - live once the switch is flicked. A trickle of dark brown liquid pools in the open palm and the casing of the drill glistens in the soft light

Dan never takes chances and spends some time searching for a suitable piece of wood with which to flick the switch. He knows, deep down, that the plug itself is safe, but nevertheless relaxes, when he comes across a foot long piece of half inch dowel.

Removing his right glove, he feels for a pulse; a strong regular beat thrums beneath his finger. Then, with no hesitation whatsoever, he reaches across with the dowel and stabs it against the switch.

The plastic click is drowned by the instant whirr, as the drill springs into life.

Enthralled, he watches as the previously limp body appears to stiffen, twitching a couple of times before, once again, becoming limp. The drone of the drill ceases, tendrils of smoke rise into the musty air from the outstretched palm and a brief blue flash sparks from the plug.

It could be his imagination, but he thinks the lights flickered once.

With the switch depressed and the plug removed, he quickly replaces his melted and blackened makeshift fuse with the original one, tucks the wire into his pocket and plugs it back in.

The pulse, only a few moments ago, strong and regular, is no longer there. The skin is warm but totally lifeless. Dan stands and looks at the corpse. Five minutes ago, no three, maybe even two and a half, this dead thing was looking forward to finishing its model. Perhaps having a nice cup of coffee then a pleasant evening meal with *Mrs* Office Boy. Simple things, simple pleasures. Never again. No more black coffee, no more cigarettes. A small detail registers in Dan's brain and he scans the shed for an ashtray or packet of cigarettes but sees neither. Perhaps the dead thing didn't smoke when it was modelling. Not something it'll ever need to worry about now anyway. Dan's fascination has always been this fragility of life; one minute, the rest of a life spreading away into the infinite distance, the next, nothing.

Oh well, not to worry.

Job done, nearly.

Dan blows the smaller fuse, the drill this time not even giving the slightest hint of life. A brief, barely audible, 'pop' comes from the plug and, although again unsure, Dan thinks the light flickers once more. He takes out his penknife, carefully cuts the cable-tie and places it and the knife back in his pocket

Time is of the essence, the dead man's wife could walk in at any minute and spoil all the careful work of the last few minutes. That certainly would not do.

Privately, he relishes the thought. Relishes the prospect of ending another life; it's what he does best. Supposed to be quite a tasty piece too; he could always have himself a piece of her. A nice session of forced sex, just the thing after a nice killing, followed, of course, by another death. At least she'd end her days knowing what a real man could do, not some meddling office boy who plays with toy cars.

Lifting the body, limp and already cooling, he raises it up to head height and stares into lifeless eyes.

He is concerned about his initial blow. Any mark could prove awkward to a conscientious coroner. Two inches below the right ear, a slight bruise has begun to form, slowed by the lack of blood flow, but there none-the-less.

Looking around for a solution, his eyes fall upon the low shelf directly behind the bench on the opposite wall. It's made of good thick wood, easily two inches deep. Not perfect but not bad at all. He holds the head steady and forces the neck against the shelf. He finds the crunch of bone and sinew immensely satisfying and considers doing it again, then thinks better of it and lets the useless carcass fall to the floor, a sharply defined crease forming on the neck and a line of splinters embedded in the skin.

Propped against the wall, the upturned face stares back at him with a look of shocked realisation that its life is over.

Gloves back on, Dan steps out into the cool evening, pleased with his work and happy that tomorrow, he'll be £10,000 better off; not that he needs it. With a sly, ironic smile he thinks he might give it to a charity or, even better, use all those lovely crisp notes to light his lounge fire.

He leaves the way he came, calmly and with a strange dignity, through the unlocked garden gate. He scans the pools of shadows for signs of evening dog walkers and, seeing none, strolls across the lawn, onto the pavement and along the street.

It's a minute walk to his car and during this time his erection presses uncomfortably against the inside of his jeans.

After the tense work of the previous half hour, he needs some relaxation, some release. He heads for a few late night streets around Wolverhampton that he knows well. He drives slowly but not too slowly - attention is not something he craves. He watches. He looks. He searches for the girls who wait for him in shadows cast by amber street lights.

Unwanted news

In my dream, the clutter of my shed, the familiar articles of my spare time; the fly-tying equipment, garden tools, old bits of twisted steel and plastic, were weighing me down. Their weight seemed to represent all the issues that threatened to crush me, yet rip me apart at the same time.

It was a strange dream, a swishing noise distracted me and made me think of the seashore. Odd names were called out, names from my past, names barely remembered, drawn from a memory made indistinct by the passage of time.

A man, dressed in black from head to foot, with the short and squat dimensions of a dwarf, crouched on my bench. He was smiling; a manic smile. The smile of someone who's lost control. All the time he was tapping a screw driver against an old saucepan. His taping rang out clear and bright, gradually increasing in speed. Louder and louder until the individual 'tings' became indistinguishable and merged into one.

Like an alarm bell.

A school dinner bell.

A fire bell.

A *phone ringing*.

I woke with a start, instantly alert and, initially, as I looked across the darkness of our bedroom, sure that the dwarf of my dream sat on the dressing table, grinning at me.

Only shadows.

I glanced at the bedside clock: 3.27. All was quiet. No phone ringing.

Rachel breathed deeply through her open mouth. Not quite a snore, just peaceful and relaxed.

Had I known then of the turmoil, the tempest of emotion and circumstance that was to break upon our lives in the following few days, I would have shaken her awake, bundled her into the car and drove far into the night.

I didn't though.

I was thirsty, so swung out of bed and made my way downstairs. Standing in the cold white glow of the fridge, swigging orange juice straight from the carton, gulping the cool, thick liquid and thinking that

Rachel would do her nut if she saw me, I stifled a snigger and looked out into the garden. I loved our garden, the work that we had put into it over two summers, gradually forming it into what it eventually became.

The ringing mobile startled me from my thoughts and, for a second, I thought I was back in my dream. I pounced on it, fully expecting to wake all over again.

"Hello."

There was nothing but silky silence on the line.

"Hello, who's there?"

"Andy, it's Steve." He was barely audible and seemed to be struggling with a great turmoil. His voice seemed lumpy, the tone rising and falling, sometimes disappearing completely, a horse croak, nothing more.

"Steve, for God's sake slow down, I didn't get any of that."

I heard the deep breaths; great lung-fulls of air. Waited, while my work-mate composed himself; waited for a message that, at half past three in the morning, I reckoned I didn't want to hear.

"Andy's dead."

"What?"

"Andy's dead. Electrocuted. I've just comeback from his house. Jane's in a right state. Christ Andy, they think he spilled some coffee on his drill, something as stupid as that. I thought your phone would be off, I was just going to leave a message … sorry mate, I wouldn't have rung at this time …" His voice broke, cracked right open, the vocal equivalent of an earthquake and he was sobbing.

I tried to calm him to ease his pain, knowing how close they were, instantly wondering what I would do and how I would feel had it been Al who'd died. I agreed to go over in the morning, struggled with a few more, hopefully sympathetic words and hung up. I sat at the kitchen table, numb, but never more awake. Rachel pushed her way through the door, hair dishevelled, groggy with unsatisfied sleep and I stumbled into her arms, crying and talking gibberish. She held me for what seemed an age, letting my sadness drain away, drawing out my grief and loss and (looking back) taking in my guilt. The strength of my outpouring shocked me.

An accident, Steve said - a tragic accident, nothing more.

Even then, I felt the stirrings of unease, the coincidence that was simply too tidy.

Irrational I know, but there just the same.

Barely twelve hours previously I'd made him and Steve privy to the information that had played on my mind for what seemed like a lifetime. Poured onto them all my thoughts, revelations, theories and concerns. They had sat, slack-mouthed and incredulous, soaking every last syllable into their memories.

Now Andy was dead.

An 'accident'.

Andy.

"Oh, Jesus, Rach, Andy. Andy's dead. What if they did the wrong Andy?"

I eventually calmed and we sat, side by side at the table, holding hands, first me speaking, generally coherent but sometimes needing coaxing. Then both sitting and saying nothing. Rachel was calm from the start - Rachel the rock, Rachel the sane.

"It was an accident, nothing more." She sighed and squeezed my hand. "Don't read anything else into it. It's not your fault, no one's after you. It was just an accident."

I agreed, eventually and felt my whole body slump with an odd sort of relief. Selfish relief. Rachel was right. I was tired. I'd received some bad news in the early hours of the morning. It wasn't about the whole CSA - Trevor Talbot - Chris Stevens fraud thing. It wasn't about me. Just an accident. Bad timing. The worst.

In the ten minutes that I felt had passed since my rising, time had defied logic and physics by racing ahead of itself. The clock on the wall proclaimed it was 5.01.

"Go back to bed Rach, I'm going to have a shower and get over to Steve's."

Her lips felt soft under mine and her hair smelt of bed and sleep as I kissed the top of her head.

"Go on, have another couple of hours. I'll come in before I leave."

An hour later, I was driving into a world damp and steamy with rising heat. I remember thinking what a great morning it would have been to spend by a shady lake, watching a bright red float tip dance amongst the bubbles of feeding fish while rising columns of mist spiralled into the air.

I never got to Steve's.

On my passenger seat lay the file that had last been out on show at the pub the previous day and in my head was a speech that would surely put an end to the illegal aspects of Mr Stevens and his empire. Hopefully, one that would bury the bastard for a long time to come.

I really do believe they thought I was mad; those early or possibly late shift policemen at Wolverhampton Station. Some nutter off the street ranting about drugs and investment fraud, waving a manila file in the air and demanding to speak to a detective. They gave in eventually, having sat me down and given me a plastic cup full of hot brown liquid that could have easily been either tea or coffee (it was sweet and burned my tongue).

A young man in a dark suit eventually poked his head around the edge of an open door, glanced nervously at one of his colleagues and received a nod of confirmation before calling out "Mr Perkins? Could you come this way please?" I followed him down a tiled corridor, turned a corner at the end and squeezed past him into an untidy office strewn with paper and about to collapse in on itself under the weight of A4 sheets pinned to the walls.

DC Spall listened to my story. He made notes on a clipboard balanced on his knee. He nodded in all the right places and raised his eyebrows intermittently, as if remembering his training from Police College about body language and the uses thereof.

He thumbed his way through the file I placed in front of him for a while before speaking. "So none of these investments actually exist? Is that what you're saying?"

I confirmed his grasp of the situation with a tired nod of my head.

"Bare with me a minute please Sir" and he was gone, along with my folder.

Three hours later my head was spinning. A dishevelled and initially muzzy headed DCI Callow joined DC Spall ten minutes after Spall's return to the office. *He* took me seriously, followed rapidly by his junior once he'd realised his initial mistake. Spall scribbled notes fit to ignite the pad over which his pen flew, nodding, smiling and pitching in with a few comments and questions during brief pauses in Callow's flow.

It turned out they'd followed up my initial gravel bin deposit and telephone call with a few discreet enquiries of their own. Known users had been questioned and an undercover policeman had already made a few discoveries that were pointing towards useful in-roads into the local drug industry. Stevens was under surveillance and had been for some time. My information had simply prodded them along a little.

It was odd, sitting there amongst the clutter of a world as alien to me as a Women's Institute meeting, strangely relaxed, smoking and chatting. Callow had a way of making everything seem normal, safe, and secure. In between his strange habits of blowing out his cheeks and scratching his left ear, he would, when in thought, gaze across the desk as if bathed in some kind of inner peace. As though he was somewhere else.

He possessed a large, round, 'piggish' head, a broad nose that appeared to be trying to spread across his whole face, small, squinty, eyes and a wide, square chin. His hair, what was left of it, seemed to want to escape. Sticking up in all directions, it gave him the appearance of someone who had slept at his desk - badly.

I got the distinct impression that Callow knew of our midnight foray into Stevens' barn, even before I made my cannabis deposit. I remember thinking that perhaps they'd got his phone tapped, or that they'd watched the whole episode from a hidey-hole in the bushes.

Of course, I had to tell them how I came to be in possession of such a large lump of illegal drug and relayed to them every detail of the operation. I left out Al's involvement; didn't see the need to tell them. I talked, they listened, took notes and nodded at each other in some apparent Policeman's sub-language. Callow puffed out his cheeks, scratched his ear and ruffled his hair. Spall scribbled, nodded, raised his eyebrows and hung longingly on his superior's every word.

Nice, to think so highly of one's boss, I thought. The hatred I felt for mine burned in me, an actual physical sensation.

"Does anyone else know about this Andy?"

I looked deep into his eyes, trying to see if there was any hidden question and whether my telling would create any more problems or awkward situations to deal with.

"Andy, listen. This ..." he struggled to find the right word, "this *situation* is, well, it's serious. Stevens is just a minion, a gofer; you wouldn't want to know where this thing goes. Believe me, if our information is accurate, and we have no reason to doubt it, he is a tiny cog in a very large machine."

A scratch of his ear, ruffle of his hair, pink cheeks puffed out.

"*Does* anyone else know?"

I told him. I had to. I thought of Rach, probably at work now unless she'd knocked off the alarm clock and gone back to sleep, then of Steve, at home grieving for his mate.

"There *was* someone else. Another lad at work. Andy Miller."

"*Was?* Sorry, you've lost me."

"He died, last night. Steve told me, the other adviser at CSA, phoned last night, well, this morning really."

"How?"

"Err, accident. Apparently electrocuted himself in his shed. I don't know the details ... sorry."

Callow nodded across at Spall and the youngster leapt to his feet and swept out of the room.

The look on my face must have told a story.

"Keen isn't he?"

I was taken aback, Callow's intuition was a little disconcerting. I thought of Trevor Talbot and his eerie second sight, and realised that I hadn't told Callow about my visit to Talbot's house and all its revelations. The revelations that started the whole sorry mess. So I told him and was glad to be unburdening myself of the information. I felt drained, utterly spent. More than anything, I wanted to go home and sleep.

"Where's junior gone? Are you thinking there may be something in Andy's death?"

"No" - emphatic, certain, but possibly, *just* possibly, a touch too quickly answered.

"No. Really Andy, but, well, after what you've told us, it doesn't pay to presume."

I went to the toilet, splashed cold water on my face and then stood at the urinal for a few minutes, forcing a few drops into the drain. When I returned, Spall was back at his boss's side, looking flushed and out of breath, as if he'd not stopped running since he left the office.

"Well?"

"Coroner says accidental death. 'Electrocution due to a faulty drill'. On the face of it, there's no sign of anything untoward, just an unfortunate accident. We'll send a couple of our lads over to have a look, but it looks pretty benign at the moment. I think maybe were all just a touch jumpy." Callow held up his hands, ready to beat off my attack, "Look, it's understandable. We just don't need to be jumping to any rash conclusions at the moment. OK?"

A distinctly awkward pause followed, during which my suspicious mind *still* came to the rapid conclusion that I was being kept in the dark or at least in a deep shadow.

"Listen Andy, have you got anywhere you can go for a few days?"

I didn't understand what he meant at first. Then it clicked, he wanted me out of the way for a while. "Rachel has a good friend in Worcester, made a fortune in a dot com company a few years back. Doesn't work now, well hardly anyway. She's always asking for us to visit."

"If you've got any holiday left, I should take it, better still, just get in your car and go. Thinking about it Andy, you don't need to take holiday do you? Lets face it, you're out of work."

That raised a smile, amongst all of us.

"Yeah, suppose so. I'll speak to Rach, see if we can get off tomorrow. That OK?"

Callow puffed his cheeks, "Of course, perfect, no rush. Just don't want you around for a while. Safer all round, understand? Just in case, better safe than sorry and all that." Callow looked genuinely troubled all of a sudden. "Listen Andy, with this information you've given us, the fraud aspect and the drugs situation, we're going to have to pay Mr Stevens a visit and it's going to happen pretty smartish, probably in the next few days. I'd just prefer if you weren't in the vicinity, all right?"

"Inspector Callow, I understand, really, I could do with a break anyway. It's not a problem, honest."

"Leave a telephone number, relax, sit back and watch the papers."

I stood and shook his hand, then Spall's.

"And Andy, thank you, you've moved our investigation forward months." Another pause, puff of cheeks and a scratch with his left hand.

"Wish you'd have come forward with the drugs though, instead of dropping them in that grit bin."

I was home in fifteen minutes, spoke to a subdued Steve on the mobile advising him to get in touch with Callow and then take a holiday. I made a coffee, spoke to Rach at her work place, asked her to come home, straight away, then dropped onto the settee and cried.

My tears were hot and free flowing, my coffee sat un-touched and on the radio, Sting sang about the shape of his heart.

Rachel said she was just about to go into a meeting and couldn't, absolutely, definitely get out of it but would leave as soon as she was through. I said I'd explain when she got back.

I rang Al, spoke to his answer machine, asked him to ring me back and then went into the garden for a smoke and a wander. I spent ten minutes kicking at the gravel then sat on the stone bench and watched my fish cruising the pond.

The shrill ring of my mobile broke my trance, the name on the screen - ⊓ᒪ山Hᒧⓞᗺ.

"Hello mate, how's things?"

"Not bad, apart from my manager, blokes an absolute twat, honest Andy I could kill the bastard."

"Why, what's he up to now?"

He told me; in angry, brilliantly colourful language.

"He's as bad as Guiseppé at National Life, honest to God, It's like the industry breeds them ... or perhaps they just follow me around ... I dunno ... anyway, how you doin?"

I told him of Andy's death, my trip to the Police and their advice to 'get away for a while'. Gave him the whole story, in all its gory detail. I also told him that they knew nothing of his involvement or knowledge in the matter but that I couldn't guarantee his anonymity indefinitely.

"Whatever Andy. Listen if you need me ..."

His words broke off, leaving a deep trench of silence that I found impossible to fill. I felt my throat tighten, gulped once and then disguised it with a cough.

"Yeah, thanks mate. I'll be off tomorrow, probably for a week, maybe longer. Give me a call, I'll have the mobile with me, OK?"

"Yeah, take care mate, speak to you soon."

I felt like a young soldier going into battle.

I heard Rach's car pull into the drive just after 3.00. I was sitting in the shed tying flies to fill the empty space in my time while her engine rumbled, then fell silent. I met her in the garden. She looked flushed and troubled, a deep frown on her brow that seemed at odds with her sweet face. We hugged on the gravel path, our feet crunching as we rocked each other, letting the warmth of our feelings ease our worries away.

"Had a good day?"

I smiled, shrugged and said that I'd had better. Not many that were more eventful, but definitely more pleasant.

I sat on the settee in the lounge and, with Rach sitting cross-legged on the floor, I spilled the beans.

I was becoming tired of telling the same story over and over again. I would have loved to have got everyone together who was ever going to want to hear and tell it just the once, then forget it; the whole terrible stressful episode. I realised though, that I ought to get used to it - the next time would undoubtedly be in court.

With a suitcase packed, we sat in front of the fire eating fish and chips straight from the paper. For the first time in what seemed like weeks I didn't feel like a thousand butterflies were flying around in my head. For the two or three hours that we sat, talked, cuddled and finally made love in front of the embers of our log fire, I was totally, utterly incomprehensibly relaxed, content and in love.

The room was lit purely by the fire-glow and in the flickering light, Rach's skin glistened and reflected the dancing flames. It was too warm for a fire really. We had the front window open and a cooling breeze wafted in over our bodies.

She pulled herself up onto her knees and, taking my cigarettes from the mantle piece, took two out, lit them against an ash covered log, passed one back to me and drew heavily on her own.

I was stunned.

I didn't smoke in the house.

Rach never smoked, full-stop.

She drew the smoke in like a veteran twenty-a-dayer and exhaled straight into the hearth.

"I just fancied one."

"Right OK, whatever."

I shook my head in disbelief.

"If I live to be a thousand, and never left your side in all my years, I swear, as I sit here now, stark naked, that I will never, *ever* understand you."

She turned her head upwards, looking straight at me, blowing smoke in my eyes.

"But Rach, that's alright by me."

I breathe, therefore I am

A beautiful June morning, perfect summer weather holding out for what seemed an age. Fabulous and vivid, the greenery flew past as I sped along country roads, shades on, window open and Ocean Colour Scene blasting in my ears. I was in Rach's car, joyously working my way across country from Al's house. I'd paid him a fleeting visit to drop off a spare set of keys so he could pop to our house and make sure the fish didn't starve.

I felt as though all the pressures of recent times had been lifted and blown away into the far distance.

Spall and Callow could do their bit now. I beat the steering wheel of the Mini in time to 'The River-Boat Song' and watched the rev-counter edge up to 7,000 before I changed into third.

Built in 1972, the Mini had spent most of its time tootling about in Bromsgrove. Officially, by its birth rite, a mini 1000, it now sported a 1293 full race spec, 'A' series engine. I'd added a pair of Cobra bucket seats, roll-cage, fire extinguisher, de-seamed body, fully re-welded joints and a yellow paint job bright enough to give onlookers a headache. The exhaust system was loud enough to set off car alarms and I loved it. The sound of it rumbling and popping out of hair-pin bends sent tingles down my spine. The feel of every bump and undulation in the tarmac coming back through the steering wheel made me want to chuck it into every bend, to feel the tyres skip and squeal then grip and power into the next one.

Magic. Driving pleasure distilled to its purest form - loads of power, low weight, no frills, just fun; pure unadulterated fun.

Rach had jumped at the chance of taking the luxury of the Nissan when I'd suggested it over breakfast; couldn't understand why I wanted to drive the thirty miles to her friend's house in her car.

We decided to take both cars in case I needed to come back to Wolverhampton to 'help the Police with their enquiries' (quite likely under the circumstances).

I'd had a quick coffee with Al and barely spoken about my situation; somehow it didn't seem right. Instead we'd reminisced about night-time forays for sea trout in Wales and how it would soon be time to don our chest waders and waist coats and go wandering in search of them once more.

It had been a sublimely pleasant hour. Sitting in his garden, me flicking ash into a plant pot while Enid hung out her washing next door. She saw us sitting in the sunshine and came over for a chat, leaning on the low fence, huge bare breasts resting on the rough wood, naked, apart from a large sun hat, dark glasses and a smile.

I waited until she'd gone, turned to Al and mentioned how bizarre it was, to have a conversation in the garden with a naked woman.

"You get used to it you know," he replied, "I hardly even notice it now."

I wondered, if she'd been a twenty one year old, five nine, blonde aerobic instructor, whether the whole thing would have been as unnoticeable.

I pulled onto the A449, leaving twisting, hedge-lined country roads for fast, efficient, wide tarmac and settled into a comfortable cruise around the sixty mark.

The traffic built briefly around Kidderminster then thinned out once I was onto dual carriageway. Speed cameras mocked the passing traffic, daring drivers to push past fifty five.

Brake lights flared in the distance and the flow of traffic gradually trickled to a stand-still.

I'd passed a recovery truck a mile or so before I ground to a halt and noticed it snaking its way through the queue behind me. I pulled over onto the central reservation's grass, parched and brittle in the mini drought we were having and let it crawl past. Its yellow flashers were going at full tilt; obviously someone had decided to behave like a lemming.

I crawled for perhaps a mile until the road meandered towards an ordinarily fast sweeping 'S' bend, left then right. I could see, across the field to my left, the road sweeping on and the blue flashing lights of emergency vehicles, already at the scene. At the time, at that point in my life, I wasn't sure whether I could see a vehicle.

There seemed to be, in the near-side lane, some sort of large object, indistinguishable at the four hundred yards or so that I was viewing it.

The view was closed off as a transit van crept past on the inside and began indicating to enter my lane. I looked in my rear-view mirror and noticed amber flashes all down the line of traffic. They were all being good for once, getting in nice and early. It was as if everyone knew a little respect was due.

I suppose, looking back through the veil of tranquillisers and alcohol that clouded my version of reality for a while back then, that I was a hundred yards from the accident when the first uneasy stirrings stole into my stomach and chest.

A hundred yards is close enough - *just about*, to make out the wreckage of a car that carries the whole of your world, close enough for your mind to put together the bits of jumbled information.

The bright red paintwork.

The black suitcase lying in the grass at the side of the road, thrown, at some point during the violence, from the crushed boot-lid hanging at an angle against the road.

Fifty yards is close enough to begin to freeze, blood chilling and thickening in a heart that is striving desperately to continue pumping.

Thirty yards is close enough to make out the twisted door, wrenched open by firemen.

Twenty yards is close enough to see the missing rear wheel, its axle twisted and broken.

Fifteen yards is close enough to see the debris of scattered wreckage amongst trees on the central reservation.

Ten yards is close enough to begin to hyperventilate; to realise that the car, utterly smashed and reduced to broken, twisted, gouged, scrap metal, every window shattered and cob-webbed, could not hold a living soul.

Seven yards is close enough to comprehend that, on its roof, like an upturned crab, it's as dead and lifeless as surely its driver must also be.

Five yards is close enough to fall to the tarmac and stumble into the arms of a nervous and unprepared Policeman who is trying desperately to get the mad-man back into his car left abandoned in the road.

It's close enough to feel the disbelieving stares of fellow drivers, to feel the pity and fear oozing from their vehicles, hands shielding their faces in realisation that this wild, screaming man is involved also.

It's close enough to realise that the ambulance has already left, carrying a soul mate so perfect, yet so still and lifeless.

It's close enough to stare at the oddments that spend their lives in the safe cocoon of a car. The CDs flung as if by a child's tantrum to all four winds. The fishing hat (mine) wide brimmed, drab and green, cast aside on the verge. The straw hat with blue ribbon (Rachel's) squashed flat on the roof above the rear passenger seat, waiting for a kindly push to pop it back into its distinctive dome. The map books, ripped and crumpled, pen-marked with bright red ink circles, marking out the streets I'd visited:- James Road, Kestrel Drive, Windermere Grove; a history of journeys past.

"My wife, my wife, my car ..." The Policeman reels as if stomach punched, colour draining from his face, lips trembling and slack, stuttering gibberish, desperately trying to pull himself into some form of order whilst fighting the overwhelming urge to turn and flee. To escape this scene of tragedy and despair, this violent soap opera unfolding all around him, dragging him in deep, making him a key performer; a part in which he wants *no* part.

I remember slipping near the drivers door, hands coming up to grab the sill, now at chest height, falling to my knees and feeling the slick, slippery liquid, deep red and cloying, soak into the material of my trousers. Feeling the same oozing sticky-ness on my palm as I steadied myself. Raising the palm to my face and staring, bemused and as if separated from my solid form by the sight of the deep, arterial blood in front of my eyes.

I had never seen such dark, almost solid looking blood.

And so much, God, Jesus, so, so much.

The young Policeman took me by the shoulder, another officer helping him. Together they struggled against my growing hysteria, raised me to my feet, one of them hugging me against his chest and smoothing my hair.

I feel sure he was crying.

Perhaps he had a wife at home, the scene reminding him of the fragility of this life we cling to.

I struggled from their joint embrace and dived into the car, sprawled on the roof, wet with more blood, as though the car itself was bleeding in sympathy. I grabbed the hat, squashed on the shattered sun roof, hugging it to my face.

Inside, all was calm, quiet, I liked it there.

I was aware of silence, save for the thud of my heart, beating like slack machinery. As if beating for us both, beating fit to explode inside my chest. Building to a crescendo of its own.

I could feel hands on me again, pulling me from this sanctuary and my ears started to work again. The sounds of an empty world I wanted no part of flooded back to surround me and for a terrible moment, time swirled and spun, back to a cold black evening, with damp roads and a sparkling velvet sky, when the empty feeling of loss flooding my stomach was for my parents, not my wife and lover. When my hands were wet, not with blood, but rain; not deep red, but clear, as if from a bubbling, crystal spring, not a slashed artery. When I was still a child, clothed in a man's body, no experience of life, or death, to draw on.

Being dragged from that wreck was like being born again, kicking and screaming into the warm air of that June day.

They were forceful then. Dragging me to a nearby Volvo, all flashing lights and day-glow decals, they sat me in the passenger seat and talked to me. Of what, I have no recollection; sympathies and calming strokes that ran off me as though I was made of Teflon.

Forty yards away amongst the trees on the central reservation, part buried under a broken birch tree, as if the owner was trying to hide its involvement, a dark green Subaru Impreza sat on flat tyres. Score marks ran down its flank, painted in with red. Its screen was shattered and, although I never actually saw, its drivers side was ripped off as though a huge can opener had been at work.

Not just my wife and I then, another soul, another life, another set of circumstances tipped into the melting pot, flung into the whole terrible equation.

I'm told that PC's Gilley and Sellbridge eased me out of my hysterical trauma with the calm, professional ease of trained counsellors. They soothed me with words, calmed me with sympathies and, when another ambulance arrived, for me this time, helped me stagger towards its open rear doors.

Like buses, you wait for ages without sight or sound of them, then two arrive within a few minutes. One for the living, one for the dead.

I was sedated and lay on a padded bed being talked to in the same, calming manner that the Police had used. I drifted in a drug hazed stupor that was neither alive or dead. I existed. I breath, therefore, I am.

No sirens for me, no rush to the hospital through red lights amongst traffic peeling away in all directions, a relaxed drive, more subdued than the one I had recently finished.

I felt that I would never drive again.

Like Rachel.

I held her straw hat close to my chest, was able to smell her perfume and imagine her touch. I held it, as though to lose it would give up her memory. Like no words that could ever be spoken, it calmed me.

I drifted.

Downtime

Strange. Hazy.

The hours peeled back to reveal layers of yet more. They built and grew with a constant, unnerving insistence. First hours, then days, then weeks. Gradually, adding time like the endless drip of mineral rich water building a stalagmite, my life began to grow again. At one point, amidst the jumbled thoughts and feelings that swirled through the empty sky in my head, I decided that, never again would I achieve any sort of equilibrium. Normality, *reality* in fact, had finished, snuffed itself out; a wet finger pressed to a candle's wick. It had ceased to exist on that warm June day; been crushed on hard, black, uncaring tarmac; died amongst scrubby trees and the yellow, brittle, sun-dried grass of no-mans-land running down the road's centre. Normality had drifted away into the clear, blue sky of that day. The candle had left its legacy of wispy grey smoke to snake away, sinuous and silky.

The soul of my life was dead. The very centre of my life had died. Crushed from all angles, it had succumbed to an inevitability as old as life itself - 'I live therefore I die'.

Massive, intensely devastating internal injuries and a skull crushing impact caused by a partially collapsed roof.

I saw my wife, my Rach, my best friend, lay still and cold for the last time amongst the clinical sterility of a hospital morgue.

For the last time.

The last time.

To see her, so quiet, so 'final' as if asleep, stretched the fabric of my existence to breaking point. As I stood and gazed down at her paleness, a strange buzzing vibration built and grew in my head, spreading through my whole body until I was trembling, ready to either explode or simply crumple and fall slackly to the tiled floor.

That night, the first alone, my dreams were filled with a kaleidoscopic nightmare of spinning colours. Every shade; but all red, swirling and twisting to the musical accompaniment of rending metal and groaning, screaming, disjointed voices.

Every time I drifted into my drug induced slumber, the noise and colours pounced. Instantly, I was awake, left to stare at the white ceiling and walls of my private hospital room. I read and re-read the fire instructions, anything to take away the fact that I was struggling to keep a lid on my sanity. I was trembling on the brink of a nervous breakdown. A terrible nervous tension, an anxiety the likes of which I hadn't imagined possible, rushed maniacally around in my head.

It was as though every single cell of my body was vibrating with a biblical intensity.

Every single cell.

I could see no reprieve from the blackness that I was falling into, no chance, no purpose for the hollow shell that, at that time, I saw as my life. The hours continued to peel away revealing yet more. The days were filled with difficult minutes of clear lucidity and hazy smudges of space.

Arrangements were made, mostly by Al. People grieved, patted me on the back and spoke of my loss as if I hadn't realised it had happened. Steve phoned, fresh from his own grief following Andy's death and spoke of the Police and their questions. I vaguely re-count a conversation with Callow a few days into my new life. He knew of my loss and consoled me as best he could, then talked of Stevens being pulled in, arrested with enough evidence to put him into a small cell for years to come. Clients had been contacted, interviewed during visits to their homes. They had explained about their investments, paid either by Building Society counter cheque or some, foolishly, in cash. Such cheques carry no designated account details, just a destination. Anyone, with the required lack of ethics could use them to open an investment.

With policy documents, produced by computer at Stevens' home and hand delivered by him ('all part of the service'), no one trusting would suspect a thing.

It transpired that on one occasion, when a client had had a cheque drawn up to 'Midland Mutual ref. J. G. Evans', the lady's name, Stevens had asked her to get another. "Putting a name on the cheque was apt to cause confusion."

It would also have meant that it couldn't accompany an application for someone else.

The trial was set for December, I was required, obviously, as a key witness. Stevens was to be held on bail, Armani traded for plain denim and cotton.

A plethora of information, sympathy and condolence poured from well-wishers but it all simply bounced off me. I had withdrawn into myself. Set up a hardened shell, an outer skin too tough to be penetrated by even the most well meaning sentiment.

I heard nothing.

Felt nothing.

And all the time, through my most distraught insularity, Al sat and waited. Always there, alternating between leaving me be, or trying to coax out of the hollow shell, the friend that he felt he had lost.

I stayed with him for a couple of weeks, ambled around his house, aimless and lost. I worked in his garden, mowing, pruning and tending the borders - often under the sympathetic gaze of his neighbours.

The first time Enid came out to chat, I didn't realise it was her. She was fully clothed. Denim shorts and a white tee shirt accompanying her wide brimmed straw hat. I never mentioned it, but hugged her over the fence, kissed her sweet pink cheek and whispered 'thank you', before pulling away and returning to my weeding, tears glistening in my eyes.

At first, my days started mid-morning, the house quiet and still, Al usually gone, visiting clients. I found that I could never ask him about his work. Feelings I held for the industry were fraught with anger and tempered with a near hatred that Al, in his own way, understood.

I wanted nothing to do with it. Blamed it for my loss, my grief.

Over the first few building weeks, my routine evolved and I began to return to the world. Slowly and tenuously maybe, but I was, I felt, returning. Early rises, walks along the lanes and fields, preparing breakfast for Al. I suppose, for a while, after the initial withdrawal, he became a surrogate wife.

I pulled up short of kissing him as he left for work though.

After ten days, I returned home for the first time on my own.

The day started normally enough, but after my daily walk, I decided to take the Mini out for a drive. It had been driven back to Al's house the day after the accident and I hadn't given it as much as a glance in all the time it sat in front of the house.

It smelled of her.

That was the first thing that struck me. I could smell the perfume and even the make-up that she used. The steering wheel felt cold to my touch and I initially recoiled, remembering the clammy, cool feel of her shoulder, touched briefly, at my first goodbye in the morgue.

The key turned and I didn't cry.

Its plucky little engine burbled lumpily into life and I still didn't cry. Even when I fastened the seat belt, the same strip of material that had hugged her breast so many times, I didn't cry. The bucket seat felt snug and firm beneath me and, as I engaged reverse and swung out of the drive,

I actually felt normal, not happy or relieved, just … normal - part of the world again.

I let the engine warm slowly, going up through the gears without building the revs too high and the little car pulled me along, apparently revelling in its outing. I let it raise my spirits.

Lighting a cigarette, I leant across and switched on the radio cassette and was instantly back on the day of her death. I never really gave it any thought, but the tape that had been playing as I fell out of the drivers door on the A449 sprang back to taunt me. *Then* I cried. I cried for Rachel, for the life she would never know, for the times I would never spend with her, but mostly, selfishly, for her leaving me alone, for throwing a great big spanner into the domestic works, upsetting my life and my plans; our life our plans.

God, I needed her.

I drove through the tears, their blurring, stinging floods threatening to spill me from the road. Coincidence, habit or whatever, drove me along until I found myself outside our house.

The first thing I thought, the *very first thing* that sprung into my mind as I looked at the pretty front garden, was that I ought to sort out the mortgage. Claim the life policy and pay it off. Strange really, but it happened a lot. I would slip from maudlin, self obsessed despair, to a state of resignation, then fear, then a physical longing that would burn with a terrible intensity. Often, once passed, a resolute clarity would overtake me, I'd shrug, take a deep breath and just get on.

Rachel was well covered, I'd already had a cheque for £136,000 from her employer. Four years salary. Four years *new* salary, for the *new* job she never really started. The salary she'd not even had time to pick up. Four years worth, for a life finished.

The cheque was still on Al's work surface in the kitchen.

There was the policy protecting the mortgage, two or three term assurances, a couple of endowments, a P.E.P. or two with various companies, last years ISA and whatever she'd had in her building society account.

I'd done nothing with any of it.

I seemed to remember receiving a form from her pension scheme asking for the bank details so they could pay the widower's pension to me, supposed I must have filled something in to receive the £136,000. It was all a haze.

The keys to the front door were on the key ring hanging from the ignition and I watched them dangling, glinting sunlight from their silvered peaks and grooves.

Could I? Was I really ready for this?

Sitting at the kitchen table, the room cool and bright, I waited for the tears again. They let me down and refused to come. I was glad. My earlier tears had shocked me, made things feel real again. Made *me* feel real again.

Truth was, at that point in time, I preferred my make-believe state.

I think I must have sat for about an hour, then slowly crept upstairs, looking at the half closed door to our room, glimpsing the corner of our bed and turning away quickly. I wasn't ready for that. Not yet anyway.

My office door was open and inside everything looked exactly as I remembered it - business like and with just enough clutter to give the impression of serious work being done there. I suddenly hated it; wanted to smash every piece of furniture, tear every single product brochure and every remnant of my career to shreds. I wanted to take the whole room into the garden, burn the lot and scream as I watched the flames consume every last scrap of my previous life.

Instead, I reached under the desk, took the filing cabinet key from its blob of blue tack, opened the top drawer, removed our personal file, descended the stairs and left.

Simple as that.

When Al returned, just after 8.00 p.m., I gave him a huge glass of whisky and surprised him with a smile.

He was obviously shocked. "Err, everything all right?"

"I've been to the house, this afternoon."

My statement hung in the air, swirled around us for a while, then disappeared.

"Right ... good ... err, OK ..."

"I'm alright, honest. Took the car out for a spin, just seemed to turn up there." I moved back to the kitchen and picked up the file that held the financial remnants of Rachel.

"I need to go through some stuff, you know, life policies and things. Fancy giving me a hand?"

"Shit, yeah of course. I was going to mention it ... just couldn't find the right time, you know?"

"Yeah. Is there ever a right time?"

We spread everything on the dining table. Sat down with a calculator, a huge bowl of pasta each, a pad of paper, pen, two glasses and a near full bottle of whisky.

By the time we'd finished, we were both drunk, both full, both tired. The table had a dozen or so small piles of paper on it and the pad on which I'd been scribbling policy numbers, account details and sums assured, proclaimed a final figure.

With the mortgage repaid and counting the £136,000 death in service payment, I was now worth a touch over £780,000, plus the house.

What had swelled the figures was an accidental death policy I'd forgotten all about - five units of £75,000 taken out years ago with the promise of radio alarm clock as a free gift. *£15 per month.* Not even the price of a pub meal. The clock packed up after six months, but the policy just kept on ticking along.

In monetary terms I was rich. I could conceivably retire. With the £12,000 per year widower's pension on top, I would certainly be comfortable.

Financially anyway.

A fortune in exchange for a life. It was what I'd preached for years, but now, in reality, with all the figures spread before me and thrust into my face with unfeeling, cold, clear-cut mathematics, I would have swapped the lot for a single hour with her.

Probably, for one single kiss.

I missed my wife.

Something other than sadness

The ground is heavy with dew as Al's boots carry him up the wooded bank opposite 'chez Jones'. In the ground cover of thick grass and clover, the imprint of each step is clearly defined and, at the top of the rise, he stops to look back at his home sleeping in the pre-dawn glow. His tracks lead back to the gate as clearly as footsteps in damp sand.

It would be a fine day. The sky is clear; the clearest, darkest blue imaginable, still sprinkled with a smattering of stars, holding on to the last vestiges of darkness as if in defiance of the new day.

Clad from head to foot in 'real-tree' camouflage, his passing is almost invisible from the road. Draped over his right arm, nestling comfortably in the crook of his elbow, naturally, as though it's *meant* to be there, is his shotgun. On his back, a similarly camouflaged rucksack that rattles with cartridges. His scrim scarf is rolled up on his head like a skull cap. Save for the addition of a couple of green smudges on his cheeks, he looks like an urban terrorist; a relic from an Oliver Stone movie set in 1960's Vietnam, not the farmland surrounding the Midlands.

I was asleep in his spare room, snoring my way through dreams of a life changed so rapidly and without warning that I was still reeling with the devastation of it all. It was barely forty- eight hours since my wife's life, my Rachel's life had simply *finished*, like a blown light-bulb, never to glow again. I had no idea of his leaving and the events that he witnessed were not relayed to me in any detail until my mind was back to some sort of normality, at least a week later. I think he was in need of escape. A need to simply dissolve into the countryside that he loved so much. To try and forget that his life too, had been turned upside down by the loss of a dear friend rendered almost catatonic by a great loss. To do what he loved, would allow him, if only for a short while to forget, to fill his head with something other than sadness.

His shoot spreads away for three miles, skirting the road that runs past his house, then kinking left over a small hill and down to another lane bordered by a mix of grazing land and a conifer plantation.

Considering his early start he's disappointed by the lack of rabbits, so he walks, letting the warmth of the rising sun, now at his back, wake him gradually. Alone, save for the scuff and squelch of his boots, the sound of his breathing and the rattle of cartridges at each step, he makes his way up the grassy slope leading to the summit of the hill. At the top he sits on the log that has been his seat ever since he started shooting this land.

He's shot here long before he moved to his present home and still remembers, with tingling excitement the moment when, one morning he arrived to shoot, only to find the house opposite the gateway to his hideaway for sale. He hadn't shot that morning; instead, he drove straight to the estate agents and sat outside until they opened. Exchanging his country seat for the warmth of his car, he'd made an offer on the property before the sales-girl had even switched on her computer and never regretted his hasty purchase.

The view from his log, is of rolling fields spreading for miles in every direction. In the far distance, the Wrekin and rounded hills of the Long Mynd are grey smears on the horizon. He loves the way their tops are picked out by the Sun rising behind him, igniting in a golden flare long before the surrounding lowlands, as if afforded a special consideration because of their elevated position.

It also takes in Chris Stevens' country pad.

He sits in silence for a while, sipping coffee from his flask, watching the greenery as it wakes. A normal summer's morning; country life going on as usual.

Then he spots a difference. It seeps into his brain like a nagging doubt.

Parked in a farm entrance two hundred yards from the timbered elegance of Stevens' residence is a dark blue Transit Van. Nothing really unusual in that; could be fellow shooters, although he knows of no one else with permission to shoot this piece of land. Poachers? Could be, there's plenty of pheasants put down for the privileged few to shoot. His gaze sweeps along the hedgerow, past the house and on for another couple of hundred yards. There, on the far side of the road is another, similarly drab, altogether unremarkable van and, right behind it, a green Peugeot 406.

He places his partially finished coffee on the log and delves into his rucksack for his binoculars. Turning the knob to bring his view into focus, he draws in a deep breath.

In the left hand van sit two uniformed Police Officers with peaked caps and waistcoats that look remarkably like bullet-proof vests. They stare out at the road in front of them, impassive and silent, relaxed even.

The car behind them reveals a further four men. Suits this time, dark and sombre. No bullet-proof vests there.

He jumps off the log and kneels behind it. Resting the glasses on the damp bark, he sweeps them along the hedgerow, past the house, stops, then reverses his sweep. There, alongside the conifer trees bordering the driveway, blending in against the branches, six, seven, eight, no ten officers. Against their chests are cradled automatic rifles.

Breath whistles through clenched teeth as he again raises his glasses.

The right hand van is pulling out into the road.

His vision blurs again as he sweeps left along the hedge, stopping briefly at the house. The officers amongst the conifers have gone. More blurring then becoming pin sharp as he picks out the left hand van, also moving along the lane, followed closely, within curling diesel fumes, by the Peugeot. At a point twenty yards from the driveway, stealth is swapped for full-blown, tyre spinning motion as they accelerate and swing into the driveway. They slew to a halt in front of the house sending a spray of gravel to clatter off the brickwork. The second van pulls up across the driveway, blocking it.

Black figures swarm from all points around the property, pouring over the gravel like army ants. Half a dozen that Al has missed, sweep out of the far hedgerow and take up station behind a rockery wall, guns trained on the house.

A vague hum of shouted instructions reach him from the teeming property and the sound of splintering glass and exploding door frame drifts back as a muffled 'crump'. Shimmering splinters of frosted glass sparkle in the strengthening sunshine. Al gasps as the sound reaches him, gawps with incredulity as the swarm pours with liquid grace and precision through the broken doorway. More shouts drift back, more curses, more destruction.

Two armed officers crouched behind the Peugeot point to the rear of the property and raise their weapons, shouting at a figure that skids across the gravel near the lawned portion of the garden. The figure spins around, the face framed in Al's binoculars, scared, angry and confused. He slips to his knees then scrabbles forward, desperate to gain his feet before sprawling headlong in the gravel.

He lies there for a moment, shouted instructions echoing around him then, raising his head towards the fir trees, he lifts his arms and places his hands behind his head. Three officers announce their intention and emerge from the conifers. Shouting at the prone man continually, one hand-cuffs him where he lies while the other two stand and point their weapons.

Dragged to his feet, his boxer shorts are pulled half way down his thighs. His captors make no attempt to preserve his dignity and, instead, lead him to the van parked across the drive.

Al watches as the semi-naked captive is swallowed into the black confines of the vehicle. The face that briefly stares at him through the binocular lenses is red and puffy, grazed down the left cheek from its contact with the gravel and streaked with tears. It's the face of a frightened, captured animal, terrified for its future and unsure even, of its present.

It's openly sobbing.
Openly pleading.
Stevens.

Dreamland

"Emily ... EMILY!"

Waking from a dream.

A dream where a little girl in a blue checked frock, lacy edged and multi-pleated, skips with a rope in a rose bordered garden. The grass is recently mown and the smell of the mower's work is strong in the air. It mixes with the sweet, almost sickly scent of rose petals and lavender. The day is warm, sunny and rich in splendour. The sky is clear and blue, cloudless for a million miles in every direction. The grass is cool and soft beneath bare skin, the heat of the day massaging the young boy's chest with its soft, seductive touch.

A yard to the left a white rat sits and cleans itself; paws moving left and right, smoothing down pink ears.

Life is good, sweet.

Life is perfect.

Dreamland is great. In this world he can play with his sister and Mr Jingles, safe from the nastiness that infects the real world, safe from the despair and hardship that unfolds its black cloak over millions of living souls each time the sun rises or sets.

Yes, dreamland is good.

Fields spread into the distance. They merge gradually into blue hazed hills, low and rounded, hung with wispy white clouds like puffs of steam from cartoon trains.

As the sun beats down, a hint of darkness seems to grow and build on the horizon. Slowly, imperceptibility, the darkness swells and multiplies until the sky is a broiling mass of dark grey smudges. Yellow tinged and ugly, the clouds roll in, building in height to awesome mountains of black vapour.

The sky darkens until the whole scene has transformed itself into an ugly non-light; a seedy mixture of day and night, neither one nor the other. Lightning crackles in the distance and, as the wind builds, the temperature falls, raising goose pimples.

The little girl has ceased her skipping, the rope hanging limp at her side, both red handles in one hand. She stands and stares at the fabulous sky, her blonde hair lifts and swirls around her angelic face. Her eyes are wide with wonder as she spins, arms outstretched, flailing in the wind. She is laughing; a cute giggle that develops into full blown laughter. Her eyes shine and she turns her face to the sky, amazed and thrilled at this storm that has enveloped the day. Growing dizzy, she stops and, on wobbly legs turns to look at her brother, now sitting upright, his palm over his eyes, staring past her, into the distance.

He seems to be searching for something, waiting for an element of the storm that is still distant. His gaze is fixed, as though he wants to be ready.

This time.

The little girl begins to feel afraid, her brother's strange, far away look scares her.

She tries to call out but her voice is carried away on the buffeting wind and she struggles to remain standing. Wobbling from foot to foot she attempts to go to him, hesitant steps at first then a full pelt run, closing a distance between them that continues to grow and so stays constant. With her young chest rising and falling, breath coming in hard pants, she ceases her run and stands weakly in the wind. She is crying now, scared at this turn of events.

The cottage behind him is dark and brooding; once it was light, welcoming, and quaint - like the cottages in the stories her brother reads her before putting out her bed-side light and kissing her forehead. As she watches, the first orange and yellow lights dance in the windows.

An explosion of glass makes her jump and she screams as the shards fly towards her. She feels the slicing of her skin, the first trickle of blood on her cheek, raises her hand to the cut and stares at the deep red smear on her fingers.

Flames follow the shattering glass and flare high into the sky, illuminating the scene in an eerie glow that is more frightening than the darkness. Her brother still watches, appears to be trying to raise himself to his feet but the same force that prevents her from running is working its magic on him.

The cottage is now an evil mix of dark and light, timbers flare into a pyrotechnic nightmare and, as the roof gives way, a shadow rises from the space as black as boiling tar. It rushes across the void between the cottage and her brother, her lovely, kind, thoughtful brother. Its coldness brushes his hair, then covers the distance between them in an instant.

He now watches as this blackness, this malignant, vaporous entity, envelopes his sister, his Emily and lifts her from the grass. Her feet flail the air briefly before she is thrown to the ground.

Her once pretty dress, now dirty and torn, moulds itself to her body, the wind acting to press it to every curve. Blackness covers her and the last he sees is her face, set in a terrible scream of fear and helplessness and, for the first time since wind and storm invaded their world she cries his name. Clear and sharp, it cuts through the bedlam and, as if it's taken on a physical form, slices straight to his heart.

"Danny ... DANNY!"

A grey light smudges out the detail in the room but, from the weak glow pressing at the blinds, Dan guesses it to be morning. Early morning, though he's not sure exactly which morning, which day he's decided to grace with his awakening. The nurses could tell him, *will* tell him once they've run their checks and the doctors have questioned him with their words, stethoscopes and lights in his eyes, but of these facts, he is, at present, unaware.

For the time being he lies still, breathing deeply and evenly, listening to the beep, beep, beep of a machine to his left. He takes stock of his surroundings, trying to piece together the situation into which he's surfaced. The bed is firm, sparsely clothed in starched white linen and a woven green blanket. A framework surrounds the bed, levers and pulleys cross-crossing his prone body. Some sort of structure is under the covers, keeping the weight of the linen from his lower body. That *can't* be good.

His left leg feels weightless. A slight flexing brings a sharp and immediate flare of pain which rockets from his knee to his thigh and then spreads its warmth across his midriff to both hips. He may have swooned at this point were it not for the fear of re-entering the dream. Instead he grits his teeth and concentrates on breathing deeply.

Gradually, piece-by-piece his thoughts relocate themselves.

An accident - definitely an accident.

He was on a job. A job his employer had told him to drop.

The memory of the 'office boy' tinkering with his toy car floods back. The musty smell of the shed, the crackle of surging electricity and the twitching of fingers. Then the shame when he realised it was the wrong man; same first name, just the wrong place, wrong surname, wrong fucking car (right colour if nothing else).

He got the bastard in the end though.

Jesus how that Nissan flew, took off when he gave it a nudge on that bend. It slew round as he braked, straight into the trees on the central reservation, flipped perfectly into a barrel roll, three times he reckoned, before landing from ten feet up straight on its roof.

He watched it slide, must have gone fifty or sixty yards, sparks flying. It transfixed him. So much so that he was on the grass before he realised what was happening, a tree the Nissan had demolished dug into the wing of his Subaru and ripped it and his door straight off.

He remembers only two things after that. The first was being flung into a tree at high speed, rolling and cartwheeling through undergrowth, things snapping within his own contorted body. The second, just before he gave into the haze of unconsciousness; a pair of legs twisted into ridiculous shapes in the upturned, totally smashed Nissan, hanging limp and still.

Yes. Stevens could go fuck himself.

He always finished a job and by God, this time he finished it big time. OK, so he banged himself up a bit in the process, but the job was done.

Over.

He has no real idea of his injuries but guesses, by the flare of pain that leapt along his thigh earlier, that he has broken something - probably fairly comprehensively.

He's fairly sure, not 100% but certainly 95%, that the office boy is long dead, so the helping hand he gave the Nissan into the trees should never come out into the open. He can pass it off as an accident, the Nissan sliding in front of him on the bend.

No problem, piece of cake.

Hopefully, his injuries won't be too bad either; be up and about in no time, collect his cash from Stevens then, who knows, Thailand maybe, travel, relaxation, excess.

He can hardly wait.

He was right about his blame for the crash; that would never surface.

He did not know, however, that, while he lay in his hospital bed, Stevens was 'helping police with their enquiries' and would stay inside for twelve years. True to the agreement, the name 'Daniel Soames' would never be mentioned, thus enabling Dan to keep a clean record as far as the law was concerned. He would never receive his £10,000 payment for the job though, his employer's bank accounts being deeply frozen. That wouldn't bother him too much.

What would, were the extent of his injuries. The fact that his legs would wither from lack of use while his arm muscles would build from six months of pushing a wheelchair. The compound fractures in his thigh, dislocated and shattered knee cap, obliterated left ankle and fractured pelvis would itch and throb for long months to come. The pins holding him together would create pain undreamed of, the wounds would become infected and require treatment while the steel-work was removed then reinserted. And his spleen would require removing.

The thing that would grate like broken glass between his teeth though, would not rear its head for a few days yet. Radiating from a newspaper article, was the fact that, yet again, he had made a mistake. That his intended victim was somewhere, living, breathing, while his wife, the owner of the dangling, twisted legs, lay in her coffin quietly rotting.

It would be nearly two years before their paths crossed once more.

The Trial

Thank God, it was mercifully swift.

I travelled back from my new home and spent a few days dossing at Al's. My involvement in the whole thing was thankfully and quite amazingly, given my *actual* input, very minimal. No details of my own drugs seizure, of any detective work involving client's money, or my meeting with Trevor Talbot ever raised their head. Well, not attributed to me directly anyway.

The defence was, all things considered, no defence; the weight of evidence was too great to deny and too detailed to argue against. With just under a million quid's worth of cocaine in Stevens' garage, they were clutching at straws for a lenient, reduced sentence right from the start. One particular straw that they clutched at desperately, was Stevens' previous good character.

It was like witnessing a pack of hounds falling on the body of a bleeding fox. The prosecution tore into the defence and any tenuous shred of hope disappeared. They literally ripped him to pieces, stating that the only reason Stevens *had* any previous good character was because he'd never actually been *caught* before. All the time, Stevens stood or sat, as directed, ram-rod straight in the dock, his Armani suit looking more dishevelled as the days dragged on in a remorseless assassination of his character.

He never showed any signs of emotion, nor did he look smug or confident. He knew he was going to spend time at Her Majesty's Pleasure - he was simply praying for as short a period as possible. So he stared ahead, unblinking, as his business life was taken apart, broken down into all of its most basic, illegal, immoral components and spread out for all to see.

I gave evidence twice and was cross examined by the defence for ten minutes, during which time I had to stifle the almost desperate need to shout that he was a disgusting, dishonest, horrible bastard that deserved to be sliced with razors and rolled in salt.

As he was sentenced, he looked at me and, with a coldness that I will never forget, smiled and nodded as if in recognition of my good work.

He got fourteen years, the judge recommending that he serve at least twelve.

For me, at the time, it wasn't enough. Even without the knowledge that came to me later, it wasn't enough.

Had I known then, what I eventually found to be the truth, I would have gladly, right there in the courtroom, taken Al's Winchester and blown Stevens' head clean off.

Richard Neath

PART TWO

Richard Neath

New beginnings

The sea lay like a dark grey blanket. It reflected the leaden sky perfectly and, on the windless morning of May 7th, it mirrored my mood.

May 7th.

A special day for me. Twelve years previously I'd waited nervously in the hushed atmosphere of a church. Decked out in top hat and tails, fresh from the pre-marriage classes I had attended with Rachel, I stood and thought of the collages we had giggled over. Bits of tin foil, paper tissues and bottle tops that had meant to represent our new lives together. I couldn't remember ever tackling the weighty issue of finding my lover's car upside down on a road, surrounded by policemen whilst dripping blood and looking like it had been dropped from a aeroplane.

May 7th.

A splendid, warm day of clear skies and springing optimism, merry, over-indulgence, dancing and laughter. It was, I thought, as I looked out over the pulsing grey expanse of sea, a similar day to this. Warm, still and calm. The greyness of the sky was a subtle, yet somehow appropriate, deviance from my wedding day. In her will, Rachel had insisted on being buried. Some vague and stubbornly clung to, religious relic of her childhood forbade cremation. For the want of what I thought of as common sense, she now lay beneath the earth, about four hundred miles away (as the seagull flew), or over five hundred if I went by road.

I wanted something closer, Christ, *needed* something closer. A place, a symbol, something that I could look at, sit by, talk to, anything that would help me keep her memory fresh and help me not forget.

My home now, is a double fronted cottage looking out across the Sound of Raasay on the Isle of Skye. In front of the green picket fence, a tarmac track gives access to the other six houses that accompany mine. Across the track, sloping away gradually, a mess of heather and gorse runs for a hundred yards before rising up to a rounded hillock of soft grass. An unwary step from this grassy mound would have the careless spinning eighty feet into the sea.

Atop this mound, set in little pads of concrete mixed by my own hands, sits a wooden bench. Set into its oak back-rest is a brass plaque. It reads:

'My dear Rachel. This view you loved so well. Now rest and look forever.'

Her clothes, well, a small portion of them, her favourites, saved from the clutches of a Wolverhampton charity shop, followed me to this distant rocky outcrop. Their ashes, gone now, some eighteen months, billowed out in the wind from the very spot on which I sat. They swirled in the rain filled air and I watched them spiral away, a grey-black vortex of dust. With them, I couldn't help thinking, went the last trace of Rachel, carried out into the wide ocean as a symbolic gesture of finality.

But I still carried the memories of her in my heart.

"Andy ... eh Andy, can ye no hear yer phone?"

Gesticulating wildly from the track, a figure clad in bright yellow oilskin trousers, grey jumper and woolly hat caught my eye.

"Thanks Iain, the answer machine will get it."

I turned and trudged back.

Iain, my neighbour, fifty five years old (or so he admits to) with the outlook and physical fitness of a sixth former and the drinking ability to match. Wind-swept and wind-tanned, his thick head of grey hair contrasted with a neatly trimmed dark beard.

At age forty, he left Inverness where he worked as an industrial chemist, giving up a £30,000 salary, four bed detached house and opulent standard of living, to live on Skye. Three years as a Council 'odd job man' and a further twelve months unemployed had passed before he got a job tending his 'flock' of up to half a million salmon, caged and secure in the bay off Portree. He spent his leisure time walking, with me generally, fishing, again with me generally and, when the wind shut us from the outside world, we would sit and drink whisky, talking and watching the rising dance of yellow flames from a peat fire.

"Hi Iain, no work today?"

"Aye, been oot all mornin'. Yeh OK?"

His dark brown eyes saw my sadness.

"Anniversary. Twelve years it would've been."

His gaze swept out across the sound before resting on Raasay and its flat topped crest.

"Aye, 'sa sad day tae remember happy times."

We both stood and looked across the narrows to Raasay, mist-hung and alone. Its greenery not yet shining to its true potential, it looked ... well frankly, it looked a bit depressing.

"Fancy a brew?"

"Is it no a wee bit early yet?"

I shook my head, "Ah meant tea or coffee yer drunken 'basturt'. But Ah s'pose given the day we could always ha' a wee dram for Rachel."

"Aye, get the kettle on," Iain replied, adding as we walked to the front door, "yer accent's still shite."

My home was 'our' dream. Having visited Skye on numerous occasions in all seasons, we harboured a deep desire to live there. The bitter irony of the situation was that it had taken Rachel's death for it to come true. In the end, after months of deliberation I put the house on the market, sold it in just over five weeks, took out a six month lease on a Ford box van, loaded it with personal effects and drove north.

Our house was sold completely furnished. I didn't need any of it. Moreover, I didn't *want* any of it. It all held too many memories. It seemed that the slightest thing could, in the few months that I rattled around in it, set me off into floods of tears. The settee on which we had cuddled, dining table at which we'd sat and eaten with friends. Whenever I sat in the kitchen, a hidden door seemed to open in my heart, out of which Rachel would step. In all her red haired splendour, she would sit opposite me, lean over and take my hand.

I got to the point where I would avoid the room totally. The cooker wasn't used for weeks and my waistline grew in relation to the take-aways I consumed.

The bedroom was the worst. The first night I slept alone in that room, my dreams were of utter despair. So vivid and colourful were the images of her that I moved into the spare room for the rest of my time there. I really struggled for a while. It was as if she was haunting me, blaming me for not being in the car. For taking her's instead. For not following her directly. For getting her involved in the whole Stevens affair. For having to go to Worcester in the first place.

I rose in the early dawn light, following my first night there alone. Full of sleep that throbbed heavily in my head like a three bottle of red wine hangover, I wobbled on unsteady legs downstairs and slumped into the cushions of the settee. I must have looked a mess. Unshaven for several days, dreary, tired eyes, puffed and red ringed from tearful outbursts. Hair dishevelled from interrupted slumber. I smelled too, stale and musky. The smell of tension and stress.

I risked a trip to the kitchen, careful not to disturb the ghost of our life together, made a cup of strong, instant coffee and climbed with leaden legs back to the first floor.

The bathroom was cold, unappealing and frankly so full of Rachel that I almost wept again; think I would have, had my tears not already been spilled.

The water was cold. The heating didn't come on until 5.30. Rachel went to work at 8.00 so didn't need hot water for her shower until 7.00.

You see, everything, *everything*, reminded me of my life before the end.

I clicked the heating onto manual, slumped back downstairs and watched cable T.V. for an hour without actually watching. I just let it wash over me and swirl about for a while; disjointed words and snippets of stories bouncing around the room and around my head.

In the shower, later, I cried again. Not for any particular reason. Nothing set me off specifically. I'd simply lost my wife. I blubbed, let the water mingle with my snotty tears and wash them away. Out of sight and down the drain. With my hands spread against the tiles, I let the water steam and boil, raise red welts on my back and shoulders, but never thought of adding any cold. It was like a penance, a pay-back to the Great God of Self Pity. I knew I was wallowing in it, knew I had to 'pull myself together' and get on with my life but didn't want to. A song kept playing in my head, over and over, jangling and echoing within my skull, '... it's my party and I'll cry if I want too, cry if I want to, cryyyyy if I want to, you would cry too if it happened to you, do-do-do-dooo-do-dooo ...', "Shut the fuck UUUPPP."

My own anger, shouted out in the now steamy, echoey bathroom, startled me.

I was alone.

And yet I wasn't.

I *was* being haunted.

My dear wife, two weeks gone, had come back to give me a message of love.

There, on the mirror, running and dripping with steam was her message, a tender note from beyond the grave.

A circle, three inches across. Two dots, an inch apart in the top third of the circle. Another dot, in the middle. A line at the bottom, gently curving upwards at both ends.

A smiley face.

Underneath, a single line of capital letters that stopped my heart.

'I LOVE YOU', then X. Just one kiss for good luck. A token of her affection.

My mouth hung open, the metallic taste of hot water strong and unpleasant. I reached for the towel, drying my face, covering my eyes, hiding from the open stare of the face in the mirror. I honestly thought I was going mad, that, when I lowered the towel and crept out from under its protective cloak, I would simply see a steamed up mirror, no message, no ghost, no haunting.

And then it came to me, the morning of the crash, our last morning together, our routine, our life, our little jokes, her silly romantic ways, *my* silly romantic ways. The message she had written on the mirror after her shower. The message I couldn't bring myself to rub off as I heard her shout her goodbye and shut the door on her way to Worcester. The message, scribed in steam with the tip of her finger that had outlasted her. The message that had lain dormant, waiting for warm moist air to bring it back from the dead so that it could proclaim its undying love.

I was cold by the time I stepped out of the shower. I was dry although the towel had never made a single pass over my body. The message was still there, but only now, because I *knew* it was there. The steam had faded and only if I tilted my head and let the light catch the glass just right, could I make out the faintest of images.

Every morning, for the next three weeks, her message was there, fainter and fainter, until, even my imagination couldn't be fooled and I admitted it.

She'd gone.

She didn't blame me. I knew that. Deep down, I knew it was another symptom of my self pity, another selfish reason to enable me to feel sorry for myself. Al had put me right. I used to appear at his house with annoying regularity, needing a place to hide, needing his company, his words, his reality.

"She wouldn't blame you Andy. You know that. It was a shitty, bad piece of luck, that's all. She wouldn't blame you, she hadn't got it in her." Draining his fourth or fifth whisky, he continued "*You* blame yourself. Don't get me wrong, it's natural, I'd be the same, but mate, let it go. Move on. Move house for God's sake, move to Skye, I know that's what you want. Just do it, stop fucking around. She doesn't blame you, it's just you."

So I did. Simple as that. His words struck me like an uppercut to the chin. Jolted me into action and, for the first time since the accident, I started to feel alive again.

I bought my new house in the November, lived in its furniture-free shell until the new year, then, during one mad weekend in January, ordered enough stuff to fill it from various mail order companies, sat back and watched it materialise. It didn't look half bad, although I say it myself. Simple, modern in an old fashioned way and nothing like my old home with Rachel. A clean sweep. Out with the old, in with the new.

Old clichés for a new life.

In the March I bought two old cottages in the north of the island and spent six weeks making them habitable, intending to rent them out to holiday makers in the summer.

The first time May came around, my world very nearly fell apart for good and, had it not been for Iain, would have. I'd found a friend in him. We simply clicked, slipped into a strange synchronisation, enjoyed each other's company and liked the same things.

I'd been up at the cottages showing Elizabeth around, she being tasked with keeping them clean and changing the bed clothes between guests. The weather was beautiful, clear and crisp, but with a stiff northerly wind that bit deeply. My parting words to Elizabeth were to "have a good weekend" and she had replied that she was going to Inverness with Alisdair, her husband, for their tenth anniversary. A weekend away from 'the bairns'.

Her words had struck a chord in my very soul and I asked her what the date was.

"May 7ᵗʰ Andy, why dae yeh ask?"

"No reason Liz. See you next week."

She'd lingered, staring at me with a barely concealed concern. "Are yeh alright Andy? Ye look a wee bit pale, like ye've sin a ghost."

I stared out of the window, watching clouds building on the horizon and, without looking at her replied, "No really, I'm OK, off you go Liz, have a good one."

She left and, as the front door clicked shut, leaving me as alone as I'd ever been, added, "Not seen one Liz, just remembered one."

The next few hours are a haze.

I drove down the coast in a rising gale, pulling into the car park at Kilt Rock as the first rain drops speckled the windscreen.

Early May, in the rain and howling gale, it was empty.

I think I sat in the car for a while, absent-mindedly flicking the wipers to clear the screen, then watching as the view faded beneath the deluge. I don't remember leaving the car, walking towards the cliff, bent over in the storm, instantly drenched to the skin. I certainly don't remember climbing the rail and sitting, legs dangling over the terrifying drop.

I *do* remember staring at the shattered rocks below. Remember how the waves, spurred on by the insistent wind, crashed ceaselessly onto the shore, far below. Remember wondering how it would feel to lean over until gravity took over and I plunged downwards. Also wondering what that spiralling descent would be like. Whether I would be conscious of any impact at the bottom. Whether they would ever find me.

I also remember being grabbed roughly from behind, for a fleeting second saw myself spinning downwards to the surf below, then falling, not forwards, but backwards, my legs flying upwards seemingly independent of my body, limp and disconnected. Remember landing on wet gravel next to a dripping wet Iain. Being lifted then dragged, half running half crawling across the car park towards the open door of a car.

He never said a word as we sat, our soaking clothes and pluming breath steaming the windows.

"I forgot Iain, Jesus. In ten years of marriage, I *never* forgot our anniversary. One year into her death and I have. Does her life mean so little that her death wipes out her memory so quickly?"

"Death does strange things tae a mind Andy. S'no right or wrong, just strange. Din'nae blame yoursen."

They were Al's words, his thoughts from the previous year, still wise and true, spoken in a broad Scots accent.

"People keep telling me not to blame myself, to move on, start afresh."

"They tell ye 'cause it's the right thing tae do. She would'nae wanted this Andy. One day, hopefully soon, ye'll understand. Ye'll believe it. For now just hear it."

That was my first anniversary without her - last year, a lifetime ago.

People were right though, generally. I'd moved on I suppose, stopped blaming myself, come to terms with the whole incident to the point where I could discuss her, calmly and with dignity. Only rarely did I feel my throat constrict and my eyes begin to mist as I spoke of her.

Only rarely.

In the cottage, I glanced at the answer-phone; two messages, I'd listen to them later. I moved across the kitchen, filled the kettle and settled it with a clang on top of the gas ring. It was a luxury I had to have, couldn't bare the thought of cooking by electricity for the rest of my life, so had a gas cylinder installed in the rear garden, surrounded it with fir trees and had it filled every couple of months. It was expensive, but hey, my wife had been well insured so I could afford it.

Iain paced the quarry tiles, stepping from foot to foot, kicking his heels together and drumming his fingers on the work surface. He looked like a small child, scared of stepping on the cracks in a pavement. His eyes constantly flicked around the room as if seeing it for the first time, the same room that we'd sat in dozens of times, working our way through dozens of bottles of whisky. His gaze would settle on an item; the jar of kitchen utensils, picture of Everest above the fridge, dried flower arrangement on the window sill. Then, as if desperate to take everything in, he'd shuffle his feet and switch his stare to something else.

He had the look of a man who had a burning desire to be constantly doing something, terrified of wasting a minute. A man who yearned to fill every waking moment with action; never relaxing fully. He did everything at full pelt. When we fished, he would cover more water in an hour than I would in the whole day, when we sat and chatted, sipping amber liquid from chunky tumblers, he would drum his fingers between gaps in the conversation, lift his head and scour the room with his eyes, always searching, searching.

And yet, for a man filled to bursting with nervous energy, he was pleasant, relaxing company. I knew I could sit and allow him to take control of the time we spent together; I never really had to think of conversation topics when I was with him.

"Have ye no listened tae yer messages yet Andy?"

"No Iain, I haven't, I can get them later. Don't worry, they're not going anywhere."

"Aye, aye. S'pose yer right."

I turned back to the kettle as it started to whistle, grey plumes of steam reaching into the air. Shaking my head at his impatience, I asked, "Tea or coffee?"

"Tea please, ye know how Ah tek it."

"For God's sake, sit yourself down, you're wearing out the tiles."

"Aye, aye, Ah'll dae just that."

A scrape of a chair and muffled thump of backside on wood. Silence for three seconds, then, like a distant marching band, the rattle of fingernails on table top.

We sat, quiet for a while sipping our drinks and for the first time since I'd known him, felt the conversation was gong to be down to me.

"You're quiet mate, everything alright?"

"Aye, well ye know ..." he looked embarrassed, as if his thoughts were stuck somewhere deep in his head.

"Last year … at Kilt Rock … Ah s'pose Ah wiz just a wee bit worried about ye *this* year, yer ken?"

"I'm OK, really, you should know that well enough. Yeah, not a day goes by without me thinking of her, but, well, you needn't worry about me taking a jump. That part of my life has passed. Honest."

He didn't look entirely convinced. Raised eyebrows said what a million words couldn't.

"What, with the sea trout and salmon only a month or two away? Miss all that? Come on."

"Aye, mebee yer right. Din'nae blame me for worryin' though, I wiz there remember, last year. If a man wiz ever goin' tae jump, ye were him."

Drinks finished and with a promise to meet later that night for a 'wee dram', Iain left. Happy that I wasn't suicidal, I watched him march down the track to his house, back-lit by the reflected greyness of the oily looking sea.

I checked the messages.

One from Al, phoning to see how I was and asking me to call him back.

One from Mrs Nicolson, gushing about how successful my exhibition was going; six paintings sold and over a dozen photographs.

I'd found my forté in the last year you see. A simmering flame of talent that had never entirely gone out since my childhood; bloomed briefly during the first years of marriage and then gradually suffocated under the pressures of work.

With time on my hands I'd fanned the embers into a roaring fire, allowed a passion for the outdoors to consume me and manifest itself in images of mountains, rivers, lochs and coast. The tourists loved them. The back end of the season had been a rush of activity; I couldn't fulfil the demand. This year I was ready. This year I had a veritable stock-pile of watercolours, prints of some of my most popular images from last year, framed photographs, mainly of sunsets and rises and a few oils that the punters seemed to like. I was amazed how well it was going. I thought my work was OK, fairly competent in a gifted amateur's sort of way, but nothing special. Filling a gap in the needs of tourists, it didn't hurt that it provided another income stream into my bank account either. Not that I really needed it.

With the house in Wolverhampton sold (very quickly, thankfully), I had, at one point, a balance in my current account of £944,000, earning a paltry half a per cent interest. Soon it was spread amongst various fixed interest deposit accounts, bonds, unit trusts and a whole host of income producing stuff; none of it with my bank.

Al benefited though. He did three months target in one appointment with me before I left to head north. I also deposited £50,000 into his bank account without telling him. My feelings at that time were an incredible jumble of contradictions. I was able to give money to a mate like a lottery winner, head north in a van to search for a 'dream house', forget ever being an employee again and jettison any money worries in one fell swoop.

Shortly after I settled on Skye, I took a trip south to Blackpool in a hired Ford, test drove a brand new TVR Cerbera and paid for it, cash. Then, keeping the revs below two and a half thousand, drove it north with a young mechanic from the factory in tow in my Ford. I paid him £200 for delivering it back to the hire place in Glasgow and drove home, arriving a day after I'd left.

I'd spent £100,000 on my main home overlooking Raasay, a further £25,000 kiting it out in one extravagant weekend, £30,000 each for the cottages in the north of the island and another £12,000 renovating them. In less than three months I'd spent more money than I could have earned in four years or more. I'd lived a dream, created a dream existence and still had change out of £600,000, churning out income and growth to add to the pension income, rental income and now the cash flow from paintings sales.

The result of sound financial planning, intelligent use of life assurance and, as I reminded myself, usually as I approached the bottom of a bottle of Talisker single malt, Rachel would have been in the same position had the tables been turned.

She wasn't though and this single thought was the one that nearly drove me to take the dive off Kilt Rock.

She'd paid the price for my comfortable easy-going lifestyle, the ultimate price as she lay in her cold grave in Wolverhampton. I would spend money; order things for the house and then my mind would thrash around in turmoil and guilt.

During the drive back up the M6 surrounded by leather opulence, serenaded by 4.5 litres of V8 and spurred along by 420 bhp of ridiculous, unnecessary power, tears flooded my eyes. I sat in stationary traffic just south of Glasgow and stared intently at the passenger seat, un-creased and useless, trying to imagine Rachel sitting there, smiling, telling me to slow down. Telling me she loved me.

The paintings saved me. Gave me a new purpose.

I could load my equipment, usually tucked into a rucksack, into the boot and listen to the low burble of the motor in the quiet of the dawn stillness. I could lose myself in the twisting roads, empty and inviting, turn right at the Sligachan Hotel and spend the day wandering in the Cuillin, or along the west coast. I could paint or take photos, using the whole of the day for my purposes, then, steal a pint in the hotel on my way back.

Like Iain, I too wanted to use all of my time, all of my days, all of the hours that continued to peel away, layer after layer, exposing new ones to be filled with life.

Since Rachel's death I was living for both of us.

Experiencing new things, drinking in life, supping on time as though I too, was condemned.

Life is short; our time finite, indistinct, uncertain. I had learned this whilst loosing the one love of my life. I had wasted time, squandered experience, missed out so many layers of living that now, on my own, I was giving back to life all the minutes, seconds, hours that Rachel would never see or use.

I lost myself and yet also found myself in the images I produced.

Every piece of work I finished, works that travelled to all corners of the country, probably the world, carried a little of Rachel with them. She was my driving force, my purpose.

A day never went by, whilst on the island, when I didn't spend half an hour sitting on her bench, my memorial to her. I would talk to her, tell her of my day, my experiences, the views I had gazed at, fish I had caught, conversations I'd had. Everything.

I probably talked to her more in her death than I did in her life.

"Mrs N ... yes I know ... great thanks, how are you?" I looked across my small square of lawn at the back of my house whilst Mrs N babbled enthusiastically about my paintings. She took 20% of the sale price, so was understandably keen to sell as many as she could.

"Really? Great, and what about the prices? No ... I mean have you had to knock any off to sell them?" She nearly took my ear off with the vehemence of her reply, putting me right in no uncertain terms.

"Well that's great, yes I'll get some more over to you tomorrow ... OK ... yeah ... yeah ... right." I counted off on my fingers, "Shots of the Cuillin, sea-scapes and sunsets are in at the moment." I listened again, loving the steady lilting sound of her voice.

"Yes, I know, the season hasn't really started yet ... yes ... OK ... I'll get painting ... yes ... OK ... see you tomorrow, bye." I glanced at the clock over the mantelpiece - four and a half minutes; a record. It was rare to get off the phone in less than ten when talking to Mrs N.

"Al, matey, how ya doing? ... No. Great ... really. How's work?"

I let him talk. It was good to hear his voice. We spoke three or four times a week but I missed his company. He'd been up for a couple of visits, once over Christmas just gone and once the previous August, that time for three weeks. Two taken as legitimate holiday then another as sick leave. The fishing had been so good I didn't think he was going to leave at all and even asked him whether he fancied moving here permanently to start a business. He declined but I'm sure it was only after a hefty internal battle.

Only when I spoke to him did I feel a pang of homesickness. It was always short lived and not really for Wolverhampton specifically, more for the Teme Valley and the Severn. Places where I used to fish, wandering with my rucksack and rod between bouts of work.

"OK mate, I'll speak to you later in the week ... and thanks for calling today ... no worries, cheers, see ya."

To the side of the house stood a remnant of years gone by; the original crofters cottage, crumbling and sad looking. In a state of semi-repair, part roofed and with glass in three of its six windows, I had been working half-heartedly on it since first moving to Skye. I had no grand ideas for making it truly habitable, simply wanted it as a work room cum hideaway. Single storied, it was dry at the far end where I'd finished the roof and housed my fishing gear. Neatly stacked or hung on hooks, it was ready in an instant if the desire to cast a fly came upon me.

Five minutes after entering the mustiness of my 'tackle store' I was strolling out into a still, calm, early afternoon, hung with drab green canvas bag, chest waders and ready-made-up, ten foot fly rod. Thirty minutes later, I was climbing the fence at the Storr Lochs, making my way down to the water as my TVR ticked and tocked at the side of the road, cooling after its blast. Ripples spread from the rises of half a dozen trout. The surface was a flat mirror, reflecting the magnificent surroundings.

It was *nearly* perfect.

The paintings had enabled me to claw my way back into the land of the living. With each finished work, improving in both competence and style, my mood lifted and purpose strengthened. When Mrs N heard of my pictures and viewed a selection at my house, brimming over with enthusiasm and instantly talking of showing them in her shop, I began to feel a degree of pride creep back into my life. When they started to sell, towards the end of the tourist season and a couple of months after my thwarted attempt to leap into the void at Kilt Rock, I began to settle back into the everyday world.

And what a world it was.

When my blinkers of self-pity and desperate desolation lifted like the drawing back of a black veil, the atmosphere of clear Highland skies and fellowship flooded in. Suddenly, Iain was just another (albeit special) soul ready to welcome me into island life. The hands of friendship were extended towards me from all directions until I felt ready to collapse under their combined weight of compassion.

I knew though, you see, that it would be like this. It was the single most important element that had dragged Rachel and I back year after year. Then, being able to live with no fear of being mugged, abused or robbed for a couple of weeks per year was enough. It strengthened our sense of humanity. To live for fourteen solitary days without litter-strewn streets, graffiti daubed walls and aggressive, foul mouthed louts. Magic, pure magic.

Now, I intended to let this life of value and decency fully consume me. It took a while to sink into my bones but gradually, over months of terrible, sickly mourning, it crept to the surface until I felt at home and settled like never before.

So, with the paintings taking off, the cottages booked almost constantly for the whole summer and Al's visit in August, I was feeling as good as I had for years. Rachel was still a big part of my life, always would be, but I had come to terms with her passing.

Twelve months into my new life, around October time, I spent a day in the Cuillin, scrambling amongst the plethora of gullies and crags, stomach churning paths and scree slopes, vertigo inducing ridges and crests. I stood on top Sgurr Alisdair for the first time, looking out across thousands of acres of pristine void. My eyes swept the steel blue waters of Loch Coruisk past Sgurr-na-Stri and onto the blue-black starkness of Blaven, the peak on which I had snapped my most treasured image of Rachel.

As I picked out the conical trig point on its summit, where she had sat, braving the chill wind, no ache of remorse or regret surfaced; just the twang of happy memories.

From Alisdair's summit, I had scrambled, working on 100% adrenaline and fear, over shattered rock to its eastern flank then, in a crazy show of unfounded confidence and bravery, crawled and slipped my way around to the start of Collie's Ledge. This 'path' clings, defying both gravity and common sense, to the face of Sgurr-mich-Choinich, one thousand vertical feet, above Corrie Lagan. A slip would result in a plummeting, stomach-lurching, bone-crunching, life-ending fall to the boulders and scree below.

I couldn't do it.

Instead, I scrambled the face of Choinich, eighty feet up and then half walked, half crawled to somewhere near the middle of its ridge and sat on the flattest rock I could find. While I sat, legs hanging into terrifying nothingness, my thoughts returned to Kilt Rock and the terrible waste that had almost consumed me.

I'm sure, looking back, that this was the point that my whole life truly turned a corner. I sat, dangling my boots into space, drank a cup of coffee from my flask, smoked a cigarette, ate an apple and watched the blue swell of the North Atlantic pulsing against the islands of Rùm and Eigg. In the far distance, just visible through a haze that hung like muslin, the Outer Hebrides merged with the ocean; dark smudges on the far horizon.

Two hours later I was back at the camp site, sitting on the bonnet of my car finishing my coffee and watching the tide flood the mussel bed at the mouth of the River Brittle.

A strange feeling of pure exhilaration almost overcame me. Life was good. No guilt flared with the thought, no pangs of sadness or remorse to spoil the moment. I was tired from my climbing, sweaty, in need of a shower and really fancied a pint.

The Sligachan Hotel, or to be more accurate, Seumas' Bar, is a wonderful mix of traditions, hospitality, steaming feet and piles of muddy rucksacks. It also serves a great pint of Guinness - just the thing after a hard day in the mountains.

Behind the bar, hung in regimental neatness, single malts tempted the connoisseur into amber liquid induced oblivion. What caught my eye though on this particular day, was not the whisky but a red-headed bar maid. Small and neat in black trousers and Seumas' Bar tee shirt, her smile stirred an army of butterflies into undulating flight in my stomach.

I'm sure I stuttered over my order and probably sounded like a blushing schoolboy faced with an awkward question from a sexy supply teacher. She smiled, took my money, turned to the till, then handed back my change.

I retreated, a defeated general, to a table near the windows and sipped my pint, cautiously watching her through plumes of cigarette smoke. The swing of her shoulder length hair, sparkle of her green eyes and slightly upswept slope of her nose enthralled me. I was captivated, smitten for God's sake.

That evening, showered and dressed in jogging bottoms, boots and a warm jumper, I sat on Rachel's bench telling her of my day. She would, I knew, have been terrified at my route on the Cuillin. Our climbing was nothing more than mildly adventurous scrambling, Rachel not being one for gut clenching drops and I felt proud to be telling her of my exploits. There were areas of the ridge that I hadn't, as yet, plucked up the courage to attempt, but I was ticking them off a list held in my head, gradually and with no real pattern.

I had, not just the span of a holiday, but the rest of my life. I was in no rush.

Arriving back at the cottage, a bottle of Laphroaig sat on the kitchen table between two heavy crystal tumblers. Each glass held three fingers of golden liquid, its scent light and fragrant in the air. The bottle top lay squashed flat on the table and, lying at an angle in my large stone ash tray, two Habana Boliva No. 2 cigars awaited a flame. The toilet flushed behind me and Iain strolled in. The squashed bottle top had informed me of his intentions (quite scary the first time a Scot takes the top off a bottle and squashes it flat), we weren't stopping until it was empty. And we didn't.

Many evenings had passed since, starting with this ritual of bottle top crushing. Autumn had past into full winter, gales had rushed in from the west bringing driving rain, sleet and then finally, a few days before Al's visit at Christmas, snow that lay deep and brilliant white.

I picked him up at Inverness, fresh from his flight from Birmingham and had crawled along in a mixture of slush and hard packed snow which crunched under the TVR's huge tyres. Now, with the budding of new growth springing all around, May rushing on towards June, the thought of snow and ice a distant memory, life had quite literally come full circle.

I'd kept a couple of brown trout, just under a pound each, perfect in their red spotted finery and, with the light fading, strolled into my kitchen and switched on the main light.

The room was large, decorated in cream, beige and a smattering of terracotta. Original beams spanned the ceiling and over the fireplace set into the gable wall, a railway sleeper size mantle sat, hung with dried flowers. I loved it. It was the kitchen I'd always wanted, the dream kitchen Rachel and I'd planned together. In the far corner, an easel stood on its sturdy legs, the picture held on its board, tilted at an angle of 45°, was my latest and, I felt, my best yet.

I stood and looked deeply at its greens and blues, letting my eyes wander at will, lighting on the rocks in the foreground then sweeping across the white crested expanse of sea to the soaring pinnacles of mountains in the far distance. A view from Elgol, the boulder strewn shoreline being the foreground, across Loch Scavaig and onto the southern end of the Cuillin ridge. Copied from a photograph in the warmth of my cottage, it was, I supposed, a bit of a cheat, but lacked nothing because of it.

The unlatching of my front door and arrival of Iain for our pre-arranged drink drew me from my thoughts. He stood next to me, following my gaze to the painting. "Aye Andy, that's a fine, fine picture. Really captures the feeling o' it. Them Cuillin are an impressive collection o' peaks are they no?"

"Aye Iain, I'm pleased with it, I really am. Think I'll keep that one for me. Above the fireplace in the lounge, what do you reckon?"

He shoved his hands deep into his pockets and nodded dramatically.

"Grand, fine picture. Would'nae mind that meself ye ken? Could'nae do another could ye?" He added, quickly, "Ah'll pay ye, yer know that."

I slapped him on his shoulder and laughed, "Yes mate, I'll do you one, but you're not going to pay me," I raised my hand to still his complaint, "you pay your way in whisky ten fold each year, I wouldn't dream of it."

With that he raised a bottle of Talisker and wagged it in front of my face.

"Here's a doon payment fer starters, ye get the glasses, Ah need tae tek a leak."

While I lifted a couple of glasses from the cupboard I shouted "Anyway, I'm selling enough at the moment, nice to give one away now and again."

His reply was muffled from the toilet along the hall, but I heard the words "Mrs Nicolson" and "bulk order." I waited until the toilet had flushed and heard his footsteps on the quarry tiles.

"What was that mate?"

"Aye, Mrs N collared me in Portree earlier, says she's had some bloke in this afternoon, strange bloke from what she wiz sayin', from your neck o' the woods. Bought all yer pictures she says. The whole lot. True as Ah'm standin' here, put doon a deposit of £500, bringin' the balance in tomorrow." My face must have been a picture.

"Honest Andy, Ah'm no windin' ye up."

I struggled with the maths in my head.

"What's he bought then, all the originals or what? That's got to be £10,000 or more. Got to be."

"Andy, yer no listenin' tae me - he's bought the lot, prints, originals, everythin'. Must be a dealer or somethin'. Mrs N told me no tae say anythin', wanted tae tell ye in person tomorrow when ye took your latest stuff tae the shop."

I was stunned, last year I'd made about £3,000 from my paintings and photos all season. If this was right (and I'd no reason to doubt Iain's word), I'd just sold over £30,000 worth of stock in one go.

"I'll phone her." I made to go to the phone but he grabbed my arm with his left hand, waved the bottle in his right and persuaded me to wait until tomorrow.

"Let's drink tae yer success, then, when it's all confirmed tomorrow, we'll dae it all again. What dae ye say?"

I shrugged, it could wait, "I'll drink to that."

Mr Salt's incredible purchase

I was strangely aware of an insistent ringing somewhere off to my left. It could have been in my head, such was the drumming and pounding that seemed to be trying to split my skull in two. My eyes were apparently glued shut, only opening with an effort that caused a pain to shoot through my whole body and a dull light to flood in and set my retinas on fire.

Confused and disorientated, I fell heavily to the floor, sprawling onto deep piled whiteness. During the night, my bed had shrunk and relocated itself into the lounge.

"OK, OK, Jesus, I'm coming."

The ringing was the phone, the time was 8.30 a.m. I had slept on the couch, the effects of which, when added to the bottle (or was it two?) of Talisker Iain and I had got through, meant that my body felt as though I'd fallen from the summit of Blaven.

"Hello, shit ..." I dropped the phone and suffered a flare of pain and surge of dizziness as I stooped to pick it up. Settling for kneeling on the floor rather than risk standing up again, I apologised to my caller.

"Sorry about that. Hello? ... Al, hya mate, how ya doin'?" His voice seemed loud and I winced at his words.

"Al, yeah, do us a favour, keep it down a bit ... yes Iain ... yes one or two ... well you know, talking and stuff. How're things?"

I let him talk while I staggered to the kitchen sink and gulped a pint of water straight from the tap that had the desired effect of ungluing my terminally furry tongue from the roof of my mouth. It also caused a white hot spear to shoot straight through the front of my skull, dissecting the bridge of my nose and killing a billion or so brain cells.

I must have squealed or at least gasped at the influx of freezing cold water as Al asked if I was OK. I explained, blearily, he laughed, loudly, I took the phone away from my ear. He chatted on for a while and I told him in a decidedly slurry, disinterested manner about my apparent sales success, adding that I hadn't *actually* spoken to Mrs N, only Iain, so it wasn't confirmed yet.

"Anyway mate, speak to you later when I've come round a bit ... yeh, cheers Al, see you soon."

The gas burner kicked in and I stood back from the jet of water, waiting. Ten seconds later and steam was rising from the shower tray. Allowing the spray to wake me, I stood, gurgling and sighing for perhaps five minutes before washing and dressing.

I needed food and lots of it, so set about preparing a full breakfast. Toast, bacon, sausage, eggs and beans, washed down with a litre of coffee and started off with a bowl of porridge. Something to soak up any vestiges of alcohol still lying in my stomach, clear my head and set me up for the day so I could miss lunch. I was finishing my third cup of coffee and just lighting a cigarette when the door bell rang.

I shouted across, "Come in, it's open," and was answered by a minor whirlwind that manifested itself into Mrs N.

"Mrs N, how are you?"

"Andy, Andy, oh mah dear, ye would'nae believe what's happened."

Mrs N is mid forties, with the air or someone approaching sixty. Short, plump and grey with the appearance of a favourite Aunt or maybe a youngish grandmother. Never still, bustling, bossy and forthright, I've always thought she and Iain ought to get together. In my still delicate state she pounded my head with the tale of the mysterious Mr Salt who was about to empty her shop of my paintings and photos. Iain had not been exaggerating; every single piece of work had been sold. Every painting, every print, every photo; the lot. She'd spent an hour totting up the bill - £32,655.

"Tell you what" I said, still somewhat disbelieving, "let him have it all for £32,000 - what the hell, let's live a little."

Her look was one of incredulity.

"Ah've never budged on price an never will. As long as the stock's goin' from mah shop, he'll pay the goin' rate," adding, with a disgruntled huff, "discounts? Huh, never."

I could see why I'd agreed to let her sell my stuff in the first place.

"What is he then, a dealer?"

"No, well he says he's no." She paused, re-running the conversation in her head then repeating it with great deliberation.

"He's bought a new house that's totally empty an wants tae fill it wi' memories of Skye."

"Jesus, must be a big house and an even bigger bank balance," I added.

"Ah'll ask ye no tae take the Lord's name in vain while in mah presence. Ye should know that b'now." She peered at me over her tortoise shell glasses, glaring at me with her sternest 'old maid' look. "Ah din'nae ask for much, but respect fer the Lord is sacrosanct."

"Sorry Mrs N, I just got a bit carried away you know?"

"Aye, Ah'll forgive ye this time."

Mrs N eyed the last couple of pieces of toast amongst the battlefield that was my breakfast table.

"Help yourself. I'm done. Want a coffee?"

"Aye, t'would be grand" she said, pulling a chair up and settling down to her toast.

I grabbed another cup. "When's Mr Rothschild picking up his art collection then?"

"Said he'd be in at lunchtime today, he's had tae hire a wee van tae collect it all."

"I'll make sure I'm there to thank him personally."

Mrs N paused in the middle of buttering her toast and looked embarrassed or at the least, a touch awkward.

"You know, that's the strangest thing. Ah suggested the exact same yesterday, ye know, that you, the artist should come in an see him, an well …" another pause for thought, then her eyes lifted to mine and she removed her glasses "… said emphatically 'no'. Said it spoiled the mystique of art if the creator was turned intae reality. He really made the point though, got all philosophical wi' me. Strange don't ye think?"

I shrugged. "As long as his money's good, I don't really care. Anyway, shouldn't you be making a move?" I glanced at the clock, "It's already 9.30, customers waiting and all that."

"Och no, Maggie's openin' up for me, bless her. She's a good girl."

Maggie was Mrs N's daughter. Mr N had been lost at sea ten years previously and her daughter had been doted on and spoiled ever since. Understandable really, but well, Maggie was the image of her Mother and Mrs N constantly tried to get us 'fixed up'. She was twenty six years old - ten years my junior, but there was a blossoming forty year old struggling to get out. I definitely didn't want to help it escape.

I watched her Land Rover chug off along the track leaving a plume of dark, oil burning diesel smoke in its wake, waved and went back to my coffee dregs.

"Didn't want to see the artist eh? Very strange … takes all sorts I suppose."

It *was* odd though. Usually punters are real keen to chat with me, get the back of the picture signed along with a little note of thanks. I had to admit to being curious.

Mrs N's shop is in Broadford, eight or nine miles from my house by boat, nearer twenty five by car. From the outside it's a wooden shell, a shed really; a large shed granted, but still a shed, temporary and just slightly dilapidated looking. Its large windows were empty that particular lunchtime, no paintings to be seen. They were stacked, or leaning against each other in a large red Bedford box van parked at the side of the road. From where I sat, in cotton shirt and sunglasses basking in the May sunshine, I could see the front door and the mysterious Mr Salt each time he came out laden with my work. Average height, very stocky and tanned, he was nothing like I'd imagined. I had an image in my head of a silver haired businessman, paunchy and slightly uncomfortable looking out of his business suit. What met my gaze over a copy of the Press & Journal was more bouncer than businessman. Undoubtedly wealthy but as far from the image of an art collector as could be possible.

I watched, enthralled as my pictures gradually disappeared into the cavernous tin box that would carry them away, leaving a shop empty and my bank account full. It must have taken an hour until he appeared at the driver's door, jumped in and drove away. It all appeared to have been carried out with the efficiency of a delivery driver collecting a parcel or a builder dropping off a pallet of bricks, sterile, unfeeling - somehow uninvolved.

Not like someone collecting thirty grand's worth of art.

"Hey Mrs N. Counting your winnings?"

She was standing at her till thumbing her way through a huge pile of notes.

"He paid in cash, the whole lot." She shook her head, amazed at such a large amount of money.

"Cash! Over £32,000. Dear Lord, ye'll hae tae go tae the bank Andy, I can'nae hae all this in mah shop."

"Mrs N please, on Skye you could leave it in your stationery drawer with the shop unlocked and the worst to happen would be someone coming in and borrowing a tenner."

I smiled at her obvious concern "And they'd bring it back the following day."

She wasn't convinced. "OK, OK, I'll take it as soon as you're done." I pointed a finger at her and wagged it, joking, "Make sure you take out your cut, OK?"

She smiled, as if it had only just occurred to her that she was over £6,000 better off, then returned to leafing through the notes, absentmindedly licking a thumb at every tenth one.

"Didn't look like an art dealer to me you know, but there again," I said, "didn't look like he had £32,000 in his back pocket either." Mrs N hadn't ceased counting or even broken her rhythm. "What do you think then, art dealer, drug dealer, what?"

Still with no break in her counting she replied "I did'nae like him. Din'nae know why Ah should say that but ... well somethin' in his manner was'nae right."

Now she did stop and, looking straight at me added "Ye know, he never looked me in the eye once. At the floor, the counter, the ceiling, anywhere in fact than at me. Strange, Ah never quite trust someone who does'nae look at me when they speak."

I made a point of returning her stare.

"Had a nasty limp though, seemed like he could'nae put any weight on his left leg. Kept hotching from foot tae foot an leanin' on the counter. Ah asked him if he wanted a seat at one point an he just ignored me. Yes," she said, resuming her counting, "strange man."

"Did he say he wanted any more?"

"Did'nae mention it, though, with what he's just taken, Ah doubt he's got any more room."

After the bank I returned home, glancing left at Glamaig as I passed the Sligachan and catching a glimpse of Marsco and Gillean in the rear view as I accelerated up the rise towards Portree. It had only been eighteen months since I'd moved to Skye, probably too soon for the view to become normal so I couldn't help glancing at the mountains whenever I passed them. Such was their draw, their mystique, their pure, undiluted majesty, that I felt I would never tire of them.

I'd dropped a car full of pictures in to the shop after Mr Salt had left and knew my attic was now empty of work. I had a busy time ahead of me and was looking forward to producing more. It would certainly mean more exploits in the mountains, more strolls along the coast, more evening sorties into sunset land with my camera. It was what I lived for, what kept me sane.

The previous August when Al had visited, I'd dragged him up Preshal More, a twelve hundred foot dome of rock overlooking Talisker Bay and the North Atlantic. The day started clear, then around mid-day a brief squally storm had swept in from the west, leaving us bedraggled and huddled beneath a rocky outcrop near the summit. We took the opportunity to eat our sandwiches and guzzle a cup or two of hot coffee while a fresh breeze blew in and swept the darkness east over the mainland.

Clear again, the peaty ground steamed and our boots squelched through puddles between the heather.

A hundred vertical feet from the summit, I stopped, holding out my arm to still Al, as below us, previously hidden by an outcrop, a golden eagle stood with its talon embedded in a rabbit. Massive and impressive, perfectly in tune with its surroundings, it seemed to be striking the remaining life out of its meal with its huge beak.

After a few seconds, it lifted its head, swivelling its eyes around the hillside, spotted us and lifted effortlessly into the air. Its broad wings beat slowly and it rose almost vertically for fifty feet, then tilted to its right and soared away, dropping along the slope towards the glen bottom. For a quarter of a mile our eyes followed it, the rabbit dangling from its talon like a scrap of brown rag, fluttering in the wind.

It was Al's first and only my third sighting and we were both awe-struck. We hardly said a word, just shook our heads and continued up the final climb. We spent an hour on the top, letting the view and raw atmosphere seep into our minds. I took a photo of Al standing astride the summit, all beaming smiles and oozing pride as if he had conquered an unclimbed Himalayan north face, before heading back.

The painting I produced in the week after Al left, never saw Mrs N's shop. I had it framed in a beautifully grained and ornately carved, deep mahogany, parcelled it up in protective bubble-wrap and sent it to Al. He reckoned it looked a treat over his fireplace.

Later in the evening, I had a pint at the Sligachan and on the way home, stopped at the bridge over the River Varragil. Silence came back at me, save for the rhythmic ticking of cooling aluminium and steel. The lights of Portree twinkled in the distance against an endless blackness and a sublime peace descended over my world. The night was warm and, shielded by a high, dense blanket of cloud, the heat that had built up over the day lingered on, trapped under its umbrella cover.

I leant on the bridge, watching the water swirl and eddy beneath me, imagining the sea trout and salmon that would soon be nosing their way upstream under the cover of darkness or high water from the bay a mile distant.

I thought of Rachel and of Mr Salt and his cargo of my paintings, travelling south in his echoing box van, full of excitement at the prospect of hanging his purchases. I thought of him heading back to the Midlands, which bought me back to Rachel. No shared cup of coffee, no battle for the toothpaste in the bathroom. No warm, cuddling discussion of the day's events and cosy drift off into sleep. Instead, solitary slumber in an empty bed.

The thought of *courting* again pushed its way into my mind and I found myself smiling, remembering the huddles under cold clear starlit skies. Sneaking into my parents' house in the early hours, long drives in old cars, underage pints with half a lager and black for the lady.

A loud splash snapped my head up just in time to see the rocking swell of broken water as a large sea trout leapt from the steady glide at the tail of the pool.

"You're early mate," I whispered into the darkness, "might be back tomorrow to see if you'll take."

Sitting back in the warm comfortable luxury of my car, a light shower broke and, in the far lights of Portree, raindrops glistened like shattered diamonds on the windscreen. Reflecting the white brilliance of the streetlights, they looked like stars sprinkled on the glass.

A visit from Emily

Dan stands in his garden; the night's blackness moulds itself around him. Millions of stars and a bright sliver of moon strive to cast their light over the stillness. He is tired; driving always annoys him and leaves him feeling drained and irritable. His leg gives him hell after a couple of hours behind the wheel and, following a really long drive, it burns with a fire from his ankle to his groin. The doctors, although pleased with their work, are surprised at the speed in which he has regained full use of it.

Dan's not surprised. Dan has a reason. A purpose that's driven him to long, sustained agony in the gym. A deep desire that's pushed him from his long walks to even longer runs. Sweating from every pore, he's driven himself on, mile after mile, breaking through the itching discomfort, the nagging throb and finally outright pain that's pulsed in his mending bones and muscles. Every pounding step, every jarring, jolting thump that's echoed up his thighs was for *the purpose*. On each run, every step he's imagined to be planting itself squarely in the middle of Andy Perkins' face. Every single throb of pain has been mentally stored, packaged away in his mind until, at some divine point of retribution, he'll call on it again. He imagines pouring out all of his reserves of pain and anguish onto the helpless twitching shell that was once Andy.

For months after the 'accident' he brooded over his mistake. He feels no remorse for Mrs Perkins. Remorse is not an emotion that figures heavily in Dan's psyche. He has however, experienced great swathes of anxiety, not over what he'd done, but what may have come of his actions. Terrified that Mr Perkins would press charges against him over his part in the death of the little wife, he spent months agonising at every phone call. Each ring seemed to take him closer to a prison cell. Every time his hospital door had opened, especially if a policeman entered his room (and this was often in the early days), he would feel a chill seep into his stomach and groin. His Solicitor, acting on behalf of his own insurance company, wrote to him explaining that Mrs Perkins' widower would not be pursuing the matter. Satisfied that the whole incident had been a terrible accident he wished to move on and grieve for his wife without the aggravation and anguish of a long, protracted court case. Although relieved at this, at the same time an element of annoyance prickled his skin. In other circumstances he would have loved to lay the blame squarely at the bitch's heels. And he could have done it; screwed Perkins for everything his insurance company would cough up rather than simply claiming he could remember nothing conclusive other than her sliding in front of him on the bend. The risk though, had been too great; too many questions could have raised their heads, not to mention police involvement, court appearances and probing lawyers. It was all just too much to risk, too close to the truth. No, he prefers the odds to be stacked a touch more in his favour. He has too much to lose and yet more to gain if he bides his time; plays a long game of seek and find.

The day of retribution is drawing ever closer. His own voice startles him in the silence, "Every dog has his day Andy. I *know* you, *where* you are, *what* you are."

He strikes a match, watches it flare brightly in the night and feels the heat against his face. The tightly wrapped newspaper in his other hand sucks greedily at the flame. It springs into life then arcs through the air, landing at the petrol soaked base of the pile in front of him.

Twelve long hours ago, he drove away from a shabby shop, fighting the urge to spin the back wheels of his large, rumbling van. For ten of those hours, he'd sat, hunched behind its steering wheel, watching as the roadside sped past. The kaleidoscopic effect of the trees and buildings had lulled him into a sort of daze; mountains had crawled past his window, agonising in their glacier-slow creep and endless in their passing. Once on the M6, at a constant 80 mph, the central reservation had set up a strobe effect that further drugged him until he was barely aware of his driving.

A blinking light, insistent and annoying drew his blurry eyes downwards and forced his only stop at a service station just north of Manchester. The petrol pump dragged on and on. He willed the fuel through its rubber pipe and into his tank. Such was his need to continue, that he nearly sped away without paying, only realising his mistake as he drove off the forecourt.

Wasted minutes, wasted minutes, get away, need to fly, pay with five £10 notes, no change, run, run, scream away and back onto the hard, black surface of the southbound M6 in a hazy smoke of tyre rubber and exhaust fumes.

His cargo is precious, no, *priceless* to him. He would have gladly paid £132,000 not £32,000 for it - and more.

Once stacked in his van, it now lies in haphazard piles amongst logs and garden waste, dripping petrol onto his lawn.

The pile ignites with a frightening 'wumph', flames leap skyward, ten, fifteen, twenty feet into the shadowy blackness above. His face remains expressionless, reflecting the orange flickering glow of the marching flames. The night fills with the tortured scream of expanding wood, the crackle of oil paint that bubbles and sparks adding fuel to the fire and smoke to the air. Prints depicting sea and mountains curl in the heat, blacken and shrivel, turn to dust and ash, then explode into brief twisting flame. Gone in seconds. Photographs disappear in the same manner; some lift and float away with the heat of the burning.

Images flash across Dan's eyes; a twisting red sports car leaps from the top of the fire and spins, only to be replaced by a motorcycle which cartwheels through space. Before his gaze, the fire takes the shape of his father's house, crumpling and distorting, collapsing in on itself. For a brief splinter of time, he watches as his father's face appears to scold him from deep within the dancing flames. Then his father's whore shouts at him, her face stretches and distorts as she melts. A piece of fence panel topples and its flat surface becomes the iron capping of a mine ventilation shaft; the log beneath it, the legs of his own whore.

Later, as the remains glow red, almost welcoming and topped with an icing-like dust of white ash, his Emily rises from its centre. She hovers a few feet above the smouldering pyre, twisting slowly, revolving until her beautiful and angelic face is clear. Despite the heat, her pretty checked dress is pristine, crisp, the lace a brilliant white. She smiles, raises her arms high above her head, spreads her fingers into the night sky, then curtseys to her brother. Her voice echoes in his head; a delightful mix of childish giggle and coy, near-sexual taunting.

"Good work indeed my brother, good work indeed. He dared to call this art?" A brief peel of laughter then, again, her voice, "There is more work ahead, you know that don't you?" Dan nods, his mouth slack and drooling. "Much more work, solid, good work. Vengeance if you like. Work for a good, good man such as you; a man who helps the innocent to live on and knows the meaning of life and all its wonders. Life and death, such opposites and yet so intricately linked as to be the same, one, inseparable. Like me and you my brother. Never cease in your quest; you know what has yet to be done."

Dan nods again, a parody of a man, unhinged and lost in his madness.

The image fades until he's looking at a dying fire.

"Always you Emily, always you. Much work to be done ... always you."

The following morning, hazy sunshine spills through Dan's open window. The curtains are open and the palest of blue skies bathes his eyes with its calming pastel hue.

Crawling out of bed he stretches his way to the window and allows the cooling breeze to swirl over his skin. A long, drawn out yawn stretches his face and makes him shake his head in an attempt to rid himself of the last traces of sleep. He leans on the window frame, breathing deeply, letting the fresh air wake him as his eyes sweep the garden and open fields below him.

His house is set on its own, well away from its nearest neighbour and surrounded on all sides by fields bursting with fresh, new growth.

In the centre of his once immaculate lawn, is a huge grey mound of smouldering ashes, four feet high in its centre, fifteen feet across. Charred logs stick out from its edge like the broken spokes of a bike wheel, too thick to have burned, far from the inferno of its core. Here and there, odd bits of charred picture frame, spared from the burning, are visible. Like parched bones of a cremated animal, they're the only relics.

Later, after a shower to remove the pungent stink of wood smoke and petrol, he moves carefully around the edge of the dusty grey mess. Where a piece of frame lies untouched, he plucks it from the ashes and casts it to the centre, building a small dome on top of the nearly dead fire. Judicious poking with a line-prop, stokes the still glowing embers until, soon and with little effort, orange life flickers from beneath. In no time it consumes every last scrap of evidence of the fire's original precious cargo.

He has no real plan, no long term strategy with regard to his 'work' in Scotland. His original plan, the one that had prompted this last trip, his third so far, was to play out the end game. See the job finished, once and for all. He stares into the distance, eyes sweeping over the once again blazing fire, viewing the distant fields through a shimmering haze of heat and smoke.

"I'd like to see you take a dive off that grassy mound you love so much. See you bounce on the rocks below like a rag doll." A smile creeps over his face, his mouth lifts at each corner, though his eyes remain deep, emotionless pools of hatred.

"I reckon I could piss on you from the top of that cliff. At low tide I could give you a real drenching, before the sea you love so much comes in and washes your worthless body away."

On his first trip to Skye he'd watched his target over a period of two days. He'd actually walked past him in the street in Portree, close enough to reach out and skewer him with his ski-pole. Information from the private investigator had been received with barely disguised glee. The search had not been difficult, yet the P.I. had gone away delighted with his £10,000 fee; five times what he'd asked.

"I think I'll wait a month or so, let June get underway. The long days and bright sunshine are good for killing." He stirs the embers, watching as bright sparks lift from the grey mass. "You know all about death in June don't you? Yes, June's a good month for killing."

A plan is forming, seeping along the rotten channels of hatred and confusion that masquerade as his mind.

A visit from Al

Darkness. Not absolute, but a silky velvet cloak of black that seemed to ooze from every nook and cranny; from every crack between every rock.

Thankfully, a sea breeze was pushing its way up the river from the bay two miles to the north and so the midges were being blown about, not able to be too much of a nuisance. The river before me flowed under the road bridge to my right, gurgling and foaming over stones and gravel then channelling powerfully against the near bank before spilling into the pool at my feet. Trees overhung the far bank, dipping their branches onto the surface of a six foot deep, slowly revolving eddy. The flow pushed round, building and growing in strength as it exited the pool itself over a gravel run fifteen yards away. Swinging to the right and then, its flow stopped by the cliff on the far side, it curled to the left and away over boulders. For two hundred yards it cascaded over a series of rocky outcrops and between jagged gullies, never more than a few feet deep, before surging under the bridge on which I'd stopped and watched the lights of Portree three weeks before.

It was the 2nd of June or more accurately the 3rd, the minute hand having swept its way into the new day an hour previously.

My cigarette glowed briefly in the darkness, then a faint, barely audible hiss accompanied the tiny, insignificant 'plop' as I flicked it into the pool to be swept away.

Nothing had stirred; no fish had shown since my arrival at 11.00 p.m. and I hadn't made a cast, preferring to wait for a sign before fishing.

A lorry rumbled past on the bridge and crunched its gears as it made the turn towards Sligachan and the mainland, then, all was still and quiet again.

A sound of water trickling against the stones under the bridge reached my ears and then again, stillness.

A footfall on gravel behind me, the sound of a zip being fastened, the warm sigh of a deep breath.

"I hope you haven't pissed in the river, you heathen."

"No mate, all on the stones. And a drip or two on my waders I think."

Al had paid an impromptu visit. Bored with work and in need of a break, he'd actually driven from Wolverhampton and had been sitting in my lounge watching the telly when I'd got home (I rarely locked the house).

"What are you going to do about the Mini Andy? It's starting to take root on my lawn at the moment, not that it's a problem you know, but, well, if you ain't going to drive it up here you may as well sell it."

I sighed, the Mini; *another* last tangible link to Rachel - so many links. He was right though, I had to do something with it.

I desperately wanted to keep it. The fact that it had been Rachel's car was one thing, but I'd put so much work into it myself, so many oily, sweaty hours getting it just right, it seemed a shame to sell it.

"Tell you what, I'll come back with you when you leave, then drive it back. Be nice to see the Midlands again."

"It starts every time you know. I make a point of giving it a run every week or so. It's bloody loud though Andy, you'll need ear plugs if you're going to drive it up here."

"Good point ..." at that, a large sea trout rocketed skywards from the shallow water at the tail of the pool. In the stillness, it sounded like someone had hefted a breeze block into the water from the road above.

"Nice fish Al, go on, get in there."

We'd agreed Al would have first cast at any fish showing and he accepted eagerly.

3.00 a.m., each of us with a whisky resting on the arm of our chair, the talk and laughter of times gone by. The talk of happy times, the laughter of two friends relaxed and at ease with each other's company. We planned nothing, hoped the weather held and let time flow past us like the river we'd recently left.

"We'll get together for a dram with Iain tomorrow if you like ..."

There was no response. Al was as still as the 4lb sea trout on the draining board. One dead, the other, simply dead to the world.

"HEY SNOOZY BLOKE! Come on, bed."

"OK, OK, you know me mate, I hate driving at the best of times and ten hours behind the wheel, well I'm totally knackered."

We both drained our glasses and within two minutes were sound asleep in our respective beds.

"Mate, you're not listening to me ..."

"I am."

"OK, but you're not hearing me then. Read my lips chappy, I ain't coming across that so-called path. At best it's a ledge, at worst a bloody tightrope and I am *not* stepping across it." Al shook his head, hands on hips, obstinate, resolved; he wasn't moving.

I looked across the void at my feet, sweeping my eyes past him to the summit of Blaven and smiled. It *was* a bit scary. We were on the ridge between Blaven's north and south summits or rather Al was. I'd crossed and was sitting on a blocky outcrop on the south side; a cigarette that I'd lit shortly after we began our 'discussion' was almost gone, such was Al's determination to retreat.

Imagine a sheep track, strung between two domes of rock, set at a height of around three thousand feet. On each side of the track, the ground falls away; on the west, over pillars and buttresses of black gabbro to the soft grassy foot of the Glen. A rock tossed casually in that direction would bounce and clatter all the way until it landed on the springy grass and heather below. To the east, a scree and boulder choked gully arrows its way down for five hundred feet to a rounded bealach, a pass.

Al was standing on the south side of this track. He had already traversed, arms outstretched from the north side without a hitch. What forced his stubborn, stoic show of obstinacy was the way the path snaked its way up the east face of a forty foot rock plinth. This formed the south summit, our planned descent route, and where I sat.

Tears of laughter were drying on my cheeks, having watched him place a hesitant right foot on the terribly slim ledge that ran at 45° up the face, then withdraw it as though burned.

"Jesus chappy, I ain't liking this one bit … not for me mate." He'd flustered and flapped, fighting an inner battle with himself that, apparently, his rational brain was winning hands down.

He'd actually laughed to himself in an extremely awkward, self conscious sort of way; but I'd seen the fear and knew his concerns.

"Andy, seriously, this is not good. Why don't we go back the way we came up?"

It was a reasonable request, but it went against my own preference of completing 'round' walks. I hated going back the same way.

He was becoming desperate. "I wanted to come on a God-damn walk, just a walk, see the views you know? Yet, in the last few hours we've scrambled up scree; up gullies that, if we'd slipped we'd be dead; across ridges that, in all honesty, scared the crap out of me; up a twenty foot rock face; across a rock tightrope and now …" he paused for breath "… now you want me to shimmy across a rock ledge for thirty feet, at 45°, step across a bloody great crack that's running with water, all the time at pain of slipping down that fucking death-slide gully …" he paused again, "… I want to live long enough to have a drink tonight and see Iain again."

I flipped my spent cigarette butt into the void and stepped down onto the ledge.

"Al, if we go back the way we came, we've got a thousand feet of horrible scree and crumbling gullies to work our way down. This way, the path's really good (I lied), a much easier walk." He wasn't having it, not yet. "Plus, you're going to have to cross that sheep track again and, let's face it, I saw how much you hated that."

He glanced back at the north summit and his mind seemed to be made up.

"Oh Jesus, please let me get through this alive."

The step across the crack running with water is the worst move, it sort of forces the body away from the face, but it's over in a matter of seconds. He looked white, all colour drained from his face, but he'd done it. We sat for a while, letting him calm down and relax. The weather had held and, as we skipped from boulder to boulder down the mountain's eastern flank, he shouted back to me "Wasn't too bad after all you know. Piece of cake really."

On the true, north summit, prior to his mutiny, we'd sat for nearly an hour, laughing and talking, taking in the fabulous views. It's such a perfectly elevated platform that, on a clear day, the whole of the island spreads itself below. The only bits hidden from view are blocked by the Cuillin Ridge to the west and the lesser, Red Cuillin to the east. Sixty miles or so to the north, clouds were forming over the Outer Isles and a similar distance to the southwest, the summits surrounding Ben Nevis punctured the hazy summer sky.

He'd known, as we sat there, that this was Rachel's mountain. He'd seen the picture of her astride the summit cairn on my desk in the office at Wolverhampton and now on the mantle piece in my lounge. He'd known and, friend that he is, had steered the conversation away from the past. I'd not been there, since moving to Skye nearly two years previously; plenty of the other mountains, yes, but not Blaven. I'd wanted to, but not on my own and it had to be with someone who wouldn't reel at my tears, feel awkward if I broke down.

I'd past the test, but so, thank God, had Al.

Sitting on the hard, age-old gabbro boulders, looking out at the splendour that is the Cuillin, I'd pointed out the peaks that had felt my tread, traced a finger along the black, saw-toothed ridge, names rolling off my tongue like a native.

It was a magical hour, every time my voice showed the merest sign of breaking, he would step in with a hasty question or comment, steering the conversation and my thoughts away from her - away from the past and into the future.

Half way down the eastern face, blocked by a twenty foot vertical cliff out of which rough steps of tottering chunks hinted at a route of sorts, he turned to me.

"You're a sly old bugger and no mistake. Thought this was supposed to be an easier route?" He gesticulated back up the boulder field we were half way down and still a couple of hundred of feet from the pass. Arms waving and fingers pointing he shouted, but there was laughter hiding in his words, peeking out from just below the surface.

"Look at it, bloody hell Andy, it's like the bloody moon," he shook his head, the corner of his mouth twitching, rising into a smile, then exploding into raucous laughter, "I can't believe we've come down that!"

I was really gone, I stumbled backwards, blind through tears. My hand connected with and slipped off, a large flat block, spilling me over so I landed heavily and painfully on my backside. Rocking and spasming with the force of my laughter, I tried to speak but only succeeded in coughing out water that I'd just drank. Al was crying, hands on his knees, literally crying, squealing like a girl, giggling fit to pass out, sucking in great lung-fulls of air at any opportunity. Subsiding, our childlike giggles died gradually, leaving us to dry our eyes on sunburned arms and gaze out across the waters of Loch Slapin, to the peaks of Beinn Dearg Mhor, Beinn na Coillich and out across the sound to the mainland.

"Absolutely marvellous Andy. You're still a sneaky bleeder getting me to scale that rock face on the promise of a good path, but bloody hell …" he spread his arms wide, theatrically, palms outwards as if about to take a bow, "… mag-bloody-nificent."

"Aye," I replied, lapsing into the trace of a Scottish accent I'd begun to pick up "certainly is. Nothing like it mate. Nothing like it."

He continued to survey the scene, his eyes devouring each facet of the view, feasting on every rise and fall of the landscape.

"If it wasn't so God awful in the winter, I could like it here you know."

I was taken aback.

Butterflies swarmed in my stomach as I thought of the endless prospects; the fishing, the drinking, the friendship.

"You've only got to say the word mate. You know that."

"Aye" he replied, taking the mickey out of my earlier lapse.

"I know. Anyway, you owe me several pints and a meal for that sneaky trick you pulled back there so, let's get going." He dropped his gaze down past his feet, taking in the drop onto relatively easy ground below. "That is, if we get off this mountain alive, I mean Christ Andy, where do we go from here? If you think I'm going down that …"

I'd lost it again, couldn't see for tears, my chest burned with laughing and my stomach throbbed from the exertion.

Once on the path running down the burn to the car park, he kept glancing back, shaking his head and saying things like - "I can't believe we've just been up there" and "I must be bloody mad."

"... that's what you do though, isn't it?"

The evening went well, I think.

Three friends, copious amounts of whisky, lively, if often slurred conversation, good food and an atmosphere of cosy companionship made it a night to remember; sketchily.

A wind had blown in overnight. The pitch black, star dotted clarity that had accompanied Iain's stagger home, had been replaced by a grey, constantly moving, wind-blown backdrop. Clouds, in every shade of depressing grey scudded across the narrows, obscuring Raasay's flat topped hill, then racing across the mile of choppy water in seconds. The tide was in and the wind-stirred waves lapped constantly at the cliff face; like a video on fast forward. White foam that sprayed into the air was immediately whisked upwards against the rocks or around the point to be lost on the wind.

My head hurt. Thumping in time and sympathy with the lapping waves, a symphony for drums and cymbals. I glanced at my watch; the hands were a touch blurry but, after a couple of second's concentrated focusing, I arrived at 9.45, give or take a minute or two. Iain, God bless him, would be out on the salmon cages in Portree harbour now, blasted by the wind and pitching in the waves. Watching him totter away down the track at half past two, weaving from verge to verge in an attempt to keep to the tarmac, I wouldn't have expected a normal mortal to be capable of such work before midday.

I was beginning to realise they were made of stern stuff, these Scots.

I leant on the back of Rachel's bench, squinting and gasping against the wind racing across the steel grey of the narrows. My hands caressed the solid wood of the bench, sliding backwards and forwards, my thumbs absent-mindedly circling the smoothness.

"Aw, shiiittt, tell you what Rach, this 'young free and single' lark is a pain in the arse." I often got a bit maudlin and depressed after a skin-full and always proclaimed it to be the last time; until the next time anyway.

I shook a piece of lambs wool from my finger and watched it soar away towards the cottage, spinning and swooping in the gale. I felt like crying, but surprised myself by smiling instead. "I'll see you later Rach, love you."

Back at the cottage all was still and quiet. There was a distinct peaty smell of last night's whisky, so I opened the kitchen window and let the wind swirl around the room. I started on the washing up; a large pile of plates and cutlery balanced precariously on the work surface and in danger of imminent collapse. The glasses were still in the lounge along with a couple of bowls, greasy from popcorn and peanuts after we'd all 'got the munchies' around one o'clock.

I took the opportunity of calling Mrs N to see how the paintings were going but ended up speaking to Maggie who was looking after things for the morning. A few prints had gone, along with half a dozen framed photos and two originals. I really had to get on with some new work to stock up the shop. I made a mental note to get some photos blown up and framed from my supply. The painting that Iain had been so fond of now filled the space above the fireplace and I spent a minute looking at it. I let the view stir me until I felt I could smell the seaweed along the shore and feel the great big emptiness of the mountains lift my spirits.

The day passed slowly and leisurely, Al rose around noon, red eyed and with a voice as gravely as a builder's yard then, as the evening rolled in, the wind dropped and we ventured out for a stroll to blow some cobwebs away.

The rest of the week flew past in a whirlwind.

We fished often. I dragged him up another two of Skye's peaks and Iain joined us for another couple of whisky tasting sessions that lasted well into the wee hours and ended with thumping heads and suitably blurred vision. As the morning for Al's departure drew closer, I began to regret my offer to go back with him, but, the Mini did need fetching and anyway, it would do me good to see a few faces in Wolverhampton. Saturday morning dawned cold and drizzly, not the ideal weather for a five hundred mile drive south but, as we crossed the bridge to the mainland and I looked back at the cloud over Kyle, the sun came out and I relaxed.

For the first time, I was leaving 'home' and going to the Midlands rather than the other way round.

And it felt good, really good.

We stopped often, sometimes to take in a view, sometimes for a drink or the toilet, then switched seats at Gretna Green, for me to tackle the M6 back to Wolverhampton. I realised, as we threaded our way along the twisting road that hugs Loch Lomond, that it was the first time I'd ever been able to sit back and look at the scenery. Having been behind the wheel on every other occasion and too busy watching out for coaches on the wrong side of blind bends, I'd never truly appreciated the views. I think, as we left Lomond behind and headed towards Erskine Bridge and the drab greyness of Glasgow, that this was the point at which I began missing Skye. It meant so much to me already that for some time I hung on the brink of asking Al to take me back. A queasy feeling of unease and sweaty anticipation made the whole of Glasgow pass with an interminable, crawling slowness.

The gradual slip of grass to concrete gathered pace until, as we sped along the A449 into Wolves, the familiarity of places overcame my sullen depression and lifted my spirits.

His 'cottage' was warm and neat; homely as always and, after unpacking, eating a meal of pasta and polishing off three or four glasses of whisky each, the evening ended. Sleep came easily, about six seconds after my head hit the pillow. My dreams were of rugged coastlines, soaring mountains and leaping sea trout.

"... that's what you do though isn't it? I mean, what we've been doing the last ten days ... *that's* what you do ... all the time."

We were sitting in the garden under blazing sunshine and a clear blue June sky. A huge jug of fruit juice sat on the stout wooden bench between us, its ice cubes clinking at each of Al's frustrated gesticulations. Orange segments bobbed in the murky liquid and a couple of strawberries had become waterlogged at my constant prodding with a spoon and sat sulkily on the bottom.

Geoffrey and Enid sat on the opposite side of the low fence, both reading, both wearing wide brimmed hats, dark glasses and nothing else, both looking decidedly pink despite the obvious smearing of sun cream. Whereas Geoffrey looked a little on the flabby side, as if he'd put on a few pounds since I'd last seen him, Enid was looking surprisingly good. I'd mentioned this already and Al replied that he'd seen her exercising on the lawn, lifting the odd weight and doing crunches.

I found my gaze creeping across the fence for a quick peak at her. God, she was old enough to be my mother, but I had to admit to being drawn. Previously her breasts had sagged, almost disappearing under her armpits when she lay down, now they remained relatively pert and shapely.

"She's had a boob job, I'm sure of it."

"What?"

"Enid, she's had her tits pumped up or something."

"Oh for God's sake, she's twenty odd years older than you. Get a grip." He filled his glass, wincing as an ice cube splashed into his drink and droplets of juice spottled his bare midriff.

He glanced across the fence, lifting himself up for a better view, then waved as he was spotted.

"Nah, she's just been exercising, you know, firmed them up a bit."

"A bit? A bit? Last time I saw them they looked like a cross between melons and bananas. Now … well, I know you think I'm a bit of a perv, but they look pretty good to me."

Al shifted his sun glasses back up his nose, shook his head and leant back against the bench.

"Whatever. Anyway, you haven't answered me."

"What?"

"Strewth, keep up will you? What we've been doing for the last week on Skye. That's *what* you do all the time isn't it?"

"Umm?"

"I mean," he struggled for the right phrase "that's *what* you do. *All* you do. Your *job* if you like."

He could see I was a little confused and started waving his arms around in frustration.

"Bloody hell … err … you fish, you climb up those God awful scary mountains, you take photos, you paint, you get pissed with that mad salmon farmer … that's what you do isn't it?"

I pondered his comments, having never really thought about it before. I shrugged, that's what it must have looked like, to an onlooker I supposed.

"There's a bit more to it than that you know."

He raised his eyebrows, cocking his head to one side and pushing his glasses back up his nose. His face willed me to continue.

"Well," I struggled, "I have to look after the cottages and … and, I have the other one going through at the moment, that takes up a bit of time as well." (I was buying another cottage and it needed a lot of work.)

"Andy, Andy, Andy; while I was there, in over a week, you had one phone call about it and what was the crisis? You had to order some pipe-work for the new drain. Hardly bloody taxing."

"OK, I agree, it doesn't take up *too* much time, but there's the upkeep of them as well."

"You have that woman who lives in the village to do that, Christ, I bet you've never even put a duster around them have you?"

I knew I was beaten on this point.

"The paintings, eh? They don't do themselves you know, they take hours. Then there's the framing, trips to Inverness to get the photos blown up if I need anything bigger than A4."

"Come on, I've seen the envelopes, the boxes you send your stuff in; how often do you actually *go* to Inverness?"

Bastard had me beat on that point as well.

"Twice a month I suppose."

"How *do* you manage to fit it all in?"

He was smiling, as was I, glinting eyes hidden behind dark shades, but our faces, the bits not hidden, told the story.

"Yes, that's what I do. I paint, I fish, I climb, I take photos. I've paid the price though. Well Rachel did anyway."

His hands flew out in defence.

"Shit, hey come on, you know I didn't mean that."

"I know mate, I know ... it does seem a bit idyllic doesn't it? Like I've got it made. Paradise really."

"Yes chappy, that it does."

"I could do with help looking after the cottages though, you know. Even thought about opening a shop of my own, to sell the paintings in. A few art supplies, paints, paper, brushes and stuff. Could do with a manager to look after it."

He was staring out over his garden, his eyes flowing over the fields in the distance. I continued.

"The pay's not brilliant but there's plenty of time off for fishing and I could always do with someone to carry my painting stuff and cameras. The property's cheap as well. For someone with a desire to buy a few holiday cottages the market's wide open." (I knew he was keen on buying property). "Anyway mate, if you think of anyone who'd like to apply for the job ..." I slapped his shoulder "... let me know OK?"

I surprised myself by hearing my voice crack on the last couple of words.

Watching

It's now the second night that the house has been in darkness.

Viewed between the branches of stunted hawthorn and birch, the white paint of the walls and green of the window frames glow in the dappled orange glow of sunset.

11.15p.m. still no sign.

The scruffy old Scot had scuffed his way along the road and into the front of the house around 7 o'clock, stayed for half an hour, watering plants and supping some whisky from a bottle on the kitchen surface.

The perfect irony of travelling five hundred miles and finding the target away, burns with an acid intensity that bubbles in Dan's guts. A rage is building, an overwhelming desire to rip and tear and maim. He'd had to bury his head in the grasses of his hide overlooking the coast and its dotted houses when 'old scruff bag' had shuffled up the track, such was the desire to creep down through the garden, sneak up behind his stocky frame and slit his throat.

"The old bastard was probably so pissed I could have walked straight up to him and stabbed him in the eye."

It wasn't the first time he'd had to wait to complete a job. Time, for Dan, is not an issue, he has plenty of it. Get the job done. Finish it with professionalism and efficiency. Leave no trace, no clues, no trail. Keep safe. If he needs to wait, he'll wait. If speed is of the essence, he'll use it.

'Adaptable' is Dan's middle name.

His plan is simple. Knock the door at sunset, knowing his target is alone. A swift punch to the face, not caring whether there is any damage. Wait for full dark, administer a little more pain and suffering in the meantime, then drag barely conscious body to the cliff and, hopefully, but not essential, while it struggles with at least some degree of lucidity, shove it over into the heaving waves to smash against the rocks eighty feet below.

Job done. Dusted. Finished.

Dan is starting to realise that this most elusive of targets is turning into something of an obsession. He never holds a personal vendetta against any of his hits; it gets in the way of the job and clouds any chance of cleanliness. If he ever needed a job doing for personal reasons, he knows a few people who could sort it out. This is different. Even without the horrendous balls up with the car crash and the months of excruciating pain and embarrassment, the job would still have to be carried through. The target has to be hit and hit hard.

He will wait, because time is on his side.

Missing humanity

The mini was almost unbearably loud.

What had, at first pleased my ear with its throaty, rasping, burbling growl was, after a couple of hundred miles, becoming almost painful.

At the service station near Gretna on the M6, I stopped and phoned speaking pages for a guest house in Moffatt. A cheery young girl, who sounded a few days past her sixteenth birthday, informed me of three in the town and relayed the numbers to me. With the charm of a seasoned air hostess she thanked me for calling her service and asked if I could mention them to the Guest house proprietors. I agreed, knowing that I probably wouldn't and hung up.

The services were quiet, at 3 p.m. on a Thursday in June and I, relegated to the far corner of the restaurant because I wanted a fag, sat in the near silence, sipping coffee. I'd given up on the cardboard tasting Danish pastry after the first mouthful and, even though I was hungry and lets face it, not short of a few quid, refused to fork out what they were asking for anything more substantial.

I left after ten minutes.

As the miles progressed ever northward, I pondered over the few days I'd spent at Al's.

Steve was working for himself now, the impromptu incarceration of Mr Stevens acting as the catalyst required for him to go it alone. The fact that he'd used the password I'd given him to access the whole of CSA's client bank and, in one evening, the day before the strong arm of West Mercia Police Force clattered down around all and sundry, had printed off the whole lot, caused me great merriment. I hadn't seen him in over twelve months since the trial and in that time he'd grown in confidence; more businessman than office boy.

Like me, Al's parents were no more and he seemed to exist in a life of almost nomadic seclusion. I say nomadic, because he appeared to wander aimlessly between groups of 'acquaintances', no real friends. A few people popped round, none that I'd seen before, including a couple of girls who lived together a few houses along from his 'cottage'.

Gail and Debbie were pleasant enough. Tarty and attractive in a sort of scary, modern, laddish, lager-drinking, kebab-munching sort of way. Definitely good fun, certainly a match for both Al and I in the drinking game and unquestionably 'up for it'. The evening was a raucous, wine and whisky affair, involved a hastily cooked barbecue, loud music, much laughter and for me, an end of evening grope.

My morals got in the way though and I called a halt as Debbie (my appointed ride) was preparing to rip open her blouse.

Al disappeared with Gail for a few hours, both reappearing as the first glow of sunrise bathed his garden in a flat, yellow-grey light.

All in all it had been a pleasant time. I spent the days driving along lanes that had grown hazy during my time away. Taking in old haunts and visiting pubs for pints and lunches, I would sit with a book, lost in other worlds; I was on holiday after all. It was a strong reflection on just how powerful a hold Skye had on me, that, after only four full days away, I was itching to return. I needed a fix of fresh mountain air, the smell of the seashore, the warm glow of my log fire and cosy comfort of my cottage. I was tired of having to take my mobile phone with me when I parked the car; tired of having to put the alarm on when I nipped into a corner shop and tired of having to take the keys out of the ignition when it was left on Al's drive.

I missed the humanity of the Island, the true civilisation.

A change of plan

The scruffy Scot had shuffled off down the track half an hour before and not a soul had stirred since.

A blanket of light cloud has settled over the island making the scene one of damp, clammy stillness. A snipe thrums its incessant call over hillside which rises steeply behind a figure standing stock-still amongst the hawthorn. Dressed totally in black, his movements are only discerned by the pale bobbing of an uncovered face that seems to hang in the night.

At the boundary to the neat, if somewhat sparse, rear garden, a brief rustle of clothes and thump of foot fall rises above the more usual night sounds as the figure leaps the low barbed-wire fence. That same weird bobbing of disjointed face, as the figure jogs across the lawn heading directly to the rear of the house. Down four steps onto a gravel path dotted with hexagonal paving slabs that unwittingly help to deaden the sound of unwanted footsteps. A brief pause at the front corner of the house, a glance left and right, checking for dog walkers or the unfortunate return of old scruff. The porch door creaks, left unlocked with all the misplaced trust that the locals have. There's a click as the interior door's handle turns and dips in the darkness, the sound loud in the silence like a rifle shot as the door swings open.

Dan stands, open mouthed and instantly confused. For a second he can't believe that the house is actually empty. Such faith, such trust is unknown to him. In a world where *taking* is the new religion, where people get what they can as quickly as they can, regardless of the consequences, an open house defies belief.

He hovers on the threshold. The house is warm and the open, trusting nature of it imparts a fear in him that he cannot understand. He is quite used to breaking and entering; not just *entering*. His skill is in taking, in forcing his will on a situation, in leaving no trace. This isn't even taking sweets from a baby. This is having them delivered on a plate by a smiling Father Christmas. It unnerves him.

He stands in the hallway, his eyes taking in stairs off to the right that twist away into the gloom and the dining room with large oak table and heavily stocked drinks cabinet to the left. At the bottom of the stairs, an open door affords a glance into a study; heavy mahogany desk, studded red leather chair, bookshelves stuffed with hundreds of volumes. An antique lamp sits over a green leather blotter. He moves quietly along the hall, all night sounds shut out by the now closed front door. A door with frosted, stained-glass panels swings silently open into a modern, well equipped, wood and marble kitchen. A pine, farmhouse style table and four chairs sits solidly on quarry-tiled floor. A half empty bottle of whisky stands on the dappled grey marble work surface. Next to this a note: 'Iain, thanks for looking after the place - have a drink on me - Andy'.

For a second Dan's hand tenses, making as if to crumple it into a ball and toss it across the room, then, with a huge effort, he relaxes and replaces it on the surface.

To his right, a large, open plan lounge turns the corner from the kitchen. A three-seater settee and two armchairs surround a large coffee table made from what appears to be railway sleepers. He wanders into the lounge, standing on the white rug in front of the fireplace.

Dark eyes take in the homely yet efficient air of the room, flicking from item to item. A pressure builds in his mind; a mind darkened and corrupted by the committing of countless atrocities. A dangerous and terrible anger claws away at him. What he *wants* to do is smash and destroy; break everything that *will* break; scrawl obscenities on every wall; leave his excrement smeared on every piece of furniture and piss all over the clothes that no doubt hang in long, expensive rows somewhere upstairs.

What he *actually* does is stand and stare.

His eyes wander over the scene that hangs above the fireplace. Even in the considerable darkness he senses a beauty that seems to pour out of the frame. He steps to the front window and draws the curtains, hoping that they will shut out the light he intends to switch on. After the darkness he squints against the glare.

The scene appears to glow before his eyes, a fabulous mixture of soaring mountains and deep blue, almost black, pulsing sea. The sky is the most appealing mix of pastel shaded blue, dotted with cloud above the highest peaks. The shoreline is crisp, clean; white and grey boulders catch the light and reflect it outwards. Boats bob on the swelling water and sea birds wheel in the ocean-blown breeze. He imagines he can hear their calls.

Slowly, reverently, he steps forward and stands up close; so close that he can smell the oil paint and heady varnish that makes the ornate frame sparkle. The ridges and whirls of paint are sensuous to his fingers' touch; deep grooves run into spiky, miniature points of living wave-caps and sharp, rocky ridges.

For the first time in his life, Dan is in awe.

He sees perfection. The skill of the artist shines out with such clarity, such utter beauty, that he feels himself begin to sway and, steadying himself against the mantle piece, bows his head in supplication. He feels he should kneel before such a work of incredible passion, bow down to the creator of such a painting.

In his mind's eye he sees the flaming fire that consumed other work by this same genius. He sees his own hand lighting the torch that ate its greedy way through the hours of toil spent in labour at the same easel. For a while Dan's thoughts fly around his head in a terrible, jumbled turmoil. That he could have committed such a wicked act begins to tear at his soul and a tear springs from his eye.

Slowly he comes to. No, the other paintings were worthless, tourist driven tat; rubbish. He looked at them all, remembers his stomach turning, his bile rising. No, he did this one, true painting a great honour by destroying the bastard rejects, the commercial garbage that hung, prostituting themselves in that wooden hut of a shop and watched over by that stupid, ingratiating woman. He steps back until his calves push against the coffee table, letting his eyes lift and soar over the scene, taking in all its emotion.

It's a long time before he lowers his gaze.

At this point he could gladly leave and return to his home. Give up the crusade that has driven him for the past two years and let life continue.

A voice in his head, his Emily, gently scolds him for his momentary lapse, draws him back to a controllable level of hatred and loathing. Only this time, it is tinged with a hard edge of respect. His plans have altered, already his mind is working towards a new plan, testing theories, probing at ideas, building a suitably glorious ending to a life that could compose such perfect, harmonious beauty.

This would be his hour, not a killing for financial gain or even one borne out of anything as ugly as vengeance. Things change. For a man driven by perfection in every aspect of his life, change is inevitable, to be used to its fullest, embraced. Change brings new opportunity, a chance to excel and move to a higher plain.

He speaks for the first time in what seems like hours. "Oh Andy, dear, talented, misguided Andy. Such beauty, such honesty." His eyes glisten with new tears at his spoken thoughts. "Cleansing you of this terrible world and all its falsity will be a glorious task. If only I'd known sooner, you could have witnessed, as guest of honour, the burning of your other foul, worthless scribblings." His arms are raised as if in prayer, outstretched in worship of the picture. He continues, "Such glory would have rained down on us, such honour," he pauses, as if a new thought has just occurred to him, "you would have been with my Emily now, in wondrous, eternal peace. No concern, no hardship. Soon my dear Andy, so soon."

Anyone peering into the house at this point would see a man in the throws of what appears to be, a frantic, zealous, religious fervour. Arms outstretched, palms spread upwards, body rocking to a silent tune.

The whole of his face is in utter rapture, his cheeks are wet with fresh, rolling tears; and his eyes are smiling,

A letter arrives

Middlemare guest house was warm, almost uncomfortably so. Mrs Stansmore, the proprietor, was friendly, also almost uncomfortably so. Originally from Milton Keynes, she'd moved in with her husband, then moved *him* out when she found him having sex with a teenage back-packer staying in room six. I hesitated to guess that this was the reason for her over-friendliness and for her offer to "plump up my pillows for me." It was about the hundredth double-entendre she'd shot across my bows since my arrival and came as I got up from the guest's lounge on my way to bed. Delivered with a theatrical flair that would have been at home in any 1970's soft porn film, I struggled to keep a straight face, but declined her offer.

A breathy "If you need anything … *anything* at all, I'm only across the landing," rang out behind me as I trotted up the stairs.

Lying in bed later, one arm out of the open window, flicking ash into the rear garden, I thought of all my years with Rachel. I was single and it wasn't as though Mrs Stansmore, *Catherine*, was unattractive. She was my age, plus a bit, short, slim, blonde and obviously gagging for it.

I kept my door locked.

She was persistent, I'll give her that. Even at breakfast she made sure I got an eyeful of cleavage, placing my napkin in my lap and bending over my table at any opportunity. I was the only one stopping there and felt a little like a hostage, a prisoner of a deranged, bored, sex-starved housewife.

I paid and left, knowing, as I walked along the street that, had I looked back, she would have been leaning on the door frame, licking her lips.

I didn't look back.

The Mini had grumbled at first, firing lumpily on three cylinders for a while. I checked my phone for messages as the oil warmed up and the firing became smoother, more consistent. Two: one from Al, enquiring about my journey and making a point of shouting his message as he thought I might be a bit deaf after so many miles in the Mini and one from Mrs N, dear old Mrs N. She needed to speak to me urgently.

I dialled her first and spoke to Maggie. Her mom was doing some shopping but Mr Salt had been on the phone, wanted to know whether we could meet; something about a possible commission. I asked her to get her Mom to ring me when she got back, phoned Al, got his answer machine, shouted a message back and hung up.

The miles droned by and the buzzing of the Mini's little engine began to vibrate in my head. "Oh for a fifth gear!" I shouted against the din, as I sped along the M74 towards Glasgow. Traffic was sparse - the odd lorry, coaches full of bored looking septuagenarians and of course the ubiquitous, dynamic, aggressive young sales executives, suited and with garish ties; laid back and driving at arms length at a steady 90mph.

Glasgow passed - slowly. Erskine Bridge appeared huge and seemed to sway alarmingly from the cramped interior of the car. The run towards Lomond seemed to take days and then, I turned right, onto the twisting, hallowed road along the shore of the Loch.

I was in Mini country.

I pulled over at the first lay by and sat on the bonnet swigging Lucozade from a plastic bottle. I took time to allow myself to be absorbed into the wild atmosphere that surrounds the billions of gallons of gently lapping water. Weak sun dappled the surface and reflected off every wave as though sprinkled with a million diamonds. A blue haze hung over the mountains while Ben Lomond towered above its neighbours in the north east, hugely domed and impressively dark against the misty horizon.

Determined that I would enjoy the last two hundred miles, I spent half an hour relaxing before pulling on to an empty road, settled myself into the snug bucket seat and concentrated on the twists and swoops of the tarmac unfolding before me. By the time I pulled up at the toll booth at Kyle of Lochalsh I was aching. I'd met few cars and managed to pass those after only a short period of frustration.

Mrs N's Land Rover was parked next to the shop and I considered pulling in and saying hello but decided against it. The phone had beeped to tell me I had a message, Mrs N probably having phoned while I was in the mountains. I was too tired to be bothered; I'd call when I got home.

I swung into the driveway and parked in front of my partly rebuilt shed, next to the TVR. I couldn't help thinking how it would be difficult for two cars to be more different. The sweeping, slippery curves of the TVR made the Mini look like a brightly painted packing case. Standing at the end of the drive, my eyes flicked backwards and forwards, from one to the other. Chalk and cheese - but both were extremes; real driving machines. It didn't matter that the TVR had an engine which made the Mini's look a little like a clockwork egg-timer and pushed out roughly four hundred per cent more horse power. They were both fast in their own way, both unrelenting, unforgiving, mechanical beasts that were difficult to live with. The TVR just had a bigger growl.

Grabbing my hold-all I shut the Mini's boot and strolled around to the front of the house, pausing at the gate to look out over the calm and deceptively serene ocean. In that instant, I knew, absolutely, categorically, knew that I would never leave Skye. Never before had I experienced such utter joy at returning home. Never before had I been stirred by such a feeling of warm belonging; of total oneness with my surroundings.

I'd have a stroll down to Iain's later, take a bottle of Tamdhu as a thank you for looking after the place. Tomorrow I'd rise late, start work on a few more paintings and nurse the inevitable hangover.

The gate creaked as it swung open and I made a mental note to oil it. My feet crunched on the gravel path to the front door and a mild panic set in when I couldn't find my keys. I checked my pockets, digging to the bottom of each one twice before remembering that I hadn't taken them with me. Iain had a set and there was a spare hidden, rather unimaginatively, under a plant pot by the front step. The door wouldn't be locked anyway; never was. This was, after all, Skye, not the Midlands. Crime was largely a rumour, just a news item from the mainland.

My home greeted me like a faithful lap-dog; like putting on a pair of fire-warmed, comfortable old slippers. Good to be back.

I unpacked, (tipped all of my clothes onto the bathroom floor, filled the bathroom cabinet with the few toiletries that I'd remembered to bring back from Al's, placed my latest Iain Banks novel back on the bedside table) then trotted downstairs to check the post.

Two statements from my bank, a letter informing me that I had definitely won one of a large selection of prizes and all I had to do was call a premium rate number to claim it, an electricity bill, a credit card application, a charity request complete with the attempted bribe of tacky plastic ball-point pen and a hand written letter, post-marked Kyle of Lochalsh, which intrigued me. I didn't get hand-written letters, didn't have anyone who wrote to me apart from Al, but, as I'd just left him in Wolverhampton, knew it wouldn't be him.

I placed the junk mail in the bin, stuck an 'addressee gone away' sticker on the charity request, stacked the bills next to the toaster for filing, filled the kettle and set about making a cup of best instant.

The neat, black print, written in fountain pen by the look of it, stared up at me from the work surface, willing me to take a peak. The kettle boiled, I made my coffee, picked up the letter and took it into the lounge.

Black coffee, a cigarette, the longed for relaxation following an exhausting journey and an intriguing letter. Surely there can be few greater pleasures.

I sat back, took a deep draw on my cigarette, opened the envelope and began to read.

Dear Mr Perkins,

Please excuse my intrusion. By sending you this letter at your home, I mean no impropriety. You are something of a celebrity on the Island I have found. As the enigmatic English artist who keeps himself to himself, your address is not difficult to uncover.

I am an art lover of whom you know quite well, although you do not realise this fact at the present. I am, you see, the man who recently swelled your bank balance quite alarmingly by purchasing your complete works.

At the time I felt it better that we did not meet, preferring to keep art and the artist separate, to help keep the magic and mystery alive. Having lived with your work for sometime now, I feel myself drawn to your landscapes, the beauty and reality that shine from them. In every view there lies a hidden depth that grows with each day and I find that such works deserve a respect, a reverence that is missing in most others I own.

I would dearly love to meet with you and show my appreciation for the quality that your talent has brought to me. I feel sure we have a great deal in common and, bearing in mind our shared love of this landscape and the images that represent it, a huge amount to talk about.

I am staying at the enclosed address for a few more days and would be available to meet at your convenience.

I look forward to hearing from you.

Yours sincerely,

David Salt

"Shit"

I re-read the letter, lit another cigarette, wandered over to the lounge window, stared our for a few seconds then returned to the coffee table and read it again with mounting disbelief.

"'*Enigmatic English artist*', is he taking the piss or what?"

I scanned the letter again, already knowing it almost off by heart "…'*hidden depth … reverence … respect*' this bloke's a bit of a nutter."

My voice echoed in the empty house and for some strange, inexplicable reason, I felt a twinge of apprehension.

Iain was slightly less complimentary.

"He's a bloody fruit cake. Nae disrespect intended ye ken, but Christ Andy, anyone who writes this in a letter is a wee bit more than odd," he waved the now crumpled paper in the air in front of his face, struggled for the right phrase before continuing, "this friggin' basturt knows where ye live. Ah'm thinkin' ye'd be advised tae tek a wee bit o' care wi' him. Aye a wee bit o' care. Mebee yeh got ye sen a stalker."

I laughed, nervously.

"Ye may laugh Andy," a stern look came over his face, a seriousness I'd not seen before "Ah'm thinkin' he's trouble."

"Aye, maybe you're right; fancy another?" I topped up his glass, took the letter from him and tucked it into my shirt pocket.

Outside, the night was drawing in, along with a high cloud cover that blocked out the stars and a fresh breeze that suggested a change from the recent warm, sunny days.

"Are ye still planning yer wee walk in the mountains Andy?"

My 'wee walk in the mountains' was a dream of mine. Involving at least three nights out in the open, all of them above three thousand feet, it was an undertaking that Rachel would never have agreed to. My plan was to trek from Elgol and along the coastal path to the start of the Cuillin ridge, the first day ending on the summit of Gars Bheinn. From there I would traverse the whole of its airy crest in one day and arrive at Sgurr-na-Gillean for my second night in the open. The third day would involve a descent from Gillean into Glen Sligachan. Resisting the urge to turn north to the hotel, I would then tramp across the glen, perhaps taking in Marsco, then onto Garb-Bheinn, Sgurr nan Eich, Clach-Glas, up onto Blaven and a third night under the stars. The final day would see me drop down the south ridge of Blaven, picking up the coastal path again and back to Elgol.

It was a hell of an undertaking and testament to how my confidence had grown in the matter of my climbing. The ridge itself presented not only technical difficulty, but a logistical nightmare. I couldn't carry enough food to complete the whole trip realistically, unless I could bring myself to survive on powdered food, re-hydrated en-route. If I wanted 'real' food, I would need to leave pre-deposited stashes, which would mean at least three trips to the ridge beforehand. I didn't mind this extra effort, but really wanted to complete it in the best possible style.

I'd already decided I suppose, that I'd need to live on unappetising but nutritious slop for a few days.

"Yes Iain, I'm planning to start my 'wee walk' a week on Monday - weather and 'stalker' permitting."

At the time, I didn't realise just how true those words were.

Moving to Tibet

An empty house, its rambling garden, untidy in its natural 'back to nature' way, strange neighbours, alone in their 'off the wall' habits. Naked as the day they were born, they sit and pick their way through a colourful summer salad, sipping occasionally at iced tea slurped through slices of lemon. Overhead, a Friday-evening-in-June-sun pours its warmth down on their pink skin. Waning now at 7.30p.m., the intensity has eased its way down to a level of pleasant heat. A flock of wood pigeons swoop low over the rural scene, wings thrumming through the still air, then clattering as they brake their flight before landing in the old oak at the edge of the garden. Home to roost.

Al starts at the sound, his eyes sweep up to the gnarled old branches, woken from his daydream where mist hangs in the glens of age-old mountains and sunlight glints in golden specks off bands of quartz.

He's bored. Bored of life in financial services. Bored of the tedium of everyday life. Bored even of the attentions of Gail or Debbie (or even, on occasions, Gail *and* Debbie). Bored of his eccentric neighbours. Bored of his life. More than even this, he's envious. A feeling that doesn't come easily to him; envy has always been for others.

He lives life by a simple code: the belief that, as far as he knows, this is his one shot, his one and only time on this world and, with this knowledge burning constantly in his mind, he lives life as he feels fit. It's the reason he's single, the reason, if he's truthful to himself, that he has few close friends. There's a band of selfishness in him like a seam of the gold-glistening quartz that scribes its way through the rock of mountains that have invaded his thoughts for the last twelve months - since his first visit to Skye.

It's a selfishness that extends to one thing, and one thing alone, in all other aspects he thinks of himself as generous to a fault. Time though, burns in him. How much left? How many more misty mornings by silted ponds; jewels in green countryside? How many more night times lit by sprinkles of stars against the black blanket of a Welsh sky? How many more electric pulses on cold fingertips as a fresh sea trout takes hold, pulling downstream and spraying the blackness with tail thrown diamonds?

Time.

He felt that his visits to Skye had *stopped* time. Although it passed with the simple fluidity of time gone by, it had seemed to gather rather than pass.

The whisky tasted better, the air clearer. The scenery bristled with a beauty that took away his breath. Seascapes, moorland, mountain ridges, wandering, peaty coloured rivers, gurgling over gravel and boulders in their journey to the ocean. He hated driving, the aggressive, ignorant actions of road users (himself included), simply raised his blood pressure and reduced the act to that of mildly subdued warfare. While on Skye, the simple task of driving to the pub became a pleasure. The quickest, fastest, most aggressive, thrusting, ambitious, ruthless attitude won; won the day, the business, the parking space, the service at the bar, the inside lane at the traffic lights. Shout loudest and you get heard, shout longest and you get noticed, work harder and longer and you get ahead. Beat the rest, beat the pack, pull in front.

Bollocks, all utter bollocks.

He looks across at his pink, rounded, naked neighbours. Having finished their salad, they are sharing a bowl of strawberries, laughing at each other, enjoying their simple, uncluttered company.

He remembers once, during a working lunch in a busy, typically 'up and thrusting' town centre wine bar, feeling a pressure build in his head and chest to such a degree that a cold sweat broke out over his body. The talk was of campaigns, the launch of the new savings product and the impact it would have on sales figures. The second quarter launch of a new bond, complete with a new managed fund. Annual premium income, profit margins, niche markets, fact finds, referred leads, mortgages; all bollocks. It had made his head spin and his blood boil.

It had passed. It always did, and probably always would, but, at the time, during the interminable hour he spent listening to overly enthusiastic colleagues piping forth with sales ideas and concepts, he could have quite cheerily got up and walked out - or keeled over and died right there amongst the shiny brass stools and cigarette butts littering the carpet.

Sitting on his own, by a window on the other side of the room, a man in his early forties slowly turned the pages of a paperback. The page-turner held a cigarette in his left hand and, with each draw on the tatty looking roll up, a swathe of smoke rolled around his head and shoulders. He wasn't reading. He was *absorbing* the book.

The cover, dog eared and cracked, showed a yellow, roughly

square section of a map set on a green background and above this, a single word: TIBET.

The calm that exuded from the space the page-turner occupied was tangible; to Al anyway.

In every corner of the bar, at every table, from all around, chatter and shouted statements rang through the air. Mobile phones blared their ridiculous, electronic cacophony, answered quickly with shouted "Hello's." Music blared from speakers set into the corners creating a wall of sound that seemed to mock at any attempt to converse.

"GO ON YOU BRAINLESS BASTARDS, GO ON, SHOUT, LET'S ALL SHOUT AT EACH OTHER. THINK YOU CAN BEAT ME?"

In his little patch of swirling sunlight, the page-turner existed in his own serene world. He was, to all intents and purposes, *in Tibet*. He could smell fresh mountain air, gaze across snow capped peaks of unimaginable beauty. He knew the simple taste of rice and vegetables cooked in blackened pots over crackling fires. At that moment in time, he was enjoying the peace and quiet of a Tibetan evening with the sun, huge and golden, reflecting off snow and rock that pushed its way miles into the air.

Al's concentration on this tiny oasis of simple existence, calmed him to the depth of his soul. His blood, a moment before, racing through his veins, slowed and its pressure dropped. The tension in his chest subsided, his headache vanished, his vision became clear and sharp.

Remembering this, his occasional cigar burning away between his fingers and whisky tinkling its ice against crystal, he glances across again at his neighbours. *They* have that peace. *They* have their own tiny portion of heaven, a simple, inner joy at their own unconventional existence. Peace with each other, with their way of life. He can see it in their eyes, it shines out from their faces, their unselfconscious grasp of a life they love. *Truly love.*

He has seen that same look, felt that same inner calm radiating out from his friend in the north. Seen it and hated it. Marked the way it seems to shadow him like a protective aura, as though surrounded by his own bubble of serenity, a passion for life and all of its possibilities. It follows him like a well-trained dog, never leaving his side.

Al has seen it and is envious.

On his bench, in the waning light of a near perfect Friday in June, he decides, whilst Enid finishes the last of her plump, ripe strawberries and the pigeons begin their cooing that, more to the point, he wants it.

He has the money. No mortgage, a property worth £150,000 and over £75000 in various investments. He has no ties (other than the ones Gail or Debbie occasionally fasten him to the bed post with). He's had a job offer. The details of his potential new employment are a touch sketchy to say the least, but, hell, he could live a little, take a risk.

He has all these things, all the makings of a new, improved life. Shifting his gaze from Enid's breasts (his mate had been right, she's definitely had a boob job), he allows himself to drift across the greenery surrounding his home. Over fields and hedgerows, away into the far distance where a wood of oak and birch sits like a domed, vibrant green hat on a squat, rounded mound of a hill.

He sees it all and yet, at the same time, none of it.

His mind is filled with soaring black peaks, deep river hewn gullies with prancing, foaming white water, beautiful green glens where sheep and highland cattle crop at the stunted grass.

He sees Skye.

He sees his new home.

Mr Salt pays a visit

Saturday morning dawned as though the island had stepped back six months into a cold, gale blown January. Thick, rolling cloud scudded across the sound from Raasay, blown by a near gale force north westerly. The track in front of the window was dry, no rain having fallen, but the clouds said differently. They said they were simply biding their time, waiting for the right moment. Wet and windy was the order of the day. They were just holding back on the wet bit.

I wandered out towards Rachel's bench, struggling against the onslaught that blew straight into my face; the salt, strong enough to dry on my cheeks and brow in a dusty white powder. Over to my right, Glamaig sat squat and massive, its summit clear of cloud. Racing up its steep, scree covered flanks were dark shadows as sparse breaks in the cloud allowed the sun to shine through. Further to the west a huge broiling mass of white vapour hurried across the mainland. I studied the cloud's leading edge, seeing instantly, a rounded brow, deep set eyes and large roman nose.

"There you go Rach, see? Up on that great big one. Right at the front. See it? Brow, eyes, nose, huge chin."

Rachel would have seen it. Probably would have spotted it before me and pointed it out with a childlike giggle and wildly pointing finger.

"Of course you see it. I know that."

The previous evening with Iain had been a fairly quiet affair. Mr Salt's letter had clearly disturbed him. He seemed to see a foreboding menace in it that I couldn't. I gave in at some point during the evening and agreed that I wouldn't call him. Agreed to 'take care', handle any chance meeting cautiously and give him nothing. I secretly thought Iain was acting a little paranoid and *that* worried me in itself. He was a hard-nosed, pragmatic Scot who didn't succumb easily to anything as unquantifiable as intuition. His concern left me feeling ill at ease.

It quite simply wasn't him.

At the gate, my phone started ringing and, as I dashed down the path to answer it, felt the hairs stand on the back of my neck.

"Hello."

Nothing - empty air space.

"Hello ... hellooo, anyone there?"

"Andy, sorry about that ... customer."

Mrs N.

I let her talk, rambling away while I pitched in with the odd "Yes" and "Oh right," "Hmm" and "OK."

"Listen Andy ... Mr Salt, the guy who bought all yer work ..."

"Yes Mrs N, I'm aware of Mr Salt."

"Well, he's been in. Popped int'ae the shop on the off chance o' seeing ye ..."

"I know ..." I replied "... he's sent me a letter."

"Really, och right ... that's ... interesting?"

"Yeah, that's what I thought," I paused, weighing the words in my mouth before continuing, "Iain thinks he's a nutter, a stalker or something. I know you didn't like him, but ... what do you really think? I mean ... do you reckon he's dangerous?"

Again, clear air space, silence and a pause that stretched on and on.

"Ah din'nae know about that. He's ... unusual, Ah'll gi' ye that," another pause and I could imagine her searching for the right words, for a phrase that would sum him up. She signed, a somehow desperate, terribly fatigued, desolate sound. "Ah din'nae like him, that's all Ah know. Ah din'nae trust him Andy. He gi's me the creeps." When she continued it was with a certainty that was at odds with her previous indecision. "It's like he's a secret, somethin' that he knows an is'nae lettin' on about. There's a nastiness about him. Somethin' dirty, unclean ... just nasty. I can'nae think o' a better way tae describe him. Sorry."

My eyebrows were raised so that the skin on my creased brow felt ready to split.

As the morning progressed and gradually became afternoon, I'd finished a simple watercolour of the view from my window. Looking from the image on my easel to the real thing, I was pleased with how well I'd captured the scene. Upon starting, I'd felt out of sorts and a touch distant; not the usual tingling buzz that accompanies time with my brushes.

"Not bad ... not bad at all." I spoke to myself, adding "It should sell all right anyway."

It had taken forty minutes; forty minutes to produce something that would sell for £300 or more, framed.

"Yeah, not bad at all."

The rumble of tyres on tarmac made me crane my neck down from the window. A dark green Subaru crept past my house, its tinted windows and gold wheels looking somehow out of place in the still blustery day full of dark racing clouds and splashes of sunshine.

I'd always liked the brutish, aggressive lines of the Subaru. From the front they always gave me the impression they were about to pounce, that the air scoop rising from the bonnet was ready to suck in stray pigeons or traffic wardens.

That all changed two years ago.

After the accident, I couldn't look at one without feeling an anger rise in me that edged towards hatred.

I knew, in my heart that it wasn't the other driver's fault. It was an *accident*, the police, God bless 'em, had been sure of that. Everything tied in with the brief information the other driver could offer, as hazy as his memory had been. Just an accident. Ridiculous that a piece of metal should raise such strong feelings within me. It wasn't the car's fault after all.

It didn't stop the rising feeling of obsessive dread.

It crept past the picket fence, past the driveway, then pulled slowly to the side of the road and mounted the grass verge, its brake lights shining out briefly. I watched, waiting for the driver's door to open and spill out a wealthy bird-watcher or photographer. When nothing happened after a couple of minutes, I stepped back from the window, shaking my head and moving towards the stairs.

Time for lunch.

My steps creaked on the stairs, the sound loud and obtrusive in the silence. At their foot I glanced out of my front door; the panel of frosted glass showed a figure opening the gate. "Jesus." It was a totally impromptu outburst, followed by a rapid, shambling run down the hallway to the kitchen. "It's him, oh shit, it's him." I flattened myself against the wall with a rising feeling of apprehension and counted out the seconds. I imagined his feet crunching on the gravel path as he made his way towards me, waiting, without breathing, for a knock on the door that would still my heart. I ran at a crouch to the telephone, not sure what I intended to do or who I intended to call, knowing only that Iain's words of caution and Mrs N's description of a monster were battling for broadcasting space in my head.

Succeeding in clattering the phone from its table, I swore, stooping to pick the tangled mess from the carpet and hastily dialled Iain's number, just as the knock I had dreaded sounded from over my right shoulder …

A ringing telephone breaks the silence, intruding on the quiet of the uncluttered cottage. At the third ring Iain reaches across from the kitchen's serving hatch, bubbles of washing up liquid drip from his bare arms onto the highly polished surface of his sideboard.

"Hello ... oh aye, how are ye? ... bloody hell ... right ... aye ... that's a turn up then ... when dae ye think? ... aye ... bloody hell ... aye, so soon? ... a surprise is it? ... well, that it will be, ye ken? ... aye, grand, bloody grand ... the more the merrier, that's what Ah say ... aye ... great, bloody great ... 'sa big step mind ... aye, aye ..."

The disjointed and distinctly one-sided conversation continues for a few minutes. "Mum's the word ... aye, see ye then ..."

Hanging up, Iain whistles through clenched teeth and, with a huge grin spread right across his face, returns to his washing up.

'... Beep, beep, beep.' "Shit, great, bloody engaged, Iain don't do this to me."

The knock on the door reverberated in my head, seeming to vibrate through the whole house. A light sheen of sweat had broken out across my forehead, my arms and palms felt damp and clammy despite the coolness of the day.

"This is ridiculous, I'm behaving like a stupid schoolgirl. It may not even be him. Even if it is, he might just be a little eccentric, not a bloody maniac mass-murderer."

I took a deep breath and made my way to the hall, strode to the front door and swung it open, my best, most friendly Isle-of-Skye-hospitality-smile, shining out in welcome.

The porch was empty, as was the gravel path and in an instant I relaxed, ready to shut the door as soon as I heard the flat-four burble of the Subaru's engine start up. Relief, sweet relief, ridiculous and stupid at the same time.

For a fraction of a second, my smile shone out genuine and sincere.

"Ah, Mr Perkins?"

I must have jumped a foot in the air. "Ahhh, strewth, sorry, you made me jump. Thought I'd missed you," adding as an after thought "... I was on the phone."

The face that peered around the porch frame, leaned further into the open door, followed by broad shoulders and a stocky frame. A tight blue tee-shirt moulded itself around a well muscled chest and thick set legs strained the material of faded denim jeans. Black, well shined footwear, like trimmed down motor cycle boots sank into the gravel. Blonde, short-cropped hair, thick and shiny, combed forward, modern looking and practical, framed an incredibly square face. A smile that was neither pleasant or welcoming showed straight, movie-star teeth. Muscles bulging in his angular jaw looked like they could propel their pearly whites through a teak coffee table without chipping the enamel.

The eyes though. 'Lizard's eyes' was the first thing I thought. Cruel, ruthless, uncaring.

Mrs N was right.

His voice was cultured, calming, relaxed and confident; it cut straight through to my marrow. In an instant my core temperature dropped a degree and I was chilled rigid.

"David Salt … I wrote to you." His thick and strangely dark eyebrows rose in question, framing steely blue eyes that did indeed seem to be hiding a secret.

"You got my letter didn't you?"

I couldn't answer; my power of speech seemed to have given up on me. I imagined my jaw working, trying to form words, moving spastically but with no sound to accompany its movements.

"Sorry Mr Perkins, I've obviously startled you, I do apologise," a pause and yet another non-smile, "should I call back at a better time?" He continued, giving me time to gather my wits "But you see, I'm only here for a few more days and I *really* would like to thank you for the way your work has brightened my home."

At that point, it could have gone either way, I'm sure. Speak or faint, dead cold on the floor, spread on the gravel of my path. I felt a strange whooshing vibration as though blood was filling my empty veins and realised I'd been holding my breath.

"Sorry, yes, yes you did startle me a little. Please, do come in, I apologise for my rudeness."

My hand was outstretched in greeting, an automatic reaction that I would rather have not bothered with; training I suppose. I must have shaken ten thousand hands in my lifetime and felt I could tell a lot from a handshake. Sweaty palms; weak grip; strong, crushing, vice-like pressure; dry skin; rough workmen's hands; slim well manicured fingers of well-to-do ladies; oil stained skin of car mechanics; single firm pump; overlong vigorous shaking that made me want to pull away; and, of course the good old 'double hander'.

David Salt's grip was firm but not overly so, his skin was well cared for; soft but again, not overly. There was no pumping or double handed grip, no roughness, clamminess or sweaty, stickiness.

The day *was* buffeted by a cool north westerly, but his skin wasn't just cold; it was like *ice*. The touch of his fingers, as they closed around mine, was like plunging my hand into an ice bucket. I tried not to, but couldn't help glancing down, almost expecting to see frost forming over my skin.

It was like shaking hands with the dead.

I turned away, desperate to relieve the dreadful effects of those cold empty eyes.

"Please, come in, come in," my voice was surprisingly calm and level. The front door clicked shut as I entered the kitchen and I fought back a feeling of being trapped; cornered like a wild animal at the mercy of a hunter. I hadn't wanted to let him in but the offer sprang from my lips in an involuntary outburst.

Fear *did* that to me. In a tight, awkward spot my mouth often ran away with itself and went into overdrive. Later I would run back through the conversation and, always, I would think, "Why didn't I say this?" or "Damn, I wish I'd said that." As I placed the kettle on the gas ring, doing the 'hospitality' bit, while wishing I was anywhere but in the kitchen, being watched by Mr Salt, the thought that I could have just said I was on my way out sprang to mind. Too late. At least I could part-remedy it.

"I haven't got long Mr Salt …"

"Please, it's David"

"Sorry, David, I have to go into Broadford in a little while." I risked a brief glance and was rewarded with another non-smile, hastily painted onto his face. "Delivery you see. I have to take some paintings in. Mrs N's running short."

David's eyes swung around my kitchen, examining apparently everything in view. His stare was uncomfortably direct and piercing. There was a mockery there, a sly knowing look, like sarcasm. His eyes, in fact his whole expression, seemed to be saying "The joke's on you mate, you don't know it yet, but the joke *is* on you." It may have been hidden behind the glossy charade of his cheesy, salesman's grin and confident, politician's demeanour; but it was there, no question about it.

At the time I felt it quite clearly; it was as if he was indulging himself, playing a part. *Taking the piss.*

"How long are you here for David?" The kettle was coming to the boil and I'd taken out a couple of my best china mugs, even though I hadn't asked him if he wanted a drink. I was running on auto-pilot, shielding myself from an unpleasant situation by undertaking a mundane, every day task. I was playing for time. I didn't care what his answer was, I just needed something to say.

"Now, that is magnificent."

I pulled away from the work surface and looked into the lounge where his voice had come from. He was standing by the coffee table, hands in his pockets, taking in the picture over my fireplace. From where I stood I could see his head moving from side to side, from one aspect of the scene to another. He looked as though he was watching the world's smallest tennis match.

"Ah, thank you. Yes, that's my favourite. Couldn't sell it, I, err, I just loved it too much really. Didn't want to part with it."

As I moved closer to the lounge he continued.

"It's the light you now. It's captured *perfectly*," he gestured with his hands, swirling them in front of the picture, "the way it picks out the detail on the mountains, every crag and peak. Marvellous, marvellous." He moved closer, peering at the shoreline. If he'd worn glasses, he would have glanced over the top of them, I'm sure. "This shoreline," he shot a look briefly back at me "the detail, the rocks, driftwood, everything. Even the way the waves are lapping at the gravel, pulling back, then surging forward." his arms spread wide and he shook his head. *"Would* you sell it Mr Perkins? I know you said you didn't want to part with it, but, well, forgive me, everyone has a price, surely?"

He delivered his pitch without taking his eyes from the picture. As if he didn't want it to leave his sight. I was beginning to feel a little embarrassed, not to say creepy.

"I'm sorry David, but I really ..."

"£5,000. I'll write you a cheque now." He smiled at me and this time, there was a difference, a degree of sincerity.

"Well ... I don't know what to say. Urrmm, it's a very generous offer, really, it is, but, well, it's not the money."

"£10,000?"

"David, really, honestly, its not the money. Phew, £10,000, that *is* a lot of money." I was tempted. Ten grand for one painting? For a few seconds the figure bounced around my head and all I saw was an obviously very wealthy art lover; Christ, my biggest fan. But then my mind focused back on that dead handshake and cruel, piercing blue eyes that shone out nothing but snide, somehow dangerous insincerity.

"No, really. Thank you, I really *am* incredibly flattered, but it's not for sale. Thank you anyway." I moved to go back into the kitchen, "Coffee?" There was no response and I turned back to the lounge.

"Mr Salt, David, would you like a coffee?"

"No, thank you, I'm fine at present." He never drew his eyes from the picture. He stood, stooped and shrunken. His voice seemed to have developed a tiny tremor, as though filled with dreadful sadness, then, as I watched, he appeared to grow and swell, filling his frame back to its previous solidity.

He turned and pierced me with the flashing blue of his eyes. "You know, I'm used to being able to buy what I want. Your high standards and morals are ..." he considered his choice or words "... commendable, they truly are. If that is your final answer, and you do not wish to 'phone a friend', could I put another option to you?"

He made a joke. Coming from him it was like being offered a cuddle from a crocodile. I didn't smile.

"Would you accept a commission? Not the same scene, you would never reproduce such a work as this and I would always find myself comparing it to the original. To this ... this ... masterpiece. No, another scene, but from the top of these mountains, looking from them, not towards them." His eyebrows raised, dark flashes over empty blueness. "What do you say? Will you take my commission?"

That was a completely different proposition.

Selling the painting was never going to be an option, it meant too much to me and the strange thing was, I didn't really know why. It hadn't followed a particularly memorable climb or sprung for my memory of a holiday with Rachel. I'd parked the car and sat on the shore, sketched the basic scene, took half a dozen photos to try and capture at least some degree of the colour and atmosphere, then started work on it back at the cottage. I was out of the car, for perhaps an hour (it had been a cold day and a stiff breeze had come in from the North Atlantic that blew me back to the warmth of the car a lot more quickly than I'd planned). It somehow seemed to work. The light *was* good. The movement of the sea on the shore, something I'd always found difficult, had just painted itself naturally onto the canvas.

I forced myself to look into his eyes. They fixed me with their icy blueness and I was transfixed like a rabbit at the mercy of a particularly sly fox. Another, surreal thought flashed into my mind that seemed totally at odds to the situation. There was a beauty there; not a traditional beauty, but one that was borne from a limitless depth of power and control. He seemed to ooze wealth and a strange blend of ruthless charm. Of course I'd take his commission. No mater how he unnerved, terrified, and repulsed me, there was a dangerous fascination to him. Something, hinted

214

at, veiled beneath shifting layers of sly cruelty, that created an incredible interest difficult to deny.

"Of course I'll take a commission. You give me an idea of what you want, I'll run through a selection of photos from my collection and I'm sure we can come up with something."

"Is there any easy way of getting to the ridge?" He patted his left knee, "Rugby accident from my twenties, you see. It doesn't take particularly well to climbing."

I didn't, at first, see where this line of questioning was going.

"I suppose the pass between Bruach na Frithe and Am Bastier is the easiest. The scree at the top of Fionn Choire is a bit gruelling, but not too bad."

His eyes seemed to sparkle with an inner excitement at my words. "What's the view like from there?"

"Well, on clear day, it's one of the finest on the ridge." I counted the aspects of the view off on my fingers. "Firstly, the whole of the southern end is visible, Bannerdich, the Inaccessible Pinnacle, Sgurr Alisdair. Then to the left, Gillean is prominent, swinging round you've got Glen Sligachan, Marsco, Garb-Bheinn and then Blaven, my personal favourite." I paused, expecting a question as to why, but when none came, I continued. "Down the middle you've got the whole of Harta Corrie, then Sgurr na-Stri right at the far south. After that, you're in the sea and, on a really clear day, Ben Nevis is just visible, fifty odd miles away."

He looked at me with a strange mixture of what appeared to be confusion and pity. The sort of look reserved for a friend who's extolling the virtues of fine wine, when it's becoming clear that quantity, not quality is the real issue.

"Take me there Andy, show me this view and we can decide a scene for my painting."

"David, really, it's not a good idea. For someone with a dodgy knee, it's a hell of an undertaking. The path, like any in the Cuillin is horrendous, rubbly, scree. I ache after I've been up there and I know most of the ridge first hand. *And* I'm very fit. I wouldn't be happy."

At first he looked totally crestfallen, his piercing blue eyes taking on the doleful sadness of a scalded puppy. Then, as I watched, the steely hardness returned, run through with a streak of anger. I thought he was about to explode, or at least withdraw his offer of a commission and storm out of the house. Instead, he turned from me towards the painting again and appeared to take a huge breath.

I imagined him counting to ten, warding off his obvious rage, trying to return to some normality.

"Fine Andy," he spoke to the painting, "I understand, I really do. Tell you what ... I'll pay you £1000, minimum for your work, regardless and up to £10,000 if you capture even a portion of this stunning example's quality." He swung back towards me, no trace of 'puppy' in those eyes. He continued, "When are you likely to be up there again?"

I told him of my planned traverse of the whole ridge in a week's time.

"So you'll be there next ... Tuesday evening?"

"I'll hopefully sleep up there over Tuesday night, so yes I'll be there then. I'll leave Wednesday morning, over Gillean and into Glen Sligachan by lunchtime."

He obviously spotted some concern in my face at his questioning. "Don't worry, I'm not gong to suggest meeting you. Just capture that view, on camera, but, more importantly, in here," he tapped his temple, "that's the thing. You have a wonderful talent Andy. A wonderful talent. Capture it, breath in the scene, the atmosphere ... then, produce me another masterpiece."

Capture the scene? The atmosphere? Breathe it in?

This was the point I knew Iain was right. David was a nutter. I just painted scenes. I wasn't one for analysing art, mine or anyone else's. If it looked nice, looked *real*, I usually liked it. I agreed, if only to keep the peace. He *was* paying me a thousand quid minimum; I thought I ought to humour him.

"OK David, you've got yourself a deal. I'll paint you the scene that greets me from Bruach Na Frithe next week."

I smiled, working hard to look sincere and added "Let's hope the weather's good eh?"

David stepped towards me, icy, dead hand extended to seal the deal, "Warts and all Andy, if it's cloudy, so be it. I want that scene. I want you to imprint it in your memory and reproduce it on your canvas." His hand met mine, that same deadness that shocked me at the front door, a brief, barely noticed shake, then solid unmoving grip.

"Remember the scene Andy. Imprint it as if it were to be your last."

I had to drop my stare. It felt like he was slicing into my brain and raping every decent thought I'd ever had.

"Sheeeet! Never?"

"I'm telling you Iain, his handshake, Jesus ... I've never known anything like it." I shook my head and took a very large drag on my cigarette, the third since David had left. "Like the dead; cold and icy. Made my skin creep."

"Aye, Ah told ye so. Ye would'nae listen. The shite's a bloody nutter ... nae right in the heid."

We were sitting in Iain's garden, overlooking the bay and then onwards, towards the southern tip of Raasay. The mainland was now bathed in glorious late afternoon sunshine that reflected the golden browns and greens of its heather clad mountains. Cloud still capped the highest peaks but the light was crystal clear and dazzlingly bright. Wester Ross would be dappled; moving patches of light and shade dancing over its hugely impressive mountains and glens.

I'd watched David's Subaru make its five point turn in the cramped space of the track and returned his wave as he'd gunned the accelerator and spattered gravel from his tyres, watched as the shiny green paintwork had glinted sunshine for two hundred yards until it disappeared, over the rise and, thankfully, out of view. Within a minute, I was knocking on Iain's door, having broken with tradition and locked my porch before jogging the hundred yards to his house. The action of turning the key was as natural as leaving the door unlocked had been for the past two years. For the first time since arriving on Skye, I felt scared, unsafe. And the feeling itself unnerved me.

"What Ah can'nae understand though Andy, is, if he scairt the shite out o' ye so bad, why ye agreed tae tak on his commission?" Iain extended his hands towards me, spread wide, palms upturned, "Why did ye no just tell him ye did'nae tak em?"

It was a valid question and one that I struggled to find an answer for. The thought of declining his offer seemed impossible. It wasn't the money, Christ I didn't need it after all. The bank account was looking good, my investments were doing OK, the cottages were pretty much fully booked all season and I was selling my artwork with scary regularity.

It was his manner, his strong determination and charming, yet forceful nature. I couldn't have refused.

I exhaled a long stream of smoke and watched it curl away on the now depleted breeze, stared at the last inch of cigarette and flipped it neatly over the fence. My shrug was enough, I couldn't have explained to Iain anyway. Couldn't have told of the feeling akin to being snared and helpless. Rachel would have understood. At a push, Al would have grasped my meaning, then called me a nancy-boy or an old girl's blouse.

Iain? Well, I just couldn't imagine him coming to terms with such fearful emotion. Such weakness.

"Ah, whatever." I looked across at him, his thick grey hair and wind tanned face. He smiled. It was the sort of smile my father would have given in the same situation. "Hopefully, I won't have to see him until the painting's done anyway. He's leaving in a couple of days - thank God. You *were* right you know. I tell you mate he makes my skin creep."

"Aye, nasty basturt." He was one of the few people I knew that could deliver such a phrase with a smile on his face. "Anyway, Ah've had a wee bit o' good news today ..."

"Aye?"

"'Sa surprise."

"Hmm?"

"Ah said, it's a surprise ... a secret."

My eyebrows raised in question.

"Din'nae press me laddy, Ah hold ma secrets like ma whisky. Ye'll find out soon enough."

I *didn't* press him, knew it wouldn't do any good. He was right, he could hold a secret, a confidence, to the grave.

"Fancy taking a rod up to Loch Fada tomorrow? See if we can catch a brownie or two?"

"On the Sabbath? Yer a bloody philistine so ye are."

"Sorry I forgot." I honestly didn't know what day it was. So much seemed to have happened.

"See you later for a dram or two?"

"Aye, that ye will. 'Bout eight?"

"Great, see you then."

I said goodbye and strolled back up to the house. My eyes kept flicking back along the road then up to the rise in front of me, expecting the rumble of a Subaru to break the quiet. Try as I might I couldn't shake a feeling of being watched.

A really sharp pair of eyes would have spotted, high on the hillside behind the cottage, a dark shadow of green squatting beneath stunted, wind-sculpted bushes. Watching and waiting.

Biding time.

A tiny touch of blue

Despite the events of the day, I managed to do another painting in the early evening. Another view from the window, similar to the morning's work but only in content, not atmosphere. The light was completely different; the harsh, stormy quality of earlier had mellowed into a pleasant golden evening. The sky was still flecked with clouds, pushed along briskly from the northwest, but the mainland horizon was shimmering; reflecting the sinking sun in all its glory.

In June, I still had another five hours of light at 7 p.m. Well, three hours of light and a further two of half-light as the day hung on, clinging to the sun until the last minute. A handful of hours later, the dark grey of the night, still with traces of glow in the northeast, would begin to change to another period of half-hearted darkness. The glow would develop and strengthen, flooding the land and sea with pastel shades until, by 2.30 a.m. another day would stretch, yawn and burst over the land.

An insomniac's paradise, no need to sit and mope over lost sleep with only darkness for company - in the summer at least. The winter months were a different story.

Downstairs, I emptied a packet of nuts into a locally made bowl with a painting of the Cuillin in the bottom, opened a bottle of Tamdhu and retrieved a couple of crystal glasses from the dishwasher.

A large pan of chilli bubbled on the stove and a couple of bowls warmed in the oven. A pack of cards sat on the table next to the whisky, ready to be shuffled and dealt later.

I walked over to the window and watched the evening develop, still unable to shake the feeling of being watched. Ever since returning to the house I'd found myself constantly looking at the doors or out of the windows, glancing over my shoulder, not knowing what I was expecting to see. "Relax Andy, relax," I told myself and sat in the chair facing the fireplace.

Over it, the picture hung, silently filling the chimney breast.

I became the watcher.

I let my eyes sweep over its rippled peaks of oil from peak to shore, from sea to land; not really looking.

Watching.

I allowed my vision to blur, as if nodding into sleep. Relaxing , at last.

David had been fascinated by it. It *was* good, but £10,000? Never in a month of Sundays was it worth that much. Perhaps £500 on a good day, £750 or £1,000 on a *really* good day. What did he see in it? What could possibly have stirred him that much to offer such a ridiculous figure?

Thinking back, his manner had been strange from the start, from first entering the house. Something, *something* had not been right. On reflection I got the distinct feeling that he'd known what was going to be hanging over the fire. He'd been awe-struck by the picture, but not *surprised*. It was as if he'd seen it before and was merely renewing old acquaintances. Ridiculous, but still the feeling persisted. He'd known, somehow he'd known.

He was right of course, the light was fabulous; the sun sinking behind the tops of the jagged peaks looked almost surreal and I'd captured its reflective quality on the scree and heather exquisitely. Compared to my commercial work, the prints and watercolours hanging in Mrs N's shop, it was in a different league. It held more depth, more detail. Like a heavy, plum-scented burgundy after a glass of cheap, sparkling perry; a connoisseur's painting, one to be appreciated rather than just something that was simply - *nice*.

Sitting there, caressing it with my gaze, I thought I understood why David had been so taken with it. He'd hung every wall of his house with my shop bought pictures. Scenes produced in half an hour, or an hour, simple watercolours of simple landscapes, pleasing to look at but often lacking depth; produced to sell, to titillate and lighten the soul.

He'd not been sipping at a glass of Lambrusco; he'd been bathing in a cellar full of the stuff for the last three weeks.

Slightly right of centre, the pointed peak of Sgurr na Stri (the Peak of Strife) poked its way into the sky. Improbably angular, it dominates the coastline, not quite breaking the horizon formed by the main ridge several miles beyond. In Cuillin terms it's a mere minion, a baby amongst monsters and despite its impressive profile, it reaches no more than half way up the flanks of its distant brethren. But its position, so much closer to the viewpoint, exaggerates its size. I struggled over the composition for days, sketching then re-sketching, knowing that it lacked the size and dominance of the distant giants but unable to get it quite right. My brain kept telling me it looked too big, but my photographs said otherwise.

An enlightening lesson in perspective, one might say.

At the base of this most Alpine of hills sits 'The Bad Step'. So named because, although part of the coastal path that I would follow in a week's time, it presents quite a barrier to the walker. A big step up onto a huge block of rock then a heave onto a crack that runs at forty five degrees along a slanting slab. A slip from the crack would propel the careless over a lip and then through thirty feet of open space, straight into the sea. It couldn't really be seen from Elgol but I'd represented it by a small lighter square of sandy coloured paint.

I was happy with it; it looked about right, how the slab would look, had it actually been visible. Artist's licence if you like.

I stared at it. It looked different somehow.

Everything around me blurred as though I was running at high speed through a multicoloured tunnel.

Something.

I knew the picture intimately. If someone had chipped off the paint of a brush stroke, I would know. It had taken over four months of hard graft to produce. Four months of squinting, staring, constant appraisal. Four months of headache and heartache, to the point where, on the final brush stroke, I sat heavily in the one comfy chair that furnishes my studio and heaved a huge, tearful sigh of relief.

Something. Something *different*.

There was a tiny indistinct splash of colour at the top right hand corner of the sandy coloured slab - a barely discernible speck of blue.

I got off the chair and stepped up close, hand extended, hoping that I could simply brush off a speck of cotton but knowing, illogically, that it was paint.

From the beach at Elgol, the slab of rock would be three miles away over Loch Scavaig. In clear weather, with perfect vision, a person standing there would just about be visible. *Just about*. With a good pair of binoculars, or a five hundred millimetre camera lens, one could perhaps make out whether they were wearing a hat or see the wave of an arm across the water.

With my face a few inches from its rippled surface I could make out a minuscule touch of blue, no bigger than an exclamation mark, without the dot, in a book of fine print. I'd never noticed it before, and would have put my house on the fact that *I* hadn't put it there.

I ran upstairs and dragged open the right hand drawer of my desk. Then, with my magnifying glass in hand, ran down, jumped the last three steps and charged back into the lounge.

I took a deep breath and peered through the lens. There, amongst the swirls and ridges of oil, nestling between them as comfortably as a trickle of water between ridges of sand, was a tiny figure. Although no more than the merest flick of blue and brown from a brush made up of half a dozen bristles at most, the intention was crystal clear.

A figure, a young girl almost certainly, standing atop the rock slab wearing a blue dress and with long, light-brown hair.

I pulled away, looking again without the glass; still there but indistinct. My analogy of a strand of cotton was about right.

I put the glass back and the figure appeared.

"Did I do that - without knowing? Could I have caught the surface with a tiny flick of paint and not realised?"

Somehow, I doubted it.

"I didn't paint it. It's as new to me as it is to you."

Iain was hunched over the magnifying glass, face pressed close to the surface of the picture, one eye closed, squinting at the image framed within the circle of shiny stainless steel. He held his breath, so as not to fog the glass and turned his head to one side to exhale and grab a mouthful of whisky from the glass in his left hand. Then, as he had been doing for the last few minutes turned back and continued his scrutinising.

"It can'nae be just a wee accidental brush stroke. It's nae possible. Too detailed, too delicate." He shook his head, straightened with a grimace and audible crackle of joints, stretched his spine backwards, hands on hips, sighed and continued.

"Its nae an accident laddy," he said and raised an eyebrow, "sure you weren't a wee bit pissed when ye finished the picture?"

"No Iain, I may have been mildly hungover if I'd been with you the previous night, but no I wasn't pissed. I never drink while I'm painting. It doesn't mix."

He shrugged again, taking another mouthful of whisky, "It can'nae be … Ah din'nae ken it. Ah'm nae a painter, as ye ken, but Ah can'nae, simply can'nae believe that's an accidental slip o' a wee brush."

There was silence for a few minutes, both of us stood holding our glasses, taking occasional sips and staring at the painting. The quiet stretched on and on, seeming to fill every space in the room until it became uncomfortable. Both of us knew what the next question was, but neither of us wanted to ask it. So the awkward, silent atmosphere continued, stretching onwards until it seemed like neither of us would ever speak again.

I braved it. "Who did it then? If we both agree that it couldn't have been an accident, that I was sober when I painted it and that you didn't sneak in and do it when I wasn't looking, who did it?"

"Ye can probably guess ma thoughts on that. It does'nae tek a genius as far as Ah'm concerned ... that nutter, that weirdo, David Salt. He's an art lover or so he reckons an he's been up here all week, while ye were at Al's." A spark of inspiration lit his face and he continued, excited, "The paint, is it old? Ah mean, has it been there long? Can ye tell?"

I smiled despite myself. "It's dry Iain, that's about it. The whole thing's not that old, so It's not possible to tell."

"OK ... OK ... so, have ye never noticed it before? Obviously not, or ye'd have told me then would'nae ye?"

"I agree, I think, but, well, in all fairness mate, I don't look at it that often. Not for any longer than a passing glance anyway. It's only since David took such an interest in it today, that I actually sat down and had a good look. That's when I noticed our *addition*."

Another period of silent reflection spread out around us, each deep in our own thoughts. Sips of drink broke the procession of shrugs and sighs.

"Bare with me a minute" I said and, placing my glass on the kitchen table as I passed it, jogged up the stairs two at a time.

We'd finished our third game of Crib. Iain had taken £3 from me, having won every one and we were halfway up the pegging board for a fourth time, at least he was. I was still near the bottom, getting trounced again.

"Fancy a game of snap?" I asked as he played his card and moved another three points up the board. He smiled and told me to play; my luck would turn.

I glanced at the picture in the lounge. Even through the alcohol-tinted vision that I was now looking, I could still see the tiny fleck of blue standing out clearly on the sandy brown rock. It seemed to mock me, taunting me that someone had violated my work. No matter how tiny an adjustment, it *had* been tampered with. It was still an impressive piece, still my best work yet and would continue to hold pride of place over my fireplace. The image though, was spoiled. I would never be truly able to look at the picture without seeing that tiny fleck of blue and the somehow tragic image of that small girl, alone at the base of the hill. Even though I had hidden all visible traces of her with a flick of sandy brown paint, I would always see her.

We never spoke of it again.

Making plans

By Wednesday, the wind had blown in and blown out again, bringing a balmy warmth, crystal clear blue sky and temperatures hovering in the mid seventies. I was sitting in the front garden in shorts and a tee shirt. Spread out in front of me, on the picnic table, was my Cuillin map. Next to that, my guidebook, detailing the route across the ridge and the technical bits I could expect.

I knew the ridge very well. Even the bits I hadn't got first hand knowledge of were burned into my memory from the books I'd read and pictures I'd studied. I could have left the map at least, at home, but, old habits die hard and, I *could* get into trouble or suffer bad weather and have to come down. Doesn't hurt to be too careful.

I was concerned about the weight of my pack. Pretty much all of the uphill sections could be 'free climbed' fairly easily and safely, but there were several pitches that had to be abseiled unless I took a route round them so, other than carrying a full set of climbing gear, I would have to do just that.

Food was as basic and light. On the table were four packs of dehydrated curry - chicken, lamb, beef and vegetable. They *all* tasted of chicken, except the vegetable which tasted like nothing on Earth. I would keep this in case of a fourth, forced night out. Also spread out in front of me were a dozen small sachets of fruit drink to be mixed with water and heated; vacuum-packed cheese and biscuits (four packs); sixteen mars bars and two packets of cigarettes.

Just the essentials.

My stove was a tiny and altogether flimsy looking aluminium affair, but it worked well enough. I thought two small gas canisters should be enough. Sleeping bag and half length mat, one mug, two small billie cans, a spoon, pen-knife, two one litre bottles of water to be refilled en-route, two lighters, half a dozen sticking plasters, a small roll of bandage, a tube of antiseptic and my camera. Stuffed into my spare pair of socks were three thirty-five millimetre films. The camera and film were extra weight that I could have done without; a luxury really, but I'd be visiting places and seeing views for the first time. If a few scenes found their way into my painting repertoire, their weight would be justified.

Anyway I had to keep David happy if nothing else.

I was determined not to allow the pressure of having to produce a painting for him spoil my trip. It was for me. More than this, the whole high level scramble amongst some of Scotland's most serious mountains was for Rachel.

She would have wanted me to do it.

The afternoon was really warm. A cloudless, infinitely blue and limitless sky spread from horizon to horizon, dotted here and there with lazily soaring sea birds. The tide was full and, in the surrounding silence, the lap-lap-lap of waves slapping on rocks drifted on the breeze.

Rachel's bench squatted on the little rise overlooking the gently moving ocean wrapped in a hazy, shimmering heat. The highly varnished surface of the oak glinted sunshine from its corners and for a moment my spirits slumped and I was swamped in melancholy.

A conversation from years gone by ran through my head but, for its clarity, it could have happened five minutes before.

Mr Jefcock had called me in to see him on the premise of taking a little investment advice. The final sorting of his wife's estate, she having died six months earlier.

In his late sixties, he had the look of a man who had shrunk into himself. Simply dissolved back into his frame once his life-long partner had finally succumbed to her fourth stroke in as many years. A faded, sepia wedding photo stood on the fireplace amongst assorted bric-a-brac and photos of friends and family. It depicted a six foot youngster, full of pride and expectations, smiling with his arm wrapped round his new bride. A full head of dark hair, wavy and thick, curled from under his RAF peaked cap.

I couldn't help thinking that the majority of his six inches height loss had happened in the months leading up to and following his wife's death.

He spoke for over an hour. All the time, I nodded and agreed with him, while he struggled to maintain some degree of control. At every mention of his wife, his voice would crack and splinter. The whole conversation was undertaken on a knife-edge of undulating emotion. His eyes would redden and large tears would spring from their corners, rolling down his old cheeks, tracing the lines towards the corners of his mouth.

He never apologised for his outbursts and I never acknowledged them, simply kept up my professional, dark-suited image, looking away at opportune moments, allowing him to wipe his eyes.

"You work all your life you see Andy, as a man, it's *all* for your family. A man on his own, well, he'd get by with the basics you know; a knife and fork, plate, mug, table and chair. But when you're married, it's *all* for the family. All your life you work for your family, working for your retirement, gathering together the bits, the things to make you both comfortable ..." he had fixed me with his stare, peering through red rimmed, swimming eyes and, for a brief moment, despite the over-spilling tears, I could see his old steel. Then he slumped, another millimetre of his 'presence' disappearing, deflating "... and it's all for what? I don't need anything, I'm all right, you know. I've got a cup and saucer, plate and fork. All your life, and then ... well, then your life's over."

I remember leaving and thinking that I'd seen the man for the last time, that I'd see a report in the local paper, tucked away on page twelve or thirteen saying that he'd killed himself. He was a suicide waiting to happen, waiting for the right reason, for the right level, the *critical* level, of despair.

At the time, I couldn't imagine how bad it had to get before reaching that level of hopelessness - nothing could be that bad, ever. There was always hope. Always.

From my bench seat, looking out over a flat calm ocean, I thought back to the previous year's episode at Kilt Rock. Remembered the stomach churning drop of hundreds of feet to the rocks and pounding surf below. I thought of the dreadful weight of utter despair in my heart and the wind blowing past my ears, mocking me, taunting me to jump; "Go on, let go, you've nothing - nothing to lose, nothing to gain."

My eyes focused on Rachel's bench and a smile creased my face, forming lines along which a single pair of salty tears crept.

I still harboured the odd pang of guilt at my life and its comfort. The cottage, the views, the money, the laid back, carefree manner in which I filled my days. At times when it bubbled to the surface, when the guilt of my good fortune stopped me dead in my tracks, I thought of Rachel and the price she had paid. It always helped, always subdued the terrible, tearing feelings, that I was doing what we'd ultimately wanted to do. She would have wanted it. No doubt there, guilt maybe, but not *doubt*. I would have wanted the same for her.

We spoke of it often, "If we win the lottery ..."

Well, I hadn't won the lottery; I'd lost my wife.

I packed my rucksack, methodically ticking every item off my mental list as it disappeared into each pocket and crevice. Laid out on the table, there looked to be a huge amount of stuff; far too much to go into my forty litre pack, let alone be lugged across thirty miles of incredibly rough and uncompromising mountain terrain. Once stuffed into the green fabric that would be its home for the trip, I was surprised that there was a little pocket of space at the top.

Immediately, I began to think of things to fill it with. My binoculars, a half-bottle of whisky to sup on the ridge while I watched the sunset or, possibly, a small jar of coffee? All highly desirable, useful items, but not my choice.

When I wound my way up to bed that night, four full days before I was due to set off, my pack, boots and sticks sat expectantly at the foot of the stairs. The little, organised collection would serve to excite and remind me as I counted down the days to my departure on Monday morning.

Each time I passed, I'd think of the fresh air and vertigo filled hours ahead of me and of the freedom at being alone amongst the rock and scree of my favourite landscape. Most of all, I would think of Rachel and how she would have fussed and worried over me, constantly going through my planned route, timings and, most importantly, re-assessing her own, meticulously planned, hand-written lists.

I was pleased that a little part of her would be with me. The space at the top of my sack had been just enough for 'Floppy', a threadbare purple rabbit with only half the normal allocation of eyes and a tuft of white thread where his tail used to be

'Floppy' sat on top of the rucksack, watching over me through his one eye, head cocked over at an angle, one ear hanging limply behind him, the other folded over on top of his purple head.

He looked somehow solemn and forlorn, but it was me that wiped a tear from my cheek as I turned off the light, rolled over and dreamt of high places.

The journey begins

High on the cliff overlooking Loch Scavaig, I hopped onto a boulder at the side of the path and, shielding my eyes from the early morning sun, waved a final farewell to Iain. He was sitting on the bonnet of my TVR looking like an ageing rock star in dark glasses and tatty jeans. I made a mental note to warn him about scratching the paintwork, smiled to myself as I stepped back to the heat-cracked ground and strolled off into the hazy distance.

Way to my left, on the far side of the shimmering calmness of the Loch, the saw-toothed ridge of the Cuillin pierced the fabulous, blue of the June dawn. With not a cloud in sight and the chill of the previous night burning rapidly away, I felt like a thousand tonnes of rubble had been taken from my shoulders. OK, I hadn't had much to worry about anyway, but still, the feeling of freedom, of care-free unashamed abandon was indescribable. I felt as though my feet were skimming from rock to rock, barely touching the ground between steps, the weight of my pack the only thing stopping me from floating away.

My route snaked its way in front of me, carving through the heather and gorse to the lower slopes of Blaven's South ridge. It seemed an interminable distance, but I knew it was simply a combination of the clear air and the way my eyes followed the glen towards Sligachan, fourteen miles away.

Choosing a focal point on the path where it dropped below a rise, I picked up the pace and walked.

At the head of the Loch lies Camusanary, a remote bay complete with white painted bothy and lumbering Highland Cattle. A river runs in at its western corner and, surrounded by some of the most remote scenery imaginable, it looked utterly serene. Blaven, to the east looked black and foreboding in comparison and I found it difficult to imagine that, in three days, all being well, anyone picking their way along the path I was now on, would be able to see me trekking back, down its steep flanks.

The bothy, three miles distant, reflected the golden beams of the sun and seemed to glow; a stone haven in an oasis of shimmering green.

Within an hour, with the sun pouring molten heat straight down from the perfect blue above, I turned left, and began to drop towards the bay. As I approached the bothy, a couple of hikers burst out of the front door. Dressed in underwear alone, the female of the pair screamed, dodging past me. Her male partner, resplendent in 'Simpsons' boxers, gave chase and, after a brief but noisy struggle, deposited a bucket of water over her before slipping on the grass and lying sprawled, wracked with laughter. The girl, dripping from head to foot, her underwear now pleasingly see-through, stood laughing and shivering at the same time. I shouted a 'Good morning' and trudged on.

A short while later, as I was rounding the headland and glanced back for a last look at Blaven, glistening ripples spread outwards twenty yards off the beach as the water fighters splashed like children in the shallows.

Blaven was in full profile, black against the blue of the sky and I followed its ridge to the summit, an airy crest three thousand feet above me.

Blaven was my goal. The whole ridge was a fabulous extravagance of unashamed pleasure, but Blaven was Rachel's place. No matter how I kidded myself, no matter my self-proclaimed reasons, this whole trip was for her. Whether it was to exorcise her ghost or just because *she would have wanted me to do it* - I didn't know; hadn't thought about it enough. All I knew was that she figured in my reasoning - in a big way. Perhaps I would get closer to the truth, closer to my true feelings during the next few days.

By 10.00 a.m. I'd deposited my pack and sat on the top edge of the Bad Step smoking my first cigarette of the day. I'd already guzzled half a litre of water and moisture dripped off my chin as I watched the first influx of tourists disembarking from the Bella Jane for their couple of hours in the great outdoors. A middle aged lady in high heels and tight skirt tottered up the broken rocks of the path, her handbag swinging in time with her attempts to keep upright. I stifled a smile and shook my head.

"It's up to her," I muttered and shouldered my pack.
I passed her after five minutes of walking. She was sitting on a rock at the side of the path arguing with her partner about how rough it was. In one hand she held her left shoe, the heel dangled at an angle, held on by a strip of glue, victim of a wayward boulder.

"Ninety pounds these cost, you should have told me it was going to be like this ..."

She was still gesticulating at her sullen other half when I skipped over the final rise and Loch Coruisk spread its grandeur before me.

Coruisk is the jewel in the Cuillin's crown. In different weather it holds different charms; its mood changes to suit the conditions. Under the brilliance of the blue sky it seemed not to exist. Someone had replaced it with a huge mirror that reflected the soaring mountains in perfect symmetry. At the far northern end of its glass flat surface, a single, solitary cloud hung in watery reflection. More mist than cloud in the true sense, it looked like a single puff of steam from a train of yesteryear. I watched, spellbound as it rose, its edges breaking away and merging with the clear fresh air.

In a minute or two its was gone, I simply felt privileged to have seen it and to have captured it in a couple of frames of film.

I planned to detour along the loch's western edge then straight up the Sgurr-Dubh Slabs having never climbed them. Huge slabs of tilted Gabbro, as rough as the roughest sandpaper, rising for a thousand feet. From near their peak I would swing south, tracing the contour lines across An Garbh-Choire, then follow the stream up into Choire Beag and up onto Gars-Bheinn, the *real* start of my journey.

Looking up to the crest of the ridge, a number of climbers were picking their way along Sgur nan Eag, the first real difficulty on the traverse and I felt a pang of envy. No worries, I would be there tomorrow, tracing a route across the knife edge of ancient rock, high in the clear air.

Half way up the Sgurr-Dubh slabs, I sat on an outcrop, swigging the last of my water and eating the first of my Mars bars. My legs dangled into space, below them, six hundred feet of fifty degree rock straight into the waters of Coruisk. There was nothing whatsoever, technical about the ground but, in the back of my mind was the thought that any slip, no matter how trivial, would end in almost certain disaster. This thought had flown to the fore-front when I'd unintentionally prised out a small chunk of the slab with my boot and watched it career downwards, bounding and spinning over and over, sending up explosions of dust. I'd followed its progress for what seemed an age until, after a spectacular bounce that sent it high into the air, I actually heard the splash as it disappeared into the loch.

With no way out of the predicament (down climbing was out of the question and shimmying crab-like across the incline would be ridiculous) I continued upwards and as is usually the case, once I reached the corrie and relative safety of boulder strewn ground, I wondered what all the fuss had been about.

Peace, absolute peace. I stood and listened to the silence of the mountains; no other sound is quite like it, there's a presence, a tangible atmosphere that's never actually devoid of sound. It swirled around me; a snippet of muted conversation from above, the sigh of a breeze springing off the sea and the gurgle of water finding its way through rock as old as time itself.

I was making great progress, having allowed a day to achieve what could be realistically achieved in half the time. Still, I was in no rush, no race to finish. Time in the mountains is always well spent; I could never have *too* much.

Three hours later I was still in the corrie, lying back and watching a pair of Buzzards float, high on thermals rising from the sun-warmed rock. I glugged a bottle of water, wincing as the cold set my teeth on edge, then refilled it in the burn. Such pleasure in the simple act of dozing in the sun, in a place where few people would ever tread. I could have whooped for joy, shouted at the top of my lungs with the pleasure of simply being alive.

Human traffic above the slabs was few and far between and, because of this, no path had been worn. I felt as if I was the first to ever tread there, my boots breaking new ground; no one to follow, no self-inflicted 'race' as I subconsciously struggle to catch up with the climbers in front, or force myself to keep ahead of followers. Just the mountains, the ground in front, rising to jagged spires of rock, like a blank page, an expectant canvas waiting for my footfall to leave an imprint, some sign of my passing.

The ground was steep and, with every step seemed to increase its angle. What path I'd been tenuously following, disappeared completely and I wandered for a while, hopping from block to block. Boulders gave way to small rocks and then patches of scree between shattered, fragmented gullies and buttresses.

My map showed a rough, potential route that followed the burn then swung towards the left, between buttresses and up the final wall. Studying the contours only told me what I could see myself. It was steep, difficult ground with some vertical scrambling to get onto the ridge. I gritted my teeth, shouldered my pack and continued.

Amongst the scree, I found a spring that I dug out with my boot until I'd formed a six inch deep pool of clear water that didn't drain away. I drank my fill, mindful of the moisture I was loosing with every drop of sweat that broke on my skin. Then, being careful not to stir up any silt, filled both bottles. The next available water would be at Fionn Choire at the far, north end of the ridge. Even this would entail a detour down two hundred feet of scree. I'd be there tomorrow night and reckoned I could use half a litre tonight, the same in the morning, then struggle with one bottle for the whole day. After another three quarters of an hour, I'd made my way through the scree filled bowl and stood, gazing up near vertical cliffs that towered two hundred feet above me. Cracks and gullies angled their way up the face, broken by bands of boulders and pots of steep scree. I deliberated, shielding my eyes from the glare coming over the uppermost edge of the ridge and finally plumbed for an easy looking gully on the far left of the wall. The holds looked good, big blocks of rock, easily spaced for the first seventy-five feet or so, skirting to the left of a prominent buttress. Once past this obstacle, the route disappeared but looked as though it would give access to the top by angling to the right.

"Just a big zigzag then," I smiled and added, "piece of cake."

And it was. It was also immensely enjoyable. Nothing too technical, but enough to keep me interested. As I pulled up over the final block onto the broad expanse of broken grey rock, sweat trickled into my eyes and blurred a view that made the toil worthwhile.

I had, for the previous few hours, climbed in the enclosed confines of a natural bowl with rock inches in front of my face and all of my concentration focused on the next hold. The final pull onto the summit of Gars-Bheinn was therefore much like emerging into sunlight after a week spent stumbling around in a mine. Shadow gave way to bright sunshine and with it, a vision of sea and sky that exploded in front of me. I had to steady myself on a rock to stop the dizzy feeling from tipping me back over the drop.

With the appearance of an unsteady drunk, I straightened my legs, stepped away from the edge onto the ridge proper and, with my hands on my hips, stared incomprehensibly over a seascape that stretched to America.

Every shade of pastel blue, green and silver was spread before me; a limitless expanse of pure wonder. Rolling grey, then green, then blue and shimmering silver as the slope of the land plunged into the shinning Atlantic. I revolved on my tired feet and took in the mainland to the south, peeling away over rolling glens. Eastwards and Blaven dominated the view, its black and oppressive summit level with me. *Now* I was looking at it on equal terms. Swinging round to the north, a gleaming, priceless 'wasteland', meandered between peaks way below me. *Directly* north, the ridge snaked sinuously and temptingly into the distance.

I traced it, picking out individual, rising summits all the way to Gillean where the ground plunged back to the glen bottom. It was a frightening jumble of peaks and troughs, terrible drops falling away at every step.

And I was going to walk it.

Three minutes to change a life

The previous week had passed in a whirlwind of telephone calls, meetings, heated conversations, tearful exchanges, hugs and kisses, frantic packing of cases, selling of unwanted furniture and the lease of a Ford Transit Van. The weekend had been, in comparison, a fairly sedate affair; a meal with the neighbours (thankfully clothed) then a visit from Gail and Debbie, late on Sunday evening (pleasantly naked after the first half an hour - both of them).

Now, on Monday morning, right about the time when Iain lets the big burbling V8 of the TVR pull him up the hill from Elgol, Al pulls out of his driveway, for the last time. A hazy sun burns away the last of the low lying mist and a dew speckled spider's web glistens between the 'For Sale' sign and its post in the front garden.

Since four that morning, he has worked tirelessly, packing the van from floor to roof with the bulk of the contents of his cottage. Beds, wardrobes, settee and dining suite still fill the dents of time that they have made in the carpets; left to make up the bits that sale particulars describe as, 'part furnished'.

A strange, tingling excitement, spliced with a healthy measure of fear sets his nerves on edge. Excitement at a new life, five hundred miles north. Excitement at falling into a mind set that he'd witnessed in the 'Tibet book' reader, years ago in a noisy and smoky pub in an equally noisy and smoky city centre. Excitement at seeing his mate again, watching as his eyes fill with tears of surprise and shock, disbelief. Excitement at the thought of waking somewhere where the front door is left unlocked and the view is not of brick and tile but rock and sky.

Fear at the unknown. Fear that he may have, just possibly, made a monumental balls-up.

His bank account is healthily stuffed with the proceeds of several investments, shares, the contents of his bonus account at work and from the sale of several unwanted household items. In what the Estate Agent proclaimed as a 'realistic' two months, it should begin to overflow with another £150,000 or so.

He'd decided to sell the house after spending a couple of days 'umming and ahing' over whether to rent it out. Richard, the young,

233

smartly dressed executive from the agents, reckoned it would sell within the week. Al hoped he was right and had waved nervously as he watched him speed off along the lane in his brand new V6 Golf.

His boss had been shocked. A week's notice was all that was required and all he gave; then took the whole time as holiday, being owed it anyway.

As he put the phone down after telling him he was leaving, a feeling of calm serenity washed over him and he took a step closer to that state which he now termed simply as 'Tibet'. Staring at the phone, dead and still, knowing that Karl, his boss, would be doing exactly the same forty miles away, he unplugged it and went into the garden. A cigar and cafétiére sat on the garden table, placed there in readiness, the coffee only just beginning to lose its heat. His boss hadn't argued. It hadn't taken long.

Three minutes to change a life.

Within forty minutes his van rumbles onto the M6, pulls into the middle lane and, as the fields and villages of Staffordshire drift past, his life continues to change.

Twelve hours later, as I stand on the airy crest of Gars-Bheinn's summit, Al pulls off the Skye Bridge, tired, bleary eyed and running on Pro-Plus. At the first lay-by, anyone watching would have seen a stubble-cheeked man step down to the tarmac, cross the road and, in the parched grass of the verge, kneel down and kiss the ground. Tears roll unashamedly down his cheeks and a large, salty drop spills from his nose as he shakes his head in disbelief at what he's done. What he's achieved.

Forty five minutes later, the van pulls into a driveway next to a bright yellow mini and within another two, the driver is being hugged and back-slapped by a large grey haired Scot. As hard as nails, the Scot sniffs his own tears in the sunshine and turns away to blow his nose.

At about the same time as I sat on my sleeping bag, the warmth of the day being replaced by the chill of a clear evening sky, Al and Iain share a pizza and the first of many bottles. Sitting on my garden bench like an old married couple they laugh and joke, sipping warming Glen Turret. Already formulating a plan, a surprise meeting befitting such a turn-up, their laughter lifts sparrows from their roost in the trees and startles sheep that wander along the track.

The calm and peace of good friends in good company; Al moving steadily towards his 'Tibet', Iain already there. What they don't know, can't have even begun to guess at, is that what they are witnessing is the calm before the storm.

Like the worst storms, the most devastating, it would rise quickly and strike out of the darkness, bearing down on its unsuspecting victims. The weather is perfect; sun dappled shadows spread below the trees and a silky flat ocean pulses against its rocky boundaries.

A storm is building that has nothing to do with barometric pressure or cold fronts coming off the sea, but a storm that is borne of hatred and pure malevolence. This storm is of the worst kind, the storm of a sick mind, a storm in the shape of a man, a man on the very edge of humanity.

A man with nothing to lose because all is already lost.

On the ridge

11.50p.m. No breeze and, amazingly, no midges.

The ground in front of me dropped away over thousands of feet of steeply shelving boulders, gradually lessening in angle as the heather and gorse took over forming a shallow, shelving plateau down to the sea. Kicking my heels against the ground released a rivulet of tiny stones and gravel that trickled amongst their larger neighbours. With a mug of steaming hot fruit drink and the last of the day's cigarettes curling smoke sinuously into the clear evening air, I viewed my horizon with awe and wonder.

Earlier in the evening I'd chatted with another group of climbers, safely bivouacked further along the ridge. Their accents had reminded me of my old home as they came from Dudley and were up on Skye for two weeks. It brought home to me just how well I'd settled in that they couldn't tell where I was from. My Midlands' accent had all but disappeared, replaced by a nondescript mix of, well … *nothing* really. I had a 'non-accent'. We talked for a while about the ridge and its difficulties and they explained their intentions to complete the traverse and head off to the Sligachan in one day. I'm sure they were envious of my leisurely route and three nights out in the open.

There were a few stars beginning to show as I made my way back to the man-sized area of flat ground on which my sleeping bag and mat lay. Sparkling brightly against the dark blue of the night sky, they seemed somehow out of place in the half light, the Sun still giving out a healthy glow to the northwest. Ten minutes before, it had sunk behind South Uist and Barra, turning their back-lit shapes into silky black silhouettes floating in a fiery glow. Even after the dome had sunk from sight, its warm orange-red light had painted the horizon in an eerie luminescence.

With my head propped against my partially empty rucksack the ridge marched away to the north. Points of light formed beacons which shone out starkly from the pointed pinnacles of rock as though each peak held its own gas lamp. From the surface of the ocean, bands of light spread, like the layers of rock onto which they reflected. Bright, almost white, into burnished gold, deep warm orange, sandy yellow that blended into the palest, most pastel of blues. From there on, the colour deepened and grew into a rich purple-blue that darkened as it stretched overhead, never quite reaching black.

Deeply cocooned in my down sleeping bag, I folded my arms across my chest, said goodnight to Rachel and the world, closed my eyes and was instantly asleep.

I stumbled as I approached the first gully, stubbing my toe and falling heavily onto unprotected, outstretched hands. A muttered curse at my clumsiness broke the stillness of the morning and I watched as a cut on my palm oozed a tiny trickle of blood.

To my left, the ridge dropped away over a dizzy expanse of nothingness, the rocks below, hidden by swirling white mist. Up here it was clear, the dark gabbro and basalt, shiny and wet looking. The sun was low to my right, just breaking above the cloud-draped mountains on the mainland.

It was a grand morning.

I sat on a large, flat boulder that seemed to defy gravity by staying on the knife edge that was the ridge at that point. Licking the blood from my palm, I inspected the skin for any flecks of rock that may have found their way in. It had thankfully stopped bleeding; a plaster would have meant digging around in the bottom of my pack. I wanted to get moving, I'd only gone a few hundred yards and was keen to press on.

I dropped a few feet, following a hint of a path skirting a bulging outcrop of heavily fissured rock and stepped onto a large slab at the base of a ten foot gully. Three or four moves later and I reached for the obvious hold at the top of the crack and scrambled onto a billiard-table sized, flat expanse of ground. For a second or two the exposure gripped me and I hesitated on bent knees before straightening.

Fifty yards away right on the crest of the ridge, a patch of green caught my eye. Lush grass swayed in the breeze, doted with wild flowers and a small, obviously sculpted bush. I shook my head and blinked a couple of times, glancing left and right, trying to get my bearings. There *was* no grass on the ridge. It was strictly the domain of boulder and scree, a hard, unforgiving place with no softness to cushion a fall or smooth the edges of one's vision.

As I watched, my brow creased with a disbelieving frown, the bush, rounded and the most lush, vibrant green I'd ever seen, shook briefly, violently. In the stillness I heard the rustle of its leaves as clearly as if it were right next to me. The sound was surreal, amplified somehow, like it was happening only in my head.

From behind the domed surface of its leaves, a head popped into view. In the sunlight, her hair shone with the vibrancy of polished brass; it seemed to reflect the golden beams like a halo. Even from the distance I was watching, I could see the beauty of her blue eyes and upturned sweep of her pretty nose. Her face was that of a cherub, a sweetly smiling angel, perhaps eight years old, maybe nine or ten.

She moved around the bush and sat cross-legged before it, settling herself comfortably, before spreading her blue and white checked dress over her knees. She was looking at the grass, watching intently - something that *I* could not see. Then, with a swirl of her long hair, she threw back her head and raised her arms, palms upturned to the sky.

Immediately, a flock of crows, their feathers black and glossy, spiralled out of the air to swirl around the lawn (I could call it nothing else). At first, there was no sound, save for the beating of their wings, a frantic flapping and whooshing as they pitched and spun. Then, as their movements became gradually more frantic, a shrill, ear splitting 'caaaww' rent the silence and in seconds, the pretty girl in the sweet, blue checked dress was sitting beneath a whirlwind of maniacally gyrating blackness. A bird split from the group, briefly lifting above its flock, then as though terrified of the solitude, dropped like a stone, drawn back into the cloud.

All of my attention was focused on the scene in front of me. The crows were now a constantly changing black mass with no shape or form, like smoke from a pyre of burning lorry tyres.

Time spread outwards, or stopped, I'm not sure, all I could see was blackness against the blue of a dawn sky. It could have been seconds, minutes or days. I had no perception whatsoever. My legs had begun a transformation from bone and muscle, to disjointed rubber with the strength of thick treacle and I knew I was about to fall.

And yet I didn't.

A sound was building, intensifying, the rushing sound a train would make, approaching at full speed, but with its engine dead and cold. The time that had seemed to gather and congeal, suddenly catapulted back, trying to catch up with itself and it felt as though the noise was all around me, that I was strapped to the front of the train, unable to breathe with the onslaught of air battering my face, forcing its way into my mouth, nose and eyes. I was falling, spinning out of control, sure I was about to die. And yet, my view of the world remained unchanged; just the blackness of the swirling birds and the little girl sitting on her grassy plateau high in the mountains.

Then, as I struggled for breath, unable to shake the feeling of desperate, deadly speed, the blackness, formless and indistinct, changed, became a single crow, monstrous, obscene, slick shinning feathers seeming to drip and melt before me. It fixed me with its stare, eyes as black as a star-less midnight.

Then it was gone.

I shuddered, stepped back on wobbly legs then held fast as I watched the grass and the tree fade to invisibility. The little girl smiled and then too was gone, shrinking away to nothing.

All this in a second, a blink of a disbelieving eye.

I glanced down at my feet. The ridge continued ten feet below me and, as I looked down, a man stepped out from the rise on which I stood. Blonde, short spiky hair, long black leather coat, swirling around his ankles.

He stared up at me, cold blue eyes like ice.

"Andy." A smile.

I woke with an undignified grunt that expelled a lung full of air I imagined I'd been holding for minutes. Above me, the sky was the same blue-black, spattered with stars. It was cold; my face, the only thing exposed to the air, tingled, feeling invigorated and fresh, but my body was slick with sweat. For a moment I thought I'd wet myself then had a brief panic attack as I struggled to free my arms from the bag.

After a moment or two I found my lighter, lit a cigarette and, still lying in my bag, held the flame to my watch.

12.35 a.m. I'd been asleep about half an hour and yet I was wide awake, as though a full night had passed.

"Shit, that was some dream." I mumbled into the darkness, dragging deeply on my cigarette, feeling its heat warm my face and throw a comforting glow over my fingers and palm.

Five minutes later, I ground the smouldering filter into the gravel, covered it with a couple of small stones, rolled over and, before I had chance to think about anything else, fell soundly asleep.

I didn't dream again that night.

By six thirty, the day already lit by bright sunshine, I'd breakfasted on vacuum packed cheese and crackers, a Mars bar and half a litre of hot fruit drink.

Feeling a great sense of occasion, I took the opportunity to scramble a hundred yards back down the ridge with my rations, choosing a bungalow-sized outcrop for my breakfast seat. Happy that no one would tamper with my stuff, I sat in delightful peace while the rest of the ridge's temporary inhabitants flustered over their early morning arrangements.

I was in no hurry. I was under no real pressure (my experience in financial services and its obsession with targets, had left me with no great desire to work to deadlines).

The sun was so bright, hanging above the mainland's glorious peaks against a pure blue backdrop, that I had already donned my sun glasses. My thighs, wrapped in the stretchy nylon of my tracksters were heating up, while my feet, hanging over the five hundred foot east face of Gars-Bheinn remained cool and airy.

On that morning in June, high on the ridge of my dreams I can honestly say I had never felt more free. I seemed to have gained a weightless quality, as if, with a simple step and flap of my arms, I could glide over the landscape, competing with the eagles and swooping on unsuspecting crows.

The thought of crows drew me back to my dream, previously forgotten and the swirling black mass that had formed above the little blonde haired girl. She was, I realised, without a shred of doubt, the girl from my picture. How I knew that, I've no idea, but I was certain. How a simple paint streak that I had thought initially, an accidental slip on my part, could have materialised into a beautiful young girl, I also have no idea. I was certain nonetheless.

Just as I was certain that the spiky haired man in the long black leather coat, had been David Salt.

My eyes settled on the sparkling, rippled surface of Loch Coruisk, three thousand feet below and I tentatively formed a link between the two.

David Salt and my painting.

Ridiculous, absurd and yet the fit, somehow, seemed unmistakable.

Like a hand in a glove.

A couple of early risers crunched their way past me, shouting a cheery "Good morning," fresh from their own high rise bivouac and their keenness galvanised me into movement. I had a ten mile trek on the country's best high level ridge to cover and needed little encouragement to get started. With my pack sitting comfortably on my back, shades blocking out the squinting brightness of the sun and a light breeze blowing in off the sea, the exquisite feeling of weightlessness had me skipping from rock to rock.

I was on my way.

By 10.00 a.m. I'd worked my way over boulders and buttresses, up gullies, broken away from the main ridge and sat on the highest point to grace the island's sky line. Sgurr Alisdair.

The feeling of weightless freedom was still with me. I felt like the king of all I surveyed. With every step, I had to suppress the urge to shout with the pure joy of being alive. I couldn't remember feeling more vibrant, fulfilled or, in fact, utterly ecstatic and, as I shuffled and half slid down Alisdair's eastern flank, even the massive drop to my right didn't bother me.

I peered northwards, allowing my vision to follow the undulation away into the distance, swinging round to the right after three miles or so before reaching the saw toothed, tri-peak of Gillean.

So far it had been a stroll. The real climbing started here.

Sgurr Thearlaich rose in front of me and I followed an indistinct path around its southern flank, avoiding its summit which was cluttered with the bright jackets of fellow climbers, then choosing to traverse around its eastern side, pretty much directly above Loch Coruisk where I'd wandered the day before. Following a smooth path, I regained the true ridge, shattered and razor sharp, arriving at the alarmingly steep drop into Bealach Mhic Coinnich.

My God, that view was awesome. To my right, a vast expanse of open space falling three thousand feet to the rippled waters of the loch. To my left, Loch Lagan shimmered fifteen hundred feet below and directly in front of me, the ground gaped in a chasm of splintered blocks a hundred feet to the tiny platform which masquerades as a 'pass'. On the other side of this 'pass', Mhic Coinnich reared upwards to the same level that I now stood, daring me onwards.

The down climb was OK, but at the bottom of the cliff I struggled to find a foot hold. Try as I might I couldn't find a shelf or crack into which to wedge my boot. I was only four feet above the pass but the thought of jumping, while all the time the drops on either side waited to claim me, was so excruciatingly terrifying, I couldn't do it. In the end, a group of teenagers, sauntering around Coinnich's western face as though out for a stroll forced the issue and I leaped backwards landing in an undignified tangle amongst the rocks.

Cheery greetings were exchanged, along with comments about the perfect clarity of the day and then, with barely a break to catch their breath, they were off, racing fluidly up the cliff down which I had just laboured like an arthritic hippo. Huddled amongst the rocks, I composed myself and gazed out at the flat expanse of the North Atlantic.

One stupid slip, a momentary loss of concentration would be all it took. I was alone. The thought hit me like a punch to the chin and for a while, my spirits sank to something approaching hopelessness. I glugged some water, ate a Mars bar and considered my options.

I could go straight on, following the ridge up onto Mhic Coinnich, a route that entailed a climb similar to the one I had just come down and one I had done before. Or, there was Collie's ledge. I unwrapped another Mars bar, lit a cigarette and, alternating between inhaling smoke and chewing chocolate I pondered my options.

Anything to put off making a decision.

Let's face it, I'd been here before and then I'd chosen the 'easy' route.

I continued to ponder, like I said, anything to put off making a decision.

On Rachel's bench

Somewhere around the time that I sat wrapped in indecision as to my next move, Al sat similarly wrapped in his first hangover since arriving on Skye the previous day. Iain had kindly stopped by to throw stones at the bedroom window of my house on his way to work at 7.00 a.m. It was the first time he'd sat on Rachel's bench. The first time he'd taken in the view as an 'Islander' and his thoughts were a jumbled mix of fear, joy, trepidation and thumping, head-pounding, whisky-induced pain.

The thought that this was his home now, the Island that is, was impossible for him to really comprehend. Realising that he wasn't just there for a week or two; that all of his belongings, those that mattered anyway, were packed into a van a hundred yards away, brought a feeling of queasy apprehension.

Imagine making a decision that would turn your life on its head; not just having a half-hearted thought, but actually making that decision and sticking to it. Then, three or four days later it's all gone off around you. You've done it, broken the ties, sold your home, uprooted every aspect of your life and find yourself sitting in a hangover induced stupor, watching seals bob in a gently swelling sea, your life packed into a van.

Pretty scary I'd say.

No time to think about your actions; no months of planning; no lists and organised change of address cards. Just 'whoosh, here's your new life mate, what do you think?'

I suppose my cogitation over whether to risk my neck on a rock face or a ledge would have seemed pretty pathetic to Al at that point.

My move to Skye had been pretty rapid as well. *But*, whereas Al had just gone and done it, I'd planned it all in my head, meticulously, over the previous years. The final outcome was somewhat different, granted, but it *had* been planned - planned as a place to retire with Rachel.

We used to dream about the uncluttered, relaxed atmosphere where no one was a total stranger. Where we could perhaps start a small business, live life simply and spend hours watching the mountains. She would talk about her painting and how it would give her the incentive to develop the skills which had rusted away under the pressures of working life.

Richard Neath

Strange, how things turn out.

Iain had promised to call in on his way back from work, grab a coffee and finalise their plans for Wednesday morning.

It had been Iain who had suggested it during one of their many phone calls over the previous week and Al, always keen on surprises, had agreed immediately.   What better way to announce his arrival, permanently, on Skye, than to be waiting on the summit of Blaven for his best friend?

They would rise early, park on the eastern side of the mountain, approach 'on the blind side', arrive in plenty of time and, with the help of binoculars, watch my progress as I made my way across the glen bottom and up over Garb-Bheinn and Clach Glas.   Three friends would then spend an evening of happy chatter and a shared bottle under the stars. Then, like three reunited soldiers, we would march onto Elgol.

Perfect.

Like I said, strange, how things turn out.

244

The ledge and onwards

Collie's Ledge scared the living daylights out of me. Imagine walking along a wide window sill a couple of floors from the top of Canary Wharf and you won't be far away. Add into the equation a few obstacles in the shape of portable TV sized boulders and you're even closer. Tilt the whole arrangement so that, at times, you're making your way up something that's a similar angle to your house's roof and you're spot on.

Nothing could have prepared me for such an experience, for the utterly terrifying exposure of it all and yet, at the same time, the freedom and exhilaration of such a high level scramble.

An hour later, my legs had just about stopped shaking. The total splendour of it all kept the weightless feeling of euphoria strong and clear. I believe that I had never been so close to death on Collie's Ledge and yet, *I know* that I had never felt so alive.

If I'm honest with myself, the whole trek was intended as a time to finally exorcise my remaining ghosts. Time for reflection, careful thought and cogitation. The fact that, if my plans went unhindered, I would arrive on Blaven, sleep overnight and wake on the second anniversary of Rachel's death, had not been a conscious consideration. The human mind though, is a complex thing and I feel sure it was more than coincidental. Perhaps my subconscious had wanted a final test?

Waking on this particular date on our favourite mountain. A final test perhaps, yes. So easy, in a renewed bout of depression to simply wake, say "Good morning" to the world, take in the splendour of the mountain vista, whisper "I love you" to the clear sky and step off into a welcoming void.

Easy also, to shed a tear and rejoice in her memory. Easy to talk to her, to listen to her sweet voice and lilting laughter. Easy to remember her smiling face. Easy to remember the love we had shared, the uncluttered companionship that had always been there.

Easy.

A time to reflect? Yes - 'Andy in the wilderness', uncluttered by modern paraphernalia or technological trumpery. Just me and my boots.

The fact is, during my time on the ridge, I'd found little time to think at all. Other than where to place my boot next or where to stop for the next Mars bar, my mind had wandered along with me in a comforting blankness. Like a badly tuned TV, my thoughts had simply remained a fuzzy, jumbled mess.

Probably having the same effect though.

Sitting on a rock on Dearg, I glanced across at the Outer Hebrides. The rounded lumps of their peaks broke from the surrounding ocean and above them, a line of benign looking, fluffy white clouds sat motionless - warm, moist air blowing in from the Atlantic. And yet there was a greyness to them that hinted at a change; subtle, but there nonetheless. The forecast had been good for the week, a ridge of high pressure to accompany my ridge of high drama. But usually the island makes its own rules, forms its own weather and sniggers in the face of such weightless prediction.

I felt pleased with my progress as I sat and watched climbers on the Inaccessible Pinnacle but, after half an hour had to remind myself that I had a lot of ridge to cover before night-time. Burying my cigarette butt in the gravel, I set off down Dearg's northern flank.

If the previous hours had passed me by in a state of 'non-thought', then the time between Dearg and Sgur a Mhadaidhs final top fled by in a jumbled mix of euphoria, joy and pure terror. Three times I clung to the rock, cursing my stupidity in thinking I was up to its challenge. At least twice I was convinced my fall from Kilt Rock had simply been delayed and once, I sat, having down-climbed thirty feet, crying like a baby, too scared to continue and yet seemingly unable to retreat any further.

It was after eight when I slumped to the ground and leaned against the trig point on the summit of Bruach na Frithe, too tired for anything other than to thank whoever it was looking after me, that I was still alive.

I suppose I sat for half an hour, breathing deeply of the clear mountain air, allowing my nerves to return to normal. I smoked a cigarette and enjoyed its taste, blowing smoke out in relieved plumes. All of the time my eyes roamed along the ridge, picking out features; rock formations I had stood upon, clambered over or sweated past.

Blaven, tomorrow night's destination, loomed over the southern end of the glen. Stark and black, its ridge sparkled in the waning sunlight.

My emotions were a chaotic, jumbled mix of fatigue and pride. I took the opportunity to tell a couple who arrived, panting onto the summit that, "Yeah, it's a great view. Really pleasing when you've done the rest of the ridge." They were suitably impressed with my achievement. Here, sitting on his rucksack, was a *real* climber. I didn't tell them I'd cried like a baby only ninety minutes before and that much of the afternoon had been spent in a mixture of abject terror and frustration.

After they left I followed them back into the corrie, dropping the couple of hundred feet to fill up my water bottles and taking the opportunity to drink and wash my face.

Back on the ridge I searched for a spot to sleep for the night and settled on a rocky ledge overlooking Harta Corrie. Below and to the left, a huge dome-fronted buttress overhung the corrie, its shadow already creeping across the heather and boulders as the sun dropped in the west. The Bloody Stone, way below me, the site of a terrible massacre hundreds of years ago, looked imposing and yet lonesome at the same time. I imagined the McLeods, backed against the huge block, slaughtered by the MacDonalds after several days fighting. Battling to the last, their limbs had been scattered around the corrie.

I'd saved the chicken curry for my evening meal and sat stirring the brown, bubbling goo, watching the bright orange flame caress the bottom of the billie-can. My mood had slipped a few notches after the euphoria of my climb and the stillness seemed to be seeping into my thoughts.

I was thinking of Rachel.

On our very first visit to Skye we had trudged up the ridge and sat taking in the view from a spot twenty yards behind where I was camped for the night. The thought of how good it would be if she had been sitting next to me forced a tear from my eye and I sniffed it back. A stroll to the top of the buttress while my meal simmered calmed me and by the time I was back at my stove, the mood had passed.

By ten, I'd finished and, with a mug of steaming hot fruit drink and a cigarette, I clambered up onto the summit of Sgurr a Fionn Choire.

The daytime walkers and climbers had departed for the sanctuary of Seumas' Bar. I was totally alone. Few climbers used this part of the ridge as a bivvy site, preferring to start from the far end as I had and then descend, all in one day. I took a few photos from the summit, remembering my commission for the first time since starting. The Glen, stretching away to the sea in the south, snaked like a lush green carpet, framed by black rock that soared upwards on both sides.

The raucous call of crows echoed back to me from somewhere far below and the lights in the hotel blinked in the hazy evening glow.

Al remembers

Al is troubled.

Something nags insistently at the back of his mind and Iain has noticed he seems to be distant, as though his thoughts are elsewhere.

It's 10.45p.m. On a whim they've driven over to the Sligachan, time for a quick pint then home to bed.

Al would say later that it was like an itch, deep in his head. Like his brain needed scratching. The buzzing of a mosquito from within, this nagging thing; this thought that plucked at his sub-conscious. His pint is half finished, Iain's drained so that foam sticks to the glass, quickly drunk.

"Are ye OK Al, ye seem a wee bit distant?"

"Hmmm?" His eyes are glazed, staring out into blank space. The hustle and bustle of the busy bar could be a million miles away.

"Ah said, are ye OK? … ye din'nae seem quite wi' it."

"What? Yeah, yeah … something's bothering me. You know? Like I've forgotten something … something important. Probably just to do with the move and all. It's got to have an effect don't you think?"

Iain slaps him on the back and calls for another from Steve behind the bar.

"Will ye no join me Al? One fer the road?"

"Errm, no, thanks. Still feel a bit rough from last night if you want to know."

"OK, just the one please Steve … aye, Black Cuillin. A pint please."

Iain pays for his drink and sups foam from the top, tilting the glass and gulping a third of it in one long draught. They stand at the bar in silence for a while then, on the entrance of a gang of girls, Iain puts down his pint and nudges Al.

"Al, Al, see them three just come in?" He points, careful not to draw attention to himself. "Right bloody slappers all o' 'em. Only come here tae flirt and get a shag." He nods their way, "That middle one, the blonde wi' the tiny skirt on, Emily Tarbet, Jesus, she's come on tae me a couple o' times." He shakes his head, inspecting his boots and shuffling from foot to foot. "Ah'm old enough tae be her father, probably her grandfather if the truth be known. The youth of tod …" Iain spins round, a sharp pain in his upper arm as Al's fingers dig through his sweater.

"Christ Al ..." Al's eyes blaze back at him.

"What did you say her name was ... the slapper, the blonde?"

"Emily Tarb ..."

"That's it. That's what's been nagging at me since we got here."

Iain just stares, his expression blank.

"Emily ... shit, as we came onto the pub car park, a car was leaving by the other entrance, towards Carbost. You know, turn right, out of the pub, up past the Cuillin. Its number plate. I know it, I've seen it." Iain still looks back at him, blank, lost.

"Emily. The plate, E-M-I-1-Y."

"Sorry Al, still no wi' yer." Iain pauses, scratches behind his ear "Should it mean anythin' tae me?"

Al's away, his jaw muscles working as he chews the inside of his cheek, a habit he always reverts to when deep in thought or stressed. Looking into his glazed eyes, Iain thinks he sees not only confusion but a tinge of fear; deep concern buried away in his mind.

"Let's sit down and I'll try to explain."

They move as one, Al indicating a round table in the corner. Above it hangs black and white pictures of the Scottish Mountaineering Club of the late 1800's. The bearded, solemn looking climbers dressed in tweed jackets, waistcoats, ties and hob-nailed boots, stare blankly from the frames, proud, fearless men frozen in time. Their outfits look out of place amongst the bright fabrics of the climbers dotted around the bar; more suited to a Sunday stroll to church than tackling some of Scotland's most challenging peaks.

Al's stare is devoid of emotion. Blank, uncertain recognition greets Iain's request for him to continue.

He takes a swig of his beer, glances once at his finger nails and begins.

"Two days after the crash ... Rachel's crash, you know?" Iain nods, "Well, Andy was keen to get the stuff out of the car, c.d.s, maps and things ..."

... The door bell jingles as Al strides into the reception of Harvey's Autos. The day is overcast, threatening showers, fittingly damp and sombre for his task.

Inside, bright fluorescent lighting casts a starkly clinical light over the red and grey furnishings. Dealer plaques proclaim that a host of staff have gained certificates in topics such as clutch maintenance, brake technology and paint spraying. A large poster looms over the reception desk. James Harvey smiles out from the bottom left hand corner, his signature and personal proclamation that 'Your delight is our sole aim' underlines the general message and a 'mission statement' of service and quality. The desk itself, a shiny grey marble effect, is littered with invoices and job sheets, there's a distinctly antiseptic smell in the air and a phone rings continually in the workshop behind glass panelling.

An electric doorbell, mounted on the desk rings at Al's push, followed almost immediately by the appearance of a middle-aged Indian gentleman whose name tag proclaims 'My name is Jagdeep, I'm here to help!' Thin dark hair, swept across his head a-la-Bobby-Charlton, threatens to blur his vision and he pushes it back into place.

Al speaks first, desperate to get his task over with as quickly as possible.

"Morning, I'm here for Mr Perkins' things from the Nissan. I rang … earlier today."

Out in the yard, haphazardly parked cars greet him in all states of repair; some mildly dented, awaiting attention, some in for servicing, some brand new.

Then there are the real wrecks, brought to the garage for insurance assessment then scrapping. Like lepers, they're parked in a mechanical huddle at the far end of the yard. Sneaked in via the rear entrance, hidden, as though the owners are embarrassed by the destruction. Automotive solitary confinement for the terminally smashed.

A four wheel drive, possibly a Land Rover Discovery, Al can't tell for sure, sits on four flat tyres. It looks as though it's made of rubber and been placed in front of a furnace, as though the heat has melted it into a tilted mess. The entire passenger compartment has been pushed over to the off side. The driver's door is missing along with pretty much every single piece of glass. The driver's airbag hangs into the foot-well like a dead balloon and a buckle from the seat belt lies in a pool of congealed oil.

Next to the leaning Land Rover, a squashed flat VW Polo hunkers down next to a completely flat backed Ford Mondeo. The latter looks like it's been rear-ended by a train.

A dozen or so cars, lined up in a casual row, awaiting Insurance companies to record their time of death. The smell of grease, oil and rubber fills the air, mingling with a tangible scent of despair. Al finds it difficult to breath, such is the thick, clammy odour.

His eyes flick from wreck to wreck, taking in the tangled destruction, the utter devastation. Thousands of pound's worth of vehicles, destroyed; millions of hours of experience snuffed out; life's slate wiped clean.

He can't imagine any of the occupants could have got out alive.

It's a while before he notices the Nissan. At first his brain can't take it in, can't register the fact that *this* is Andy's pride and joy. No panel has survived; the roof is almost devoid of paint, the bare metal deeply scared, each of its four corners is crushed, each of the three remaining tyres is flat. They look like dead slugs squirming beneath the buckled and cracked alloys. The front and rear screens are cob-webbed and bulging.

Al stands, a few yards away, while slack-mouthed and incredulous, he takes in the spectacle.

His gaze switches from dent to dent, from bulging, misshapen panel to twisted door pillar, his mind blank. The whole car is dripping with water, as though it's recently been liberally and forcefully hosed down, inside and out. Deep stains still cling to the driver's side upholstery. On the tarmac, a dark pool of red-brown water looks slick and oily.

Realisation as to the origin of the stains dawns slowly, building with a gradual, terrible certainty. Al squints at the grey sky, tears spilling in silent sobs, rolling down his cheeks to pool in his ears.

A silent stream of salty despair.

It takes a minute to realise that little in the car can be salvaged. He gingerly picks up sodden maps and street guides between thumb and forefinger, dropping them immediately. A couple of wet, but unstained c.d.'s and a hat of green canvas, is the sum total of his salvage work.

He turns to leave, a terrible weight pressing onto his shoulders, as Jagdeep strolls over.

"Quite a mess don't you think." It wasn't a question. "How did you know the driver?"

Al explains, his voice a quavery, reedy gasp.

"We thought the husband was coming over, that's why we washed it off." He shakes his head, "Man, there was a *lot* of blood."

They stand for a few moments in silent reflection at the obvious frailty of life.

"That's the other car, you know, the one involved in the accident," he points to a green Subaru parked in the corner. It hangs lopsidedly, canted over at a drunken angle. Otherwise it looks pretty normal, shiny even. A couple of long scratches are obvious on the near-side wing and the arches are mud-splattered, but, of any damage, the sort of damage that surely should accompany such a crash, there is no sign.

Al does a double take, frowning at Jagdeep.

"What? This car? ... I don't understand.   It looks ... well ... perfect. The driver's in intensive care isn't he?" Trailing off, his voice fades to a murmur and his silent stare is the only question Jagdeep needs.

"Yeh, I know what you think. It's a right off though." Al's eyebrows raise. "Take a look at the driver's side. Go on, have a look."

He feels as though, for no apparent or logical reason, he's approaching a dangerous animal. Stepping cautiously over oily puddles and around a pile of buckled wheels he squeezes between a Transit Van that has obviously hit something very hard and a Volvo that appears to be the injured party, its rear end concertinaed into a rising tangle. Gradually the Subaru's driver's side comes into view.

He remembers an eightie's rock star who would paint one side of his face as a snarling grim reaper, whilst leaving the other side normal. He remembers the video to accompany his single. Remembers the gothic, moody lighting employed to heighten the transition from human to ghoul. Bright flashes of white light would accompany each snarling view of the painted image. He was thirteen at the time and, although he never admitted it to anyone, the video gave him nightmares. Three nights in a row he woke, sweating and flushed, goose pimples raised all over his body. Staring into the darkness, expecting, at any moment, the snarling grin to appear from the black depths of his bedroom, he fought to stay awake.

He got over the scare but doubts whether the image unfolding before his eyes, twenty years later, will *ever* leave him.

The rear bumper is ripped away at the far driver's side corner and the light cluster dangles from a cable like an internal organ hanging from a black artery. With the subdued light shining on the paintwork, he can see ripples on the surface of the boot but they're minor blemishes; nothing that couldn't be repaired in the body-shop.   The rear wheel is missing, accounting for the lopsided cant and the whole car rests on the snapped axle. No brake assembly remains. The rear panel slopes down from the boot and then ends in a jagged tear, its wheel arch exposed to the daylight. Al's eyes sweep along the side of the car, unable to believe what he's seeing.

The whole of the driver's side is missing.

Where the rear door should be, a horrible empty socket stares back at him, twisted and buckled. Bedraggled scraps of foam dangle from the rear seat. To Al, they look like the result of a vicious disembowelling. The sill, running the length of the car, has been peeled back from front to rear. It ends just forward of the rear arch, sticking out in a jagged snarling maw and torn off to leave four inches of twisted steel. The door pillar, between front and rear doors has snapped, six inches down. Amazingly, the sleek dome of the roof remains unaltered. The pillar pokes backwards at forty five degrees like a fence post snapped in a winter storm. Inside, the front seat has twisted from its interior mounting and sits at a distorted angle facing towards the hole that used to be the driver's door. The seat belt has been ripped off at two points and dangles from the remaining anchor. Lying on the tarmac, it looks like a coiled and dangerous, sleeping, black snake. Air bags have gone off in the steering wheel, door pillars and passenger compartments. Hanging flaccid and useless, he can't help thinking of spent condoms. At the front, like the rear, an axle ends where there should be a huge disk brake and calliper. The front wing is also missing. Cables and pipes dangle from the cavernous wheel arch and a pool of green coolant has gathered amongst the oil and grime.

The overall effect is one of utter devastation.

If Jagdeep had told him someone had taken out their considerable wrath on the car with a heavy duty chain-saw, he wouldn't have been surprised.

Not one bit.

He starts at Jagdeep's voice, close behind him.

"It flipped right up in the air when it mounted the central reservation, so they reckon. Must have been really flying though; eighty, ninety, a ton, who knows. The damage came about when it clipped the side of a big tree." He shakes his head and cups his hands around a cigarette, flicks off the Zippo lighter and offers the pack of Bensons to Al. "Thanks." He takes one without thinking and inhales deeply as the Zippo's flame touches its tip.

"I was in the station wagon when we went to collect them. Shit, the Scoobie's panelling was everywhere, all scattered amongst the bushes. We got most of it, but there's probably still some there."

Silence descends, each lost in his own thoughts. Al thinks of the twisted shards of metal and plastic lying in the grass, a silent testament to the loss of life.

"You know the amazing thing? Just *where* the Scoobie had hit the tree. It was a great big fucker ... sorry, 'scuse my French and a huge slice was gouged right out of it, the bark missing, all peeled and white it was, you know? Eight foot in the air as true as I'm standing here talking to you ... eight foot up. I tell you mate, he was going some."

They both turn to leave, Al shuffling past Jagdeep in the cramped space between the wrecks. After a couple of steps he feels the material of his jacket sleeve tugged. He looks back as Jagdeep points to the rear of the car.

"Strange number plate for a bloke though, don't you think?"

The black letters and number are spaced evenly against their bright yellow background.

He takes them in. E-M-I-1-Y. He shrugs, the strangeness lost on him.

"Sorry, I don't see it ..."

"EMILY. You know ... a girl's name? Weird, for a bloke like, don't you reckon?"

"I suppose so ... it's up to him ..."

"... an ye reckon ye saw this number plate on a car as we arrived at the pub?"

Ian's pint is a bare splash of brown liquid in the bottom of his glass, Al's unchanged from when he started his story.

"No question about it. Gave me the creeps when it sank in a moment ago. It was the same car, OK the same type, a green Subaru Impreza. Big spoiler though, like on the new ones."

There follows a strange moment of intense silence, thought and clarity. Al would state later, much later, that it was as though their minds mingled, joined, computed a host of information and came up with the same answer. Different and yet the same.

"Daniel Soames" "David Salt."

"Who?"

"David Salt." Iain offers, swills off the last off his pint, then, with his hand to his mouth, issues a large ripping belch. "'Scuse me. David Salt, Andy must ha mentioned him no? Bought a load o' his paintings, thirty odd grand's worth all told." Al's face is blank. "Aye, aye, true as Ah'm standin' before ye. Tried tae buy that painting over his fireplace as well. *Ten grand* he offered ..." "Yeh, Andy told me about that. But Iain, the bloke in the crash was *Daniel Soames*, believe me I remember from the insurance paperwork. Definitely Daniel Soames." They both stare at each other, a long drawn out space filled with their own jumbled thoughts.

Al continues, "Daniel Soames, David Salt. Same initials, same number plate, same car. Coincidence?"

"Well it's a wee bit strange an' no mistake. Are ye thinkin' he's got himsen a wee bit o' bother or somethin'?"

Al's face is a blank sheet, devoid of any obvious thought or emotion. His eyes are glazed and distant. After a moment Iain begins to worry also.

"Did he know about this trek that Andy's on?"

"Aye, wanted tae meet up wi' him at Bruach Na Frithe. The daft wee basturt's gone an agreed tae dae a picture fer him. 'Sunrise over Blaven' or somethin' like that. He was wantin' tae meet up an' watch the sun rise wi' him. Andy put him off. He's no even s'posed tae be on the island now."

"How would you get to this mountain, this Bruack ne wassissname?"

"Bruach Na Frithe. If ye look from the road, up the glen, Gillean's o' the far left, then Am Bastier, Bastier Tooth, a wee lump on the bealach …"

"The what?"

"The bealach, the pass. It's pretty much where he's gonna be sleepin' the night. Bruach Na Frithe's the next one along, tae the right."

Al considers the geography for a second or two.

"So you'd get to this mountain from the road up here?" He points behind him, "The one the Subaru went up?"

"Aye, ye would, Ah s'pose. Yer thinkin' Andy's in danger are ye?"

"I've no idea mate. Let's face it though, if this *is* the same bloke, the one in the crash, it's a tad spooky that he's changed his name, got pally, with Andy, given him a great big commission, bought his entire stock of paintings, found out where he's going to be, right about now and, just happens to be leaving the car park heading in the same direction someone would take if they were going to walk up Bruach Na Frithe. Too bloody coincidental mate, too coincidental by half."

He stoops and picks up his jacket, "Come on, let's go and have a look."

He doesn't wait for an answer, leaving Iain to scuttle along behind him as he bursts through the door and into a car park bathed in subtle grey light. It's a perfect June evening, warm but with a cooling breeze to keep the midges off. Good walking weather.

Al spins the TVR around in a gravel spitting circle and rumbles slowly past the bar. Children are still playing on the swings and slides of the play-ground, watched by parents supping pints, their tents abandoned on the camp-site across the road. He glances left and right, then powers away, tyres squealing momentarily before finding grip and propelling them up the hill.

"Din'nae go tae fast Al, the first parkin' space is just round the corner."

They both peer into the lay-by. A camper van, parked illegally for the night, its only occupant.

"He's nae there then. The next one's about four hundred yards. There's a wee derelic' shed. Ye'll nae miss it."

"Right."

The rear wheels squeal again as Al tramps the accelerator; first, second, then third gear, the revs rise to fever pitch each time. At ninety, Iain points out the corrugated iron shed on the left and Al lifts off, letting the engine scrub off speed. He breaks heavily near the entrance to the lay-by, sluing round on loose gravel.

There, tucked behind the far side of the shack, the green paintwork of a Subaru Impreza glints in the half-light. Partially hidden and ominous looking; as though it's actually *trying* to hide.

They swing into the crescent of gravel, illuminating the interior with the TVR's headlights.

Empty.

The number plate tells them all they need to know and causes a chill to run up Al's spine and goose pimples to rise on his bare arms.

E-M-I-1-Y.

A light in the glen

I tried to sleep but every few minutes I'd open my eyes and gaze back along the ridge. Grey stone and lighter coloured scree curled away on my right in a seemingly endless, undulating skyline. Much like the previous evening, the sky was clear; but there *was* a difference. Now, as I watched, peeking from under the hem of my fleece hat, mist curled around the boulders in the glen bottom and rose like the spectres of long dead climbers from sluggishly flowing stream courses. At various points, the ridge itself was swathed in white vapour, Alisdair itself appearing like a witch's hat with white fur around its base.

And it was cooler.

At half eleven or thereabouts, I struggled to release myself from my sleeping bag, stretched, yawned and strode the little way back up the scree to the bealach. From there I peered north over dark, rolling hills and glens, along the Trottenish Peninsular and away to the Outer Hebrides. Barely visible in the gloomy distance, they were dark, rounded smudges in the ocean.

The clouds I'd seen earlier were now thick and boiling. Dark grey, massively tall and tinged with a pink glow on their eastern edge. They were utterly beautiful; a natural outpouring of nature's brilliance.

Despite their beauty, they poured a real potential dampener on my plans for the rest of the trip. I didn't fancy scrambling over Gillean's summit, arguably the most difficult and downright scary climbing on the whole ridge, in a howling gale and sheeting rain.

A wind was building from the northwest. With any luck, I thought, the clouds would slip by to the east, pouring their rain on the mainland.

As my cigarette burned down to my fingers, I tossed it into the wind and watched it spiral away before exploding in a shower of sparks on the rocks to my right and almost behind me. It didn't look good for tomorrow - the thought of waking wet and cold holding no real attraction. I watched the cloud and nearly, oh so nearly, chucked it in right then. The escape route in mind was to traverse along the ridge of Sgurr a Bhastier, then follow its eastern flank down into Glen Sligachan. Providing I could get a room, I'd be in bed in three hours and asleep five minutes later.

"Nah, it'll be all right in the morning."

My voice drifted in the breeze and I turned to trudge back to my bivvy site. I'd not completed my turn when I spotted, out of the corner of my eye and way down in the glen to the north, a tiny speck of light. I turned back. It was probably three miles away, coming along the path from Sligachan.

I was intrigued, so sat back against one of the boulders, lit another cigarette, and watched.

In the time it took to finish my smoke, the bobbing light had moved perhaps two or three centimetres across my vision. At the distance I was viewing, it couldn't have been more than fifty yards.

I ground the filter into the gravel and, as a shiver of cold shook me, returned to the warmth of my bag.

A sheep-kill for Al

"I don't like it Iain, not one bit."

Al is standing near the front of the Subaru, the first signs of a cool evening breeze forcing his hands into his pockets. "You reckoned he was a bit loopy right?" Iain nods rubbing his fingers through his beard, "In fact, your exact words were, that he was 'a total and utter creepy wee basturt' am I right?"

"Aye, s'about right."

"So what are we waiting for? He's probably way up there by now and Andy, Christ, he's cocooned in a sleeping bag knocking out the zeds, totally unaware of what's going on. Shit, we gotta get after him, cut the bastard off or something. I mean …"

"Al, Al, Ah'm wi' ye, but fer God's sake, ye din'nae just heid off up the Cuillin at eleven o'clock o' the night in a tee shirt an trainers, June or no." He waves his hands to quiet Al's protestations. "Come on Al, gi' that thing some revs an we can be home, changed an back here in half an hour." Al looks as though he's been allocated every frustration in the world, "Half an hour? He'll have an hour and a half on us by then, we'll never catch him. He could have rolled Andy straight off the fu …"

"He can'nae walk so good. He's got a terrible limp, drags his foot somethin' awful." Their eyes lock in the darkness and Iain smiles, his best, most fatherly, 'don't worry' smile, "We'll catch him, fer Andy's sake, we'll catch him." His hand strays to his chin again, twirling his beard like a child with a comfort blanket, while Al stands and chews the inside of his cheek as though it's his last meal, his face etched with a deep concern.

"We have to."

The TVR leaves thick black lines for fifty yards back towards the hotel …

****

Blackness.

Despite the glow in the west which highlights the odd wispy cloud and late flying gull, in the glen, the path is just a hinted at grey stripe leading him onwards.

After an hour, he rounds a grassy mound and stumbles on a boulder. Falling heavily onto his weaker left leg, he rolls onto his side and lies there for a moment before struggling onto his right knee, supporting himself with outstretched hands. To his left, a foot away, maybe eighteen inches, the heather gives way to stunted grass overhanging a thirty foot jagged cliff, straight into the slow waters of Allt Dear Beag.

Glancing back down the path he sees that the lights of the hotel are hidden from view by the rising ground. A pair of headlights move slowly along the coast road three miles away. He rummages in his pack, dragging out a head torch from the tangles of his waterproof jacket and in the yellow glow of its beam he inspects his knee, pulling the scuffed trousers tight. No blood, but the pain is there.

"The pain oh yes the pain … flares like a bastard sometimes … since that day, that fateful day. You paid though didn't you … bitch? Oh yes you paid all right, but the mountain man? Well he still owes a portion or two. No worries, all will soon be remedied."

The path is a mix of gravel and carefully placed stone, winding its way upwards around grassy mounds. Heather hangs over it, snagging both boots and laces - Dan doesn't like it.

Shouldering his pack, he moves on.

Stationary, on a flat piece of rock, a caterpillar reflects the yellow beam. From end to end it measures almost four inches and with its alternating black and yellow stripes, it looks like the world's largest wasp. Dan's first step pulps it into a sticky writhing mess that leaves a smear of green juices on the sole of his boot. He smiles. A real smile that takes over his usually stony face. A genuine smile that touches his eyes.

"You'll do for starters Mr Caterpillar, my main course is way up there though."

His steps, slow, painful and faltering, scrape over stone and gravel, ever upwards.

****

Twice on the way to the cottage, Iain shuts his eyes and whispers a small, silent prayer to whatever God watches over people travelling in fast moving cars, the first time, barely half a mile from the hotel. The road rises over a crest, then, after a hundred yards traverses over a narrow, flat bridge, kinks left then right. Iain knows the road well having travelled it for many, many years, but never in a four wheel drift at over a hundred miles an hour.

The TVR drifts out over the empty road, tyres squealing. A roaring, scraping thrum vibrates through the whole of the car and he's aware that his eyes are shut tight, his eyelids vibrating in tune with the abused chassis. A timeless, weightless feeling washes over him, like floating and, for a second he's convinced they've left the road and are flying through the air. He opens his eyes and illuminated in the headlights, black and white chevrons alert drivers to the next right hander. They've covered two hundred yards since the last chicane in a matter of seconds, apparently, mostly sideways. Glancing at Al, he sees a face, set in such utter determination and concentration, that he relaxes a little. The car powers through the corner, clipping the gravel on the far side of the road then the grass on the near side. He glances at the speedo and utters a moan; the needle is indicating one hundred and thirty miles an hour. Now they're breaking hard, the needle dropping rapidly, one hundred, eighty, sixty, hard left then right into the junction, bottoming out over a dip in the tarmac. Single track road now. Down to thirty for the right angle, right hand junction, left, right, then hard right at seventy, a blind dropping bend into a dip then over a stream. Now they *do* take flight, the roar of the V8 fills the cabin followed by a squeal of tyres and a slide from the rear.

On, up the straight, then right again. Blind again.

The road is full of sheep.

A dozen lambs and ewes begin to scatter in their subdued, half hearted manner and Iain flashes a glance at Al. His knuckles are white on the leather steering wheel but only the slightest sign of alarm shows in his eyes.

Then they're through.

A ewe, straggly and forlorn looking, half its fleece gone, breaks to the right and is lifted thirty feet in the air, landing high up the grassy bank, twitching. Another disappears under the car and for a second, Iain is sure he can feel and hear a scraping beneath his feet.

He doesn't open his eyes until they pull up at the cottage.

"See you back here in five," is all Al says before sprinting up the path.

Iain sways, his legs having turned to jelly, an effect no boat trip has ever achieved and promptly relieves his stomach of two pints of bitter, the remains of his evening meal and, it seems, most of his breakfast too. It splatters the tarmac and his shoes.

He's already running for his house.

****

Blackness, silent, breeze rippled blackness.

He sits on a large stone, gazing into a massive, hollow, rock amphitheatre. The corrie's entrance is still over half a mile away, open, boggy moorland, criss-crossed with streams and sheep tracks between him and it.

Just past midnight. He's been going for two hours and although his left leg throbs with an insistent pulsating ache, he feels good, feels strong. He knows it's taken him a long time to get to where he now rests, probably twice as long as a guide book would suggest.

"Good things come to those who wait." His voice is gravely with the exertion of breathing hard. He smiles, another good smile, a real smile that lights his eyes in the darkness. Smiling is good. It's a new thing to him - real smiles. Not the sham, half smile that usually creases his face when in company.

Directly in front of him, at the back of the corrie, Bruach Na Frithe rears up against the blue-black night sky. Its sweeping curves drop to the left along a broad pass and then transform into a jagged, crinkled horizon.

There, three miles away, two and a half thousand feet up. There, in the clear night air. There, amongst the scattered rocks and boulders.
His pack rustles as he digs into a side-pocket. Pills rattle in a bottle, two shaken into his palm - painkillers.

The bottle is replaced and now, in his hand, is a battered old tin that once held strong mints. Again, the rattle of pills, but only one this time. Something to raise his game a little, something to improve the odds. It starts to dissolve on his tongue. Bitter. A rush of energy. An almost instant tingle through his muscles and joints.

He could walk up Everest.

Three more hours, he thinks, three gruelling hours of pain to reach his goal. He *will* stumble, he *will* fall again, of that he is sure, but he also knows he will see the sunrise, pure and brilliant gold.

Another smile breaks over his face, another real one.

"Hey, hey, me and Mr Speed ... we're gonna have our finest hour. Oh yes a fine, fine time. You hear me?" His voice rises, unhinged, strangled, utterly manic. "You hear me you bastard? Our finest hour."
Shouldering his pack he limps on, feeling real good now. A real buzz courses through his body and he begins to sing, more of a chant but with some, small semblance of a tune. It rises in volume and raises crows from their roosts amongst the rocks.

"You can run but you can't hide, run but can't hide. Dan gonna get you, gonna sort you out. You hear me? YOU HEAR ME OFFICE

BOY? HEY FUCKER, YOU LISTENING TO DAN?"

Silence descends again, save for the scrape of boots and the odd call from the crows.

Upwards, ever upwards.

****

"Listen Al, Ah din'nae *ever* tell a bloke how to drive, yer ken? But … well, Ah can'nae stand another ride the likes o' the last one … sorry, but Ah threw up a bucketful …"

Al's brow creases in the glow of the interior light, develops into a full blown grin then a deep guffaw of laughter.

"No bother Iain. To tell you the truth, I had to change my boxers." Iain slides into the leather bucket seat as Al continues "We'll take it a bit easier on the way back OK?"

"Aye, may no be a bad idea. Ah din'nae reckon the sheep population could tek much more o' that wild drivin'."

Al nods, "Don't remind me, that was horrible … I couldn't have done anything though could I?"

"Nae bother, nae bother, the bloody things are a pain in the backside anyway. Are we gon'nae get goin' then or what?"

The trip back to Sligachan passes without incident. Fifteen minutes instead of ten and no increase in the dead sheep tally. They stand for a moment, looking up at the classic Cuillin view. They both feel their time is short.

In front of them is the vast green space of Glen Sligachan. The rising slopes of Gillean and Am Bastier scribe black arcs against the sky. The desolation is humbling and although neither of them admit it, terrible fear grumbles in their stomachs. It bubbles and builds and, for the briefest of moments, they both struggle with the urge to turn and flee. The vast emptiness seems to mock them, egging them on into the unknown.

Al presses the key fob and they're bathed briefly in a yellow glow as the alarm arms itself and the central locking activates.

Anyone watching would see the fear on both of their faces.

The girl in the picture

Cool.

Very nearly cold in fact.

The wind from the northwest seemed to have swung around to a full blown northerly, but it was probably just the action of the corrie channelling the rushing air through its funnel of rocks. Whatever the reason, a strong breeze was pushing over the top of the ridge behind me, lifting dust and debris from the dry paths to swirl around my bivvy site.

I'd pulled both arms into my bag, not something I generally do - I don't like the constriction of being fully enclosed. Usually I'll leave an arm out, but in the last hour, since eleven thirty, the temperature had dropped significantly. So I lay there, my face showing from the quilted warmth, like a cross between an Eskimo and an Egyptian Mummy.

I couldn't sleep. Despite, or possibly because of the exertion of the ridge earlier in the day, I was wide awake. I think I dozed for a while shortly before midnight, but woke with a start and didn't know why. I'd struggled to glance at my watch, dimly aware that I'd heard the faintest of shouts; a distant call from distant miles that had plucked at my sleep and jolted me into consciousness.

I'd spent a few minutes listening, straining to hear any sound but hearing nothing except the steady drone of the breeze.

Twice since waking, I'd succumbed to the pull of a nicotine fix, despite beginning to run low *and* having to rummage one handed in my rucksack (which was doubling up as my pillow), for the partially crushed pack.

There's something intensely comforting about smoking when all around you lies emptiness and, to the uninitiated, desolate wasteland. As each exhaled plume of smoke dissipated in the breeze, the view would shimmer for a second and then snap back into focus. Subdued and faded in the evening dimness but its beauty enhanced because of this. Subtle shades of grey, more numerous than I would have believed possible, spread away on all sides. Gradually blending and mingling with the black velvet sky over the mainland, they seemed an impossible task for a painter. Concentrating on all their differences I attempted to submit as much of the scene to memory as I could, determined to at least *try* and replicate it on canvas.

The thought of painting allowed a thought to simply barge straight in to my head, muscling in like a bore at a party and wrestling all my other thoughts out of the way.

David Salt and his stinking commission.

I shut it out as quickly as I could, but still it seemed to linger. I rolled it around in my head, picking over the details; the offer for the painting over my fireplace; the bulk purchase of all my work at Mrs N's; the cold, dead handshake; the equally cold blue steely gaze.

The girl in the picture

"That wasn't necessarily him," I muttered through a breath full of Marlboro's finest.

But there it was.

My brain, at least the deep subconscious part of it that sorts out the crappy bits, had decided that he *was* the phantom artist, the 'micro-painter'; more than that, the house breaker. Realisation that, deep down, I believed him to be the culprit, set off a squirming anger which built within me. I closed my eyes trying desperately to shut out the vision of him in *my* house, delicately flicking a tiny brush on *my* work. Adding his own touch.

"Bastard," my low curse set me chatting to myself, to the dark mountains; "you can shove your commission up your icicle encrusted arse. Any painting I do as a result of this trek will be for me or my friends, not some creepy, cold hearted bastard like you." I exhaled and again the far crags shimmered amongst the swirl, then cleared and became sharp. "Go to hell."

I think I slept for a while then, more of a light nap really, drifting in and out in a hazy mix of full sleep and dozing.

At one o'clock I was fully awake, alert and as far from sleep as I could possibly get. I dragged my fleece from inside my rucksack and, zipping it fully against the wind, jogged back up to the ridge, stamping my feet, forcing blood to flow. Another cigarette flared, this time the smoke obscured the corrie falling away in front of me and the far isles floating in their black sea. Their cloud capping had shifted, the billowing grey and white bulk now hung over the Mainland, leaving behind it a light dusting of bright, almost glowing vapour that hovered a thousand feet over the island's small rounded hills.

My eyes scanned the path down the scree, through the huge, hollowed out bowl of the corrie and then on. No light. No bobbing head torch. No tortoise-like progress along the path from Sligachan.

As I stood, watching the night getting on with passing the time, I was aware of the wind decreasing. As if someone had flicked a switch, the rush of cool air slowed to a barely discernible trickle and I waited, expecting another gust to blast its way over the ground.

Nothing.

After five minutes I flicked my finished smoke out into the void and watched it fly, twisting end over end, straight and true. No breeze caught its flight. Where earlier, the iridescent speck had curled around, almost landing behind me on the stones, this one stayed straight as an arrow, dipping towards the scree, bouncing, sending up sparks. I glanced to my right, tracing Gillean's summit to a tiny point in the clear air. It looked awesome, scary and magnificent all at once. Not for the first time, I silently questioned my decision to climb it. The drops between the three jagged pinnacles that make up its ridge are amongst the most exposed places anywhere in the UK. I looked straight up, into a dark sky as beautiful as I had ever seen and felt a great sense of serenity. Suddenly confident that I could tackle anything that the ridge could throw at me, I was back in my bag within a minute and fast asleep in two.

Lonely soldiers

From the main path, across the boggy ground to the first slopes of short-cropped grass and intermittent scree, the going is hard. After heavy rain, the peat is sodden and slippery. The path will meander for a while then peter out at a ditch or stream, only to reappear fifty yards away to the left or right or straight ahead. All the time, in the distance, the summit of Bruach Na Frithe seems to watch, sniggering with smug glee at lopsided, stumbling progress. The axe blade of the Bastier Tooth, 'The Executioner', peeps out from its rocky home, also mocking. In the day-time it's possible to allow your eyes to wander up to these high places, to spur tired legs onward.

In the darkness of a Cuillin night, the pleasure is lost ...

A great shadow rises, thousands of feet above and still a gruelling three miles distant, a seemingly impossible task, but the speed is working, allowing a torrent of energy to course through an otherwise tired body. Dan stumbles on.

His face is set in a grimace that is one part stubbornness, one part determination, one part chemical reaction and seven parts hatred. He's given up on the path; now his head is down, eyes cast at ground eerily illuminated in his torch beam.

He's decided the path is a loathsome thing that constantly tries to lure him off course. The idea has built to a point where he believes the path is in collusion with his intended quarry, a mean spirited, twisting weapon that wants him lost and broken. He needs no part of it. He can make out more solid ground, perhaps fifty yards away, the scree and bouldered pathway representing the start of the real climb.

A bray of laughter shoulder-charges its way into the silence and anyone hearing it would surely cower back into the confines of their warm sleeping bag, try to convince themselves that it was the wind rushing through rocky outcrops above. Its raucous edge teeters on the edge of humanity and crosses the threshold of a rational mind into the no-mans land of the utterly depraved. Sometime in the period between his rest on the path, the taking of the speed and the point at which he now stands, Dan has lost his mind.

He's mud splashed; dirty water dripping from his face and hands make him appear born from the peat itself. As though, in some terrible ritual as old as time itself, the peat bog has spawned an infant in the form of a man, before which, good, mortal souls will fall to their knees and quake.

A large pool of water, left by the last rains, lies in the earth before him; a hazy reflection, a face, dripping with streaks of dark liquid, stares back. It ripples as drops of water break the film, distorting the image, making it sway and spread. Beside it, looking angelically over his shoulder, the innocent, blonde haired girl smiles with all the sweetness of a pre-Raphaelite cherub and Dan spins, desperately grasping for his beloved sister, his Emily. His hands grasp nothing more than clear Scottish night, a greeting half way from his lips and he stumbles backwards, arms pin-wheeling.

The pool is shallow, soft bottomed and the water as cold as his heart. He falls heavily, feeling a muscle tear and burn deep in his weak leg.

Lying on the soft heather, the pool now some way behind him, the empty night sky pulses with images that block any feelings of cold or pain. In his mind, a cloud, solitary and utterly benign, tears open from within and the face of his Emily breaks free. Gone is the angelic smile, the cherub's face crowned by curly blonde locks hanging in ringlets. Instead, the snarling face of a demon, blue eyes, now black, screaming out a malevolent rage that rips into Dan's soul. Her pretty, upturned nose is now a black beak, a Raven's 'caaaaww' breaks free from her with a force that spears through his conscious brain and twists deep in its pulp like a knife.

In an instant, as quickly as he can blink his terrified eyes, the vision changes.

Beautiful and alluring, the red haired woman smiles meekly at him, her face filling the sky. As Dan watches, her features switch and flicker, the background a flashing, strobe-like mix of trees and tarmac. He has the feeling of being on a bizarre fairground ride; a spinning, thumping roller coaster that can only have one ending. Sounds steals into his ears; the breaking of glass, rending of steel, scraping of metal on concrete. Blood begins to flow from the pretty eyes of his gyrating vision, then from the mouth and ears; it sprays outwards in crimson jets. The sound dies, simply ceases and, as he watches, he realises he is looking at a corpse. Lifeless eyes, open mouth, still and quiet.

Then, it's gone.

Cool air flows around him, chilling his body beneath sodden clothing. Dan gets slowly to his feet. Water flows down his legs and arms. In the distance, way down the glen, the lights of the Sligachan twinkle once more now he's gained height.

Darkness all around, but more than that. A darkness within. As he once more begins his plod upwards, even the pain in his leg, only a moment ago, a screaming agony, has gone.

The frightened hiker, cowering in his bag, would not see a broken man with a painful limp, but a headstrong, determined force. The frightened hiker would stay low, keep quiet and, at all costs, avoid the look from those terrible eyes.

****

A sheen of sweat has broken out over Al's face and neck. Despite the chill, he can feel the trickle of moisture on his back beneath his rucksack. The steady tramp of their feet is the only sound and, with their steady beat to accompany him, he ponders on their quest and whether it's simply an overreaction. And quest it is, or at least that's what it feels like. Lonely soldiers marching into an unknown arena, through the stillness and blackness of a mountain environment that's both alien and yet welcoming at the same time.

The silence *does* seem to welcome them. It calls them on, beckoning them into its hidden depths.

Up ahead, Iain has stopped. Against the backdrop of the still glowing western sky, his silhouette takes the form of a statue soldier, his walking stick a gun on which to lean. Al feels a surge of strength and willpower just from knowing he's not alone.

"Taking a breather? We really need to be pushing …"

"We ha' a wee choice tae mek Al," Iain cuts in, not a hint of breathlessness. "See here?" He points at the path winding its way towards Glenbrittle, "That's the path our man will ha' taken. The thing is, dae we follow, an try tae catch him up, or …" even in the darkness, Al's sure he sees a glint in the old Scot's eye, "… or dae we try tae cut the basturt off?"

Al waves his hand "Go on."

"He's got a gammy leg has he no? He *will* ha' gone up the way there. Nae question. Easiest route up the Cuillin … an' he'll ken it."

"OK, go on."

"Ah'm just thinkin', if we wiz tae cut across the base o' the mountain here …" he points south with his stick into a pitch black emptiness "… we can flank him. We're travellin' twice his pace, got tae be. Even wi' his heid start, Ah fancy we can beat him tae the bealach …" a pause, "… the pass, where yer man, Andy is."

"What's the ground like though? It looks steep, let's face it, it looks bloody awful. I'm no mountaineer, a few walks is …"

"It's quicker. It's no dangerous. Well," he adds, "no much anyhow."

"Ah, shit, you're the leader … yeh go on , let's do it."

Iain's away with a nod of his head, taking the southern path that leads towards the base of Gillean and its sister peak, Sgurr a'Bhastier. Al starts after him, quickly getting back into his rhythm. The distance seems to fly by, the path is good, occasionally uneven and often indistinct, but basically good; level, easy going.

"Hey if we get above him and cut him off, perhaps we could lob a few rocks at him?" Al laughs at his own joke, a good wholesome chuckle, well received by Iain who shouts back "Ah'd like tae bounce a few rocks off his heid ma sen. We could mek it seem like he's had himsen a wee tumble. Aye fuckin' right."

A brief ripple of laughter flows between them in the darkness and then, once again, silence, save for the their footfall and Al's breathing; back to work.

He's never walked in the mountains at night before. Plenty of times along river banks and around pools, but never amongst mighty mountains. The midnight sea trout rivers are intimate, enclosed places, tree hung and vegetation rich. They are places where one can stop for a chat with other anglers, still able to mingle with like-minded souls.

This is different.

After half an hour, the ground is rising steeply over a series of grassy hillocks. On the horizon, the three improbable teeth of Gillean soar high into the air. Al thinks they're quite likely guarding the gateway to Hell. Massive and impenetrable, they strike a deep fear into him.

Ten minutes on and Iain's stopped again. He's sitting on a rounded boulder, his head torch illuminating a patch of heather at his feet. As Al approaches, his own torch flashes briefly into Iain's face, making him squint and hold up a hand, "Jesus Al, ye tryin' tae blind me?"

"Sorry mate, they tend to shine where you look don't they?"

In the briefest of moments before Iain raises his hand and then turns away, Al sees terrible tiredness, almost resignation. He's un-shouldered his pack and, with a careful deliberation, removes his flask, pours a coffee and drinks in grateful gulps. Al does the same and, for a while, they sit in silence.

"Listen, I know you think I'm being a bit of a wimp, but …" he points to Gillean, "… we're not going over *that* are we? I mean, I really don't …"

"Relax junior, ye'd nae get me over that thing. Nae bloody way."

Al fills with relief as Iain continues, pointing straight ahead. "Nae bother, *that's* where we're heading. Sgurr a'Bhastier."

Al looks stunned and scared while Iain swills his coffee, shakes the dregs from his cup and adds, "It's still a bit o' a basturt, but really, it's nae so bad." He continues as he re-packs his sack and throws it onto his back. "It's all rock, after the first wee bit o' scree. Good solid ground. As I remember, there's nae much o' a path really. Bit scrambly, few boulders an' stuff. Nae exposed though, din'nae worry ye sen Al, ye'll be OK."

A brief but crystal clear image of the pass between Blaven's North and South peak springs into his head and the fact that he's *heard that phrase before.*

"Ahh, God I hate these bastard mountains. I swear Iain, if we get off this alive, I'm never setting foot up here again. I'll become a mountain 'watcher'; I'll sit me down in the Sligachan with a pint of something cold. I'll watch the loonies who enjoy this, watch em coming back after a day up here and say 'how-do' and order me another pint. I'll buy books and read about them, look at photos and 'ooh and ahh' at Andy's paintings. But all from sea level. I tell you …"

Iain is thirty yards away, just starting to climb the scree at the base of Sgurr a'Bhastier. His torch is bobbing along, the pool of light its beam creates, swinging left and then right. In the darkness Al can hear him chuckling.

"Wait then you big hairy Scot, a bloke could get lost here you know."

Iain roars with laughter and bends over his stick, helpless.

"Ye din'nae stop talkin' enough tae get lost; Ah reckon they heard that last piece o' rantin' in the bar."

He turns and continues, his feet shuffling on the gravel sized scree ...

****

... The scree is awful. A shifting, sliding, unstable mess and Dan has already lost count of the number of times he's slipped to his knees.

But any trace of pain in his left leg has now gone and for the first time since his 'accident' he feels strong, back to his old self.

Dan the invincible. Dan the super-hero.

It's Emily that gives him his strength, the will to continue.

She has come to him twice now, urging him on with tender words of encouragement. She calls him 'Danny' when she speaks to him. An old, nearly forgotten pet name he vaguely remembers being called by his mother. No one would call him that now. No one has called him that since he was a boy.

It simply doesn't fit anymore.

He stumbles heavily and sits down on the slope. All around him the huge walls of the corrie tower like a massive rock stadium. Behind him, the land sweeps away. There are no lights now. The slopes of Sgurr a'Bhastier to his right hide the hotel and the road is a distant memory. No tarmac up here, just nature's materials; rock and heathery patches of green, the trickle of water to his left and the empty expanse of nothingness above.

A sound behind him has him spinning around, sending a cascade of stones away from his boots.

Way above, the pass that separates the two converging ridges of the corrie, stands out against the skyline. Snaking its way up towards this, he can see his path, more distinct now that he's gaining height. The top appears close enough to touch if he were to stretch out his hand. His arm is outstretched, reaching forward, then he's lying face down, his breath blowing tiny particles of grit from between the stones.

"You can't fool me, you sister-killer. But don't worry, you're mine. Oh yes, you're mine."

His mind is still slipping away a fraction at a time. He's now convinced he's stalking the murderer of his Emily. The memory of the accident has faded, not gone entirely, but drifting. He knows that he took something from his intended quarry but can't remember … it's hazy … unclear. It *will* come back, of that he's sure. If not? Well, it doesn't matter.

He knows his work is dark at the top of the pass; knows that there, sleeping like a baby, is someone that has to, simply must, die.

That he can't remember *exactly* why, is irrelevant. Emily has told him.

And the wolf.

The wolf spoke to him earlier.

It said the same.

He thought that the noise behind him had been Mr Wolf returning to egg him on, keep him going.

Mr Wolf has obviously slipped away - off stalking his own prey.

At the entrance to the corrie, the ground flattens off, lush grass and heather spreads in all directions; an area the size of a couple of football pitches. In the centre there's a huge rock, as big as a two-car garage that marks the way forward. Its sheer faces glistened as though sprinkled with diamonds, each one picking out what scrap of light remained in the west. Patches of moss clung to the cold surface, seeming to glow with an effervescence that was borne of the rock itself.

He stood, open mouthed as he took in the spectacle, dimly aware that he was sinking to his knees.

A huge shadow was being thrown by the beast that stood on top of it. Although there was no moon to backlight its shaggy head and shoulders, it seemed to throw its own black image towards a now sobbing Dan.

He shut his eyes, convinced, in his rapidly degenerating mind, that he was about to be devoured. For long seconds he remained, kneeling, eyes tightly closed, a warm trickle of liquid spilling down his leg to his knee.

"It's all right Danny. I'm not going to harm you. You should know that."

The voice was familiar. Desperately, he scanned through his memory, picking at snatches of conversation, rejecting, sifting again. Finally, after what seemed like a lifetime of searching, he settled on a match.

His father.

Last seen as a face at a window, surrounded by raw heat and flame, crackling timbers and roaring, scorching fire, the memory rushed back. It enfolded him, wrapping him in a claustrophobic blanket of sorrow and shame, then anger that he should be bothered by this voice from the grave.

He opened his eyes, hatred glaring out from their cold black depths, ready to scream at his tormentor.

His vision was filled with the power and grace of a magnificent, shaggy coated animal. Its teeth were exposed in a snarl, saliva dripping in tear-shaped drops that glowed as they fell to the ground.

The voice of his father snarled at him. "I *said* I wouldn't harm you and I meant it. But ..." the wolf shook his head sending a shower of sparkling droplets into the darkness, its teeth flashed, long and curved, wickedly effective, "... don't piss me off. That's a nice piece of advice Danny-boy, don't even think about it." The wolf sat on its haunches while its tail flicked in a lazy arc left and right. It yawned. The full expanse of its teeth flashed and Dan felt his bladder give way again.

"We have lots to talk about Danny. Lots to say and yet time is short and getting shorter all the time." It turned its head towards the high pass and its nose wrinkled, twitching and glistening in the cool air.

"You stink like a disused toilet you know. We have to sort out some things, set some old stuff straight and I'd prefer if you could do it without ... well ... *leaking*."

"Sorry." Dan hesitated, chewing over his words carefully, then added, "Dad?"

They talked for a while, sharing old times, not the thing anyone would expect between a victim and his murderer. Had the sleeping bagged hiker felt brave enough to follow Dan up the slope into the corrie, he would have seen a man, on his knees, holding a one-sided conversation before a huge boulder. The smell of urine would have been strong, but the rancid stink of madness would have been stronger.

Dan scratches his chin, an absent minded, confused and pathetic gesture. His khaki canvas trousers are damp, the stain, once dark, is fading, becoming less noticeable. The stink still lingers but he's unaware of this, in his state of madness he's unaware of anything much.

Somewhere, deep in the recesses of his tangled thoughts, there *is* the knowledge that he has to climb, must continue upwards; something or someone up there, is waiting for him. The darkness that presses in on him from all sides scares him a little. The huge, towering rocks scare him a lot. His head flashes from side to side as he stumbles along the steepening path, watching out for the rock faces closing in. Never, has he been in such a desolate place. The breeze rushing over him is like the moaning of lost souls and forces a blubbering sob from his quivering lips at each caress. Soft and yet empty as an old grave, the rippling touch of each blast of air raises fresh goose pimples and shivers that turn him to jelly.

His limp has returned, but he feels no pain even though the speed he popped earlier has almost worn off. The stream that he has followed up the whole of the corrie, is dwindling as he gets higher. Now, the deep gorge, once filled with the sound of gushing water is a boulder filled, shallow depression with sluggish pools.

Dan stands, hands on hips, surveying the ridge above him.

Three hundred feet?

Maybe a touch more. Surely no more than four, four fifty at the absolute most.

"Not long Danny." The voice startles him into a frantic panic, he spins to his left and before he knows what's happening, his boots have tangled together, spilling him onto his right hand side. Still searching for the source of the voice, he continues to turn and, in mid air, executes a perfect roll that sets him barrelling down the slope towards the almost dried up stream.

A large rock, angular and wickedly sharp, strikes his right temple and his fall ceases along with his consciousness. It is only a minor tumble, a silly slip. On the ridge he would be dead.

Had he known he'd jumped at his own voice, even in his insane stupor, he would likely have smiled to himself.

The rock is cold …

****

"… bloody cold, freezing in fact."

"Aye junior, wakes ye up though. Dae ye no agree?"

Al is half way up Sgurr a'Bhastier, swilling his face with handfulls of freezing cold, clear mountain water. Iain is twenty feet above him, resting against his stick, leaning nonchalantly, despite the steepness. He was right though, the exposure is minimal and Al is coping well.

"How much further?"

"Ah, difficult tae say in the dark," he scans across to the south, letting his eyes travel across the void to Gillean and the Bastier Tooth, "probably a wee way yet ye ken? Three or four hundred feet tae this wee summit." He glances down at Al, already trudging towards him. "We've med good time junior. Aye, reckon we'll catch him yet, heid him off at least. Ye fit?"

"Aye Senior, s'pose Ah am but Ah've nae felt tae good fer a wee while now."

"Hey, that's nae tae bad Al. Keep practisin', we'll hae ye as an honorary Scot yet."

"I'll settle for getting off this mountain alive thanks."

In the darkness, Iain nods and turns, heading off up the rock strewn ridge. His head torch illuminates a patch of ground ten feet in front of him.

"Aye, wise words junior, wise words indeed."

Nearly dawn

I woke from a deep sleep.

Squinting into the darkness, I was aware of the faintest of glows over Blaven to the southeast, its ridge quite clear in the strengthening light. It looked black and dangerous. The sky was an amazing silvered screen, glowing with the imminent arrival of a new day, the darkness above being shoulder-charged away by shimmering light for another twenty hours or so.

I glanced at my watch. In the distinctly eerie dawn glow, the face shone with a reflected luminescence - 2.45 a.m.

I lit a cigarette, inhaled deeply then, once again, the view to the south swirled, as I exhaled. Craning my neck, I peered up the scree to the ridge above. It was still dark over Bruach na Frithe to the west and Sgurr a Fionn Choire was a black jagged lump framed by a sprinkle of stars. The storm that I'd been concerned about had skirted the island, leaving the sky clear and bright. I thought that anyone on top of Slioch or An Teallach on the mainland would be trying to dry themselves out by now. The temperature seemed to have dropped a few degrees further and I shivered as I lay and smoked, thinking about the day ahead.

I was still concerned about Gillean and my ability to traverse it safely. The scrambling itself was not an issue, generally good holds on rough, grippy gabbro. But God, the exposure, the sickening, stomach churning drops on both sides, the steepness of it drawing the eye away to the glen nearly three thousand feet below and giving the impression that a careless slip would result in one landing on the hotel roof.

I didn't know whether I could cope with that.

Twisting in my bag, I leaned on my left elbow and allowed my gaze to follow the fractured rock upwards to Gillean's summit. It looked ridiculously pointed. Not difficult on its own, but the three peaks separated by gaping chasms on the eastern side were hidden. Waiting.

I flipped my finished cigarette into the darkness and lay back down, determined to get another half hour's sleep.

I'd make up my mind when I had to.

A boot print in the gravel

In the last few minutes, Al's head has begun rolling from side to side.

His breathing is still good and strong but his legs, specifically his thighs, are screaming. The pace is gruelling. Seasoned hill-walkers would raise an eyebrow at the speed they're ascending the ridge. For rank amateurs, it's crippling.

The ridge itself is sharp, uneven and hard-going although the rock is wonderfully rough. It in-stills a confidence in the two friends; they both feel invincible, as though a slip is unthinkable.

He glances up and his torch beam illuminates Iain who turns and shouts a message of encouragement.

Al smiles, a tired, resigned smile that seems to conflict with the throbbing, raw pain in his thighs. He shakes his head and watches as Iain's head torch snaps upwards, shinning its beam into the sky.

Then all is black and empty.

For a split second Al thinks Iain's torch batteries have failed, then, a scream and shouted curse cut through the night followed by a rumble of rolling rocks, more shouts and the terrible sound of sliding over loose stone.

"Iain, IAIN!" Nothing, just the sound of the still mountain, its breeze sighing over the rocks. Silence; absolute, save for the pounding of his pulse, thumping out its increasing bass line in his ears.

Al has never felt more alone.

In five seconds of confusion, the world has dropped away, leaving him standing, perched on a slab of rock, the gaping hole of Coire a Bhastier gleaming blackly to this left and the pointed summit of his chosen route highlighted high above him in the pre-dawn glow.

With a terror building in his chest, he makes his way onward, ensuring that each footfall is placed directly into the yellow pool thrown by the head torch. He's not aware of what's happened, only that Iain has fallen, that in the second it took to shout encouragement, his torch light has missed something; a drop off, a gully or a crack in the rock.

Al is not going to make the same mistake.

Ten yards on, his beam stretches out over a void, a gap in the ridge and he kneels then lies flat on the cold, rough rock.

He peers over the drop, seeing the steep fall of scree plunging ever downwards.

His cheek is flat against the rock …

****

… the rock is cool against his face. It feels damp, but it's not water. A thin trickle of blood is seeping from a gash on his temple and his first attempt to move causes Dan to swoon. A sickly feeling of nausea sweeps over him and he lies still. After a few moments through which he travels in a semiconscious drifting haze, he feels well enough to lift himself into a sitting position. Knowledge seeps back into his head, gradually clearing away the stupor that has enfolded him.

High on the ridge, the first real signs of the new dawn are illuminating the craggy horizon.

He sits, limp, like a rag doll, his eyes shut, coldness seeping through his trousers. His palms are wet, his fingers sinking into cooling gravel.

He's sitting in the stream bed.

Between his knees his head torch illuminates the trickle of clear water, its movement causing a resurgence of the earlier nausea.

As it clears, Dan realises that there, right at the edge of the small, crystal clear pool of water is an imprint of a boot. The pattern of the tread is clear and there, right at their centre is a name. It takes him a while to read, as the letters are inverted - 'Salomon'.

He *knows* that name.

The recognition rings in his head as clear as a church bell.

Where has he heard that name?

OK, it's a well known brand among the climbing community so why should it matter?

"Andy fucking Perkins."

He remembers a brief conversation, where they discussed the footwear needed for a trek over the Cuillin.

"Andy wears Salomon boots."

Thoughts flood in; the reason for this ridiculous night-time climb; the paintings; the accident, but most of all, the real reason why the sleeping man on the top of the hill has to die.

His madness is more acute now. Conversely, a re-gaining of some knowledge, some small degree of reality has now strengthened his loss of sanity.

He stands and surveys the ridge above him.

Very close now, it seems. Ten minutes and he can place his feet on flat ground and begin the search. He may sit a while and watch the sun come up for himself; he doesn't need a painting - he can memorise the real thing.

Bruach na Frithe looks like a good spot, a fine place for some quiet contemplation before a spot of retribution.

Yes, Bruach Na Frithe looks fine and dandy.

As he moves away, lurching back towards the path up steep scree, he hears the stones rattle away below him ...

****

... a rattle of stones breaks through the stillness, the sound chirping and clattering from way below. Al tenses, ready to shout, then hesitates, tilting his head to one side, trying to get an accurate fix on the source of the sound.

"Iain," a pause, "Iain," louder this time.

Time stretches onwards and for a moment he is truly alone.

"Shite ... I tell ye Al, Ah din'nae recommend sliding on yer arse doon that basturt."

"Iain?" A sense of relief like Al has never experienced in his life, surges through him. "Are you OK? I can't even see you. Hang on I'll come down."

He drops the four feet behind him onto the flat plateau of the gravely path then, oh so cautiously, steps around the bulk of rock to the top of the scree filled channel.

Iain's voice filters up from the darkness below. "Ah'm OK, really Al, jus' gi me a wee minute Ah'll be wi' ye in a mo."

Al ignores this and begins descending, his head torch searching the unstable blocks beneath his feet. Dark and foreboding, the shadows are silky and black, the rock, wet to the touch of his outstretched, probing fingers. He can't imagine an uncontrolled fall through this terrible hell-hole. One minute striding along on good, solid, rough rock; the next, plummeting through space and sliding in an uncontrolled tangle of arms and legs through a black void.

After what seems an interminable time, Al sits next to a prone Iain. His rucksack has split and lies at an angle behind him. Al can see that his fleece has ridden up from his waist and is bunched around the middle of his back and shoulders.

They sit in silence for a while.

Together again in their quest; it's enough for the time being.

Al speaks first.

"Are you alright?" The question is timid, tinged with a decidedly nervous edge. "Jesus mate, you just … well, disappeared."

"Aye, nae a bad tumble Ah reckon." He pauses weighing his words, keeping the fear at bay. "Ah would'nae recommend it one wee bit. Scairt the shite out o' me, an no mistake."

"Are you OK though? Any breaks? Any pain?"

"Aye junior, plenty o' pain. Ye try slippin' doon tha' jumble o' crap on yer arse. Aye plenty o' pain. Nae any breaks though," another pause, "none that Ah can feel anyhow."

"I tell you what, I thought you were dead. You *just disappeared*." Al giggles, his laughter building. The relief of finding Iain alive and more to the point relatively *unhurt*, is incredible.

"Your … torch … it … just … flipped up … in the air! Whoosh … and you were gone!"

Iain turns his head, looks straight into Al's eyes and literally explodes with laughter. For a minute or two they rock in uncontrollable bouts of giggling. Gradually their mirth subsides and silence stretches between each bout of sniggering.

"S'pose we'd better be away, dae ye nae think?"

"If you're sure you're alright?"

"Aye mate, s'nae tae bad really. Feel like Ah've been in a rugby match, but aye, s'nae tae bad."

They shuffle and slip back up the slope; ten minutes to complete a journey that took Iain about three seconds on his way down. Back on the ridge, Al takes the opportunity to inspect Iain's back. Red scratches and grazes oozing thick, viscous blood, extend over the whole of his lower back but the majority of the force was taken by the cushioning effect of his fleece, shirt and thermal vest. Deep slashes above his trousers are freely bleeding and Al wipes them, applying pressure with his own fleece sleeve.

"Sit down for a minute Iain, I really need to have a look at these cuts."

He doesn't complain, just sits on the nearest rock, bending forward at the waist to expose his bare flesh. He sits with his head in his hands while Al searches through his own rucksack.

The fact that he doesn't really need his head torch now is a surprise. He finds a battered tube of antiseptic cream in one of the pockets and turns back to his friend. The sky over Gillean is now a beautiful pale blue, getting brighter as each minute passes.

"It's really getting light now mate."

"Aye, a new day an' all that. Tell ye what, Ah'm bloody knackered. God, Ah can'nae remember ever bein' this tired."

"Seems like we've been on this mountain for days." Al pauses, stretching his back with his hands on his hips, "It feels like my thighs are going to explode."

He bends to his task, smearing the pink goo over Iain's lower back, smudging deep red blood over his skin. He doesn't have time to ensure the blood has fully stopped, doesn't have time for any of this really. They *have* to keep moving.

The blood and cream have left light and dark whirls of colour like a child's finger painting. It looks a mess but at least it should help stop infection. Al thinks a couple of the deeper cuts above the waist will need a stitch or two.

He pats Iain's back, replaces the tube of cream and shoulders his pack.

"Thanks. Tell ye what, it stings somethin' terrible."

Iain stands and tenuously flexes his arms and then his legs, rolls his head from side to side, an alarming crack coming from his neck as he does so.

"Ohh, shite, that hurt. Better now though. Rheumatics ye see junior. Comes tae us all ye ken?"

"You're not doing so bad for an old un."

Iain bends for his own sack, lifting it by its broken strap. Useless.

"Hey junior, Ah din'nae like tae ask, but could ye see yer way tae carryin' a few bits an bobs fer me? Mah pack's sin better days."

They are only twenty paces further on, both looking stiff, cold and tired when Al, in the lead now, stops and turns back.

In the new dawn, the view is impressive. The craggy ridge over which they've travelled snakes its way towards a point where it simply vanishes six or seven hundred feet below. The glen, bathed in the early morning sun is fifteen hundred feet below the ridge but the effect is of seamless continuity. Iain's pack lies on the path. Ragged and forlorn, it looks like a small, dead animal left to rot.

"We're too late aren't we? We spent too much time on the ridge, drank too much coffee, dallied too long."

Iain's face is one of stern determination.

"Din'nae think like that youngster. Never, never, gi' up hope. It's nae over till the fat bloke sings, ye ken?"

"Yeah, you're right I suppose, but … well I reckon he might be taking the applause by the time we're up there. How much longer?"

"Ah reckon ten minutes an' we'll be on the pass, mebee fifteen - give or tek."

They continue, no torches needed now, their feet fall on stone bathed in dim grey light that grows in intensity with each step.

Breakfast

My stove lit at the second attempt. Spluttering into life, its flame glowing bright orange then settling itself into an even blue. I sat and waited for the water to boil, comfortable on my sleeping bag and sleep-mat. Boots on, dust covered and damp looking after their night out in the open. My fleece felt cold and clammy, recently relieved from its job as ineffective pillow in my rucksack.

I added a juice sachet to the pan, munched my way through a packet of crackers and cheese, lit a cigarette and watched the new day grow. Shadows shrunk back from the low-lying peaks in front of me and a wisp of mist, as sinuous as smoke from a damp fire, rose from the stream bed in the glen.

I sipped my drink.

I thought of the day to come.

I analysed my chances of success.

I thought of Rachel.

I peered up the main ridge to the west. The slope down which I had travelled the previous day was grey and dusty, rising steadily to Bruach Na Frithe. A fellow climber had taken up station on one of the far rocks. He sat, cross legged, facing away from me and towards the southern end of the ridge. He was over a hundred yards away so I couldn't make out any detail, just the shape of a similarly lonesome mountain traveller, taking in the beauty of a June morning in the Cuillin.

"Blimey, he's keen. Thought I was up and about early."

I thought I'd have a stroll up the path and say 'Good morning' once I'd finished my drink, then turned back to my own view and my own thoughts.

A chill sped through me and I shivered enough to spill some of my juice.

Recognition

As Dan arrives at the summit, the sun's glow bathes a face as cold and stony as the surrounding rock. The still weak, but gradually building heat of its rays have no effect on the iciness of the dazzling blue stare sweeping to and fro along the black rock of the ridge.

For Dan, the abject horror of the previous five hours has been eclipsed by the view that spreads before him. He's forgotten the cold embarrassment of his ducking in the peat stained water and the childlike misery of urinating in his pants. These details have faded to a dim jumble of thoughts that could easily originate from his pre-school days. He remembers something about a wolf. It could be from a trip to the zoo, but for the fragmented belief that he - as ridiculous as it sounds, even to him - *held a conversation with it.*

He is focused now, the killer's gleam in his eye.

The 'Ice Man' is back.

A fluttering rise in his heart rate sets his nerves tingling. Adrenaline courses through his body. Externally he is almost comatose, blank, seemingly unmoved by his surroundings. Internally, he is a buzzing, rapidly building force; a tsunami pushing up from the ocean depths, building in height as it rushes coast-wards, rising and growing, speeding forward. Soon, his full force will be unleashed.

He sits, cross-legged on his chosen rock, his pack, snug against his back. His boots, dripping and mud splattered, leave brown streaks where they slide back and forth against the rough, grey gabbro. His hair, once blonde, sporty, is smeared with peat and flecked with mud, leaves and grit. It clings to his head like a skull cap. A patch of blood, the size of a playing card, is drying in the breeze high on his left cheekbone. The remains of its trickling path have dried, leaving vein-like, branching streaks that extend to his jaw-line. His mouth is set in a strange half-smile. Straight, brilliant white teeth peep through thin, dark lips. A run of drool has crept from the right hand corner of this grinning cavern. Speckled with a mix of blood and peaty water, it looks as though a slug has crept from his mouth and down his chin.

Dan - the tsunami, avalanche and mud-slide all rolled into one, handy, man-sized package. The madness is the necessary energy but the memory of the job un-done provides the momentum to push onwards. His *reason* was lost for some time during the climb to his summit, but now it's clear.

He's aware of the climber, his target, reclining on the green sleeping bag. He senses, rather than sees, the acknowledgement of his presence, the hasty sweep of eyes that follow the grey rock upwards, resting briefly on the back of his head.

Recognition?

He doesn't think so, but, senses attuned as they are, clarified and sharpened by the knife-edged quality of his madness, he feels a drawing back of his quarry.

Maybe a shiver?

"You'll shiver soon you bastard. Oh yes, you'll shiver." Dan is staring out towards the southern tip of the mountains. In the far left of his vision he can see a blur of colour nestling on the ridge, the tiny movements barely noticeable. He continues to stare, biding his time. His time to finish the task is short; he knows this.

"Yes I'll make you shiver," his lips barely move, a mere ventriloquist's flicker. "Before you die, you'll shiver *then* good enough."

He stretches, arms wide and stands, leaning against the rock.

A Christ-like image.

A black cross, sharp against the early morning sunshine, breeze-blown clothing flaps against his body, against his own crucifix, set as though in stone. He swivels, the movement for one with such a damaged leg, is seamless, almost robotic. It appears that way, because that's exactly what it is.

He is past the point of no return.

The machine set in motion.

Running on auto-pilot and incapable of halting.

The swivel continues, his arms drop to his side and he stares down the path. Gillean, black and angular, a spiky, evil looking beast of a summit is a blur, a dark smudge at the far corner of his vision. He is staring at a point one hundred yards away. Staring at a man sipping a hot drink from a tin mug, a cigarette cupped in his left hand, its smoke drifting away in the breeze. Staring with all of his mental power into the back of a head filled with dreams of mountains, climbing and the memory of a lost love.

After what seems an age, a gradual dawning of recognition seems to creep over the figure sitting below him on the ridge; an uneasy feeling of being watched. He sets down his mug, takes a long draw from his cigarette, exhaling the smoke in a long protracted jet and, with obvious hesitation, turns to look up the ridge.

A hand is raised in greeting - a hand that stops somewhere around shoulder level, fingers splayed, then curling closed into a half-hearted fist.

Recognition.

A surge of fear from one set of eyes; smugness, domination and knowledge from the other.

****

They haven't spoken for over five minutes, each concentrating on the crunch, crunch, crunch of their boots on the splintered shards of rock. Their progress has slowed although neither one knows it; to them both, they are still pushing along at the same punishing pace that they set from the start. Both sets of legs are complaining, both pairs of lungs are now burning, desperately trying to draw in enough oxygen to fuel their work. Al's head has slumped and now rocks from side to side. Iain's is set straight ahead in grim determination; his eyes though, are glazed and vacant. He wanted to stop twenty yards ago. He picked a spot on the path, a large oblong boulder, but once reached, he patted its surface with the palm of his right hand and continued past, his mouth set in a stubborn grin of pain.

Al's doing a little worse.

"Enough! Iain, I gotta stop for a minute, my legs, God, they're on fire."

Al had chosen the rock as his rest point also. Unlike Iain, his legs had simply continued their rising spiral of agony until he felt that if he continued for another step without resting they would simply explode. Iain stops and turns round, chest working to draw in deep breaths, hands on hips, feet splayed wide to stop him from teetering.

Neither of them speak.

Al pulls his pack from his back, drops it unceremoniously onto the boulder and, hunched over it like an old man, desperately rips open the draw string, searching for his water bottle.

It's nearly full light now. The sun, although still fairly weak, imparts a soft billowy heat on their faces that is so welcome after the cold clamminess of the previous hours.

He drinks deeply, the water setting off sharp, icy stabs of pain behind his eyes, in his temples and in the fillings in his back teeth. His throat is soaking the liquid away, turning from sand paper roughness to silky smooth satin as the coolness soaks in and a shower of sparks goes off behind his eyes, stars flashing briefly then fading as he glugs the half litre bottle in one, long, greedy swallow.

He rummages again, looking for more, not for him this time, but his partner, his cohort in this quest that, surely, please God surely, must be nearing its end. His fingers close around the bottle and for a moment he thinks how good it would be to swill this one too. Perhaps just a few mouthfuls, enough to set off another firework show behind his eyes?

Now the bottle is out, held aloft for Iain.

"Aye junior, Ah think Ah will."

Iain steps his way down the slope and drinks slowly, without the mad, impetuous clamour that Al displayed. He takes each sip carefully, swilling it round his mouth, letting it soak into his skin before swallowing.

Time slips by as slowly and languorously as the slide of the water down Iain's throat; time that they can ill-afford to spend in quiet resting.

Al leans his head on his hands, linked together on the boulder. Water and sweat droplets spin down onto the rocks as he shakes his hair from his eyes. He gives a small, surprisingly lady like belch and then doubles over as half a litre of water splatters over his feet amidst a retching that echoes off the mountain itself.

"Shit, ohh God that hurts … cramps … massive stitch in my side."

Iain watches the colour drain from Al's face; high red splotches on his cheeks fade to a pasty cream then white tinged with a hint of green.

"Ah nearly said ye were drinkin' tha' a wee bit quick." He shrugs and adds "S'pose Ah should ha done. Och well, it'll pass junior, Here ha' a wee pull on this. Nae tae much though, I din'nae want ye chuckin' tha' up as well."

"Are we nearly there?"

"Aye, s'no tae far the noo. Top o' the wee hill there, then two hundred yards an we're on the main ridge. Andy ought tae be there somewhere. Mebee we'll be able tae see him. Mebee."

Al sighs, a sigh that speaks of tiredness and frustration. He re-packs the rucksack and lifts it, swinging it onto his shoulder.

The top is in sight. A small, conical plinth smoothed by countless thousands of boots over the years.

The feeling that they are at the end of a great journey is strong in them both.

Their footsteps begin, the crunch of gravel and scrape of scree against rock, accompanies their journey like an old, familiar friend.

Nemesis

The path from the summit is a gradual stone strewn ramp over the broad ridge leading towards Gillean and the Bhastier Tooth. I was dimly aware of a figure making his way down from Bruach na Frithe like some dark cowboy, dust covered and dishevelled.

I'd seen the blonde hair, the thick set of his shoulders and stockiness of his general frame. Not really much detail but (and this is a fact that will remain inexplicable forever more) still I knew, absolutely knew, it was David Salt. His eyes, those cold, icy blue holes, entrance to a mind as warped and disturbed as I could ever imagine had touched me with their evil. Even from that range, I swear I felt his madness.

I watched him make his way towards me then drop behind the blocky, rock outcrop that rears up from the southern edge so he was blissfully out of sight for two or three minutes. I was aware, at some level, of a terrible need to flee. From what I didn't really know. Why exactly this man should create such a fear and loathing in me, I also had no real idea.

Yes, without doubt, he was a loony; a total head banger, nutter, "Nae fucking reet in the heid" as Iain would no doubt have said. Yes, he'd possibly broken into my house and skilfully doctored a painting, a painting that was extremely dear to me. Yes, he'd also got the coldest, deadest eyes and handshake that I'd ever had the misfortune to witness. And yes, his apparent obsessive need to own my paintings gave me the creeps.

But this was the same man who bought the entire stock of my work - well over £30,000.

In my days as a financial adviser, I would have worked for the best part of a year to bag a sale like that.

That was a previous life though.

His gaze, from high on the summit of Bruach na Frithe had seared its way directly to my soul and filled me with dread. The effect was devastating.

My drink sat untouched on a rock to my left, steam curling from its surface. I leant forwards and switched off my gas burner, reached into my rucksack for a cigarette, lit it and stood, my legs shaking uneasily. I allowed Blaven, that beautiful, twin peaked rock bastion, to fill my head with its grandeur, traced its southern flank until it almost sank into the sea and turned to face my visitor.

My nemesis.

The path, in fact the whole ridge between me and the trig point was empty.

****

At the outcrop, Dan sinks to his knees, crouching low on the ridge, blending in behind the blocks of stone. He is sweating lightly, not through heat, as the morning is still cool and fresh, a light breeze rippling over the rocky surfaces like wavelets on a beach. He sweats through excitement and rushing adrenaline. This is what he *loves*, what he *does*, what he *lives for* and *has* lived for, through years of efficient killing, rape, mutilation and pain.

When it comes to quick and painless or horrific and excruciating, Dan very much favours the painful version. He thinks that this will almost certainly be a pleasant job; pleasant for him that is but very nasty, very painful for his intended.

He slides a short way on loose scree down the north side of the ridge, gains his feet and scrambles along, twenty feet below the path. Keeping hidden is a speciality of Dan's.

He moves quickly, no sign of his previous, pronounced limp. His clothes stick slickly to his body, his face is set in a constant grimace that sits squarely between ecstasy and horror, his eyes firing out blue icy fire from beneath his thick blonde eyebrows. The machine, once in motion, runs on well greased bearings, deficiencies forgotten, pain blocked out - pay for it tomorrow.

At the zigzagging path below Sgurr a Fionn Choire, he slips carefully and in near silence, upwards, heading for the sunshine pouring over the rocks.

Ten feet from the top, he rests and stares at his feet, composes himself, allows his emotions to cycle down a little. The turbines that are pumping the blood and adrenaline around his body ease off - they need to. Coming upon his target as he is will likely have him running off the mountain unaided. He knows he looks … well, scary before a kill.

That simply will not do, so he takes a water bottle form his pack and empties it over his head. He then washes his face, slicks back his hair and dries himself with his fleece as best he can.

A facade of calm is needed. A little light conversation perhaps, maybe a shared cigarette, a cup of whatever is on offer then ... well, let's wait and see.

Dan is fairly sure that one of them is going to take a very long bumpy fall, straight into Lota Corrie.

He has no intention of taking it himself.

Twenty shuffling steps and he emerges onto the ridge again, full sunlight bathes his features and softens the grinning evil that shines from his face.

He steps across the ridge, ten steps, then down onto the plateaux on which his target stands.

For the second time in five minutes, two pairs of eyes lock.

****

Al scrambles upwards, false summits over and, above him just the vast, open expanse of a clear, Scottish blue sky, dotted with swirling patches of vapour that burn away before his eyes. The massively long and fractured ridge that rises endlessly to Bruach Na Frithe's crest undulates in front of him, a mile distant, but in the clear air it looks close enough to touch.

He stands and looks over a swelling expanse of green. His legs, complaining and wooden, burning with a pain that almost beat him, forgotten; his feet, battered and sore from their ceaseless tramping over rough terrain, simply numb.

Had he, at that point, looked south, he would have spotted a figure slink over the ridge and drop out of sight behind the rocky nub that is Sgurr a Fionn Choire.

He didn't. He chose north.

Iain struggles upwards, breath heaving from his mouth in laboured, gasping lung-fulls. He steadies himself on the rough, unstable cairn and scans the surrounding mountains, searching the paths down into the corrie for any sign of movement.

"Aw bugger, we've missed him, must hae. Shite Al, along the ridge ... go, go ... he's nae doon in the corrie, he must hae' med the top."

Two hundred yards to the left, the narrow ridge on which they stand meets the sharp knife-edge that is the Cuillin. Ten yards further on, just out of sight, a drama has commenced, building rapidly to a crescendo.

Careful, so careful, their steps trace the narrow rock. On either side, five hundred feet of emptiness beckon them to make an error, to slip and to fall.

"Oh Jesus, Iain, *this* I do *not* like. Not one bit."

Through the lens

One minute I was watching a figure that I was sure was David Salt making his way down the ridge towards me, the next, I'd only the breeze and view for company. I peered at the outcrop behind which David had disappeared, expecting him to appear over the rock at any second (it would take less than a minute to scramble the ten feet to pass it).

Nothing.

Three or four minutes must have passed and I found myself thinking that I'd imagined him. I *had* been a little on edge and he *had* got under my skin, what with the painting and his 'commission'. My mind began batting the thought around that maybe he'd fallen; it was a tricky little scramble and, to the inexperienced, quite exposed, hanging over the southern edge of the ridge as it did. I surprised myself by hoping it *was* him and that he *had* fallen. A strange thought really, after all, what had he actually done to me for certain? Spooked me a bit, that's all.

A noise to my right, a clatter of rolling stones. It startled me and I spun round.

"Mr Perkins!"

I looked straight into his eyes, those fathom-less pools of non-emotion. They sparkled in the early morning sunshine, shone out their glowing, frosted stare with an almost impish, cheeky-young-lad abandon.

"Jesus … David, you startled me." My voice was a breathy expulsion spliced with an obvious, but unintentional stab of fear. "I … I … saw you, a little while ago on the ridge. I was starting to think you'd fallen off." My voice rose slightly, trying to instil a little humour into the conversation.

His eyes stared back, and though his mouth curled in the vestige of a smile, any trace of humour stopped there.

"I didn't really fancy the scramble over that outcrop. All too scary for me, what with the old leg aching as it is." He gestured with his thumb over his shoulder and continued, "I dropped down onto the path. Sneaked up on you." This time his eyes flicked with the barest hint of a smile. "Only joking - ha!"

There followed a gap, no longer than five seconds, but it seemed to stretch on and on, growing deeper as each hour-long second ticked by.

I continued, the only way I could think of "Well, this *is* a surprise. I know you suggested meeting me up here, but, well, I thought you'd left the island last week?"

"Change of plan, that's all. How could I drag myself away from all of this? Hey? I mean, fabulous isn't it?" He winked, one eye closing, blonde eyelashes flashing. As he did, his remaining, open eye seemed to flash with double the intensity. As if all his iciness switched between them.

"Think I might buy a place on the island you know, somewhere to 'escape to', somewhere to grow old, settle down." He shrugged and winked again, flicking his shoulder towards me in a ridiculous, Monty Python-esque parody, "May even take myself a little woman, know what I mean?"

God, he was loathsome. I felt the hairs prickle on the back of my neck and my eyebrows scrunch together in a frown. I couldn't help it; I must have looked utterly disgusted.

His reaction was strange. At first, his face opened up, bright and innocent; he looked, to all intents and purposes, like a child, admonished by a stern parent. I realised, there and then, that I didn't fear him. Yes, he was a disgusting loathsome individual but - and this I had only just realised - he was also terribly insecure.

I watched as he tossed my reaction around in his head, as though he was carefully weighing up its meaning; trying different caps, to see which one fitted. The child remained for a little while, the silence spreading out again, feeling awkward again. Eventually he broke eye contact and looked to the left, over the Glen towards the southern coastline.

"David, I didn't mean anything, you know, if I looked strange, I was just shocked, that's all."

"No bother, no offence taken. I'm a very wealthy man Mr Perkins …" I interrupted, couldn't help it, "Please, it's Andy," hearing him call me 'Mr Perkins' was like chewing a sandwich dipped in grit.

"As I was saying *'Andy'*," there was a sarcastic, childish tone to the way he pronounced my name and I wished I'd left it at 'Mr Perkins' "I'm a very wealthy man, not in bad shape. I think I'd be quite a catch for a simple island girl. Don't you agree?" I didn't, I thought he'd be an absolute bastard to live with. An insecure control freak with a shitty character. "Yes, David, of course, of course, like I said, you caught me off guard that's all."

"Hey, forgotten already." His smile was back, a half-smile, almost a non-smile.

He continued, "Have you taken any good shots for my painting then? I can see it now, pride of place over my fireplace. What a view."

"I haven't yet … I was just about to," I lied.

My old Nikon was tucked into my rucksack. Wrapped securely in my waterproof jacket, it was fairly safe from clouts and scrapes. It unravelled itself as I delved into the sack's depths.

"Ah, Nikon, reliable, trusty engines aren't they?"

"'*Engines*' - never heard them called that before," I thought, and stifled a smile, "Yes, never let me down and takes some lovely images. Sunsets and sunrises are when it's at its best. This should be good."

I framed up a shot incorporating the bottom of Lota Corrie, Sgurr na h-Uamha, Sgurr Beag, Marsco's southern edge, Clach Glas and Blaven. Back-lit in brilliant early morning sunlight and with a strip of blue framing it from above, it looked magnificent.

"What do you fancy then David?"

"Oh, I don't know, something, anything that captures the magic of the place, the grandeur. The real magic begins when you touch paint to canvas anyway, wouldn't you say?"

I clicked off a shot then panned out to 28mm capturing the whole of the vista including a border made up of the southern tip of the main ridge. "Well, I don't know, photographs can do a pretty fine job of capturing a feeling, if they're done right." I re-framed at 70mm, just Blaven and a small triangle of water at Camasunary "I've taken many a fine picture then totally ballsed it up trying to put it into paint."

"Do you ever see *Rachel* through that lens?"

At first, I thought I'd misheard him, he was leaning quite close to my left side, his breath a warm draught against my neck. My mind fumbled with his words, trying different phrases, anything that *could* fit. An icy chill spread from my stomach, up, deep into my chest, then prickled the skin on my neck and shoulders. My head felt as though it had been plunged into a chest freezer, stars went off behind my eyes and I was conscious of a deep thrumming vibration in my temples, pulsing in time with the blood surging into my brain.

I was shocked and incredulous, terrified and hurt all at once. I maintained the pretence of looking through the lens but the view was blurring to indistinct shades of green and grey.

"*What* did you say?"

His mouth was close to my ear now, like a lover leaning in to whisper sweet words of love.

"I *said*, 'do you ever see Rachel through there?' Her image, you know, her ghost. Perhaps on the edge of a shot, just a brief glimpse that turns out to be something entirely different?" His breath was caressing the skin around my ear, his words a lazy, languid stream of whispered questions. *"I* would, I'd see her long red hair, slim, trim frame, slight hips, full breasts, I'd see them all ..."

I spun round shocked, terrible anger flaring. My cheek smashed into his nose and he recoiled, fast as a striking snake.

"What the fu ... who are ... what do ...?"

I was utterly lost for words. Questions formed in my head then turned to jumbled mush as I tried to articulate them. My head spun and I felt on the verge of a faint, wobbling on shaky legs. He smiled for the first time, a real, honest-to-goodness smile that transformed his whole face. His eyes lit up and flashed their cool icy blue power and, leaning towards me again, he looked deep into my own eyes.

"*I*-am-you-worst-fucking-nightmare-*Mr Perkins*."

I actually saw his right arm fly backwards then piston forward. Saw it flying towards me, a blurred battering ram. I never even attempted to duck and it connected with the bridge of my nose, sharp shocking, with no follow through. I felt and heard something snap, felt the blow explode in my ears, as if a small charge had gone off in my head, tasted blood briefly and felt a gagging sensation in my throat. I think I shouted out in shock and pain, then toppled forward as though someone had taken my legs off at the knees.

I have the vaguest of memories of being held up, saved by my attacker from collapsing to the floor, then, blackness.

Deep, dark, complete blackness.

Gripped

Al's head is spinning. Ten yards in front of him Iain is stepping from rock to rock, sometimes arms outstretched like a tight rope walker, at others, held low, stabilising his movements, fingers clasping onto rocks. For a man well into his fifties and much closer to sixty than he would admit, he's doing well, breathing easily with no sign of suffering from the exposure of the ridge.

Al's not faring so well. He's tired, legs feeling like useless lumps of wood, his back aches with a deep throb at its centre and his knees sting with every jolt after every tentative, carefully placed step.

Worse though, much worse, is the terrifying feeling of being perched on the ridge tiles of the world's highest roof. The sensation of being utterly exposed, totally at risk, on the brink of a painful death, has fully consumed him.

His legs are jelly; no control whatsoever. On the brink of a faint he drops to his knees, slowly reaches forward, and grips the rock in a lover's tender embrace.

"Iain." His voice is a quavering, feeble thing, almost blown away on the breeze. "Iain, mate … I'm in a bit of trouble here."

He looks comical, like a drunk at a wild-west evening, struggling to stay on the bucking bronco even before it's turned on.

"Ye all right there Al?" Iain turns and skips back to his prone friend with the confidence of a child walking along a low wall. He smiles and stands, hands on hips perched on top of a four foot square block.

"No mate, I'm not alright … seem to have lost it … my legs … they don't seem to want to work."

"S'nae bother, yer jus' 'gripped', s'natural. Let's face it we're a wee bit high here. Ye jus' need tae tek a breather."

He sits down on the block, facing Al and the way they've just come. The trig point is a good hundred and fifty yards away, the knife edge ridge snaking onwards, before appearing to simply end.

"We've nae far tae go now." He looks behind him, the Bastier Tooth less than a hundred yards away. "An' Ah'll say this mate, we've naer a lot o' time." He bends at the waist and touches Al's shoulder. "Ye need tae sort yersen oot, we've got tae be movin'. Andy, ye ken?"

Al raises his head, his eyes searching Iain's for assistance, for support. He looks like an injured animal, lost and scared, fearful for its life.

In the breeze, drifting over the millennia-old rocks, a brief but audible shout creases the silence.

Their eyes lock in recognition and instantly, Al is struggling to his knees, then shakily, to his feet. With arms outstretched, hands searching for the security of any form of purchase, he stands and grabs hold of Iain's sleeve.

"That was Andy, I don't know how I know, but it was."

"Aye, ma thoughts tae junior. Are ye OK tae go on?"

"Yeah, let me hold onto your arm for a bit. Jesus Iain, this is bloody scary. Remind me never to try this again."

"Aye, if we get oot o' this, Ah'll dae jus' that."

Just under fifty yards of Hell for Al.

Never in his life has such a short distance seemed so long.

They struggle on, Iain directing Al's feet to each safe step, each flat rock. He talks constantly, easing his friend's fears, calming his nerves, telling him everything's OK. Time stretches on, the layers peeling away still. Stretching and extending, growing and collecting as though the distance over which they have to travel has become elastic. Like walking in a dream the main ridge remains obstinately distant. The tension is palpable and Al is close to tears. Tears of frustration, of inadequacy. After what seems an age, Iain helps his friend down onto the path, a solid, steady base on which to stand. Confidence floods back, along with tears of relief.

"OK Junior?"

"Yeah, thanks mate, that was a bit scary for a while. Come on, lets go, I've wasted too much of our time already."

The main ridge looms over them, a hundred feet above, its profile glowing in the sunlight streaming from the glen to the south.

Without knowing, they tread in the same steps that, twenty minutes before, Dan took before turning right, towards his spot of trig point contemplation.

"… it's your call."

In my dream, I'm a small child, full of sleep, grumpy and irritable after a busy day playing in the green hills behind our cottage. My Dad is carrying me, my head resting against his shoulder, his jacket a soft pillow, his comforting strength and warm breath on my neck aiding my shallow but satisfying slumber. A deep throbbing pain strives to wake me, the pain stabbing at my forehead from some point between my eyes. I can remember the sharp agony of impact on my face. I must have fallen, tumbled while scrambling over rocks. My Dad's always telling me to be more careful, to watch my step, to stop charging about all over the place.

So, I've had a tumble, he's carrying me home and when we get there, Mom will get out the 'Big Red First Aid Box'. The cottage will be warm and welcoming, a fire will crackle in the hearth and, once I'm sufficiently bandaged and liberally smeared with antiseptic cream, I'll sit and watch the flames. Dad will ask if I'm alright, offer to have a game of chess and we'll sit in the firelight drinking hot chocolate.

In my dream there's a chill breeze blowing against my face, drying the sweat on my forehead and ruffling my hair. A voice nags at my sleep, somehow alien, not the deep rumble of my Father but a harsh, manic grating that pricks at my subconscious.

I don't want to wake, I'm happy sleeping. Waking will mean accepting … something. Something that I don't want to acknowledge.

Something nasty.

Something that will hurt me.

"Wake up Andy," - I don't want to, I want to sleep.

"Wake up you fucker." A shake lolls my head backwards and forwards. At each shake, I catch a glimpse of green and grey; rocks and grass; streams and sky.

"I SAID WAKE UP!" A slap against my cheek shocks me into consciousness and, like racing along a tunnel at incredible speed, everything screams into focus; mountains, blue sky, heather and stunted grass. In the far distance, a black, twin-pointed mountain grabs my attention.

Blaven.

And I remember.

Richard Neath

Everything.

Beneath my feet a gut-wrenching drop pulls at my vision.

I'm standing on the edge of a buttress, on the very lip, the last few inches; the rough rock beneath my boots ends at the balls of my feet. My toes are already sticking out over hundreds of feet of empty space.

Strong hands hold me at arm's length, gripping my fleece from behind and pulling it into a tight concertina of folds. I struggle and the grip tightens further, followed by a gentle shove that inches my upper body over the void.

Instinctively I shout for the second time in as many minutes, arms flailing outwards, pin wheeling, desperate not to fall.

"I suggest you stay still Perkins. We've got a few things to talk about, you and me. It's up to you, listen to what I've got to say, or take a jump right now. I'd rather have ourselves a little chat but well, its your call ..."

Just ten minutes

Iain stops dead, head cocked over to the left, listening, like an obedient lap dog for his master's call. Al stands, likewise, his left hand gripping the sleeve of Iain's shirt as though his life depends on it.

They are eighty feet below the ridge, a tiny distance and, compared to the near three thousand they have already climbed it's a distance to be covered in a matter of a few minutes. But their legs are tired, no - more than tired - utterly exhausted, even Iain, used to a hard life of strenuous work in a hostile environment, is close to his limits of strength and stamina. Al, strictly white collar and used to jumping in a car at any opportunity, passed his limit some time ago. He knows that, with a ten minute break, he could jolly his way up the last, seemingly endless portion of scree whistling 'she'll be coming round the mountain'.

Just ten, tiny, insignificant minutes.

They both know they have no such luxury and, as they look at each other in the still subdued light of the Cuillin dawn, they fear for their friend.

"He's in trouble. You heard that shout as well didn't you?"

"Aye, Ah did that. Ah tell ye though junior, Ah'm absolutely knackered."

"Me too. Come on, not far now."

With calves like knotty hardwood and thighs burning fit to explode, they shuffle up the final climb, constantly slipping and sliding. Iain manages ten steps before having to stop, bent over, hands on knees, swearing at muscles that just want to rest.

Al manages eight.

They plod on.

"... what do you say, call me Dan?"

Below me, something like two thousand feet, the green of the corrie was still dark, still bathed in a shadow cast by the low lying hills within the glen. It looked cold down there; patches of mist hung sullenly around rock outcrops and along sections of stream. Up on the ridge, I was squinting against the sun, its warmth on my skin and glare in my eyes.

The hand at my back gave a tiny, gentle shove and my feet skittered on the rock, sending a few pieces of stone clattering away into the distance. I watched them fall and tumble, spinning out of sight. Remarkably, I felt calm, at ease, as though I was being held from falling by a kindly hand rather than being taunted with death.

If this were to be my last sunrise, I was going to enjoy it. I truly felt that if I had to die, then dying in the mountains amidst the stunning spectacle of a Cuillin dawn was not a bad way to go. Not as good as in a nice easy chair on the last page of a really good book, a couple of days after my ninetieth birthday, but hey ...

A voice behind me jolted me back to a vague version of reality.

"Are we going to talk - or do you want to take a dive right now?"

"That's not really much of a choice is it David? I mean, I don't *really* have much of a choice do I?" My voice was quiet, relaxed. It showed no sign of the fear that was tearing apart my insides.

"No, I suppose you're right. Not *much* of a choice, but, hell, *some* choice is better than *none* don't you think? I mean, to have *no* choice must be awful." He sniggered behind me and the vision of child flashed briefly in my mind once again. When he continued, his voice was edged with a manic cackle that chilled me to the core.

"Name's not David by the way, it's Daniel, Dan to my friends and hey, we're *nearly* friends don't you think? So, what do you say, call me Dan?"

"If we're nearly friends, then how come you're holding me at arms length over a three hundred foot buttress? Why do I get the distinct impression that, any second, I'm going to be falling?" My words cracked at the end of my question. To me, I sounded scared now. To my 'pusher' I must have sounded terrified.

He completely ignored my question. It was as though I'd simply not spoken.

"Yes, you may remember my name. You may *not*, in fairness though, I believe you were a little 'cut up' at the time I was involved in your life." His grip tightened and I felt the material of my fleece stretch across my shoulders; my arms, hanging at my side were pulled backwards a few degrees.

His voice was a warm breath against my ear as he leaned in close.

"Soames is the name, Andy. Daniel Soames ..." a pause, then "... ring any bells at all? Anything in your memory? No? OK, how about this then ..." His voice seemed to be coming from behind a thick pane of glass, muffled, the words mingling and running into one long monotone drawl.

I remembered the name. Remembered it very well.

"... green Subaru, red Nissan 200 SX, fatal accident on the A449, real mess, pretty young woman crushed when the roof of her car partially collapsed, young man in hospital for months with all sorts of broken bones. Ringing any bells *now* Andy?"

Instinct told me to spin round, punch this foul murdering bastard in the face, pummel him then push him off the cliff. A wish to survive said otherwise but I couldn't help tensing and clenching my fists. I was rewarded by a hefty shove outwards, then a sharp pull back as my body was thrust out over the drop.

"You should have seen it Andy. I only clipped the back of her car, a gentle nudge really, Christ we were going some. Liked a bit of a race didn't she, your missus?" He laughed as though telling a funny story to a mate over a pint. "Right on a bend we were, left hander, not sharp though, a real good sweeper. Must have been doing ninety, ninety five, something like that. Just slued right round in front of me, no warning, nothing. Thought I was going to broad-side her, then whoosh, the fucking thing flew into a barrel roll. Incredible ... I'd hit the brakes and swerved into the outside lane to get out of her way."

I could feel him shaking his head, replaying the scene as if he still couldn't believe what had happened.

"Straight up in the air she went, one minute I was looking at a nice red Nissan, the next, shit, a whole load of exhaust and drive shaft. I tell you Andy, it must have gone four or five times. Over and over, sparks flying, bits of trim, all sorts of stuff. Amazing ..."

I was hearing his words from a distance, clearly and yet still through that closed window. A voice from behind, from some ridiculous distance was speaking to me about the destruction of my wife and of the life I once knew and loved. The tone of his voice was one of controlled excitement, as though he was a teenager telling a mate about a recent sexual exploit. I could imagine his face; eyes tightly closed, a grin on his face betraying the pride in his work. His voice droned on and on. It felt like he was going to talk forever, repeating the story over and over until one of us keeled over and died on the spot or went mad and simply took a twisting dive off the rock and into the void. Perhaps, I thought, I've already died and this is my penance, my Hell, to listen to a running commentary of my wife's death until the end of time.

His arm twitched as he spoke. The fists holding great bunches of fleece jumped backwards and forwards making me totter like a rag doll over the drop. My own arms spasmed in unison, thrown first into space and then back against my body. I was trying to maintain some degree of balance but was convinced that, whether or not he *actually* intended throwing me off the edge, I *would* end up going over.

Whether by accident or design, I was taking a fall.

"... the thing is Andy and, you know, this is the most amazing thing. I swear to you it's as true as I'm standing here, until I read a paper in the hospital, until I was awake and catching up on the news, I thought you were driving the car. How about that for a jolly old turn up heh? I thought it was you, convinced of it, you were the target, not *Mrs* Andy, you the meddling office boy, getting involved with stuff you shouldn't have, poking your nose in ..." He broke for a breath, the silence rushed in and all I could hear was the pounding of my own heart, pushing blood at full pelt around my body. The pulse was loud in my ears and I thought, at the time, that it would be the last sound I heard, that he would begin talking again and I wouldn't even know. All I'd hear would be the 'thud-lup' of my heart. It would stop when I landed at the bottom of the buttress - then and only then ...

"... so yeh, when I read the paper and found you'd slipped by again, well, Jesus, I could have really flipped out then, I mean gone absolutely friggin' ballistic, apart from the fact that I couldn't walk and was anchored to the bed by steel pins, pipes and tubes, I'd have come straight round and finished it ..."

'Thud-lup, thud-lup'. Every time he stopped talking, every time he stopped to draw another breath, I was left alone with my heart beat. When his voice started again, droning on and on, it drowned out my heart; it was as if his voice stopped its beat. I worried that, if he talked long enough, managed to draw enough breath to continue for a couple of minutes, I would simply pass out, my heart a useless piece of meat, dead and lifeless but still warm in my chest.

"... twice, I *mean* God above, I've never, I repeat *never* failed a job before you, I was good, take that back, I was the fucking best ... you listening to me Perkins? the best ..."

'Thud-lup, thud-lup', my thoughts were spinning; *twice* I'd evaded him? What was he on about? He was the best? The best at what? I desperately spun my memory back two years, sorting and shifting through the junk. So much had happened, so much to clog and infest my memory bank, seemed like my brain was stuffed full of crap. I imagined the packing cases again, humping them around trying to find the relevant pieces of information. Now I imagined my brain as a huge cave full of the things, dusty and seldom used, millions upon millions of packing cases, yet somewhere, in one of them, was a key, a key to unlock a memory, to allow me access. I searched and yet all I could see was a red sports car, flying and twisting through the air ...

"... maybe a hundred, maybe more, I dunno, I didn't keep count, but God, must have been at least that many, not in this country though, maybe twenty or so in the UK, mainly Thailand, Christ that's a place, cheap you know, very cheap, sex, however you want it, whenever and wherever you want it, really cheap, life? equally so, no one gives a shit, or at least that's how it seems and I never, *never* messed up, every time, sweet as a nut, clean, no hitches, then you, you come along, simple job, ha ..."

'Thud-lup, thud-lup', simple job, me? What? I remembered a time when I lost a friend, a colleague with a fat face and a habit of wearing big jumpers. A bloke with a secret smoking habit, just the occasional one, on a fire escape in Wolverhampton. Another place, another time, another world. Hell another *life*. A man with the same name as me, a man who I let into my confidence, a man who died in a shed with his tongue lolling out and a half finished die-cast model sitting on a wooden bench ...

"... right name, right colour car, OK wrong make and model, but hey give me a break, they *looked* the same from the back, I must have gotten sloppy, who knows, you were a simple job, a simple nancy office boy, no threat, no problem, follow you, wait, kill you, get you out of Stevens' hair, simple, piece of piss, make it look like an accident, bread and butter work really, do it with my hands behind my back, easy peasy lemon squeezy ..."

'Thud-lup, thud-lup', there's that name, the name I once respected, then grew to loathe as a worthless low-life. Stevens, he was my boss, my friend once. Wow, he was going to have me killed. I must have really got to him. Al had been right, I was in over my depth; worse than that, I was drowning and didn't even know. The revelation hit me like a rock to the temple: No accident, none of it - Andy, Rachel, nothing …

"… 'Leave it be now, Dan, leave it be', that's what Stevens said, 'it's getting too heavy, too dangerous, I'm going to split in the next few days', well thanks for nothing, I'd been given a job to do, can you imagine the embarrassment? the loss of pride I felt? can you, eh? Jesus, never, absolutely definitely fucking *never* had I messed up on a job, I'd had to pull back a time or two, re-group if you like, but do the wrong target? kill the wrong bloke? well Lord love me and shit a brick, *never*, no way would I let *that* go, no way was I walking away from the job, no fucking way José …"

'Thud-lup, thud-lup', an accident, but *not* an accident then; no consolation really, the same result, same outcome; ruination, despair, loneliness …

"… so, I think, I'll do you anyway, simple car crash, swift nudge at the right time, spin you out of control and into the trees, risky, *well* risky but, hey, let's live a little, it'd be like being back in the Far East, just driving on a different side, wind you up a bit, goad you into a bit of a high speed race, then, WHAM, into a spin, straight to heaven, do not pass go, do not collect £200, worked an absolute treat too it did, like I said … did I tell you how it flipped over? spun through the air? all but did a God-damn cartwheel if the truth be known, wow … a-fucking-mazing, I tell you, I watched it fly, thinking that I'd never seen anything quite like it, never, nothing like it before, it was … well … I have to say … beautiful, poetry really, poetry in motion, BANG, CRASH, then a flip, then another, wheels, roof, I tell you I was that freaked out by it, I never even watched where *I* was going, next thing I know, I've clipped the curb on the central reservation, mounted it, onto the grass and 'good night nurse' … into the trees, hit a great big bastard about ten feet up, the whole side of the car came off, can you believe that? … the whole side, just 'whoosh', gone … my safety belt snapped and I flew too, I remember seeing a lot of branches and leaves … strange … I remember the leaves, thinking how green they were, perfect, a perfect green … I dreamt about them in hospital, kept imagining I was in a rain storm, only the rain was leaves, thousands upon thousands of them, amazing really … I think they actually found me in a tree, well hanging from one anyway, a springy landing all told … still managed to get banged up pretty good though, must have hit something pretty hard in flight I suppose …"

He paused at this point and I heard him take a huge, gulping breath followed by a long exhalation that seemed to go on forever, as though it was the first breath he'd taken in minutes. He seemed to relax a little then, his grip on my fleece loosening a fraction, a *tiny* fraction; when you're hanging over a three hundred foot rock buttress you notice that sort of thing.

His words had left me punch drunk, dazed, incapable of digesting their meaning. I felt, as I stood perched on the edge of my own personal terror, as though I'd been privy to an overheard conversation, a ranting argument of words spoken without thought for their consequences; they held no meaning for me. I was not involved.

Below me, *directly below me*, the open face of the buttress fell for three hundred feet to scree and boulders. The face itself was not actually vertical. Not quite. The top twenty feet was a jagged, black overhang, running with tiny, diamond sparkling streamlets of water. Beyond that, the rock sloped outwards slightly, perhaps ten degrees off vertical.

First I was going to fall, then I was going to bounce and roll a while, then I was going to spin and flail downwards until I smashed on the rocks.

I was going to die.

No question about it.

If I went off the front of the face, I was going to die.

A strange thought really. Not scary at all. I felt no fear, just anger and a sense of sadness.

To my left, about ten feet below me and six feet over, a second buttress joined the one on which I stood. Its surface was heavily fractured, splinters of sharp rock sticking up at disjointed, haphazard angles. The whole surface looked flaky, as if it was simply biding its time before falling away and joining the rest of the rock-fall three hundred feet below. It was hardly a ledge, more of a lump really, a blob of rock, linked to a still steep, but more gently sloping outcrop than the one I was looking over. It continued away to the left, its angle gradually getting shallower before eventually turning into scree. Below it, a large platform of flat slab hung at sixty degrees, then, below that, more broken, heavily fractured rock, just off vertical; an easy scramble under *normal* circumstances.

"... I guess I'm going to have to find someone else to do my painting now." He seemed calmer now, as if purged of his hatred, as though his earlier ranting had left him deflated, empty almost.

"It's a magnificent work of art you know ... the one over your fireplace. Missing some human interest though. I hope you didn't mind my little 'addition'?" I heard myself answer, the words coming from a great distance, subdued and muffled.

"I painted her out, didn't take much, just a flick of a brush really.

She's gone."

His hand tensed and I felt the his anger building again, knowing that I'd said the wrong thing and not caring. If I was going to die, at least I'd go with the knowledge that I'd annoyed him, really pissed him off prior to my death. I felt the pressure building at my back, a terrible gradual build up that forced me over the edge. My whole body leant outwards, my arms hanging down, my neck bent so that I was looking past my feet, down the rock face to the boulders and heather below.

Another couple of inches, five more degrees and my feet would slip; I'd fall; he'd let me go.

He stopped his push and I stood, hanging over the void.

He didn't pull me back.

"She's *never* gone. She's always there. You and your commercial crap that you sell as art, you could never truly erase her image. Never."

Despite my predicament, I tensed at his words, "What? ... but you ... thirty grand ..."

"I know what you're thinking," he cut in, "thirty two grand, plus a bit is a lot of money to pay for what I consider a pile of crap." He sniggered, the sound so hollow, so utterly devoid of emotion. It was the sound of a mind totally lost, beyond all hope.

"The most expensive bonfire I've ever had and no mistake. But, and you may not believe this, worth every single penny. I cleansed your art, made it true, made it worthy. The flames, the sounds, the crackle of the wooden frames igniting ... it was a real pleasure. Oil paint burning has a wonderful scent, beautiful even."

I could feel my boots straining to maintain a grip on the rock and flinched when my left one slipped forward from one tread to the next.

Five millimetres. No more.

When you're hanging over a massive cliff, you notice five millimetres.

I shifted my eyes to the left, to the rocky lump, my only chance.

"You do realise that you're totally mad don't you?" I said it with as much conviction as I could muster. Kept my voice as strong and as steady as I possibly could. Amazingly, it didn't let me down.

He was silent for a while, perhaps as long as ten seconds but I couldn't say for sure as time had become elastic. I felt I'd been standing on the edge of the cliff for at least a day already. He spoke, eventually, and when he did his voice had a chill that reached straight into my bones. I wanted to recoil from its sound, but couldn't. It was utter evil, utter depravity. Completely lost.

But somewhere, deep within, there seemed a profound sadness; so intense, so entangled within his mind that, for a fraction of a second, I felt a twinge of pity.

"*Madness?* What do you know about madness?"

And I felt a strange calmness enfold me.

I thought of Rachel.

I thought of Al and Iain, whether I would see them again.

And from the depths of my memory, from some end of the evening, bottom of the bottle conversation, came a snippet of a language that I'd not had the chance to learn.

It seemed somehow apt.

I spoke, quietly but clearly. Again, my voice held out; did me proud.

"Pòg mo thòn ..."

I jumped.

****

The ridge is a bright band of sun-washed rock, thirty feet above them.

Al is behind Iain, they are both bent double, scrabbling for grip on shifting scree. Their boots slide, their fingers hold onto unstable chunks of rock. A faint smell of oranges wafts in the breeze, my mug of hot juice still sits cooling next to my sleeping bag.

Iain thinks he hears voices.

He stops, holding out his hand to Al.

They listen, straining their ears against the quiet whistle of breeze. For a few seconds, it's all they hear, just the gentle sigh of air moving across rock. Iain shrugs and is about to move on, then, in mid step, a phrase comes to them, the voice, they recognise, is clear, strong and determined.

"Pòg mo thòn ..."

****

Some time before, way back in another life in fact, I had dropped from a platform in a barn, to the stone floor, ten feet below. The fall had been measured, calculated and benefited, in a way, from taking place in the pitch black.

In contrast the drop to the shattered lump of jagged rock was like jumping from a plane.

My eyes, although focused on my landing point, took in a vast expanse that spread into the distance for fifty miles over the mainland. As I fell, I felt Dan's grip tighten momentarily at my back, then it was gone and I was committed - I'd never been so committed in my life.

Five feet of space to land, no more, no less. I couldn't roll, couldn't slip. *And* it was ten or twelve feet below me, at the end of a rushed and terrified jump while being partially held up by a madman with a couple of handfuls of my fleece. For all I knew, the whole lot could give way and deposit it and me in the glen below. I never gave it a thought; I was convinced he was going to push me off anyway. I had nothing to lose and everything to gain.

I don't think I shouted, although of this fact I couldn't swear.

The fall was a disconcerting blur and, as it seemed to go on forever, I felt sure I'd missed my intended landing spot and was in free fall. The wind blew against my face, I felt the air rush from my lungs and my stomach lurched and seemed to relocate itself somewhere in my chest. My landing was neither pleasant, nor particularly pretty. My legs buckled beneath me and, as I struggled to stay upright, my right knee connected with my chin and flooded my mouth with the salty taste of blood. I howled with pain as I bit into my tongue on the right hand side, fell heavily onto outstretched hands and felt a sharp piece of rock puncture my skin. My right boot skittered on the loose stone, shooting out over the edge to dangle briefly in open space. I pulled it back immediately (if I did it quickly, I could pretend the drop didn't exist) as a few pieces of rock clattered away, exploding a couple of seconds later, hundreds of feet below. I felt as though I was watching my antics on a wide screen TV, as though it was all happening to someone else and the fear and adrenaline didn't belong to me. My heart thumped heavily in my ears; good old 'thud-lup' come back to keep me company. I could sense, rather than hear a scream building in my chest; for the tearing in my knee, the punctured skin on my palm and for my tongue, bitten clean through on one side. A scream of relief that I'd escaped the madman's grip. A scream of victory that bounced off the rock and echoed with the falling stones that sparked and shattered below me.

Dan stared from above, his face a picture of shock and rage. The sun shone around his head giving the impression of a halo as a grin spread across his face. He nodded and clapped his hands in recognition of my move and for a moment it looked as though he would turn and drift away, that the madness and terror was over. He moved from the edge of the cliff and I took the opportunity to begin working my way to the right. Facing the rock, I picked my way along rough, narrow ledges, while above, the plateau on which Dan stood, dropped slowly towards me. I could see my route, downwards and across, crab-like and careful for fifty yards towards the scree. Once there, I could descend, reach the flanks of Sgurr Beag and drop into the corrie below. The flat ground above petered away to an area of broken blocks and steep cliffs below Sgurr a Fionn Choire; in twenty yards I would be clear; Dan couldn't follow.

I concentrated on down climbing, putting as much distance as possible between us.

A rock, fell from above and exploded three inches to the left of my hand, a piece of shrapnel drawing blood on my wrist. I instinctively flinched and raised my arms above my head, hunched my shoulders and glanced up to the ridge above.

A grinning face peered down at me. A face that would have fit with chilling ease into any cheap, 1980's horror movie. His eyes reflected the sunlight and his mouth was set into a terrifying parody of a smile - white teeth like tombstone and gums revealed by drawn back lips.

"Not this time Perkins, no way, not this time." He hefted a rock, the size of a house brick, jagged and lethal, from hand to hand, "This time you *will* die. This time ..."

Now I *was* scared, I could escape a pushing hand, but dodging rocks thrown by a psychopath while traversing a steep face would be pretty much impossible. I kept moving and never even flinched as the missile whistled past my head.

When I next looked up, I was surprised at how much ground I'd put between us, having dropped forty feet from the plateau. To my right, a boulder, roughly the size of a large TV sat angled on the steep ground, partly buried in the surrounding rock. I made for it.

Ten yards is a huge distance when expecting to be smashed by a chunk of mountain thrown by a murdering madman.

I nearly made it, was lucky enough to glance upwards and watch as the rock spun and cart wheeled directly towards me. Thrumming air pounded my ears as I ducked, pressing my face flat against the slope, squashing my chest and forcing my legs to hug the contours. It sailed past my skull and connected with my right thigh, crushing my groin into the rock face. A pain flared in my hip as though I'd been kicked by a horse. I screamed, breathing in grit and dust and at the same time feeling my grip falter and my trousers ride up as I slid, out of control.

I was desperate to gain some, *any* grip, so searched with my fingers as I slid, knowing that the gradient increased to near vertical, twenty feet below me. A flap of skin peeled back from the base of my right thumb and two nails bent backwards, a searing pain flaring as they were pulled from my fingers. My boots, jumping and stuttering against the jagged face came up against a small ledge and my fall stopped. Whimpering like a wounded animal, I sucked the blood from my nail-less fingers, desperate to ease the pain, then risked a glance upwards. Dan was stooping again and I could imagine his fingers, damp and clammy like dead fish, prying up another rock.

"Oh shit, no, please no ..."

Below, branching away to my right, a good, solid, foot wide ledge, led to the scree. Above, the rock soared upwards vertically, impossible for Dan to follow. It would entail a tricky, six foot down climb, awkward at the best of times, but damaged as I was, it would be near impossible. I had no choice; below the ledge, an almost vertical slab of gabbro, devoid of any useful holds, sloped for thirty feet. Below that another rough, sloping buttress ... then nothing.

Empty space.

It was two moves.

Just two.

A lovely little pointed rock for my left foot a couple of feet below me, then beneath that, a decidedly dodgy looking crack for my right.

A shuffle, a swing across and I was on the ledge.

Piece of cake.

My fingers, greasy with drying blood and screaming with white-hot agony didn't agree. I gritted my teeth against the pain and lowered myself, finding the pointed rock easily and taking most of my weight on my relatively uninjured left hand.

One more move.

An explosion of light in my head caused me to swoon. *I actually saw stars* and swayed like a sailor up a mast, leaning outwards and then collapsing back against the rock.

Direct hit.

Blood flowed freely into my left eye and I swear I could feel a lump pushing against my skin, rising with cartoon-show speed.

I fell. Just let go. Dropped like a stone, for three feet - straight onto the ledge.

My knees buckled, struck rock and almost pushed me off. I gripped, digging my raw fingers into a crack and felt fresh blood spurt as my skin split open like a squashed grape; flesh peeling back right to the bone.

The ledge looked like a tight rope, unfeasibly narrow, spreading

onwards at a slight angle downwards to the scree.
I thought it was ten yards, possibly a touch more.
It may well have been a thousand miles.

Back on Death Gully

The dream had returned.

Gone though was my father, my saviour.

Gone was the feeling of security, warmth and the promise of a comforting fire to crackle in the hearth.

Gone was the glow of dancing orange flames and the soothing sweetness of steaming hot chocolate, cupped in hands tingling with new heat.

The dream was of darkness, of cold blasts of north-blown Welsh air. I could feel the damp moss and slate, smooth and dripping with icy spring water. I knew, if I chose to glance upwards, to crane my neck to the dark, broiling clouds hovering above, what would meet my gaze. The gully would rise into the darkening sky, running with water and slippery with greasy mould.

Death Gully.

So this is what it all came down to? Trapped and vulnerable, stuck in a memory from nearly three decades before. Waiting for help, help that this time, was not going to come. No lights, dancing through the heather and gorse. No calls from concerned parents, no strong arms to help me from my perch. But this was no dream and I fought to drag myself back to reality. A swirling mist clouded my eyes and the sound of crashing waves beating ceaselessly against roughly carved jagged rocks pounded my ears. Visions of memories past ghosted in and out of my mind; Al with a prancing rod, laughing and shouting as a sea trout sent sparkling jewels into the night air; Iain stuttering and slurring over a simple sentence, tears rolling down his cheeks, the ability to speak sabotaged by half a litre of single malt; the picture above my fireplace, gleaming in sunshine that streams in from my front window; Mrs N, hustling and bustling like a broody hen over goods in her shop; a gleaming red-gold sunrise over Raasay, the sky alight, burning the heavens with its fiery glow; Rachel's bench, solid and unmoving, its varnished grain glistening with sea-blown rain; and Rachel, her face warm and radiant, flushed with exertion and emotion, her eyes, tear filled as she takes in the view, Blaven beneath her feet and the splendour of the Cuillin ridge spreading its jagged magnificence into infinity and beyond.

Wonders that I would never see again. Pleasures that were to be taken away forever.

A fog, like smoke from a damp November fire, black and yellow tinged, swirled in front of my eyes. I shook my head, desperately trying to focus again and fearful of another blow from above that would tip me into the glen below. Stabbing pains, like arrows through my skull, exploded from my eye sockets as a dull scream. Like the dying moan of a gut shot soldier they echoed back from the rock in front of my face while gradually my vision returned. There in front of me was the mangled remains of my right hand. Jammed into a horizontal crack, the fingers looked like a road kill. A *nasty* road kill. Bleeding and mashed, the skin had split exposing mushy pink meat that oozed bright red liquid.

The crack appeared to me as a dirty plug-hole down which my life, the red slippery liquid seeping from my flesh swirled.

I watched as the image cleared, seconds trickled by, during which time my will ebbed away with my blood. Suddenly, it was just rock. Just a crack, green tinted with lichen and red smeared with blood.

I *had* to make the scree.

"Had enough yet Perkins?" His voice was a high-pitched maniacal scream. Madness had degenerated into total loss and any thread of sanity had snapped like cotton. A bone-chilling cackle pierced the mountain stillness and I lurched to the right, groping madly with feet like lead and hands that throbbed with howling agony.

I heard the falling rock quite clearly. I heard the thrumming of its edges spinning towards me and knew it was going to hit. An image of a child, blonde haired and complete with cap and loosely hung tie filled my mind. His arm was extended and, with all of his might, he willed his thrown wooden block to connect with his prize. Carnival lights flashed overhead. *I* was his prize, the coconut balanced on top of the pole.

I was going to fall.

I ducked my head and shuffled to the right, pushing my boots along the ledge. Their tread snagged and caught on the rough rock. I held my breath, pressing myself against the cliff face and was rewarded by a whooshing missile that glanced my shoulder with the caress of a lover's kiss before spiralling down towards the corrie floor.

Another shuffle, another foot along the ledge, another smear of blood on rock that would have forgotten my passing before the stains faded or were washed away by the next rainfall.

I could hear laughter, not the madness that came from above, but good honest mirth. I realised the sound was coming from me and, involuntary and unwanted as it was, it unbalanced me. I stumbled, twisting headlong to the right, my knees turning to jelly and striking the ledge as I groped, arms outstretched, desperate for anything that would halt my fall.

I was still laughing as I executed a perfect barrel-roll, off the ledge and into oblivion.

David and Goliath

On stumbling, slipping feet and fingers digging deep into abrasive scree, Iain reaches the ridge. The early morning sunshine makes him squint and he shields his eyes against its brightness. Al reaches the top and grabs a handful of his friend's fleece, desperate to stop his legs giving way. He has never felt so tired.

They stand and take in the scene before them, piecing together parts of the puzzle, allowing information to sink in.

A mountain bivvy site, nothing more really.

A lightweight sleeping bag, mat, stove, rucksack and items of clothing, nothing out of place, nothing untoward. A mug of juice sits on a flat rock, its steam rising and strong scent heavy in the still air. All very calm.

"Well junior, he's no here."

Al hobbles past the campsite, his legs stiff but wobbly at the same time. Hands on his hips, he stands on what appears to be the top of a huge cliff, nothing but rolling green and grey mountains and glens beneath his feet.

"Iain, come here mate. We've got company."

There's no emotion in his voice whatsoever; it's the voice of a man at the very end of his reserves of both patience and tolerance. A man who's given everything, has no more to give and yet knows, there is still more to be done. Iain trudges over and stands at Al's left hip, lets his eyes follow the slope downwards for twenty yards to a point where the ground falls away.

A burn, way below, snakes its lazy way, glimmering in the sunshine like molten silver and the whole of the glen is bathed in an exquisite shifting mix of mottled sunshine and shade. Its beauty is obvious and somehow touching; lost amidst the unfolding drama, it continues its show regardless. Were it not for the circumstances and the figure standing below them, they would both feel the walk had been worth it, just for the view.

Al speaks first, his voice a reedy whisper. Dry lips and throat, sore from laboured breathing strain with the effort.

"Mr Soames, Daniel, I believe we need to talk."

At first there is no recognition. No sign that the blonde haired man has heard. No flinch or movement, just the same statuesque stance; arms hanging limply at his side, his head set at a slight angle, as if watching something below him. Then, with the air of a high powered business man, he acknowledges them as if he's addressing the office junior for the first time.

"Sorry, I think you have the wrong man. David Salt's the name ..."

Al speaks, slowly, as if to a deaf old aunt, "We know *Dan* who you are. I saw your car at the garage, after the crash ... the number plate 'EMI1Y'. It was next to my best friend's Nissan, the same car in which his wife died. What we don't know is exactly *where* Andy is. We thought you may be able to help shed some light on that ..."

Dan shrugs his shoulders, his eyes flashing cold blue and the merest hint of a smile touches the corner of his mouth.

"No idea, I came up here to meet him ... he's doing a painting for me, you know, a commission, quite a handsome figure involved."

"We heard him, you were talking to him. What we'd like to know is, *where is he now?*"

Both Al and Iain stand watching, unable to believe what they're seeing. It's as if the man is transforming before their eyes.

Dan's head lowers until his chin is touching his breast bone. At the same time his arms raise at the sides, coming up fully until he's standing with them outstretched above his head. His hands and fingers shake as though he's limbering up before a gymnastics routine. When his head lifts and he fixes them with his stare, a chill blasts both of them. His eyes are frozen pools of hate. His lips, drawn back over teeth, a perfect pearly white, sneer a madness that forces them both to take an involuntary step backwards. His voice is that of a horror movie demon.

It's not his at all.

"I'm simply taking care of unfinished business. I suggest you both trot back over the ridge and disappear. This *does not* concern you."

"Where is he?" The voice is Al's though thinking back, he would swear he never spoke.

Dan shakes his head, a tiny, almost unnoticeable movement and lets out a little exasperated sigh, as though dealing with an annoying child.

"Last I saw, he was sliding down a big slab about a hundred feet below me. Upside down I hasten to add. I'm fairly sure he will have, how would you say ... expired?"

They do not show any reaction, simply return his stare.

Seconds tick by, silence filling in the spaces left by the passage of time.

Al falls to his knees, holds out his hand to steady himself and begins struggling with the straps of his rucksack. His movements become more frantic until he's tearing at the straps, finally flinging the sack to the floor in front of him, pulling the rip-cord then delving into the depths, his hands searching for something.

"Don't cry little boy, it's not so bad. He should have died two years ago. He was strictly on borrowed time." He raises his arms again, palms outstretched as if in apology. "Like I told him, I *never, ever* fail on a job. It was a done deal really."

Al pulls his hand from the bottom of the pack. In it, entwined in his fingers, is a length of black rubber. Strong elastic attached to thick steel arms. He flips down an arm rest, the plastic cup nestles against his forearm, a leather pouch dangles against the rock beneath his knees.

"What's this? You think I'm going to be scared of a fucking catapult?" Al doesn't respond, with his free hand he gropes the ground before him, picking up pieces of rock, weighing them, feeling them. His eyes never unlock from Dan's.

"I say, little boy, little boy, why don't you go toddle off and scrump some apples or something?"

Al stands; in his right palm, the catapult sits comfortably, his fingers wrapped tightly around the handle, in his left is a small rock. A piece of rock that has sat amongst the mountains for thousands of years, waiting for the next Ice-Age to carry it away. It sits neatly in the leather pouch.

With tears forming tracks down his grimy, sweat stained cheeks, Al raises his head, stares straight at Dan and takes up his stance. It's the same stance that has seen the downfall of dozens of rabbits in the fields surrounding his old home. The same stance that pigeons have witnessed a fraction of a second before their lives have ended, muscles beginning to work in their wings, desperate to lift off but always too late.

Dan slaps his thigh, shakes his head and speaks in the same manic tone. It's pure evil, but within it, the first hint of unease.

"What? Listen to me chum, you ain't no David and I certainly ain't no Goliath. Put the catty back in the pack and piss off ..."

Al's face never changes as he draws back the elastic. No emotion, no thought, no nothing.

"Fuck you ..."

Iain flinches at the 'thwack', unsure whether the noise is the elastic being released or the rock striking its target. Al lowers his arms, drops the catapult to the dust at his feet where it clatters against a block of stone. Iain's eyes follow its fall. When he raises his head, his stare takes in a look of utter shock on Dan's face, his eyes, once a fiery blue, are glazed and vacant. A bright red welt appears in the centre of his forehead and a thin trickle of blood runs into the corner of his eye. For a second he seems to be trying to speak, a frown wrinkles his brow, then a blankness descends over his face.

Like a huge fir tree, succumbing to a chainsaw, Dan topples, straight legged, backwards over the lip of the buttress and out of sight.

The sound of his falling drifts back. Like a sack of soil, his body bounces and slides away from them. Noise builds as rocks break from the face, joining the tumbling rag-doll that was once Dan. Gradually, the rattle of rocks and gravel cascading to the glen below fades to nothing.

Silence descends, filling in the gaps left by the falling stone.

A Fall of Stone

I remember spinning through space. I remember the sky constantly swapping places with the glen, then the grey rock face. I remember feeling an impact that forced the air from my lungs, setting my features in a gasping, silent scream. I remember twisting backwards, my legs following as though only loosely connected; then the back of my head struck the scree and again I saw stars. They exploded across the white screen that had replaced my vision as a bright and multi-coloured firework display. I remember a kaleidoscope of greens and grey and blue, of pain and noise and fear.

I groped for any purchase, sometimes my hands striking rock, sometimes flailing uselessly in the air, grasping emptiness before once again slamming into unyielding stone.

After what seemed like hours, I slid on my back over the lower buttress and felt, for a fraction of a second that my fall was about to end; then I was in free-fall. The ground dropped away from me in a stomach-lurching plunge that felt like a thousand fairground rides rolled into one.

I remember thinking - "This is what it feels like to die."

I had no notion of direction, of whether I was facing up or down.

Flailing through space with arms spinning, over and over and over as though caught in some gigantic tumble dryer.

Time had ceased to exist along with any comprehension of basic perspective. My vision was a blurry mess of drab green, then grey.

A pain like having a red-hot iron bar driven through both feet and up, into my calves and thighs forced a scream from me that seemed to pierce my brain. Whether it was real or imagined I could not say.

To me it was real.

As real as the pain.

My legs buckled, forcing me into a whiplash, spastic, gyrating dance and springing me forward into a rubber and disjointed cartwheel.

And then ... *the strangest thing.*

In a tiny fragment of the split second I spent upright, I saw, as clearly as ever before, Blaven, ringed in a wondrous golden halo of summer sunrise. Clear blue sky provided its backdrop. Above it, spinning heaven-wards in a gentle, delicate arc, was my left boot. I saw the deep tread of its sole swap places with the fabric of its upper. I saw the laces follow its path in a lazy spiral.

Then my whole body struck rock, my arms outstretched before me as though I was attempting a dive into a swimming pool.

I rolled onto my side and tumbled into unconsciousness.

Time.

A strange thing indeed, elastic and yet rigid.

Time, spreading outwards, dragging by at a snail's crawl during periods of boredom. Time flying by, a jet stream rush when all that's wanted is continued enjoyment; when you wish it would just hang back, drag along and spread a little, prolong the pleasure.

Time.

No friend of enjoyment, no partner to pleasure.

God, it dragged its heels while I waited for *my* time to end.

I wandered my way in and out of lucidity, meandered between sight and sound, sleep and broken, screaming agony.

Bolts of grinding heat pulsed up my legs, exploding into my pelvis. Everything felt swollen and someone had replaced both of my feet with unconnected, useless, burning blocks of wood.

I swear I could smell their smoke.

Gasping, I jolted as something flew past me in a limp and disjointed tumble. Careening down steep rock to my right, a barely glimpsed black sack that, incredibly, looked much like a body. It landed with a wet slap just out of sight behind a car-sized boulder. A few seconds later a fluttering, white lace handkerchief floated down from the heavens and settled like a wayward swan's feather on the rock near my shoulder. Pure white, edged with the most intricate lace, it twitched with the breeze, rippling like wind blown silk. I watched, unable to tear away my eyes, its beauty seemed an antidote for my pain. In one corner, nestling alongside its delicate edge, was a single embroidered letter in a blue as deep and dark as a midnight sky.

'E'

I reached across, desperate to grasp it as a gust of wind spirited it away. It lifted from the rock and disappeared, suddenly, as if never there; as if conjured by a mind desperate for some gentleness. Some soft beauty.

Then blackness.

Warm and painless blackness that caressed me with its tender strokes and kept me safe. A dark cocoon that wrapped me in a bubble of tranquillity.

I crept along in the dark, feeling my way deeper and deeper, not looking for a way out, but rather a way further in.

My travels took me to a glorious place deep within my mind. A serene place, set with trees and lush green grass. Ripples spread over a gently ebbing pool that reflected a sky of blue so intense, it must have hung over heaven.

Not so bad really.

The pain had gone so I'd obviously given in and died.

No, not so bad at all.

****

With a huge, reverberating splash, a rock bombed the water, throwing droplets in all directions. I winced at the intrusion and the pain was back, rushing in with a frantic, vengeful insistence. Another splash seemed to distort and fracture the scene entirely, the ripples spreading outwards until the trees and sky were rocking in time to their push; the sky split open with a rifle-shot crack and I flailed my arms to protect my face.

The glen spread once more, in an endless green carpet. To my right, the ridge rose and fell as it had done in jagged majesty for thousands of years. To my left, Gillean seemed to hover above, its three pinnacles mocking me, the failed climber. In the far distance, appearing like an old friend, brought back from the dead to visit in a surreal dream, Blaven shone out its blackness. My eyes took in the view; the peaks, the trickling clear burns, the climbers on the Inaccessible Pinnacle, the never ending glen, rolling far, far away.

"Watch that bit, it's well loose. Nearly had me then ... yeah, keep left then you're on the scree ..."

I knew that voice but, try as I might I couldn't place it. I searched my memory for a while, desperate for an answer.

Another rock crashed to the ground, sparking and throwing up dust and smoke. Not this time into cool, clear water, but instead, hard, unyielding ground that screamed at each hit. I shuddered, amazed that I was alive.

"Please ... puh-puh please ... no more rocks ... careful ... please ... be careful."

It was a harsh, cracked, trickle of words, barely audible even in the silent stillness of the glen and surely not enough to carry even a yard from my resting place.

Yet it did.

"*Andy?* Iain, keep still, I heard him ... he's alive." Louder this time, "Andy, Andy, stay still. We're here mate. Jesus Christ, oh my God, Iain he's alive, he's really alive."

Iain, yes, Iain, Not 'Liam'. Iain my friend, but who was with him? Again my memory sifted through banks of unwanted information, drifting my way along the cave full of stacked packing cases - searching for the key again.

An image of a sea trout leaping through black swirling water, into black swirling night air, forced its way into my mind. As it spun, throwing off droplets of sparkling, molten silver, I found my voice. This time, as strong and powerful as the fish in my head it forced its way into the limitless expanse of glen and mountain.

"Al, AAAAlllll ..."

As my voice faded, I heard, from above, a resurgence of bouncing scree. Boots clattered over deeply piled, insecure stone and a shout that drifted on the breeze came back to me. Tinged with a bubbling emotion that verged on hysteria - "Andy, Jesus mate, don't worry, don't worry, we're here. Just hang on, don't move."

Why I should have been having a conversation with Al, when, surely, he was five hundred miles away in the Midlands, was lost on me. I was simply ecstatic that I had some company, that there was someone, anyone coming to my aid. I longed for any tiny scrap of comfort; after Dan's hatred and vengeance, I would have gladly swapped everything I owned for one sentence of kind words.

Suddenly, all sounds were drowned by a continual hail storm of rock-fall, clattering on all sides and exploding into splintered fragments of smoking, spinning shrapnel. The sound of rocks cleaving the air and the clattering explosion of their impact; the sight of their flight and disintegration, the dust drifting away like the impact of artillery shells in a desert. But most of all, the smell, pungent and acid, like a thousand swiftly struck matches.

I lay, twisted and broken. Pain wracked, with distorted and shattered legs. I closed my eyes. What would be ... well, it would just have to be. If my lot was to survive Dan *and* a fall over three hundred feet of jagged rock, just to be finished off by a falling missile dislodged by one of my friends, then so be it.

A rock dropped from the heavens and disintegrated a foot from my left shoulder, its fragments lodged in my hair and a piece sliced across my forehead, drawing blood and opening up a gash that oozed into my eyes.

I never flinched; I simply lay still as if I was already dead.

Thoughts of the last two years drifted across my memory.

As each image flitted like a flickering flame across my mind, I couldn't help thinking that the events that had sculpted my life had been as insistent and relentless as a fall of stone. Like a rock fall, scary and deadly, unpredictable, violent, infinitely changeable; moulding events as easily and freely as a sculptor with a lump of clay.

I drifted, peaceful, at ease.

****

A face loomed above me with eyes that were red-ringed and blood-shot from swirling dust. Tracks in the grimy cheeks made by freely flowing tears glowed, white amongst grey.

My friend.

"Al ... you alright mate?" My voice was like a faint breeze through a field of corn.

He coughed, spraying dust and grit into his open hand, shook his head, then looked back at me.

"Not bad thanks." He looked around, taking in the quiet surroundings, thoughtful, weighing his words carefully, "I heard there was a job going ... on the Island like ... thought I might ... you know ... apply for it."

Despite the pain that burned through every single cell of my body, I felt a shudder ripple its way from head to foot. It felt like the beginning of hysterics, as though a huge reservoir of self-pity was set to burst through its dam and blast its way through me.

Instead, I smiled ... and started to laugh.

Life goes on

Broken bones, twisted, ripped muscles. Dislocation, cuts, bruises. Internal bleeding, concussion, damaged organs. All heal, all mend in that wonderful, magical way that nature has of repairing us. Life goes on; we get on with living to the best of our ability, make the best of our lot and try to enjoy.

Try to forget.

Try to forget the pain and discomfort endured through weeks and months of agonised healing. Try to forget the betrayal by a man who was once my friend, then my boss, then the mastermind of my intended death. Try to forget the pure evil and hatred of a mind that could knowingly, with premeditated calmness and gleeful pleasure, inflict pain and torture on a fellow human being.

I *tried* to forget and, most of it I did, I could. The pain passes, the bruising fades and cuts seal themselves to leave red tracks where once we bled.

But God, those cold blue eyes, those hate filled pools that shone with mocking laughter. They haunt me still, visit me in the long, dark nights and force their way into dreams of a red haired girl who captured my heart and made my life complete.